Happy Hellidays

Curated by Theresa Scott-Matthews

HellBound Books Publishing LLC

A HellBound Books LLC Publication

Copyright © 2023 Paul Kane
All Rights Reserved
Cover and art design by Tee Art for
HellBound Books Publishing LLC

www.hellboundbookspublishing.com

Happy Hellidays

Happy Hellidays

CONTENTS

Easter Bloody Easter
By Dan A. Cardoza

The last seven years have been hell for all of us, including Bobby, the Rabbit King.

I'm visiting him in prison. It's late August 2021.

Bobby, or as he prefers, RK (Rabbit King), is housed at Mule Creek State Prison in Ione.

Mule Creek is in the foothills of Northern California, east of Sacramento. It's where the infamous Menendez Brothers were housed. They blasted their parents to death in 89. In fact, Lyle Menendez was married here in the visiting room. He's been reunited with his murderous brother, Erik, in San Diego.

"When you were a child, Bobby, I watched from a distance when you were out in the schoolyard. You were 7 back then. You looked at the ground. It looked like you had the world's weight on your shoulders."

Silence!

"You were in foster care. CPS had taken you away. Your mom had physically abused you. I'd just gotten out of jail."

Nothing!

Bobby rarely responds.

I imagine his cell as this fantastic waiting room.

Bobby once told me how he enjoys the cooling touch of the concrete walls. How comforting the restrictive space feels, the cold feel of the metal door.

Most of our family has disowned RK for what he did.

He surprised me a few weeks back. He explained how his hands feel like decaying flesh, unsuitable for holding others.

"It's my hands that got me here, dad," he says.

I visit Bobby mostly on Sundays. He's calmer on Sundays. That wasn't always the case. He rarely interacts. I know he doesn't mind the visits. They're mainly for me.

RK still sketches a lot. I'm curious to know how he does it. You are not supposed to have anything sharp in your cell. My best guess is that the guards feel sorry for Bobby, his not leaving his cell that often.

What does he draw? We'll get to that soon enough.

***

For now, let's go back in time. It's early September 2015. Bobby is 14.

"Mr. Ferguson, it's late. CPS is waiting. They have an attorney who'd like to speak to your boy."

I am Marty Ferguson, Bobby's father.

The detective's voice snaps me back to reality.

"I didn't mean to startle you, Marty, but they want a few minutes of alone time with Bobby before he goes to juvenile hall in Rancho Cordova. Since he's so young, they need to prepare him for his first court appearance. He will also be assigned a public defender. I understand you don't have the funds, correct?"

I hesitate. "No, I don't, detective Hammer." I feel ashamed.

Before I go, I stand at the table and look over my boy on the chair. I ask myself, *how could you have done such a thing, Bobby?*

The detectives had taped my son's full confession. What he'd said was shocking.

Before I turn the corner, walk down the hall, and out to my car, I look back at Bobby. It's crazy how good he looks in his white papery jumpsuit. There is something pure about the mental picture to this day.

Forensics has his bloody jeans and his threadbare Metallica tee shirt. The pants and shirt were more blood than fabric.

"See you soon, son," I say. Bobby doesn't respond.

I'd shed some serious tears returning to my cheap studio apartment. It's the only kind of place a convicted druggie can afford these days. When your life is a turnstile of good and bad and a revolving door of in and outs, this is what you get.

No one needs to remind me how my life's wrong choices have led to a lifetime of grief for most of those around me. Some people even blame me for what RK did.

At my local donut haunt the following day, I read about the murder on my newspaper app. RK's story is in the Sacramento Bee, page 2. Bobby will be tried as an adult.

The headline reads, "It's the biggest horror fest since Richard Chase, Sacramento's only Vampire Killer."

I nearly gagged on the last few bites of a maple bar.

***

My Ex and I have always supported Bobby, especially in his attempt to rescue Easter rabbits left in the woods. Somehow, she'd talked her new husband into agreeing with his collecting.

I know precisely when Bobby got the idea to save rabbits. Bobby was only 6 then. Martha and I were still married.

We'd driven from South Sacramento to this Ancil Hoffman nature preserve on the other side of town. We went the weekend after Easter.

Bobby and I walked through the woods beyond the golf course. After we reached the nature center, we saw a rescued owl. He was behind a glass cage. We joked about setting him free.

From the nature center, we trekked downhill to the American River. We'd done this before. A few deer, some wild turkeys, and squirrels. It was peaceful and quiet that day. It was fun.

On our way back to the picnic area, where his mom was waiting, Bobby spied something moving under a small bush. As we got closer, we discovered it was a rabbit. Not just any rabbit. It was a giant, fluffy white rabbit.

Bobby insisted on petting the thing. An Easter-fatigued parent had clearly released it into the gorgeous park. Indeed, their child had grown tired of feeding and cleaning up after the hapless creature.

"Please, dad, can we bring it home? It won't survive out here!"

"I'm not one to correct somebody's bad choices, Bobby. My own mistakes keep me plenty busy. So, it's a no. I never feel guilty."

"Please, dad, Mom will let me keep it. She always gives in. She feels guilty because she works late. I promise to take good care of it, dad."

"If a body catches a body coming through the rye…"

"What does that mean, Son?" I asked.

"It's part of an old poem. This situation reminds me of the poem. We read it in class. It's about saving children from growing up. The poem was written by Robert Burns in the 1700s."

"Interesting, son, that stanza reminds me of someone. It was Holden Caulfield. In the important novel, he said he wished he could save all the children from growing up."

Looking back, that's the last time I observed my son smile. His smile was wide and understanding.

"What the hell, son? Let's give it a try?"

"Really, dad? I love you!"

Bobby swooped up the large floppy eared creature. It was docile and clueless.

It didn't take long to get back to the picnic area. Once we arrived, Bobby extended his arms and presented the clumsy rabbit to his surprised mom. His mother was the challenge.

Bobby knows his mother very well. He knew how she didn't want any more children with me. That was my fault. I own that. So, after a good amount of verbal arm wrestling, Martha gave in. She let RK keep the tiny beast.

We'd later agree it might help Bobby ward off his feelings of loneliness, the loneliness of having no friends at school, and how you can feel without a brother or sister.

I'm sure he felt isolated as a child, the way one feels when you know your parents aren't meant to be together.

"You can keep it, Bobby. But you better damned well take good care of it," said Martha.

So, for the next several weeks, mostly evenings, Bobby and I built his first rabbit hutch. Google and YouTube pointed out the way. We'd used a lot of scrap wood and screws that had littered my workbench. Luckily, I'd stored a leftover roll of chicken wire in the rafters. I'd used it instead of rebar. I'd cut corners on one of my employer's concrete contracts.

We purchased rabbit feed. We found a watering bowl at a flea market. Bobby insisted on a padlock for protection: hawks, cats, raccoons, even those pesky coyotes.

Two weeks passed. RK kept up on the rabbits. He asked if we could have another picnic at the park. We knew what he was up to.

After we finished our bucket of KFC, Bobby pulled me up and insisted that we hike back down to the river. Strangely, we ended up near the bush where we'd found the first rabbit. Bobby looked sad. He must have thought another rabbit would be waiting for him.

We made it all the way down to the American River again. We skipped a few stones. Bobby chatted about how unpredictable nature could be. I agreed to take another trail on our way back.

Bobby spotted it at most twenty feet ahead. It was pure white except for some rusty red blotches. I attempted to hold onto my boy with everything I had, but he was strong with love. He'd forced himself free. When I reached the horrific scene, Bobby was scraping body parts together in a pile. It was mostly bloody fur, an empty skull, and a few unlucky rabbit's feet. He stared at the stinky pile as if he wanted to reanimate it.

Snot bubbles percolated out of his nose. He sobbed uncontrollably. His hair turned sweaty and wet as if he'd been fighting at school again. He shook. He'd become a coiled spring of grief. He turned red faced and angry and pounded the dust.

"Why, what, who, dad?" he said.

"Son," I grabbed RK by one of his bloody hands, "let's go. Your mother is waiting."

"No, I never want to go home, dad," he says.

"Bobby," I was firmer, "let's go, now! There are coyotes out here, son, along the river. They have homes in the clay banks and fields up and over the levy. They eat anything they can catch cats, lost dogs, and even dead salmon in the fall."

"No!" he screamed.

"Yes!" I shouted. Nature can be cruel.

On our way back, I mostly drug Bobby alone. We had another 100 yards to go.

That's when this damned thing appeared. It was at most ten feet to our right. The tiny creature was nearly invisible under the shady sagebrush. It was skinny and shaking, hyperventilating. Its beady eyes were guarded, the innocent before slaughter.

"Dad, look, he's white too, only smaller. He looks so thin, poor thing?"

"We can't take it home, son." I pointed toward Martha, who was waving for us to hurry up.

"Please, dad, I have to save it. I won't ask you guys to take me back here anymore. Please, dad, please, I promise? It will haunt me forever if I don't rescue this rabbit."

Bottom line—Bobby got to save another rabbit. I saw the innocent thing as just another promise or bribe that some irresponsible parent had abandoned in the woods shortly after Easter.

I get it. Working moms and dads are often guilt ridden. They give into their children's whims as we did. But that's how we end up with discarded Easter rabbits.

The Evil Easter Rabbit King knew this too well. It angered him to the core.

Like most working parents, it takes a lot of energy to prepare dinner, eat, and then help their kids with homework before a few minutes to recharge. And so when Easter comes around, feeling guilty about not sharing time, they give in to their children's unrealistic demands. Little do they know if they gift their child an Easter rabbit, they are, in truth, assigning the rabbit a death sentence. This goes for chicks and ducklings too.

Across America, thousands and thousands of silly white rabbits get discarded a week or two after Easter. White Easter rabbits get dumped by the millions, far away from any notion of parental responsibility as possible.

Surely the tame little things will be spared the tooth and claw of the jungle, right? Wrong!

The Easter Rabbit King knows better. Fresh, white rabbits, in droves, will be led to the cruelest kind of slaughter.

Kids don't miss their rabbits, hell, they have more important things on their mind: school on Monday, summer vacation plans, posting to Tik Tok, and taking selfies for Instagram.

And the following week, they'll be off to soccer or go skateboarding, or their doting, exhausted parents will drop them off to see one of the latest Marvel Movies.

Once the kids at school learned of RK's salvation scheme, they teased and bullied him mercilessly. From that day forward, they never let up. The kids shamed him close to the dark edges of silence over the next few years. Clear up to the beginning of high school. All Bobby had left in his shrinking universe was the rabbits he saved.

***

Martha was done. She divorced me. I got my ass incarcerated again.

In only a few years, Martha remarried. Oddly, she married this younger, beefcake-looking guy who despised children. Bobby had turned mostly silent and angry by then, especially around his new stepfather. I'd learn in jail how Jake had physically abused my Bobby. As if the psychological abuse at school wasn't enough? RK's life had become a living hell.

Over time, Martha had turned into a co-dependent conspirator with Jake. She'd fallen into the cycle of love and abuse.

Based on what a few relatives had discussed, it's my understanding that Bobby had continued to save abandoned rabbits. His stepfather hated the idea, but it kept RK away from the house.

I'd heard about the new cages. Bobby and I had briefly discussed them. He'd built them along the back fence line of his stepfather's backyard.

At first, there were two. Eventually, there were four, and soon after, there were 13 of the raised hutches. Jake, Bobby's newish stepfather, wasn't happy with RK's extensive collection of 'pests.' That's what Jake called the rabbits, 'pests."

When I'd gotten out of confinement, RK was nearly 14. I'd take him out for pizza on rare occasions, mostly on Sundays. To divorced dads, Sundays are leftovers.

While at lunch, RK pretended to be happy. I tried communicating with him like all the divorced dads do at the Sunday pizza parlors, but he never responded.

I did my best to be a good father. How could I have known the level of darkness RK was experiencing?

Over time, I observed cigarette burns on his arms and neck. They'd mostly healed. But I sensed the sinuous scars over his heart would continue to grow. His mother mentioned something about self-harm and how he'd been working on a discarded dirt bike. She'd said they might be muffler burns?

I was skeptical as hell. But I supported my son. It was apparent how much saving rabbits meant to the RK.

Apparently, out of guilt, Martha supported Bobby's obsession. She let him continue to save all those Easter rabbits. He'd built 13 in total. Each cage housed three abandoned rabbits.

It didn't take Tarot Cards to figure out how much Bobby had grown to hate his cruel stepfather. It felt like a fuse had been lit.

***

I finally got an appointment with the school psychologist. His name is Harry Daniels. He's a nice man. He looked competent.

"Mr. Ferguson, I'd like to show you some of Bobby's artwork. He's very talented, by the way, but his art is dark."

"Thank you, Mr. Daniels," I think?

"Look closely. It's a graphic novel," says Mr. Daniels.

Mr. Daniels twisted Bobby's manuscript around on the desktop. He says the graphic novel is 200 pages, but only the top page has content.

It's like when Jack Torrance wrote in The Shining, "All work and no play makes Jack a dull boy."

199 of Bobby's pages have been ghosted.

That frightened me. It was hard to take in?

I scoop Bobby's graphic novel closer. I stared at the gifted artwork and captions on page one, the only completed page.

This Evil Easter Rabbit King is displayed in the upper left panel. He's a teacher in a classroom full of children.

He's lecturing his students about the evils of animal cruelty. The tips of his ears nearly touch the classroom's imaginary ceiling. Evil is holding a cigarette. His long whiskers are droopy, nicotine stained.

The first caption reads: (Me Evil smells of a rabbit hole, and mange kids don't mind the stink).

The second panel to the right shows the Rabbit King's angry face. He's wearing old-school spectacles.

The second caption reads: (Me muzzle is more pit bull than a rabbit, much more prominent and vicious, better for meat. Me breath is toxic and foul. Me Evil is ancient and alien.)

The Evil Easter Rabbit has black, beady eyes like Bobby.

The third panel takes up half of the bottom page, below the gutter line. The magnificent artwork shows these dancing coyote figures eating cats, small dogs, and Easter bunnies in a nature park. I know it's crazy, but the artwork also shows these scary children eating their pets and, after, their parents eating their children.

The panel's adjacent caption bubble reads: "My stepfather is evil. The world is evil."

I attempted to take everything in, but I couldn't. My mind short circuited. Anxiety shot electronic currents through the wired synapse throughout my brain. I tried to catch my breath.

Not knowing what to say, the counselor and I shot the breeze for maybe 30 minutes, and then I had to excuse myself. On the way home, I exited the car and vomited my throat raw.

***

In just a few weeks, things went to hell. Bobby had returned from a day trip to one of his parks. It happened to be the week after Easter Sunday. He'd picked up another fluffy, white rabbit, a small one.

RK entered the house. It was deadly quiet, except for the grandfather clock that insisted on sounding like death metal. The foyer smelled like a gym where someone had been wrestling. Martha and RK's stepfather were sitting quietly in the adjacent family room.

As he walked past the doorway and saw them, RK could tell the couple had been fighting again. Martha was sobbing into the palms of her hands. Her lips appeared puffy. Black vampire mascara streaked down her face.

Stepfather Jake had his oily leather recliner all the way back. He was applying a lotion of fresh blood to his swollen knuckles. Jake couldn't contain himself. He'd chuckled under his breath.

"Got you another rabbit, boy? That's some lame shit, son."

RK could smell his mother's fear from across the room. She was a stiff, waxy corpse in a seat.

"You're getting to be quite the hoarder, aren't you, boy?" Jake crushed a Coors can flat in his hand.

Little did he know that RK was all stocked up on bullshit and bullying. The last thing he needed that Sunday was another argument with his stepfather. He'd attempt to walk past the dysfunctional mess toward the patio door and the backyard.

By now, most of the bullies in high school had learned their lesson that Bobby Ferguson was someone to fear. RK had gotten much taller and more muscular. Apparently, stepfather Jake didn't get the memo.

Bobby rolled open the sliding door. He shut it, not looking up.

He walked in the direction of his rabbit hutches. Halfway there, RK raised his head. His stepfather had dropped a hydrogen bomb.

It was getting dark. But Bobby could tell all the cage doors had been opened.

As he approached the hutch on the far left, the last living white rabbit squirmed in the corner of the cage. It wriggled like this toad that had just been trapped in RK's skull. It screamed, it shrieked, it bawled.

The small creature thrashed about, unconcerned that it was hurting itself.

RK's newest rabbit chirped and squealed in the carry-along. The small thing screeched like it had been stung by 1,000 hornets.

Standing directly in front of the last rabbit cage, RK dropped the newest baby rabbit in the carry-along to the ground. He looked left and right. RK was furious about how his pet rabbits had been disarticulated and killed. He'd finally arrived at the Mad Hatter's tea party. Rabbit parts and bloody red fur steamed in the chill of the evening.

Suddenly, Bobby could hear this loud train whistle go off in his head. He could feel the tracks tremble under his feet as the locomotive rounded the corner toward him. The locomotive's sound was harsh and mechanical, the whistle, a thousand fire alarms.

The evil engineer's bloody hound dog face grew more prominent as the train approached Bobby. Bobby could smell and see that the giant rabbit locomotive handler's facial skin was raw and sweaty, so vile. He had baked blood on its fur. The motorman wore a wicked smile.

Somehow, he could hear the Evil Easter Rabbit King's voice.

Kill the motherfucker! It spoke.

After the collision in RK's mind, everything in his world ignited. The only thing inside his skull was red vapor if there was anything.

The Sacramento County detectives had taken long breaks. They'd been issued vomit bags. The county pastor did his best to comfort them, but he had to leave early. They'd all been sickened to the edge of insanity. What they'd discovered in the backyard wasn't just a massacre. It was an emphatic statement.

They photographed every body part, rabbit and human, the smelly guts, the severed heads with vacant eyes, the shit, the piss, the stench of blood stains. Surely this time of year, something so fowl should not have been wafting into the chill of a beautiful evening.

They'd also taken pictures of Bobby's stepfather, what was left of him. Parts of him were found in most of the cages. Jake's head had been tossed into a tree in the neighbor's yard. It had been discovered ten feet off the ground between some branches.

Bobby had been systematic. Like Salvador Dali, he'd warped space and time using blood as paint. It would be his best work of art.

***

What does Bobby draw now, you asked at the story's beginning?

I'm not going to lie to you. He draws bloody rabbits. I don't know how each sketched rabbit can turn out more horrid than the last, each one a satirical, evil monstrosity, but they can. His pictures appear subhuman. Disgusting sketches you wouldn't want your children exposed to.

When all the visitors leave in the afternoon, I drag Bobby's clumsy ghost of a heart through the visitor's room and out the solid metal exit door. Once it's closed behind me, I drag his heart down this long dark corridor and the sidewalk through the prison grounds. It's a red balloon.

I exit the main pedestrian gate.

Eventually, I reached my car. At the car, I release the balloon. I open the car door. Once inside, I slump forward and look up through the windshield until the red balloon fades out of sight.

As I drive out of the parking lot, I wonder which one of us really needs the company of the other.

Ghosted
A Tale of All Hallows' Eve
By Greg Patrick

"Anything could move out there in the darkness, I think. A hook-handed man. A ghostly hitchhiker forever repeating the same journey. An old woman summoned from the repose of her mirror by the chants of children. Everyone knows these stories—that is, everyone tells them, even if they don't know them—but no one ever believes them."-Carmen Maria Machado

To nervous children daring each other to stray into its forbidding shadow, the decaying mansion stood a gaunt glowering ruin by moonlight. It was a pellucid specter, haunting the imagination and dreams of generations of neighborhood children. It was an eldritch structure, the product of a mad architect that seemed to construct a frankenhouse of Victorian and gothic styles, of gables, spires, and columns. That urban legend in stone dared the children with an annual rite of passage, to climb the creaking steps to touch the gargoyle knocker with trembling hand and smite the ornate door. Then they prayed nothing would stir in the shadows and answer. It remained a grisly relic that children hastened by in the twilight, shivering as they crossed its misshapen shadow as it was cast long by the crimson dusk. "Blood manor" stood aloof from their daily lives in solitary darkness, mummified by swathes of cobwebs like ghostly tapestries.

On moonless nights it appeared more mausoleum than manor. It was rare to find a "ghost house" that lived up to its name, yet that "urban legend" in crumbling mortar, had a dark past that seemed to whisper its disembodied confession with the wind that hissed through its broken gables. Not all of it was mere lore a certain young man had found. While cleaning up the old attic Patrick, a local high school student had found yellowed newspapers headlined "murder house" detailing the horrors investigators found inside. The prime suspect was never found.

Another man convicted as his accomplice was sentenced to the chair, tearfully denying his guilt.

He swore he did not remember anything.

Later Patrick researched for a class assignment, delving in the town's historic archives,
he was chilled to uncover more of the history of "red manor." Patrick pored over grim headlines on yellowed pages and old faded images of crews taking cartloads of bones from the garden. A man was pictured being taken away smiling madly, while an elderly woman stood
defiantly at the threshold holding a tommy gun and meat cleaver. That standoff would end with her falling in a hail

of bullets still scarring the walls, a bloody end to a deranged murderess.

The article left little to the imagination, detailing the horrors investigators found inside. The manor was known eternally for its infamous tenant, but it had traded hands many times. Even the most unwitting tenant seemingly found themselves infected by the evil that seemed to ooze venomously from the walls.

Rumor and urban legend swirled around the manor like a reveling or danse macabre of dark ghosts haunting imaginations and dreams. It bore a charmed afterlife, enduring a number of plots to demolish it and whatever secrets remained buried under its grim foundations. That ominous shadow was cast long in the crimson dusk and passersby shivered in its shadow as they hastened by that foreboding presence in the falling night. It was all something older generations never spoke of to the younger. "Life goes on" their elders repeated stoically. To that end, Patrick hurried to don his costume for his eagerly anticipated Halloween date night. It was a Jon Snow costume he had been working on for weeks. Unbeknownst to him as he adjusted his costume in the mirror, that night his paths would cross with the mansion once more and we would again ascend those steps to challenge whatever haunted the grim bastion of nightmare.

Patrick had taken the long way back from school that chill Autumn day to avoid the mansion, yet it seemed all roads led back to its ominous shadow. He found himself inexplicably facing the manor as if standing before an old enemy forcing a confrontation with a reluctant adversary...*as if it wouldn't let him go*...Patrick shook his head as he observed the graffitied walls along his path. The enigmatic vandal behind the display had proven elusive, despite the generous award for his capture. The vandal had graffitied his trademark cryptic symbol always painted in sanguine red. On his way to the meeting spot to a much-anticipated date, Patrick paused suddenly as his eye caught an enticing shimmer spotlighted by a lamppost. A mysterious cache of candy beckoned invitingly in front of the uninhabited murder house. His date's favorite kind of candy he observed. And it was untouched strangely.... or predictably so. The house was infamous.

"Take one," the sign offered with a winking jack o lantern lit on the table.

An ominous foreboding gave Patrick pause. Then something else drew his gaze. He cursed. The vandal had struck again. The new graffiti had been painted red in the blood of a ritually killed puppy.

"Sick devil whoever he is," Patrick growled.

A graffitied jack o lantern face smiled back red at him gloatingly, its seemingly following him. The paint seemed fresh. Patrick wondered if he was being watched by the vandal from the shadows. Suddenly he thought he heard the hiss of a spray can. Then he spied a stranger watching. He followed the dark shadowy figure furtively before shouting and giving chase. The vandal eluded him. The stranger seemed to dissolve into the wall known eternally for its evil tenant. And in the nights leading to Halloween, he was haunted by recurring nightmares with the mansion at the center of it like a dark lord enthroned in shadow beckoning for him.

As Patrick blinked in the bright dawn, he looked in bemused wonder at the grisly spectacle before him. As if a mad carnival rolled into town, the leaf-strewn street of the quaint picturesque village seemed to transform overnight in ghoulish metamorphosis into a riotous necropolis with skulls grinning and witches leering at every corner and lamppost. Like nocturnal or crepuscular scavengers emerging from their dens to feed, costumed children raced from their homes and gathered in the dusk to infest the streets with costumes representing the denizens of Halloween lore. Between the phantasmagoria of lavishly skull and witch-festooned houses lit welcomingly to bands of trick or treaters, was a dark gap where the long abandoned Victorian mansion, a gaunt shadow of its former stately grandeur, slowly rotted. It was shunned of course, hurried past to another lit house. Meanwhile Patrick stood in solitary vigil.

"Sweet for the sweet" he had rehearsed pocketing the gold-wrapped candy he found before the "red mansion". Looking across the dreamscape of lanterns and the interplay of light and shadow he envisioned her, Clare, the night of their first dance. It was at a themed masquerade ball. He felt painfully awkward yet rallied enough courage to ask her for the first dance of the night. Patrick sighed at how radiant she looked in her golden gown and cascade of red hair. A vision of beauty behind green eyes.

He remembered the softness of the fabric of her gown as he held her tenderly. Song lyrics became incantation. Steps were lost in the sensation of flight. Candles became constellations in the turns and sweeps of her gown and hair. They had danced every song together, losing all track of time till the lights went on and he escorted her outside and they laughed under the stars. He awoke to the present and he checked the time on his phone again. He desolately imagined her laughing at him with her popular friends. He lingered there by their appointed meeting spot by a lonely street lamppost. In his lonely vigil, he listened to the incessant creaking of decorative skeletons swaying from the bare branches of an old sycamore. The streets became eerily quiet otherwise.

"Where is everybody?" Patrick wondered.

He paced restlessly as the minutes then hours crawled by like a procession of insects crawling over his skin. His heavy sigh steamed in the chill air. He stood awkwardly.

He distracted himself with trivia, morbidly reflecting on the metamorphosis of Halloween from an ancient feast ritual to a wild party night. Suddenly he was jarred from his musings by a goblin-masked figure. It was just some impish brat with his marauding gang of trick or treaters.

He jeered, pointing. They howled with a chorus of laughter.

"Look at that guy just standing there all night! Ha-ha!"

Their mocking cackling echoed back at him in passing as they ran past euphoric with the thrill of their hunt for candy. Dead withered leaves fell as if hailing him in mockery. Their cackling trailed away, and the streets became eerily quiet.

Where did they all go? Had he really been there that long?

Patrick paced restlessly. The lamplight sputtered then went out, leaving him in darkness.

Tempted to stress eat, he unwrapped the candy he found in front of the mansion. Then something strange caught his eye. It was handwriting in red on the pale underside of the golden wrappers.

With startling recognition Patrick realized it was in Clare's handwriting. He recognized it from notes they passed in class. It had a simple desperate message:

"Help me. Please!"

Suddenly the phone lit up. He jumped. It was her finally.

What's this? A video?

Patrick raced the dying bars on his phone, texting frantically…He downloaded a video.

He was horrified at footage of her trussed up in some warehouse like chamber, struggling against sinister figures.

There were other messages…A photo of her chained in a dark room.

A prank? No. The fear in her eyes was real. She wasn't acting. That was real terror in her eyes.

"Where are you?" he texted.

"You know…" came the reply.

Then a picture of the mansion and a sinister figure standing in front of it.

"Think you can rescue her?"

A laughing face and devil emoji appeared.

For the girl of his dreams, Patrick would face nightmares. He ran for the mansion. In his memory the decaying mansion had always stood a gaunt ruin by moonlight yet by some eerie metamorphosis, some eldritch trickery woven by a master illusionist's art, of moonlight and shadows, the manor's facade rejuvenated to an opulent stately mansion by some eerie resurrection. Shadow and moonbeams caressed its newly restored walls as "the red mansion" loomed before him in lordly malevolence. Patrick had seen the symbol graffitied on random walls in the days leading to Halloween. Now he stood looking at it painted gigantically on the gate that was left ajar and swaying creaking in the wind.

Patrick heard what sounded like ritual drums in the dark depths under the floorboards.

He drew two butcher knives embedded in the jack o lanterns, their carved smiles leered crimson in reply. Patrick clutched the blades between his fingers like metallic claws ready to slash at anything skulking and lunging from the shadows. Patrick found himself in the midst of a sumptuous Edwardian era drawing room.

He found shelves brimming with occult books. He almost retched as he realized some were bound in stitched human skin. Old newspaper front pages reporting on the news of the mansion murders were framed proudly on the walls as if boasting. Deciding on a bold approach rather than stealth, Patrick strode through the labyrinthine catacombal tunnel. Patrick pulled a dark medieval chest plate from the wall and donned it. He wrenched a torch from the wall to guide his way as well as a sword from the dark gauntlet of one of the suits of armor lining the halls.

"Winter is coming bitch," he growled.

Patrick recognized the music that he had summoned up his courage to ask the girl of his dreams to a dance. It was being eerily played on an antique gramophone as he infiltrated the shadowed halls. He had been expecting a dilapidated abandoned house littered with years of broken bear bottles and thoroughly vandalized. Instead, it was sumptuously furnished with antiques. "Help!" was written on the wall in red letters. Patrick found a heart graffitied on the wall and touched it. A portal opened into a dark passageway descending into the sinister depths.

He felt inhaled by darkness as he ventured further through the serpentine passageway. It seemed as if the mansion had been built over an elaborate subterranean cavern. The fluttering torchlight illuminated strange carvings on the wall like ancient petroglyphs. Patrick strayed further as his way slithered through a series of chambers.

Smuggler tunnels from prohibition, he guessed...*or something more sinister?*

Patrick recoiled at the grisly sight of the corpses of girls in brightly colored gowns like exotic tropical butterflies pinned as specimens to the wall. It was like some mad huntsman's trophy hall. He scanned their faces searchingly as the torchlight fell on their pale bloodless features. He was dreading seeing a familiar face among them, yet Clare was not there. Then he heard it, the eerie maddening sound of hearts beating in quickening palpitations…pulse quickening to rapid tempo.

Patrick recognized the symbols painted in red on the wall as the ones graffitied on the walls of the vaulted chamber. Among them were the red handprints by desperate captives trying to claw their way out of that hideous torture chamber. He suddenly gasped as he saw Clare. Her arms were splayed against a gargoylian statue like a gothic idol on a candle-lit altar. Her transfixed eyes saw through him. She was unresponsive. Patrick severed her bonds as he heard chanting in a strange tongue drawing nearer.

"I'm getting you out of here. Lean on me," Patrick urged.

Clare was frail and disoriented from enduring some horrific ordeal. Suddenly the gowned corpses pinned to the walls opened their eyes, seemingly revived and screamed as if in grisly alarm. Confronting him was a blind-folded crone. The wizened figure pointed an overgrown curved fingernail like a talon in a cringing wordless screech that echoed through the hallway in choir. Shapes moved then with a simian gate, closing in. He could make out lurching misshapen forms and grotesque hybridized features as if some mad scientist had bred some cave-dwelling creature to guard his chambers. Patrick ignited the torch and suddenly gasped as the deformed servants of these underground halls massing in the vulnerable interval of darkness were revealed. They were reaching for him with taloned hands.

Patrick brandished the torch to hold their pursuers at bay. They hissed and recoiled. The serpentine corridor echoed cringingly with their screeching echo locative cries, seeking them in the darkness. The torchlight cast the corpse-like pallor of their faces in hellish crimson. Their soulless eyes gleaming red in reply to the flame like smoldering embers. Patrick cast down the torch to cover their escape. Flames rose enveloping one in midstride. The others shrank back with a chorus of hideous cries. Patrick and Clare raced the flames and ran the gauntlet of cave-dwelling creatures lunging from the shadows. Patrick slashed machete-like through a mass of cobwebs shrouding the walls like ghostly banners of a netherworld. Patrick and Clare emerged from the grisly abattoir as the floor collapsed behind them and they burst into the night, inhaling the night air greedily.

Patrick was haggard and disheveled. He halted at the gothic threshold as he and Clare stood against a background of flame. The mansion burned behind them like an enormous bonfire. A horrific scream filled the air as if a living thing burned in agony. A solitary figure confronted them. The stranger had just turned from graffitiing his trademark symbol on the wall across the street. The vandal traced a red Cheshire cat smile and eyes on his blank soulless featureless darkness yawning under a black hood. The grin appeared like a reopened wound bleeding out.

"*Ah. now I see you,*" the vandal smiled.

His hissing voice was like a serpent's coils slithering over dry dead grass or flies buzzing around carrion.

"I trust the hosts of the manor have not been remiss in their hospitality and you feel quite fortunate to be alive. Alas, I assure you that sense of relief is premature and your doom is quite imminent indeed. An avid follower of my art it would appear. Well tonight my dear friend, you will be witness to my final masterpiece. In

fact, you will be quite instrumental in it...far from a mere spectator, " the vandal said.

The trickster locked eyes with Clare's.

"Now my acolyte," he commanded.

Suddenly Patrick felt Clare grasp his hair from behind and place a knife at his throat.

"The offering is ready master," Clare whispered in a ventriloquized transfixed voice.

"What are you doing?" Patrick cried out in alarm.

"You know nothing Jon Snow, " the vandal mocked.

"She was never the intended victim. She was always merely the bait to lure you in. Yes, you were led astray by love. And to what end you wonder? You see the ingredients were listed very specifically. One heart betrayed in love. That is where you come in. And don't bother to struggle in your last moments. You are quite outnumbered, " the vandal smirked.

Silhouetted against the fire-reddened moon the trickster raised his arms as if in the act of conjuring and a horde of figures lurched from the darkness as if restless shadows were granted form and hideous face. Ranks of masked figures massed at his back in a chanting horde. They spread out, encircling them, like a besieging army. They clutched scythes, carving knives, and sickles. The blades shimmered crimson by the firelight as the mansion erupted in an inferno of flame. The vandal raised his dark-gloved hand to signal a halt. His possessed thralls were chattering like nocturnal insects. As if ritually-masked worshippers, the trick or treaters gathered with bags of offerings. They gleefully forced a candied apple into Patrick's mouth.

"So many hungry mouths to feed and such ravenous ones. There there my brood. I promise you a true feast of Samhain. But hark. Whatever is that sound? " the vandal asked.

Meanwhile in the chasmous depths under the mansion, a myriad of living things stirred as flames devoured the manor. A vast colony of bats infesting the subterranean darkness was roused by the fire. The darkness was lit in harsh crimson light and their eyes shimmered in the firelight. First instinctively alarmed, then their senses tortured as they burned and choked by the smoke pouring into their lair. The first Patrick heard of them was a shrill chattering, merging in a tidal-like roar. Suddenly Patrick shielded Clare from a showering of sparks and burning smoking debris as the horde of bats erupted explosively into the night like a torrent of underworld flame. Uttering shrill cries of agony, the bats rose in a great undulant wave towards the beckoning orb of the moon.

The rush of night wind extinguished some yet many were aflame, their membraned wings burning and constellating the night. They hovered in a maelstromic phantasmagoric mass of crimson and black obscuring the crimson orb of fire-reddened moon and casting onlookers in an interval of darkness. The vandal laughed in maniacal rapture as several fell dead in mid-flight as they burned alive, trailing flame as if hailing him in nightmarish tribute. He basked in the crimson resplendence cast by the blaze.

"Trick or treat. Trick or treat. Give us something good to eat," a disembodied choir haunted the air.

"They all serve me now. At a word I can have them dismember you, yet I need you intact for now…Yes, they are entirely under my power…Perhaps demonstration?" the vandal smiled.

The vandal pointed at two masked figures in the mob. They bowed and broke ranks.

Cheered on by the others they staggered straight into the flames to jubilant cries.

"Not to flaunt my power...but enough of false modesty..." the vandal boasted.

"This is a dream. This has to be a dream!" Patrick gasped.

"You can keep telling yourself that mortal...It was a quiet Halloween night much like this one when the eccentric master of Red Hall manor held a séance. He dabbled in the occult... a bored amateur merely, yet his coven delved far too deeply into the ancient ground's secrets. As they were playing at necromancery in the underground chambers of his manor they awoke something that night from its ancient slumber, then sealed it back with ritual sacrifice vainly believing they could harness and wield its power. They flattered themselves. That dark spirit gorged on their souls and infected them with its evil and insatiable hunger for victims. It lay dormant, all those years till I awoke it again and the portal to hell was reopened in all its fiery glory and power! Behold. Make way for your queen!"

"Hail! Hail!" they chanted.

They passed through the masked ranks. The torchlight shining sanguine red on their grotesque features.

"O grim lord Samhain accept this sacrifice, we humbly beseech thee, " they uttered in invocation.

"Test the blade for sharpness," the trickster bade.

A masked trick or treater offered his arm. Clare opened an incision as he laughed.

"Sharp indeed. Let the ritual commence unhindered. Bring forth the sacrifice my acolyte!"

She had donned a ritual mask of flayed skin like a grisly executioner mask.

"Priestess, bring me his heart!" the vandal commanded.

"Sacrifice! Sacrifice!" they chanted as they writhed in wild atavistic rapture, cavorting against a foreground of flame as if dancing before a towering bonfire. He handed her a golden rune-inscribed sacrificial dagger.

"I assure you that your mortal weapons are quite useless against me."

He spread his arms exposing his torso.

"See for yourself. Allow me to be sporting. You may retrieve your blade," the vandal offered.

Patrick stabbed and stabbed desperately to the vandal's mocking laughter.

"Hahaha. Tickles. You, see? I am entirely invulnerable to your weapons. You imagined this was a duel. Do not flatter yourself. You are merely an offering. Now my thralls. Take him," the vandal commanded.

Patrick was grabbed and carried in a chanting torch-lit procession to a crude alter. A goat mask was forced on his face. He saw his own terrified eyes mirrored in the varnished blade. They forced a candied apple into Patrick's mouth.

"So many hungry mouths to feed this feast of Samhain...and such ravenous ones. Fret not young master. You will be avenged. Your lady will perish screaming once she holds your sliced out heart dripping in her palm," the vandal gloated.

"Hasten the hour grows late. Do not tarry," the vandal urged.

"You can stop this, Clare. Wake up!" Patrick urged.

Patrick looked pleadingly at her face, yet she was entirely mesmerized and unmoved.

He cringed and closed his eyes bracing for the agony of the curved blade slashing through his flesh. It never came. Her hand faltered as the dagger hovered over his beating heart, as the first tolling of the steeple bell for midnight echoed sonorously over the rooftops.

It shook her from whatever trance held them. The vandal screeched like a carrion bird deprived of carnage to scavenge by an advancing lion's roar. The mob shuddered convulsively as an impact ripple swept through them. Like a restless menagerie of dark spirits breaking loose at feeding time and consuming their captor they dropped their weapons and collided with him in wild disarray.

"I will not be thwarted by some lowly mortal! I will sacrifice you myself without these thralls!"

Gripping a reaper's scythe, the vandal launched at him with startling feline-like agility, evading Patrick's knife slashes. Finding an opening Patrick thrust the knife to the hilt with grim finality. The trickster's cry betrayed pain and his waning power. Its red smile shuddered like a speared eel as it faded. Like something cold-blooded and mortally wounded it still sought to kill his slayer in his thrashing death throes.

"I will carve you like a jack o lantern!" the vandal hissed.

Patrick then thrusted a torch setting his cloak on fire. Now enveloped in flame the demonic figure, charged at Patrick like a red ghost. Then as the last bell tolled midnight skeletal clawed hands reached for Patrick. The vandal drew back a hand to swing the scythe and decapitate his nemesis only to disintegrate in midstride. The scythe chimed on the pavement.

Meanwhile the trickster's "servants" exhaled dark vaporous mist that took human form before dissolving amorphously. The exorcised trick or treaters milled around, aimless and disoriented.

Approaching sirens were heard. Patrick placed a coat over Clare's shoulders.

"Let me take you home," Patrick said softly.

He escorted Clare into the bright dawn.

Winter Solstice
By Steph Minns

I crossed the main road, squinting against the driving rain. Dreary weather, dreary pub, dreary life, I thought as I stepped around puddles and shouldered the outer door of the 'Spotted Cow' tavern open. *My* dreary life. The door swung shut behind me, blocking the monochrome scene of the industrial cranes of Avonmouth once more, and I wandered into the fug of warm dampness, human breath mixed with wet coats and scarves. The bar is a traditional old pub style, dark wood, beer-stained green carpet.

I'd recently been made redundant from the docks as fewer freighters came into Bristol now. My daily existence now meant being holed up alone in my small flat, scraping by with a distinct lack of money. My old company had promised to re-employ me if things picked up, and meanwhile I'd been trawling the streets of Bristol looking for anything, shelf stacker, delivery driver. No luck so far though, and the future didn't look promising with so many in the same position. Twenty-six years old and this was my life, so I'd jumped at the chance of a pint with my old mate, Matty, when he'd called.

Matty was already at the bar, dressed in his usual leathers, his motorcycle helmet propped by his elbow.

"Gottcha one already, Dave," he shouted above the jukebox din, pushing a pint of my usual towards me.

"Cheers, mate."

My friend beamed his usual boyish grin, and I could tell he was just bursting to tell me something.

"So, what's new?" I asked.

"Fancy a winter solstice night break in a remote caravan?" Matty replied in a conspiratorial tone. "Could be a spooky one."

"Really? Where?"

I considered myself an open-minded fence-sitter to my friend's full blown amateur paranormal investigator persona, but an overnight break out of the city appealed, grim weather, ghosts or not.

"You remember my Aunty Jess?"

"Yeah."

I vaguely recalled Matty mentioning his aunt, a doctor, who lived over the bridge in the Wye Valley, somewhere near Tintern.

"Well, she's got a short contract on at a clinic in Newport, helping set up some new health project for a week, but asked me to go over to just check on the animals once or twice while she's away. Said I could stay all week if I wanted in the caravan at the end of the garden. Of course, I can't do that, but midweek is the winter solstice so I thought that would be a good time for a wee overnight break. We can chill, smoke some weed, few beers. It's beautiful out there, even in winter. Her place is surrounded by lots of ancient forest, and of course there's a good real ale pub in the village."

"Sounds good," I replied. I knew why Matty couldn't stay away for more than one night.

"Will Shelly be alright with your mum on her own?"

"Yeah. Mum'll have Meals on Wheels delivered during the day and Shelly doesn't mind stopping over to help her get to bed on the Wednesday night."

Matty's mum was disabled, and he acted as her carer, with some help from social services.

So, with the winter solstice looming on the Wednesday, I looked forward to a trip out into the Forest of Dean and the wild acres of the Wye Valley.

***

Perched on the back of Matty's bike, wearing Shelly's helmet, I drank in the beauty of the forest as we sped down the country roads. It was a bright day, the thick forest either side of the road offering a contrasting dark gloom to the winter sunlight that patterned the road. We reached his aunt's cottage around lunchtime and settled ourselves into the slightly battered old caravan at the end of the garden before wandering down to the small pasture beyond.

"No need to go into the house," Matty explained. "There's an outside loo there, and an outside tap for water."

I shuddered at the thought of the huge spiders probably lurking in the wooden outhouse but decided I could brave it.

"Hey there, fellas."

My friend started cooing to the three goats in the pasture, then went back for the hose attached to the outside tap to re-fill the tin bath that served as a drinking trough. I fussed the goats, which were pretty friendly and had come over to the fence, as Matty tossed a bale of hay over for them to supplement the winter grass.

"She had one of those pot-bellied pigs here too until last month when it died," he turned to explain, squinting against the sun which was now low over the trees as the afternoon faded.

"That was a rescue animal too, like the goats. Even when I was a kid, I remember coming out to visit and there were always animals, a Shetland pony, chickens."

I knew of Matty's love for animals, which ranked about equal to his love for Shelly and his mum, along with his fascination with photography. He'd won a national competition last year with his picture of hares fighting in a field. It had graced the cover of some wildlife charity calendar, I recalled. I'd seen the telephoto lens jutting out of one of his bike paniers as we'd set off, so assumed he'd brought some photography kit along.

It looked like nothing had changed out here for centuries. Despite being a doctor, Matty's aunt seemed to live modestly in the ancient stone cottage with its long sloping garden which ran down to meet the surrounding woods. The flower beds were now a tangle of dead, dried seed heads, still dusted with the previous night's frost in places. The sun was setting over the trees as we walked back to the caravan, and I noticed a distinct chill had crept into the air. The forest appearing impenetrable, silent, brooding.

"Let's get some beans on toast going," Matty suggested. "It's going to be a clear night according to the forecast, so we should get a good view of the night sky. That'll give me a chance to try out my new telephoto lens, well, second-hand really from a guy on the Bristol photography forum. There's a stone circle too in a field down the lane. Spooky place. But I bet it would offer some great photo opportunities under a full moon."

I always admired my friend's enthusiasm for life. His favourite saying was 'you can always find a small beauty in even the grimmest of days.' And he did, indeed, seem to manage that. You could pick that up in his photos, from birds in the park to staged 'character shots' of his workmates at the Royal Mail sorting office. Everything seemed to be a source of creative inspiration to Matty.

His cheer diminished a little though when he discovered the gas bottle for the little camping stove in the caravan was empty.

"Shit!" He muttered.

A hunt around his aunt's outhouse didn't turn up a spare. At least the electric fire worked, running off a buried cable that ran out from the cottage.

"Would your aunt mind if we borrowed her kitchen?" I suggested.

"Nah she wouldn't mind but I know she's locked the place up and set the alarm. I don't have the code, or a key for that matter. Nothing for it but to go to that garage shop we passed on the road. I know they sell camping stuff for the tourist caravan sites around the valley. I won't be long, Dave."

"Shall I come to give you a hand?"

"Nah, mate. I'll need the pillion space to strap the gas cannister on. See y' in a bit, twenty at most."

I watched my best friend pushing his long hair out of the way as he put on his helmet, before swinging a leg over his motorbike. The grumble of the engine faded away as he set off down the narrow track towards the main road.

It was the last I saw of Matty, ever.

***

When Matty hadn't returned two hours later, I started to worry. Darkness blanketed the woods behind the caravan now and only the small oil lamp on the table held back the shadows inside. At first, I wondered if he'd had to go further afield than the petrol station in search of a gas bottle, perhaps into the nearest town, but it still seemed like a long time. I'd amused myself at first in exploring the tattered paperback collection on a shelf above the seating area, mostly old 70's pulp fiction and sci-fi, but now I decided it was time to go and look for Matty. Perhaps his bike had broken down or he'd had an accident. Although there was no cell phone signal out here at least my phone flashlight would still work, so I shoved the phone into my pocket. A glance at the map my friend had left on the table showed me the route he would have taken, the winding rough track which cut through the woods, down the valley, and then met up with a local B road, the way we'd come in. The garage and shop were actually marked on the map, and I calculated that it might take me thirty minutes on foot.

The moonlight lit up the cottage garden and I thought I saw strange shadow figures skuttling back into the hedge for a moment as I stepped outside onto the crisp grass, panning my phone torch around. Jumpy city boy, I told myself. This was certainly a different world, no road noise, not even birds now the sun had gone down, and a vast sky of stars that I never noticed in the city when I looked up, due to light pollution. Aware of conserving my phone battery, I switched the torch off as I walked down the rutted track beside the cottage, able to see quite well by the moon, but had to switch it on again once I entered the wood. Here the blackness was intense, and I could hear many scuttling animal noises off to the sides.

I walked for a while before I came out of the woods again and alongside some fields. Gravel crunched underfoot in places where an effort had been made to surface the track, I guess by Matty's aunt as she was the only property along this access. When I spotted Matty's bike pulled up in a small layby, just big enough for two cars to pass each other, a wave of relief swept over me. Then I realised that the bike, parked on its stand, was facing downhill, towards the main road. Was this as far as he'd got?

"Matty. Hey Matt!"

My shouting received no response. I rocked the bike carefully on its stand and heard petrol sloshing in the tank. So, he hadn't run out of petrol. Maybe he'd stepped into the field for a piss, I wondered, fallen in a pothole, broken his leg or hit his head perhaps and was lying in the darkness nearby, unconscious. Treading carefully, I started to comb the field beside the track, calling. Nothing. But I did see the stone circle Matty had mentioned and wondered if he'd stopped to photograph it. I approached the stones, foreboding and other-worldly, as they sat like huddled old men under the moonlight. I remembered then that Matty's camera had been on the table next to the map I'd looked at. I searched the field on the opposite side of the track too, scrambling over a rickety barbed wire fence.

If something had happened and the bike had broken down, I guessed Matty had decided to walk on anyway to the garage shop to get a small bottle of gas he could carry back. I decided to walk down there, hoping I'd get a signal nearer to civilisation. As I passed the bike again, I spotted there were no keys in the ignition, lending weight to my theory.

The traffic on the B road to Tintern was minimal but a shock anyway after the half hour walk of silence through the wood. I remembered from the map that the garage would be to the left once I hit the road, so I started in that direction, cars zipping past me. The phone sprang to life as I came within mast range, and I stopped to call Matty, but his phone just rang and rang before going to voicemail. I tried it several times, hoping he'd pick up. Puzzled, I walked on, spotting the glaring neons of the garage forecourt in the distance at last.

The garage was oddly old-fashioned. A bell jingled as I opened the shop door and I noticed the shelves were stacked with old style retro stuff as I walked up to the counter, sweets I remembered from my school days, like Parma Violets and Spangles. No Perspex screens here, just a check patterned plastic countertop and a strangely out of place chunky punch button till. Maybe this remote little garage just hadn't caught up to the 2020's yet. The old guy serving was wearing normal enough clothes, saggy-butt jeans and blue shirt, and I asked him.

"Hi. Have you had a biker guy come in here recently, long dark hair, wearing leathers? He would have been looking for a portable gas cannister for a camping stove."

I'd seen the camping stuff, including cannisters, in the corner as I'd walked in so saw no reason for the man not to remember him. He ignored me to continue pricing tins of soup with a clicker gun. Maybe he was deaf, partially sighted or both as he didn't react to my presence until I walked right up in front of him to ask again, and then he jumped, as though he'd seen a ghost rise from the floor.

"Has a biker guy been in recently to buy a gas canister?"

"No, er no, no," the old guy stammered nervously, stepping backwards, and I wondered why he was so obviously ill at ease, even scared of me. Maybe he was fearful of being robbed alone out here at this time of night. No other customers had followed me in and the pumps, old-style and not the modern digital units usually seen on a garage forecourt, were empty of cars.

"OK, thanks."

A little irritated by the man's odd reaction, I turned and walked out to try Matty's phone once more. Still no joy. I called his girlfriend, Shelly, instead.

"Hi Shell. Yeah, it's Dave. You haven't heard from Matt in the last couple of hours, have you? No nothing wrong I hope, just weird that he left to get a gas bottle for the stove but hasn't come back. I found his bike up the lane, not crashed, just parked and left. Seems he hasn't made it to the local garage on foot either. No, there's no sign of him anywhere."

I chatted to Shelly a bit longer before she rang off, promising to call a couple of hospitals in the area. I decided to walk back and search the fields by the bike for Matty again on the way back to the cottage, not sure what else I could do. It would be too soon to call the police as there was no evidence anything had happened to him yet, but I felt a chill of concern that was growing by the minute. As I approached the stone circle for a second time, I had an uncanny feeling of dread, of something wrong, and my gut feeling told me to turn back, not to step up inside the ring.

As I stood pondering the massive, looming stones, I thought I could hear whispering voices, like hoarse old men chattering and cackling together. I stopped calling Matty's name to listen. The voices were indistinct, as though underground, or emanating from the stones themselves and, as I stepped away from the circle, the voices suddenly ceased. I became even more alarmed at the silence now, as though someone or something was aware of my presence and listening to me too, my breathing, my steps on the frosty grass. A ground fog had gathered on the fields by now, lending a creepy vibe to the scene.

Totally unnerved, I climbed the fence again and turned back up the lane towards the cottage. As the route took me back into the woods, dank and dark to the point of making me feel I was walking in limbo, I became aware of rustlings and twig cracking beside the track, louder than on the way down, closer. My phone torch didn't pick out anything and I guessed it was some woodland animal, a badger maybe or a deer. The sounds spooked me, all the same, and I began to walk faster. Frost had started to rime the hedge and I could see my breath misting, wraith-like, as I reached the garden gate.

As I stepped through the cottage gate, an unearthly cry rang out from the woods directly behind me. It sounded like a woman yet had some unearthly quality to it that chilled me to the bone. Something was running towards me through the trees. I could hear it on the forest floor, determined, heading straight for me. I had a gut feeling that I was prey, something being hunted.

I'd left the caravan door unlocked and so was able to run inside. I rammed the bolt across the flimsy door and fumbled for matches to re-light the oil lamp on the table. Its cheerful glow flooded the small caravan. Matty clearly hadn't returned here. I heard the weird animal cry again, just outside the caravan now. Then something thumped against the door and began scratching frantically at the bottom of it. I could see the door flexing and prayed the bolt would hold. A fox, I told myself, it was just a fox. But then why was it trying to get inside, not something a fox would do, surely?

Peering out of the grimy window when the scrabbling stopped didn't help. I could see nothing outside the door, but I was sure I could see eye-shine at the bottom of the lawn, twinkling green discs that bobbed up and down, staring directly at the caravan. They were far too high off the ground to be any natural woodland animal I knew of. I thought I could make out a second and third pair of twinkling eye-shine discs too, and tall white shapes that stretched up into the trees. The shapes looked humanoid but were definitely not people. I watched the sight in horror until the lights blinked out again, minutes later, and the white shapes faded.

I spent an uneasy night after that, worrying not just about Matty now, but what prowled outside in the garden and woods beyond. At one point, around 4am, I was woken from an uneasy doze by footsteps pottering across the caravan's tin roof. They were of something two-legged but not heavy as a person would be. I followed their deliberate progress across the roof before I heard whatever it was leap off to land beside the kitchen window and scuttle away. An hour later, just as I was drifting back to sleep again, I heard an inhuman muttering outside, two individuals talking in that raspy whisper I'd heard at the stones. Terrified, I listened as the voices faded away and the silence returned. I huddled in my blanket on the pull-out camper bed, ears straining, senses on fire to pick up any further noises, and stayed that way until dawn.

***

The watery sunlight was temporarily blinding as it hit the snow blanket, which spread out across the garden lawn beyond the cottage. It had snowed heavily during the night. There was a silent beauty about the scene, about the ice crystals glittering on the ground as far as the eye could see, the tree trunks spangled with diamonds. I came slowly back to life as I sucked on a cigarette, the chill air punching me awake.

Last night I'd dreamed of Matty, some fleeting images that unsettled me as I struggled to piece the dream together again before it was lost, like a gossamer web disintegrating under a thoughtless touch. I'd been speaking to Matty in the dream, and he'd been begging for help, terrified and lost.

"I don't know where I am, Dave. It's dark here and I can hear the stones talking in my head."

"You must come back, Matty. You can't stay there. This is your world," I remembered pleading with him in the dream. "You have to find a way back."

But his desperate voice had faded away then. The memory disturbed me and seemed somehow real, not like a dream at all. Matty and I had talked for hours about parallel dimensions, UFO's and timeslips. He had been convinced of the reality of such things. For me at this moment it was too disturbing to even contemplate.

The reborn sun climbed higher into the pearly sky, and I realised that this was the day of the winter solstice that Matty had been so keen to be here for. I cautiously unbolted the caravan door and stepped outside but was stopped in my tracks by some odd footprints in the snow, winding up to the caravan. They were large, like nothing I'd seen before with three toes and a broad pad, as big as a large dog's print, but something bipedal, walking upright. I followed them as they made their way around the caravan, stopping below the kitchen window. I recalled the noises last night and the muttering, odd voices with a fresh chill.

I was puzzling over this when the sound of a car approaching shook me back to the present. It was a small red Fiat, bumping over the frozen track towards the cottage. Shelly. She must have set out at the crack of dawn to get here.

"I was just about to walk down to the road to call you again." I hailed her.

Shelly looked as though she'd barely slept, her dark hair scraped back into an untidy twist.

"Hi Dave. I haven't heard from him, and his phone is dead now. I think we should go to the police in Tintern."

"OK. I'll just pack my bag. You saw his bike down the lane?"

"Yeah. It'll be ok there for now. Let's report him missing."

I packed Matty's photography kit up and gave the goats some more hay, as I'd seen Matty do, then Shelly put the caravan key under the van steps. As she did so, I noticed the scratches on the buckled base of the door and was about to blurt out about the weird stuff of last night when I thought better of it. Would Shelly believe me or just think I was causing a selfish distraction, all about me?

Just in case Matty had fallen in the woods or fields near his bike and I'd missed him in the dark, we searched again now it was light and we could see better. The stone circle, even in the daylight, creeped me out but there was not a sign of him. Tintern was a left turn once back on the B road and I suddenly realised how hungry I was. I'd not had anything to eat except a packet of crisps and no hot drink since we'd arrived yesterday, due to the stove not working, so I asked Shelly if we could stop at the garage I'd been to last night.

As she pulled into the forecourt, I was surprised that it looked somehow different. The petrol pumps looked like standard modern ones. Last night I'd thought they were vintage yellow Shell pumps, the sort you see in films from the 70's. The building looked the same, but once through the door I began to feel distinctly uneasy. The interior was bright and modern, the shelves stacked with snacks I was familiar with, and the counter, when I approached it, had a Perspex screen and modern computerised till. I wondered if I was going crazy, or was somehow mistaken in where I was, so I asked the young woman serving if there were any other garages along this stretch of road.

"No love," she replied. "We're the only one until town now, so I'd fill up while you can if I was you."

"OK thanks."

I took my pasty and coffees for Shelly and myself and left. I must have looked strange as Shelly asked me when I got back in the car.

"You ok, Dave? You've gone white."

"No, I'm fine thanks. Fine."

But ten minutes further down the road I told her everything, including the dream where Matty had been in some parallel universe, begging for help. And the eyes in the garden, the strange, inhuman shrieks, and the feeling of foreboding at the stones. Then the something stalking round the caravan during the night, trying to get in and leaving odd footprints. She didn't laugh at me.

"It is the same garage, except I visited it thirty plus years ago," I blurted. "It's definitely the same garage. I don't understand it."

We drove on in silence. I'm sure Shelly believed me, at least she didn't tell me I was talking a load of cods, but then we were at the police station and being interviewed about Matty's disappearance, Shelly fumbling for a good picture of him on her phone, so everything else was put aside.

***

Back in Bristol, I kept in touch with Shelly. She went back to the cottage with her brother and his trailer to collect the bike and talk to the aunt, but there was no news of Matty. The local police investigation turned up nothing. I struggled to pinpoint any tiny thing that I'd over-looked in the following weeks, but I came up with nothing that could throw any light. It seemed Matty had, literally, vanished into thin air as though taken by the pixies.

My Waifu
By Scott McGregor

Gripping his bag with one hand and the latest issue of the Nakamura Chronicles in the other, Egor strolled to the nearby flower shop in the Tokyo Haneda Airport, fresh off his thirteen-hour flight from Toronto. In every direction, he spotted the signs and billboards repeating the same message in Japanese and English: *Happy White Day!*

He rubbed his heavy eyes, barely awake. The jetlag drained him harder than he anticipated, fatigued and uneasy. As he set foot on the plane, he told himself he'd sleep during the flight. But how could he possibly rest when he was hours away from meeting the love of his life?

On a nearby terminal screen, the animated woman materialized, dressed in a pink and polka-dotted Lolita to complement her vibrant, cherry-blossom color hair. She waved at the new arrivals, and Egor's stomach filled with butterflies at the sight of her beauty.

There she is… Ayumi Nakamura.
My waifu…
Egor glanced at the cover of the Nakamura Chronicles. At the beautiful, enchanting girl who winked back at him with a playful smirk, cheeks rosy red. "I love you, forever," he said, catching a few glances from new arrivals passing him.

Ayumi Nakamura, the lead character in Egor's favorite manga and anime, the Nakamura Chronicles. Ayumi Nakamura, the girl who stole Egor's heart halfway across the world without meeting him in person. He'd seen her name on every episode of the Nakamura Chronicles, all 1226 episodes, released and distributed over the last fourteen years. He dared not admit it to anyone, but spent his most private, secluded moments of his life watching Ayumi on his computer screen. She was everything in a woman Egor could dream of: Educated, sophisticated, sympathetic, ambitious. Beautiful. Kind. Talented. Imaginative. He could go on for hours if he wanted.

But as charming as Ayumi Nakamura appeared, Egor could not say the same for the voice actress. Nobody could, as her identity was kept secret from the mass public. Across the internet, hundreds of conspiracy theories arose to debunk the mystery. Some claimed there was no actress behind the character—voice entirely composed by the studio. Egor also couldn't help but wonder why her name never appeared on the credits. But those wonders often faded when he saw Ayumi appear on screen and heard her soothing voice, for that's all Egor needed from her to make his days pleasant.

Soon enough, he'd meet her in person, a dream come true.

And on White Day of all days, precisely one month after Valentine's Day

Though they never celebrated the custom back in Canada, Egor was all too familiar with the Japanese Holiday. March 14th, White Day. A holiday for those to reciprocate the gifts and affection they received on Valentine's Day back to those who expressed their love.

For the last fourteen years, Egor consistently showered Ayumi with his affection on Valentine's Day. He expressed his love for Ayumi through letters, gifts, and flowers. To spice up his presents, he forwarded a voice recording with elaborate details of his devotion to her character.

At first, he regretted sending the recording, fearing he might come off as creepy. But to his surprise, Ayumi reciprocated. Days ago, Egor's inbox received a personal message from Ayumi Nakamura's team:

Dear Mr. Egor Bennett,

On behalf of the creators of the Nakamura Chronicles, we are thrilled to invite you for a unique opportunity to meet the wonderful and incredibly talented voice actress behind Ayumi Nakamura's character on White Day, March 14th! This invitation is a testament to your years of valued support as a fan, and we believe it will be a memorable experience that you will forever cherish.

As our team is excited to meet you in person and share our passion for the character you admire, please let us know if you can accept this invitation, and we will make all necessary arrangements to ensure your visit to Japan is enjoyable.

Should you be interested, please arrive at Marufuku Coffee at 7:00 PM UTC at the Tokyo Haneda Airport, where you will meet Ayumi in person. We look forward to your response and sincerely hope you can attend this unforgettable experience!

Once he read the message, he immediately agreed to the invitation and purchased a one-way ticket to Tokyo. He couldn't think of another woman he would be more honoured to spend White Day with than Ayumi Nakamura, for she deserved his unrequited love and devotion.

So why was he so nervous to meet her?

Maybe it's because you never learned how to talk to women.

He hated to admit it, but Egor had never had a girlfriend, forever single, and embarrassingly, still a virgin. As unlikely as it sounded, the voice of his subconscious kept whispering to Egor, *maybe that'll all change tonight when you meet Ayumi!*

All he needed to do was meet her at the designated spot in the airport: Marufuku Coffee at 7:00 PM. He wouldn't miss it for the world. Hell, what was he talking about? *Ayumi Nakamura is my world.*

Walking toward the nearby flower shop, he thought of episode 273 of the Nakamura Chronicles—where Ayumi travelled to Kyoto and slept in a field of cherry blossoms, one of Egor's favorites. He purchased a bouquet of Himawari Sunflowers. Cherry blossoms might be the most common flower in the Nakamura Chronicles, but any real fan of Ayumi knew her favourite flower was the Himawari. Surely, a bouquet of sunflowers would win him bonus points when he met the real Ayumi.

On his way out of the shop, Egor said, "Arigato."

Despite years of consuming Japanese manga and anime from his computer desk, Egor's fluency in the language amounted to hello, goodbye, and thank you. Good thing the voice actress for Ayumi handled both the Japanese and English dub of the Nakamura Chronicles, otherwise he'd be in for a long night.

Outside a coffee shop, Egor read the words *Marufuku Coffee* written below the Japanese text. *Thank God this place has signs in English.* He checked his watch periodically: 6:43 PM, seventeen minutes until his meeting with Ayumi.

As he sat down and pulled off his jacket, he told himself to stay calm and composed. Women do appreciate a man with confidence, after all.

But how could a man like Egor abide by such a notion? Back home, no woman offered affection to him. No woman paid him attention. After a failed coffee date, a girl once told him nobody would be caught dead loving someone as creepy and revolting as him.

He was tired of being alone.

Thirty-two years old, and nothing but rejection after rejection to tell his sad dating life. He longed for the day a woman would show him compassion. Showed him appreciation. Showed him he deserved to be loved like all the rest. If there was any lesson he could take away from his failed attempts at love, it was one harsh, painful truth that men like him needed to follow.

Find love where you can.

Everyone deserves a hand to hold in times of comfort, even if it's animated.

***

A young Japanese woman with spectacles approached the table.

"Egor Bennett?" she asked.

"Uh, yes?"

Could this be the famous Ayumi? He examined her from head to toe, face stern, eyes reserved and cold, rarely blinking. In his dreams, he always pictured the voice actress for Ayumi with a vibrant smile and expressive eyes, wearing a cherry blossom dress with long, dyed pink hair. Even thinking about it aroused him.

But nothing about the woman who stood before him reminded him of the woman of his dreams. Late twenties, possibly early thirties. Dressed in a well-fitted brown suit, all business, no casual. Face stoic and expressionless, presence formidable, not like the charming, bubbly demeanour of Ayumi. A bit disappointing, really.

She extended her hand toward Egor. "Pleasure to meet you."

Egor reciprocated and accepted her stern, tight shake.

"Wow, you're not how I imagined—you're beautiful, obviously."

She squinted her eyebrows, unimpressed. "Umm, thank you?"

Be cool, Egor. Be cool. "And your English is excellent."

"Forgive me, but we should skip the small talk and get down to business, Mr. Bennett."

"Wait…" Egor paused and looked at her again. *Her voice… It's all wrong.* "Pardon me," he continued, "are you not Ayumi Nakamura?"

"I am not. My name is Kyzuki Ryo, and I am one of Ayumi Nakamura's associates."

"Oh?"

Why was one of Ayumi's *associates* meeting with him?

"I'm here to escort you to Ayumi Nakamura," she said. "She's quite excited to meet you."

"Really? The invitation said I'd meet Ayumi at the airport outside Marufuku Coffee?"

"Yes… and that's where we've reached an impasse. Ayumi's schedule is extremely tight and hectic, and she doesn't do in-person meetings. Not in a place like this, at least."

"But the email said differently? Why go through the trouble of meeting me here? Why not tell me to meet with her elsewhere?"

"That's confidential, I'm afraid. Ayumi Nakamura is very private about these matters."

Why does she keep using that name, Egor wondered. "Sorry, you keep referring to her as Ayumi Nakamura, but that's just the character's name. Mind if I ask what her real name is?"

"Again, confidential. You must understand that our team takes great precautions with concealing Ayumi's true identity. Revealing such information in such a public place draws… issues. I'll have to ask you to come with me."

"Come with you where?"

"To Ayumi Nakamura, of course. That is why you've travelled all this way?"

"And if I say no?"

She chuckled. "Please."

Egor found Kyzuki's snippy attitude unamusing, the complete opposite of Ayumi's personality. Still, she was absolutely right; he wouldn't dare forfeit this opportunity. He closed his manga and gazed at the cover in the latest issue of the Nakamura Chronicles—into Ayumi Nakamura's warm, cherry-blossom eyes. How could an anime character possibly be so pretty?

"You're right," he said. "I'm ready to meet Ayumi."

* * *

As Kyzuki drove the Honda, Egor sat in the backseat, fidgety and nervous. She drove for quite some time, already two hours outside Tokyo. He tried his best to make idle chitter-chatter with Kyzuki, but her taste in fashion matched her cold personality—all business, no casual.

"So, what exactly do you do for work? Like, how do you contribute to Ayumi's team?"

"Complicated. You could say I handle Ayumi's day-to-day activities that she isn't positioned to do herself, such as picking you up from the airport."

"You're an assistant then?"

In the rearview mirror, Kyuzki glanced at Egor, lips grimaced. She looked back at the road, ignoring Egor's comment. *Guess she didn't like that very much...*

"How would you describe Ayumi in one word?"

Kyzuki paused for a moment, then said, "Brainy."

"Right, I always pictured her as a highly intelligent woman."

"It won't be too much longer, Mr. Bennett."

He held the sunflowers with care, not a petal out of place. Everything must be perfect for Ayumi Nakamura. *I hope she likes me...*

Kyzuki turned off on the main road and drove down a new path. Approaching a driveway gate, she rolled down the window and spoke into the speaker. "It's me."

The gate opened, and Egor's eyes caught a view of the emerald dojo. Kyzuki pulled toward the parking lot, no other cars around.

"So, this is Ayumi Nakamura's home?" Egor asked.

"Not exactly." Kyzuki parked. "More of a studio."

"Studio?" His stomach tightened. "Are you saying we're outside the studio where Ayumi Nakamura does all her voice recordings?"

"Correct."

"Why does she work so far outside the city?"

"As I mentioned, Ayumi Nakamura is very private. All her personal and professional relationships must be handled delicately. You should feel honoured to meet her face to face, figuratively speaking."

"Figuratively? What's that supposed to—"

"Mr. Bennett, I previously mentioned Ayumi Nakamura's schedule is tight. Please save all your questions for inside."

"Don't you think now would be a good time to tell me her name? Her *real* name? It's not like we're at the airport anymore."

"Let me ask you this, Mr. Bennett. Would you rather I tell you her real name, or would you rather hear it from her directly?"

"You know what the answer is."

"Then I suggest you walk right in. You don't want to keep her waiting on White Day, do you?"

Absolutely not. Egor opened the door, stepped out, and approached the dojo's doors.

"One more thing," Kyzuki called from the car. "Ayumi is rather self-conscious about how she looks. Please refrain from staring, if you think you can manage that."

He was about to meet the love of his life for the first time; how could he possibly not stare? "You won't be joining us?"

Kyzuki shook her head. "Happy White Day, Mr. Bennett," she said as she rolled up the window and exited the lot from where they entered.

Be cool, Egor. Confidence is key.

"Okay, moment of truth."

He opened the doors and entered the dojo. If it weren't for hours of consuming the Nakamura Chronicles, Egor would not have been able to appreciate the four portraits on the dojo walls, leading to another doorway down the hall. Four portraits of cherry blossom flowers in rose pink, cobalt blue, mint green, and tangerine orange. Each represented one of the four seasons in the fictional land of Kyanto where Ayumi lived. Her taste in art matched her bubbly personality. Perfect taste for a perfect woman, as a proper waifu should be.

He remembered all those sour interactions he shared with women. All those girls who scoffed at him. Who laughed at him. Who called him creepy. Who made him feel lonely and unlovable. They were worthless compared to Ayumi. Nothing compared to his waifu.

My waifu would never make me feel that way. Egor felt more closer to Ayumi than any person he met in the real world. *Ayumi is my world…*

He glanced down the hallway. *She must be waiting for me in the next room…*

As he walked toward the door, his legs and hands shook, petals out of place. Moments away from meeting Ayumi, he nearly lost his footing in excitement, typical Egor. Is this what love is supposed to feel like?

He opened the door and entered an empty room, dimly lit by the grey, shiny walls. No, not walls, but black mirrors illuminating his reflection. *Are those screens?*

"Hello," said a gentle, arousing voice from the overhead speakers. "It's nice to finally meet you, Egor."

I know that voice anywhere…

"Ayumi Nakamura?" Egor asked.

"Who else would it be?"

"Wow… I can't believe I'm actually talking to you. This doesn't feel real." Egor almost professed his unrequited love for her, but he kept his mouth shut. No need to gush right now. Important to make a good first impression. His waifu deserved to be treated like a proper lady, after all. "Where are you?"

"In the next room." Ayumi giggled.

"Can't we talk face to face?

The projectors switched on, and an animated Ayumi materialized on the walls. She wore a green silk kimono, hair tied in a bun. "How's this, handsome?" she said, followed by her classic wink.

"That's not what I meant." Egor paced left and right, and Ayumi's animated eyes followed his every movement. "Is this animation in real-time?"

"Indeed."

Egor inspected the background, a green hillside next to the ocean. *Of course, this is the arc where Ayumi travelled to the Kyanto region in search of her grandmother. How could I possibly forget!*

Ayumi glanced below Egor. "Did you bring me flowers?"

Right, the flowers! "Yes! I brought you a dozen sunflowers."

"Aweh, that's so thoughtful. You're such a sweetheart."

Egor blushed. This moment brought him back to his high school graduation, the first and only time he landed a date. Her name was Samantha Gradbury, a girl he shared classes with since middle school. The first girl Egor loved from afar. It took all the confidence in the world to muster the courage to ask her to the graduation dance. He couldn't believe she said yes, too.

He still savored the memory of that night when he picked her up. He vividly remembered that look on her face when he gave her the tulips. That beautiful, inviting smile that put all his stresses at ease. *You're so sweet*, she told him.

But later that night, Samantha Gradbury ditched him. Chose to dance with the captain of the swim team instead. Her rejection left Egor heartbroken, never able to love a woman again. Not a real one, anyway.

He hoped for a different result tonight.

"Is there anything you'd like to know about me?" Ayumi asked.

"How about we start with your name? Your real name."

She giggled. "Ayumi Nakamura is my real name, silly."

"Really?" None of this made any sense to him. "So the Ayumi Nakamura character isn't fictional? That's actually you?"

"It's what I imagine myself being. It's me telling the story of the life I most desire to live, even if it's only animated. Everyone deserves to turn their dreams into reality, one way or another."

Egor admired her ambition and drive. What was a girl as profound as Ayumi Nakamura doing talking to a guy like Egor? "Ayumi… why did you invite me to spend White Day? You must receive hundreds of letters from fans."

"Hundreds of thousands, yes." Ayumi blushed, reluctant to usher the words, "A few of them called me their waifu."

"That's weird. Gross too."

Ayumi raised an eyebrow at him and smirked, teasing him.

Egor sputtered, "I meant the fans. The ones who called you that are gross. Not you. You're not gross, of course…" He bit his lip in shame. Why did he have to be so bad at talking to women? "So why me, Ayumi?"

"You really wanna know?"

Egor nodded, speechless.

Again, Ayumi smiled. Not teasingly, but softly; lips sealed, care written across her animated face. "It's your voice. It sounds heartwarming against my ears. A tad sexy, even."

Is she flirting with me? His lips tightened, hands shook, and loins stirred. "Really?"

Ayumi presented a different smile, one Egor instantly recognized. The one she reserved for the boys she deemed worthy to flirt with. "You sound surprised?"

How could he not be surprised? Her words marked the first time a girl complimented him. And from the woman of his dreams of all people. Egor wanted nothing more than to feast his eyes on her.

On the real Ayumi.

"Ayumi… I want to see you," he requested.

She dropped her joyful smile at the remark. Breaking her animated trance on him, she shied to the side.

He tightened his grip on the flowers. "Please, for me? How else am I supposed to give you these flowers."

"But what if I'm not like how you imagined? What if the second you see me, you no longer think I'm beautiful."

Egor was never well-versed in person-to-person contact, but he imagined this would be the moment he'd hold her hand and tell her everything was okay. To let her know she could trust him with anything. Anything for his waifu.

"You could never disappoint me, Ayumi," he reassured.

Her vibrant smile radiated the room one last time, until she said, "If you insist."

Another door opened, splitting the screens in half, along with Ayumi. The animation vanished, filling the room with darkness. Egor stood in silence, thinking back to that day he waited on Samantha Gradbury's porch with those flowers. Why did he always get so nervous when he was about to stand face-to-face with his crush?

Because you're in love with her, just as you loved Samantha, he told himself.

"Why don't you join me in here, Egor?" said that voice again, tone arousing.

That's not a speaker, he realized. *That's really her voice, right in front of me.*

Egor stepped inside the next room, adjusting to the humid air, hotter than a Toronto summer. And with the change in temperature came the sound of dangling chains rattling against each other. "Ayumi?"

He paused when the warm-white color dimly lit the room. At first, Egor assumed he stared at a bizarre decoration dangling from the ceiling, similar to bones at a dinosaur museum—some oversized human cranium. But his eyes traced the surface of the rotten skeleton and watched the veiny, exposed brain pulsate.

Whatever dangled from the ceiling was alive. A single eyeball detached from the socket held up by a cord made eye contact with him. In the spot where a mouth should have been, he saw a voice box dug beneath the skeleton, attached to a mixture of tangled wires and vocal cords leading down to a bare larynx. The creature reminded him of all those human anatomy sketches he saw in his biology textbooks, only far more intimidating in person. As the brain throbbed with unnatural rhythm, the creature wheezed and struggled to form words.

"Hello, Egor," said the creature, voice all too similar.

He grew accustomed to Ayumi Nakamura surprising him, but he never reacted to her with such dismay. "You're Ayumi Nakamura?"

"In the flesh."

She giggled again, and Egor watched her vocal cords vibrate with each word she muttered. Normally, he found the sound of her voice soothing. Addictive, one might say. Perfect for calming himself after a bad day at work. Perfect to help him sleep when he faced insomnia. The right balance of sweetness, confidence, and teasing to leave any man longing for her affection. For her touch. For her love.

But listening to her voice come from the hideous, rotten brain made him want to cry, run away, and vomit all at once, the exact opposite of love. He brought his fist to his mouth and resisted the urge to yack.

"You don't look happy," the abomination told him, voice screechy and distorted. From behind, a screen flickered on, and Ayumi's animated body returned. "Would you prefer if we talked like this, Egor?"

He'd be lying if he said yes. Egor's antsy nerves moved him into a pacing motion, left and right. How could he possibly form words at such a revelation?

Blue fluorescent light filled the room. Attached to the back of Ayumi's skeleton, he spotted the black cords. He followed the trail of cables upward, bewildered at the spectacle across the ceiling. Above, he watched Ayumi-like brains and larynx muscles dangling, each grunting and gargling. There must've been hundreds of them, all hooked up and wired to the back of Ayumi's cranium.

"Ayumi, what is all that?"

"Meet the cast of the Nakamura Chronicles." The animation pointed to the top of the room. "Over there is Hiroshi Nakamura, my father, then Kazuki Yamamoto, my childhood friend, and Satoshi Tanaka, my rival at Hideo Academy—"

"Wait." He nearly toppled over again, disturbed and shocked. "Are you saying all those *things* up there are voice actors?"

"I know it sounds crazy, but look at me, Egor. I'm lonely. I can't exactly leave the dojo and meet people. My associates have done a great job keeping me alive and building a platform where I can express the story I wish to tell to the world. But at the end of the day, I need people to talk to."

Egor wanted to empathize with her. He wanted to show Ayumi compassion, especially since she had been there for him in his most private and painful moments without ever being in the room with him. But he would be lying if he said Ayumi Nakamura wasn't as appealing in person as he imagined. "Okay… but what does all this have to do with me?"

"Like I said, I'm quite a fan of your voice."

The implication of those words horrified him. He stepped backward, dropped the sunflowers, and said, "Absolutely not."

"You told me in your audio submission that you spent most of your life dedicated to watching the Nakamura Chronicles. Dedicated to *me*. If that's how you feel, then why not spend the rest of your life a part of my project? Spend your life with me, Egor."

He longed to hear those words. Picturing a life with his waifu was an everyday occurrence. But not like this. He imagined everyone who rudely vocalized his bizarre infatuation with Ayumi—his friends, family, and colleagues. All those people who mocked him. Those who said it was crazy to fall in love with an anime character.

Maybe he should've listened to them.

After years of fantasizing about the day he'd meet Ayumi, all he said was, "You're bat-shit crazy."

The animated Ayumi's smile faded, now pouty. "Pardon?"

"You're asking me to abandon my life. If you genuinely believe I'll sacrifice that for you, you're apeshit. All those letters were for the woman of my dreams. But I don't even know what the fuck you're supposed to be."

"But… you told me on your recording that you loved me, forever. Don't you still want to spend White Day with me?"

"Fuck no!" he shouted. "You're not the woman I thought you were. I'm not in love with you; I'm in love with this make-believe fantasy you've created. Nobody in their right mind would love something as hideous as you."

The animated Ayumi shed a tear and wiped her eyes. "That's so hurtful to say, Egor."

"So was pretending to like me. All you want is another sad sap you can bend to do your bidding. That's your specialty. Pretending to reciprocate the love you receive from others. I refuse to be a part of it. I deserve to be loved too, not manipulated."

"I didn't want to have to do it this way…"

"What are you talking about?"

He wanted to scream at the top of his lungs. He wanted to tear his copy of the Nakamura Chronicles in half. He wanted to return home and burn every disc, book, collectible, and merchandise tied to her. He wanted to let everyone know the truth behind Ayumi Nakamura—the ugly truth connected to a never-ending chain of larynxes.

But when he turned around, a familiar, unpleasant face greeted him and blocked his path.

"Hello again, Mr. Bennett," Kyzuki said, pushing a tazer into Egor's abdomen.

The shocking ripple that coursed through his body swept Egor off his feet. He hit the ground and squirmed, glancing back and forth between Kyzuki, the animated Ayumi, and the dangling brain and larynx.

Coming from the entrance, three men dressed in surgical scrubs encircled Egor. For the first time all evening, Kyzuki smiled, not nearly as pleasant as Ayumi's.

"Don't worry, Mr. Bennett." Kyzuki squatted and stared into Egor's electric-frozen eyes. "The procedure is mostly painless. Mostly."

Egor tried to tell her to *fuck off*, but his pain-ridden body put him in silent paralysis. The three men lifted him off the ground and placed him onto a trolley. A tear rolled down Egor's face as he glared at the love of his life.

"Happy White Day, Egor," Ayumi said. Behind the dangling monstrosity, the animated version of Ayumi blew a kiss toward him. His heart melted.

God, she is still so beautiful…

Find love where you can.

As the doctors injected a needle into his forearm, he wondered what kind of character Ayumi would create based on his voice. Maybe when he awoke, he'd voice a sharp, dashing young man seeking to win Ayumi's heart, as he always dreamed. Moments before he fell unconscious, he glared at Ayumi's animated, radiant smile one last time, ready to embrace his new life on the Nakamura Chronicles.

Her voice was all he needed to remind himself that true love does exist. His waifu was there for him when no one else was. And now he could return the favour.

His voice would be with her.

His love would be with her.

Forever.

Elijah
By Rachel L. Tilley

Alex perched on the steps, her palm supporting her chin while she waited. Other than when her mother had sent her back upstairs to put on a necklace and hairband – so she looked more *presentable* – she had been ready for ages. Well, more accurately, she had been ready on time.

Her father was trying ineffectively to hurry everyone else along. He'd requested her help too, asking her to get Joel dressed, but she had quite promptly informed him that no other fifteen-year-old girls she knew helped their little brothers put their clothes on and maybe he should do it himself. Disappointingly, even watching her father trying to get a toddler to stop wriggling long enough to pull up his trouser legs hadn't provided much entertainment.

"Eleanor," he called up to his wife, before clearly thinking better of it and running upstairs to try and hurry her along. It wasn't a big enough house to prevent Alex overhearing their conversation. "Come on, everyone will be waiting."

"So, they'll wait." An exasperated sigh. "Every year your family insist on doing the first seder night, and you always say we'll attend, despite knowing full well I'd rather do one at home."

"I know, I'm sorry and we can work that out later, but for now can we please just get there so they aren't all complaining about us holding things up?"

"I'll be down shortly. I can hardly go with no makeup on." That was the cue for him to leave her to it.

Alex heard him shuffle across the hallway, before knocking on Carly's bedroom door this time. He received no response. She could imagine his frustration mounting, even though this situation could clearly have been predicted, as it was the same every time they went out for dinner anywhere. She cringed as she heard her father push gently against Carly's door – not a wise move. "Hey! Get out I'm getting changed."

"Just checking you're alive in there. Besides, you should already be ready by now, why are you still changing?" He found the door closed on him, and that was the end of the conversation. Joel, in the meantime, had kicked off his shoes and was peeling away one of his socks. She toyed with the idea of putting them back on for him, but selfishly decided to get herself a glass of water instead, before returning to her observation post.

When Carly did come downstairs, Alex nearly spat the water back out again in amusement. Carly simply raised her eyebrows at her, smirking… daring her to say something. She didn't. Predictably, her dad, however, rose to the bait. "What on *Earth* are you wearing? How do you even own a skirt that short!" She dismissed him with a wave of her hand. Alex reckoned her father was yet to realize that under her sister's jumper was probably a skimpy top to match the skirt.

She wasn't even wearing tights; she was going to be freezing.

Not long after, her mother appeared. Her dad gestured towards Carly – the universal symbol for '*you* do something about this' – but it turned out to be two against one. "We hardly have time for her to get changed now, darling. I thought we were late. Anyway, she's going to a party after. It's only five, we'll be done by half nine. She may as well be allowed to have some fun."

"It's twenty-three minutes past five…"

"Yes, so let's get going."

Alex was prepared to enjoy the short journey in silence but alas… "Alexandra Epstein! What have you got on your feet?"

She looked down at the slightly muddy, white sneakers she was wearing. They did look a bit silly with her dress, but she didn't see what the big deal was. "We have to take our shoes off inside anyway. I can't see the point in lacing my boots on just for the thirty-second walk from the car."

Her mother was not appeased. "Dan. Turn the car around."

"I am *not* turning the car around. Besides, no one will be looking at Alex with Carly dressed like that." She wasn't sure whether to laugh or be affronted. Before she could decide, he made a left turn, down a street she hadn't been expecting. Had she forgotten, or had her parents omitted to mention, that they were spending the first night of Passover at Aunt Dina's this year.

Her great aunt was something of a mystery, and Alex could never fully remember exactly whose sister or cousin she was, to make her part of the family. They paid her a visit once a year; having seder night there would be a first. Aunt Dina lived alone on a secluded estate, in a house so large it astonished Alex every time she saw it.

In reality, she probably did leave the house to do all manner of things that ordinary people did – like buy groceries, or meet friends for walks in the park – but Alex could never imagine her as being a separate entity from the house.

As they drove up the private approach, the classical music on the radio turned ominous. Alex squirmed, and tried to pull her shoulders back, but there wasn't enough space.

There were five cars already in the driveway, serving as unnecessary proof they were the last to arrive. From her middle seat, Alex's vision was too restricted to see the full mansion, but as soon as Carly exited, she was able to climb out and stretch her arms. They'd parked further away than she'd expected, and it had been silly not bothering with a jacket. Although, watching Carly struggling in her heels across the uneven stones was enough to make her forget all about her own worries.

The handful of other houses in this neighborhood were of a similar size, but this was the only one that gave Alex an eerie chill. Probably because it was the only one she actually had to go inside. A three-story brick monstrosity in the Victorian style, it was well-maintained, and Alex knew the dense ivy growing up the exterior was intentional.

On one side, the roof led into a turret. Unless you had been inside, and knew this was only for decoration, it looked to be the kind of spire in which you might find Rapunzel waiting, or even better, stumble across a secret alchemy lab.

She mentally reminded herself to smile, whilst she tried to remember everyone's names and backstories.

"Who the hell are all these people?" she whispered to her mother.

"Don't say hell, Alex," she replied through clenched teeth.

"Sorry... but it's not *really* swearing, mother," she countered.

"That's not the point. Jews don't believe in hell."

There were so many siblings of her grandparents present that even her parents were counted as 'youths' at these gatherings. Alex hugged her way through the relatives – noting at least two disdainful looks pointed towards her shabby footwear as she slipped her feet free – and made her way to Becs.

Her cousin, Rebecca, was only a year older than her and easily the best choice of company here. "They've been complaining they want to get started. I'm glad you got here before they were forced to begin phoning to see where you were."

"I haven't seen Hannah yet though?" Alex briefly worried her older sister may have decided not to come back from university for the evening after all. She'd promised to meet them here instead of going via home. *Why hadn't she thought to look for her car in the driveway?*

"She's in the kitchen helping plate things up. When did you last see her? She's really changed since she moved away."

"It's been months! I guess 'accounting' is treating her well." Alex made air quotes as she spoke. Unfortunately, despite being highly respectable, economics was a relatively new subject – and her family had wanted her to gain a profession; hence the deception that, as far as she knew, only herself and Becs were aware of.

The subject of their discussion emerged from the kitchen and called everyone into the long thin, dining room. The maroon curtains were pulled across the window, with a small gap in the middle where a hand-width sliver of orange light, the last vestiges of the setting sun, slipped through. On the other side of the room, there ran mahogany display cabinets filled with knickknacks and treasures – items brought back from holidays and birthday gifts – many of which were arbitrarily horse-shaped, or equine-themed.

Given their number, not only had the table extension been applied, but a small kitchen table had also been placed at one end, for the 'children'. Alex and Becs therefore found themselves both slightly lower down than the rest of the family, and on babysitting duty for Joel.

For the last two years, her mother had insisted Joel sat on her lap, but given at three and half years of age, Joel was now dexterous enough to use a spoon, apparently the rules had changed. Becs's two older brothers, Aaron and Josh, had been allowed to sit with the adults this year, much to Alex's dismay; although it also meant they were free of Carly.

One Haggadah seder book had been provided for the three of them, but Becs had brought her own from home. She felt a pang of envy as she saw how beautifully illustrated her cousin's was, though at least it meant they didn't have to share. For all the rigidity of the evening, Passover was by far her favorite of the festivals.

Her father moved round the table filling glasses with kiddush wine – until he got to hers and switched to grape juice. She rolled her eyes, but didn't bother complaining. Forgetting to lean to the left, as soon as the blessing was finished, she took a sip. It was a bit sweet, but looking around at the bemused faces, she realized it hadn't been as unpleasant as the wine. She stifled a laugh as she observed the adults looking at each other, unsure who was going to speak first; no one wanting to be the one to offend their host.

"Unusual wine, Dina," her grandmother eventually piped up.

"Thank you, deary." Dina at least looked diverted. "It was a gift, that until now I'd been saving. I believe it's a rather expensive vintage. Perhaps that's why it tastes so… *unusual*. One might even say bitter."

At that, the whole table burst into full volume – everyone plucking adjectives out of the air, the entire family forthwith wanting to get a word in – it was mature, pungent, sophisticated, and more. Even Hannah was joining in the fray, although Carly remained her disinterested self.

"He's coming," declared Uncle Solly quite suddenly and at high volume, ending the furor.

Becs mouthed, 'He's the senile one' across the table in response to Alex's frown. Her grandad's brother, she now recalled.

As sense returned to the party, they washed hands and dipped parsley in salt water. Alex scouted around for extra parsley pieces, settling for eating Joel's in addition to her own. Their grandfather broke the matza, wrapped it in a napkin, then went to hide the afikomen.

Apparently, finding a good hiding spot was important enough to keep everyone waiting for quite some time. He was gone long enough that the guests' patience almost ubiquitously began to wane. Her father even got sent to look for him – but his own dad found his way back in the meantime and then her poor father became the subject of the irritability instead. It *was* rather annoying; however, Alex couldn't help but feel there was a slight irrationality to the way the grown-ups were acting.

For some reason, perhaps economy, the same much-derided wine was used to refill the glasses for the second blessing. Whilst facial expressions all round showed clear distaste, there was no accompanying excitement this time.

"A gate from hell is opening," shouted Uncle Solly, who had risen to his feet so abruptly his chair fell backwards. It clattered loudly as it hit the parquet.

Whilst Becs bit her bottom lip, and Hannah picked up his chair, everyone else ignored him – except Alex. "How come *he's* allowed to say hell?" she called out, clearly directed at her mother. Everyone ignored *her* too. As a seemingly unanimous decision, the seder was resumed.

Joel was declared old enough to ask the four questions, so Alex and Becs whispered the words, in the hope he would repeat them aloud. The results were somewhat unpredictable. At first it was amusing; everyone laughed and declared him adorable. It quickly became frustrating. Alex found she was the only person willing to call the thing to a halt. In the end she resolved to ask the first question herself – yes, they were still on the first one. Everyone acquiesced but there were some unappreciated murmurs claiming she 'wasn't very cute'.

The next thing Alex did wrong was let Joel dab the wine during the reading of the plagues. Admittedly, she had been so busy being careful to make her own neat spots, she hadn't paid much attention to the fact he had grabbed his cup of squash and was trying to join in. It was mostly water in there though, so she wasn't sure what the fuss was about, or why everything seemed to be *her* fault.

Carly, on the other hand – Carly, the immature one – was being praised for whatever she did. Every time she smiled and flipped her hair, Alex couldn't help but glare at her. Not that she'd noticed.

By the time the meal finally arrived, she was relieved. Most of the food was what she'd been expecting and therefore comfortingly familiar. She leafed through the pages on the four brothers while she ate. Other than another outburst from Uncle Solly – comprising a declaration of, "He's coming for her!" – there was minimal diversion.

When it came time to look for the afikomen, she was nominated to take Joel to go look for it. Seeing her exasperation, Becs volunteered to take him instead; Alex was more than happy to relinquish the duty.

Everyone had been acting relatively normal for a bit, but as they once again drank their wine, the levels of agitation in the room increased. It must have been particularly potent. She was reconsidering asking for a sip, as she thought her father might give in, when Uncle Solly piped up again.

"The time is coming!" No one paid him any heed.

A glass was poured for the Prophet Elijah and Dina set it by the door. She heard a jarring creak, then footsteps, as Dina returned.

"She's not actually leaving the front door open, is she? We never usually do that!" Alex exclaimed.

"Coming, coming, coming," Solly was reciting.

The sun had fully set now, so the only light in the dining room was coming from candles. The breeze sailing through the now ajar front door was strong enough to make the flames flicker vigorously and she worried they might go out entirely.

Her family considered using electricity on the first two nights of Passover a no-no, and if lights hadn't been left on in some of the hallways, Joel and Becs would really be struggling. "I'm going to go and help Joel now," she said, excusing herself from the table. The adults still seemed a bit distracted and not quite in full control of themselves.

Her mother was attempting to help clear the table but seemed to be taking only one plate to the kitchen at a time. Her father kept turning his wine glass upside down, then flipping it over and looking inside as if he was expecting it to have spontaneously refilled.

Aaron and Josh were pulling faces at each other and laughing.

The eldest generation were subdued; if anything, they looked concerningly vacant.

Alex had intended to go find Joel and Becs, she truly had… but the cozy study at the foot of the main stairs proved too great a distraction, and she popped in to look at her great aunt's book collection. As she leafed through a historical biography of Henry VIII, she heard the sound of something breaking. *Was that a plate smashing?*

Then several more?

The disturbance continued – strained, high-pitched shrieks reached her. She tensed up, clutching her elbows as she tried to compose herself.

The cries ceased almost as quickly as they'd started. Next came crunching sounds.

Alex was frozen. She wanted to see what was happening, but equally *didn't* want to. The more time passed, the more she convinced herself the sounds hadn't really been screams. She could easily have been mistaken; maybe it was weird laughter, or someone playing a record.

Only when it had been quiet for several minutes did she feel brave enough to investigate. On stepping into the hallway, she saw the front door was wide open.

Of course, it wouldn't have surprised her if Dina had opened it that fully to begin with. Or the wind could have blown it… although, the wooden door with iron bands was heavy even for her father.

Peering outside, which she was less hesitant to do than check the dining room, she saw what she could only describe as a rip. It appeared as though a tear had been made in the air; something in the middle of nothing.

Not overthinking it, she touched the edge – she couldn't quite believe she wasn't imagining it. It buzzed like static, and when painful spasms shot through her, she pulled her finger away. The tip was red, and hot to the touch, but it was more numb now than painful.

Peeking through, she caught a glimpse of an ochre plain, peppered with rocks, and stretching indeterminately.

When she looked again, the vision had gone.

Alex rubbed her head and wondered whether perhaps her father had accidentally filled her cup with wine after all.

No longer feeling fully lucid, she meandered back to the dining room.

Alex didn't quite register what she was seeing at first.

Her grandmother's head was tilted backwards at an impossible angle; unseeing, glossy eyes gazed towards the ceiling. A bone jutted out from the break in her grandfather's arm, the surrounding skin already mottled purple from the bruises.

Blood splatters newly decorated the wall behind them, a stark contrast to the bland magnolia paint.

Holding only a candle, she couldn't see much further. She dreaded to look.

The silence was now more worrying than the piercing sounds had been. Nothing and no one moved. Alex's heart thumped loudly against her chest; her food threatened to resurface.

Noticing the light switch, she briefly considered breaking the shabbat rules. She didn't mind personally, it wasn't like they hadn't driven there, but she wanted to respect Dina's wishes. *Why am I even debating this?* She flipped the switch back and forth. Nothing happened – the lights must have fused somehow. Maybe it was just as well… she wasn't sure she could bear to see the full truth of the present scene in stark light.

Swallowing nervously, she tiptoed further into the room.

Oddly, Uncle Solly looked much as he had in life; but whilst his injuries weren't visible, he certainly wasn't moving. Aunt Rose could have fared the worst – at least Alex *hoped* the worst wasn't still to come – her rib cage had been torn out, her entrails dripping freely.

Aaron and Josh's heads had been bashed together. Again, she tasted bile.

A dull plodding sound, a *thunk… thunk… thunk…*, panicked her. Snapping out of her reverse reverie, she came back to her senses, and thought only of Joel. Avoiding the door she'd entered by, she left the dining room by the adjacent arch, and found the back stairwell. Still holding the candle, she could see two or three paces in front of her but no further.

Running up the stairs, with her heart already racing, left her panting slightly; she tried to recover so as to quieten her breath. It was easier to focus now she only had one goal – her mind was clear of all thoughts except finding him.

Swinging open the first door she came to, she found an empty bedroom. The second door revealed the same. Alex found a bathroom, two more bedrooms, and a small balcony overlooking the garden, too shrouded in darkness for her to make out any details.

Beginning to lose hope, she made her way up another flight to the top floor. At least up here, a plugged-in night light was providing some measure of illumination. She was about to look round the master bedroom, when she heard a scuffling noise.

"It was that bad downstairs?" asked Becs.

"Excuse me?" Her eyes widened. She was baffled as to how Becs had become aware of the situation, and more so, why she sounded slightly flippant about it.

"I've never seen anyone look so relieved to see me. It must've been really painful once dessert ended?" She *didn't* know.

Alex shook her head at her. "We need to H… I… D… E… J… O… E… L. Something is W… R…O… N… G downstairs."

"That was my name! You spelled Joel!" a little voice chirped up. Alex cringed.

"Where did you find the afikomen?"

"In here! We got it now! It tastes yukky." Joel pointed to a dumb waiter. This house was full of strange quirks.

She bent down on her knees, so she was at the child's eye height. "We're going to play hide and seek now, Joel. Can you curl up and climb in there for me? Mama is going to come looking for you. I need you to be really quiet, can you do that for me?" His inner brows rose, but he nodded, and she breathed a sigh of relief.

"Can I take the light?" he asked, pointing at her candle.

"No, not this one, sweetheart. It's very hot."

"Too dark in there." His lips began to tremble.

"I know, but it'll be okay. How about… you do this for me, and I'll get you a present for your birthday. A huge one, I mean."

"A new bicycle? I want a purple one please."

"Sure, why not. A purple bicycle. If you climb in and stay quiet until they find you. Don't worry, Becs and I will wait right outside." She managed to cajole him in. Luckily, once she shut the door it seemed reasonably soundproof.

"Okay, what's going on?" Becs demanded. Alex shushed her until she was comfortable they were out of earshot, then relayed what she'd seen.

Becs immediately ran in the direction of the danger. Alex facepalmed, unsure what to do at first, then followed, cursing.

Reaching the foot of the stairs, she caught up to Becs in the doorway of the dining room. Some… *thing* was pacing around the table. Every now and then it would grab a handful of hair, lift up whoever's head it belonged to, and examine them.

Alex grabbed Becs around the waist and dragged her away; her cousin didn't resist. Backtracking up the stairs, they took a seat on the floor of a wardrobe inside one of the guest bedrooms.

Becs was wailing slightly, and having tried to shush her – to no avail – she wrapped her arm around her as a form of comfort instead. "How, this, had, what?" Alex looked at her friend in sympathy. She encouraged her to try again, hoping for sense this time. "Who, how many?"

"I don't know." She didn't want to tell Becs about her brothers if she hadn't already seen; and Alex was aware she herself hadn't seen the full extent of the carnage either. Realizing her answer wasn't helpful, she added, "It looked bad though. It looked like a lot. I don't think there's anything we can do but keep hiding."

As if her words were a summons, they heard those ominous thudding footsteps. Becs clasped her hand over her mouth; Alex held her breath.

When they stopped for a second, Alex took in a new gulp of air – before wincing, and tensing her whole body, when they started up again. With one swift movement, the doors of the wooden wardrobe were ripped from their hinges.

Before them stood a hulking beast. Alex looked up, from the clawed toes to the elongated limbs and scrawny wings, but could not bring herself to raise her eyes any further; would not look him in the eye as she shook from fear. Whatever this fiend was, prophet or not, it had never been human.

The demon looked from Alex to Becs, then back. A taloned hand reached out, grabbing Becs around the neck, and lifting her into a standing position. Inexplicably, he *smelt* her – the incongruous noises were unmistakably sniffs. Letting out a groan of anguish, he lashed out, tearing her apart.

Alex did the only thing she could – though it felt like the wrong thing to do even at the time. She ran.

Her mind had become blank. She couldn't remember where any of the doors led. Instinctively, she knew *Elijah* was coming after her next. Joel was safe in the dumb waiter – he *had* to be – making downstairs the only logical place for her to go. She needed to make it outside.

Except, disorientated, she somehow found herself back on the balcony. Alex had no idea whether she was low enough to jump or climb down – she couldn't see. She also didn't know how close the demon was behind her. With her candle doing nothing but giving away her position, she blew it out and threw it onto the grass below.

Listening for it to hit the grass didn't help her determine how high up she was but at least she felt more protected now.

Unless he could see in the dark.

A roar resounded.

Deciding against the unpredictable jump, she ran back into the hallway, hoping, more than actually expecting, she might stumble across one of the two sets of stairs. Luck – as it had in a sense been with her when Becs had been chosen for death over herself – was with her once more. She managed to not only find a staircase, but also to not fall down it in her haste.

Turning away from the dining room, Alex had intended to head straight for the front door, which she assumed would still be wide open. She was thwarted by an arm reaching out to grab her. Had she not been certain she hadn't been followed down the stairs, she likely would have screamed. Instead, she acquiesced; and found herself being dragged into the study.

On seeing her parents standing there, a rush of emotions swept over her, and she burst into tears, despite knowing this wasn't really the time. Her father pulled her into a hug. "It's okay. I'm sorry. You were right. We should never have left the door open for Elijah."

"I told you, that isn't Elijah!" her mother huffed. It seemed an unimportant thing to be focusing on right now. "Joel?" she continued, seemingly confused he wasn't with Alex.

"He's tucked up in the dumb waiter." Both parents breathed sighs of relief.

"Hannah?" she asked. They shook their heads. "Carly?" They looked at each other in dismay and shook their heads again. Alex felt the shock hit her right in the chest, even though it was the news she'd been expecting.

"How are you okay? I saw the dining room." She knew they shouldn't be lingering, but she needed to make sense of how they were actually standing here.

"Quite simple really. That brute Elijah…"

"Not Elijah," her mother interjected.

Alex's father frowned. "As I was saying. He started at the other end of the table, and we hid – in the pantry to begin with, but he seemed to still be looking for us, and we had no way to close ourselves in there. So, then we came in here, and it turned out he couldn't get through the thick study door. We've been watching out for anyone passing by since then."

Alex and her mother looked at each other. Someone obviously needed to find help and her father was the logical choice.

Once they determined they couldn't hear footsteps, they gently pushed open the door and checked the way was clear. It wasn't; there was a beautiful stranger standing in front of the door. His movements shimmered; his entire body lit by ethereal light.

"*That's* Elijah!" Her mother exclaimed.

"Sorry I'm late," the gentleman atoned, "Did I miss anything?"

At her parents' stunned silence, Alex piped up, "There's a beast straight from hell, running rampage throughout the house!"

"Ashmedai. Not from hell," he replied somewhat condescendingly, saying the name as if it were a curse. "Give me a moment to deal with him; I need only remind him of the rules he is breaking simply by being here." As he disappeared up the stairs, Alex heard him mutter, "It's no surprise he's appeared with this foul wine you've put out for me."

Her mother made a vague attempt to prevent Alex following him up the stairs; but when her father had started heading up, she'd backed down, and all three of them had gone to watch.

After all, they had to make sure Ashmedai was truly gone.

He was. Even in the context of the rest of the evening, Alex felt stunned. True to his word, Elijah overpowered Ashmedai, before banishing him back into the rent through which he had clawed his way into the world. He made them look away as he sealed the tear, as though he were afraid one of them might try and reopen it. Perhaps some humans were truly that foolish.

With prophet and demon both departed, Alex closed the front door. Hurriedly, they retrieved Joel – who, not unexpectedly for the time of night, had fallen fast asleep, rendering him oblivious to the amount of time he had been playing hide and seek. They laid him down on one of the beds and returned to face the scene downstairs.

Casting her eyes over Hannah's body, which lay slumped against the kitchen wall, she started to hyperventilate and had to sit herself on the floor to recover. "Where's Carly?" she asked belatedly, only now feeling guilty for years of sisterly rivalry.

"He took her." her mother replied.

"What do you mean he *took* her?" It was insensitive as her mother was crying, but what she'd said… well, it sounded ridiculous.

"It was Carly he was looking for." Her mother's face was flushed – but was that from crying, or embarrassment? "I'm sure of it."

In hindsight, she had seen certain behaviors which Alex could agree were consistent with him having been looking for someone, but…. "Why on *Earth* would that monster have been bothered about Carly? And if he had taken her already, then why was he still looking?"

"She has a point, Eleanor. Maybe he didn't find Carly after all."

"No, I'm sure of it. He wanted Carly." Both Alex and her father tried to encourage her mother to search the house, in case Carly was still hidden somewhere, but she was in too much of a state to be calmed down. "I..."

"Shhh, it's okay."

"It's not. It's all my fault. I... I had a dalliance. With Elijah. Nineteen years ago…" If the situation hadn't been so serious, Alex might have laughed. "Remember that seder when I said I had a headache and went to lie down? He did *say* the demons would covet his offspring, but I thought… I thought he meant it in jest." her mother continued.

Her father, calm as always, took it in his stride. "Let's just go look for her."

After once around the house with no success, her father called the police while they continued to search. Her mother checked the wine cellar in the basement – which Alex hadn't even known existed and was more than happy to miss out on – while she wandered the upper floors almost at random, hoping she might stumble upon a room that had previously remained undiscovered.

They didn't find anyone else alive, nor did they find Carly's body.

After hours of police questions, and even a visit from forensics, the early hours of the morning approached. In no fit state to drive home, the three of them laid down on the bed next to Joel for a couple of hours' sleep. Or at least, an attempt at it.

Hearing footsteps, Alex bolted upright. Looking at her parents' concerned faces, they had both already heard them. They clasped hands.

As Carly walked into the room, her mother wasted no time in running over to hug her.

"Explain yourself, young lady!" Her father's voice boomed.

"Well, when I got home after the party I just went straight to bed. When I woke up this morning and there was no one there, I wasn't sure what else to do but come and look for you here. Plus, I thought maybe I'd be here in time for a nice breakfast!" They all just stared at her. "I left straight after dessert. I did tell mother I was calling a taxi!"

Their mother looked sheepish. "I guess with everything going on, I forgot."

"Why?" Carly asked. "What did I miss?"

The Climb Up to Hell
By Sean Eads and Joshua Viola

After Chet and David's candles were lit, the five of us gathered at the base of the tree and Jake put his flashlight under his chin.

"Time to explain the dark secret of Kingwood, ladies. This treehouse was built by John King himself for his twin sons after he discovered they weren't his. Once his wife's secret was out, he poisoned her. It was a long time ago and everyone thought she just died, but his crime was discovered decades later when his diary was found. He was going to poison the boys as well, but he stopped himself."

"Because he knew they were innocent?"

"No, he thought poisoning was too good for them. He wanted them to suffer. So, he built this treehouse and made the boys live in it. Spring, summer, fall, winter. All the time. And he put two big Dobermans down at the bottom to attack the boys if they tried to leave. So, they

didn't. Even when they started to get hungry and thirsty after John King quit bringing them food and water. In the diary, he says he finally let the boys go and told them to never come back. That he didn't care what happened to them. Then he wrote that he tore the treehouse down. But all of that was a lie. The treehouse is here, isn't it? Randy, Mark, and I were the first to discover it–and the truth on Halloween night. We climbed up and saw the skeletons. It was gnarly."

"That's right. Gnarly."

"We buried their bones, but the skulls keep coming back every Halloween."

"So . . . they're up there now?"

"Yeah, numbnuts, just like we said. The three of us have taken our turns appeasing them. Now it's up to the two of you, rookies. Start climbing."

My face felt as hot as the lit candles David and Chet Somerset were being forced to carry, part of the dumb prank being played on them. The little flames flickered as the brothers made their climb with David in the lead. Jake, Randy, and I stepped back several feet and aimed our flashlights up at them.

"Dude," Randy whispered. "They bought every word of it. Holy shit."

"Did I tell it as good as you, Mark?" Jake said.

Randy aimed his flashlight into my eyes. "Sure you don't want to go up there with your buttbuddies?"

Jake snickered. I told them both to fuck off. "Chet made all that up."

"He sure knows what your room looks like."

"I told you my mom let them come over. I didn't have a choice."

"Sure."

Jake, Randy, and I had been best friends since we were seven. We were fifteen now and I couldn't tell where I stood with them after Chet started talking about him and David hanging out in my room. They didn't say it outright, but I knew I had to help them scare and humiliate Chet and David. Restoring myself in their eyes required this Halloween sacrifice, and the idea the Somerset brothers believed this was some friendship initiation rite just made it better to Jake and Randy.

"Keep climbing, girls," Randy said, his tone filled with merciless joy. "And don't forget, if the candles go out, you have to climb down and light them again."

Jake lowered his beam a few notches to Chet's ass. He snickered. "Is that a brown spot I see?"

I joined Jake and Randy's laughter just enough to keep up pretenses. But in my imagination, I saw David slipping and falling. He was already ten feet off the ground with another twelve rungs to go. I trained my flashlight beam on the next rung so David could see it. There was just a little sliver of moon, too weak to reach through the trees. Appropriate for Halloween.

Inside the treehouse were two large pumpkins and two carving knives, courtesy of Jake. The pumpkins came from a little patch his uncle kept, and the knives were swiped from his mom's kitchen. It'd been a bitch hauling the pumpkins up there one at a time in an oversized backpack, but they'd insisted I do it, a bit of hazing I endured to keep them happy.

David reached another rung and looked down to check on Chet. David was my age, Chet a year younger. They had almost the same face, freckles, and a pug nose. But Chet had brown eyes and David's were blue. They walked side-by-side everywhere, in lockstep. It was hard not to picture them being joined at the hip, so it was weird seeing one ahead of the other.

They entered the treehouse. The light of their candles made the windows yellow, and I exhaled a long-held breath.

#

The whole thing started on the Fourth of July, when Kingwood's population of 2,000 milled around the town square eating ice cream and hot dogs, listening to the high school band play John Philip Sousa shit, and sweating out lemon aid and Coke under a blistering sun. Jake, Randy, and I were hanging against the brick wall of Kingwood Community Bank. I had a bag full of snaps and was still throwing them on the sidewalk a good hour after the novelty wore off.

"Look at those two," Jake said, nudging us. Chet and David walked past, backs straight, arms limp. Chet had on a blue and red plaid button-up and David had on a white polo.

"Put 'em together and you've got the flag," Randy said, and gave a smart salute at their backs. "God bless the USA."

"Let's follow them," Jake said.

We tailed them through the crowds. The brothers acted like tourists. Sometimes they stopped to point out something, like the big white banner hung across Main Street, stamped with Kingwood's motto–*Friends Growing Strong Together*. Kingwood kids got a lot of flak from other schools for that slogan. We followed them for twenty minutes and word got around that Jill Clarke had changed into a t-shirt that was almost see-through, and since she was the senior captain of the cheerleading squad, we three kings went to investigate. I didn't get the fuss. Sure, there was the dark suggestion of Jill's black bra, but so what? Jake and Randy meanwhile almost shook their fist at the encroaching sunset. I listened to them talk about sucking Jill's tits and getting their hands up her shirt until their voices got too loud and scornful adults gave disapproving looks. Then I put some distance between us and wandered off as the fireworks started.

Downtown Kingwood had plenty of nooks and crannies, private places. What was I looking for? That question ended when I stumbled upon the weird brothers around the back of Fitzhugh's corner store. David had his back against the brick as Chet bent to press his left cheek against his brother's chest. David ran his fingers through Chet's hair. How strange, how comforting, how different, how very real compared to the shadowy importance of Jill Clarke's bra.

I spent a moment just standing there before I realized they were looking right at me. The shorter brother broke away and took a few steps, his trembling hands stretched toward me.

"Please don't say anything."

I shook my head.

"We're. . . new here."

"You mean you aren't visiting?" I said.

"No. We moved here two weeks ago. I'm Chet. This is my older brother, David."

David nodded and smirked.

The fireworks bathed us in changing colors. We turned blue, green, purple, and bright red. We didn't speak until a starburst made us white as ghosts, our shadows dancing.

"What's your name?" David said.

"Mark."

"Be our friend, Mark," Chet said.

"A *real* friend," David said.

Um, sure...

The answer felt more like a thought, but I must have spoken it because the brothers smiled at each other.

"Our first friend," David said, and Chet nodded.

They opened their arms as if to hug me, but I was having none of it and ran off. The fireworks were ending, and I found my mom with her boyfriend Jeff, who planned to be my stepdad by next year.

Why did I tell those two freaks I'd be their friend? I went to bed remembering them holding each other and I dreamt that the three of us were huddled together, arms across each other's shoulders. Tighter and tighter, like there was something small in the middle we didn't want to escape. It was an uncomfortable dream and I seemed to still be in it when the doorbell woke me at almost noon. I stared at the ceiling and listened to Mom open the front door. Half a minute later, two sets of footsteps sounded on the stairs. I figured it must be Jake and Randy. Mom had been letting them storm up into my room ever since I could remember.

Then my bedroom door opened, and Chet and David stood there.

"How are you?" Chet said.

David stepped forward. "Yes, how are you, Mark? Did you sleep well?"

I was just in my underwear, and I pulled the sheet up to my neck. David frowned. He looked at Chet and said, "I told you it was too soon."

"What?" I said.

"To come over."

"We're very lonely," Chet said.

"It's true, Mark. Until now, we've only had each other."

That's still all you got, I thought. I dressed and stole a look out the window, afraid I'd see Jake and Randy riding up the street. The neighborhood seemed deserted but there were eyes everywhere and I didn't want to risk being seen outside with these weirdos. So, I pulled out my Atari and told them to choose a game. Then I went downstairs. Mom was already making peanut butter sandwiches for us.

"Your new friends seem interesting."

"They're not friends."

"They said they met you yesterday."

"That's sort of true."

"Well then."

"I didn't tell them where I live."

"Don't have to be a detective to use a phone book."

"Mom—"

"They smell much better than Jake and Randy."

"They're probably wearing perfume or something."

"It's called *soap*. Here. Take these up."

Mom handed me a plate of sandwiches and three Cokes.

"What if Jake or Randy come over?"

"The five of you can play together."

"Would you tell them I've been grounded? *Please*?"

Mom rolled her eyes. "Whatever you say."

"Tell them I was caught sneaking one of Jeff's Bud Lights."

"Your reputation will never be greater."

Back in the bedroom, I found Chet and David sitting beside each other, the Atari untouched.

"We're not allowed to play video games," Chet said. "Our parents only let us watch television for sixty minutes a day, and it has to be the news."

I took up my sandwich and cracked open my Coke. "They sound like dicks."

The brothers looked at each other. It was slow at first, but all of a sudden, they were both cracking up. Red in the face and shoulders shaking.

David gasped. "You're so funny, Mark!"

"Very funny," Chet said, breathless. "It's great to have a friend who's funny."

I couldn't believe them at first. Whenever I hung out with Jake and Randy in a larger group, they'd be cracking everyone up, and then I'd say something that made everyone quiet. No matter how funny I tried to be, it never worked. Jokes don't when they reek of effort. But here were Chet and David almost rolling on the floor over something I said. Their reaction was as weird as everything else about them, but also so–*genuine*.

I polished off my Coke and belched. They laughed at that, too, and I held up the two Atari controllers.

"Who wants their ass whipped first?"

The new King of Comedy had his minions.

#

We didn't ask questions when we found the treehouse two years ago. We just climbed the rungs straight up through a floor hatch. Outside, the treehouse looked like a small Victorian mansion stretched across the cradling branches of a maple that might have been two hundred years old. It loomed high against the cloudless sky. The dilapidated structure was flanked on both sides by turrets that framed the peak of its partially collapsed roof. It looked like the house in *Psycho*, that movie we watched at Jake's last Halloween. The interior wasn't nearly as spacious, taken up by a mess of strange, disorienting angles that left just a small practical space tailor-made for three people to hang out. There were windows here and there and they were all sorts of irregular shapes too.

It was one of those strange things waiting to be found by the right kids, the kind of kids who sneak cigarettes from their mother's purse. We weren't the first ones inside, but it'd been a while between occupants. We found broken beer bottles, cigarette butts, and used condoms. There were scattered pages from titty magazines, faded and water damaged in the most frustrating way possible. While Jake and Randy obsessed over them, I found a rolled piece of paper in the corner. It was yellowed with age, but not crinkly at all when I unrolled it and realized it was a wall calendar with all the months printed in little square blocks above a flowery script–*Fitzhugh's Apothecary*. What the hell was an *apothecary?* The calendar was from 1916, several years after Kingwood's founding.

"Look at this, guys. Figure it means this place was built 70 years ago?"

Randy and Jake weren't interested. They'd discovered more ripped pages from some porno mag and knelt on the floor in a desperate effort to fit the jigsaw scraps together.

Fitzhugh. I thought of the town drug store. How long had it been there?

"Mark, get over here," Jake said. "We're like three scraps away from seeing pussy. Help us find the missing pieces!"

"Hunt for the cunt," Randy said, and soon we three kings chanted it together and giggled. I wasn't any help, though. My thoughts were on that calendar. On questions of time and who'd built the treehouse. I sat back and thought about it. A story sprang to mind so readily it was like someone spoke it to me.

"John King built this," I said.

"The statue guy?"

"For his sons. Twin boys. But he discovered they weren't really his kids, so he . . ."

They applauded when I finished telling the story. "You should be a writer," Randy said. "That was fucking awesome. Especially that line about the one starving brother realizing you can climb *up* to Hell."

I shook my head. I couldn't explain how the story just came to mind. I guess I'd made it up in a burst of imagination.

It wasn't important. Whoever built the treehouse didn't matter. It was ours now and we spent damn near every day that first summer here, cleaning it up, making it *ours*. We pledged to tell no one about it except girlfriends, when we got 'em. We vowed to lose our cherries up here. That summer in the treehouse, life was more real than ever before. The three of us did the same shit we would have done in the park or the woods, but we did it in our own world. Our dreams carried more weight in the treehouse, and our friendship was never stronger than when we occupied it together. I went there by myself only once, when Jake and Randy were off on family vacations. I don't know why, but I thought the treehouse was almost angry with me for coming alone. I got creeped out by the sound of the groaning wood, the creaking of the branches and stood up. I went to look out one of the windows and something seemed off. The world outside was different, like the picture on an old postcard. I didn't even feel like I was looking out of my own eyes.

I left a few minutes later and didn't return until Jake and Randy were there. Then it all felt right again. Our fascination with the treehouse lasted through that summer and stayed strong into the second one and was still going good in the third. We went there almost every day, up until that Fourth of July. Then I began hanging out in secret with the Somerset brothers and my room became a sort of treehouse for the three of us and we never left it. Mom kept covering for me whenever Jake or Randy showed up. I started feeling like I had two separate lives that mustn't intersect. They'd have to when school started, I supposed, but that was a ways out.

I didn't ditch Randy and Jake, of course. When I was determined to hang out with them, I set off early on my bike. As far as I knew, Chet and David didn't have bikes, but I always kept looking around expecting them to be running after me. I never saw them once, but only felt hidden from them once we were a quarter of a mile into the forest.

"Dude, what's been up with you?" Jake said after we'd climbed the rungs and could lounge in privacy.

"What do you mean?"

"Sneaking beers? Flipping off your mom? You got a death wish or something?"

I grinned. "A man's gotta do what a man's gotta do sometimes."

Their look of respect was priceless.

"You're going to be grounded the whole summer at the rate you're going."

I shrugged. "It's totally worth it. Fuck that bitch."

I winced inside. As moms went, mine wasn't as lame as most. Her excuses were making me look badass, but how far would she go if Chet and David kept coming over?

Jake had scored a copy of Playboy and had the magazine open on the treehouse floor. As the three of us knelt around it, Randy took out several cigarettes. They were bundled in a paper towel and were a little squished and bent. He had a lighter and kept flicking it until he finally gave up.

"I don't get why my lighters never work up here."

"Maybe it's out," I said.

"I just got it."

He sighed and went to the hatch door.

"Light one for me," Jake said.

"Me too."

Randy flipped us the bird as he descended the ladder. This took about half a minute. Then he shouted, "Hey, guys!"

We went to the door and looked down. Randy was small on the ground, but I could see him grinning and holding up the lighter. The flame flickered.

"See? Fucking weird."

He put all three cigarettes into his mouth, passed the fire across them and inhaled.

"Don't get the filter wet with your spit," Jake said. He pulled back and I followed. "I fucking hate a wet filter. It's like I'm kissing him or something."

We sat with our backs to the wall as Randy poked through and climbed inside, billows of smoke around his head. He plucked two cigarettes from his lips and handed them to us. Mine was damp, but I didn't mind. I smoked and thought how I'd like to take David up here. David and Chet, of course, but more David. I thought he'd love the treehouse.

They both would.

#

Both brothers screamed, and Randy and Jake giggled and fell against each other.

"Guess they found the skulls," Jake said. "Those pussies are too freaked out to even realize they're fake."

Randy ran to the base of the tree and hollered, "Get to it, girls! Carve a face in the pumpkins and put the skulls and candles inside. The brothers want their new heads!"

They screamed again.

"I'm going up there," I said. "This needs to stop."

Their flashlight beams lanced at me.

"It really is true, isn't it?"

"Chet was just lashing out because you were bullying his brother and he knows me. He was trying to get me to stop you. They're just desperate for friends. They wouldn't be out here if they weren't."

The brothers screamed again. Randy stormed back to the tree, climbed up three rungs and shouted at them to shut up and start carving.

"Dude," Jake said, his voice softer. "I don't know what to think."

I didn't either. Memories of the end of summer and the start of the school year flooded me. David and I playing Atari as we sat on the edge of the mattress, with Chet asleep behind us like a little kid. David flexed his calf against mine. I flexed back.

"Look," I said. The candles had gone out in the treehouse. We listened. Silence.

We waited. Several minutes passed.

"Let's go up there," I said.

"*You* can."

"They're up there in the dark. They're probably too scared to move."

Jake and I were about to argue when Randy shouted, "Gross, what the *fuck*?"

He dropped his flashlight and fell off the third rung and landed on his side, holding his hands up. His fingers glistened wet and red in our flashlight beams.

"Dude, did you cut yourself?"

"No, man, it just started dripping on me."

Randy got on his knees and began scraping his palms against the dirt. Jake and I stood next to him, pivoting our lights up the length of the tree. The rungs were wet, and the dripping became a steady pour.

"David?" I shouted. "David, are you up there?"

Jake got Randy to his feet. "Come on. Let's get out of here."

I grabbed Jake's arm. "How much red paint did you put up there?"

"What?"

"You had a can rigged to fall on them like pig's blood, right?"

Jake pulled his arm away. "I didn't have any paint, Mark." His voice was hoarse, every word like straw.

"Randy, did you have paint–"

"I'm *out* of here, man. I don't even care."

They took off. I followed them a few steps, begging them not to go. Then I made a helpless pivot and ran back to the tree.

"David? David, it's okay. Jake and Randy left. It's just me."

A minute of silence lasted longer than an hour of noise.

"Come on, guys! Chet?"

You've got to go up there, I told myself. I put my foot on the first rung and my sole slipped off. I whimpered. There was no way I could make it up without falling.

"Please, David."

A whisper came from the opening. David? Chet? Both? Then something appeared. Thank God, I thought. The prank had gone on long enough. I pointed the flashlight for a better view and only just dove out of the way of the pumpkins as they fell. But it wasn't the pumpkins. It was David and Chet's decapitated heads.

I ran into the darkness. The huge maple tree shook behind me. It sounded like a roar. I tripped and scrambled to keep going. The whispers became more distinct. Chet and David. But how could it be–when their heads were–

I turned. The Somerset brothers were there, but not on the ground. Their forms hung suspended in the air, substanceless. *Boneless*. It took a moment to comprehend just what I was seeing. Their skins had been peeled away and seemed draped like sheets. But what were their skins draped over, and who did the draping? The pumpkins were there in place of their heads, and each bore the face of one brother, carved with the exacting detail of a photograph, and lit from within by the very candles they'd been forced to carry. We stared at each other, and I couldn't help but remember what they'd said to me outside of the drug store.

Be our friend, Mark.

A real *friend.*

David floated toward me.

"The story was wrong, Mark," he said.

"The brothers were never twins," Chet added.

They hovered over me as I fell to my knees.

"Then–then–what were they?"

"Triplets."

Rabbit Uprising
By Yvonne Lang

Bobby sat in the hardbacked chair, packed in with the other rabbits as they restlessly waited for the meeting to start. In his paw he gripped the letter that had started all this and wondered for the hundredth time if he was doing the right thing by being here. They were going to launch their demands today, a pivotal moment that would go down in history if all went according to plan. Bobby was anxious as he wasn't sure yet how it would go – and which side history would record them as being on. He wasn't keen on trouble, and his nose was twitching madly in anticipation of exactly that.

Bobby was jerked from his spiralling thoughts by a white rabbit in a red waistcoat and bow tie bounding up onto the small stage in the town hall. A hush fell over the crowd."Good evening, everyone. Thank you for taking the time to attend the first ever meeting about rabbits' rights. I'm delighted to see so many of you here for our debut, it shows how much this issue matters to you all."

Bobby was starting to wish he'd stayed home. The white rabbit (he must use a dye surely, or have never worked a day in the egg factory in his life to remain that pristine) was ploughing on, enthusiastic about his mission. Or loving the sound of his own voice.

"My name is Keith and I called you all here to address a great injustice. The total lack of appreciation for the gruelling work us Easter Bunnies do. We can't prepare too early like Santa; the chocolate would go off. We always have to do most of the work near the event – which they keep moving instead of celebrating on the same day like Christmas. The tooth fairy only has to visit a couple of households a night and collect one tooth from each! Such a light load and all the work is inside. We're toiling away in our egg factories for months then having to not just deliver at night, but hide the eggs! What do we get in return for this? Nothing."

Keith finally paused to take a breath as he surveyed the crowd. Murmurs were rippling through the audience. Keith ploughed on,

"Absolutely nothing. The tooth fairy receives money for her efforts. Her reward is now measured in pounds rather than pence! Santa has ornaments and idols that look like him worshipped for months in advance. They've made films about him, written songs about him. On the night itself they leave snacks and refreshments out for him in their gratitude. It's not just that the humans ignore animals either. Food is left out for all of Santa's reindeer. Rudolph is coining it in from all of his merchandise! Yet the army of Easter Bunnies who work tirelessly to deliver out carefully crafted eggs are taken for granted. It's disgusting and I called this meeting as I don't think we should allow ourselves to be walked all over anymore. This is a call to form a union to represent our rights and campaign for recognition. I am proposing a small monthly fee – paid either in money or vegetables – to become a member. There is strength in numbers. My first point of action will be to craft a letter to the King and an identical one to the Prime Minister, signed by all the members of EARS – Executive for Advancing Rabbit Suffrage – asking for recognition and gratitude. We deserve acknowledgement."

"That's it? A letter? Do you think that will work?" A voice from the back called.

Keith nodded, his large fluffy ears flopping in time with his head movement.

"I would hope so. It is a very reasonable request demanded by a large, essential group. If they ignore it, then we escalate. The suffragettes didn't win their rights by leaflets alone."

The crowd buzzed with excitement as happy chatter broke out. Rabbits surged forward, hopping over those who were still sitting, to register for the new union. Bobby stayed in his seat. He did not share the excitement. He already sensed that escalation would be needed, and he didn't trust the glint in Keith's eye.

Bobby slipped out of the meeting and retreated to the factory where he worked. They were just gearing up for key season. The January frost was retreating as they welcomed February and a few brave snowdrops put their heads above the parapet. The Easter egg factories that were dotted around the world were kicking it up a gear. Not going at full capacity, but starting to get ready for the oncoming rush. Over the coming months it would go from a steady drip of production for those organised early buyers and to make some eggs for the decorators to experiment on, to needing all paws on deck and machines at full capacity to meet shops demands and have enough for their own distribution baskets.

There was a constant churring and whirring of the machines and their conveyor belts as they poured varying types of chocolate into egg shaped moulds. Cocoa powder dust floated lazily in the air, its aroma all encompassing. There was also the gentle bubbling of the vat where the chocolate was melted down. Bobby found it all very soothing in its familiarity and the comfort in the predictable routine. He was proud of what they created here, of the masterpieces he decorated and the joy they spread. Did they need external validation? Or was he being a doormat and he and his kind were being taken advantage of for their usual placid nature?

His colleagues started filing in and getting back to work, all chattering about the meeting.

"Do you think the letter will work?"

"Well, it's not much to ask for after all we do is it?"

"Yeah, as Keith pointed out, others get recognition. We're only asking to be treated equally."

Bobby couldn't bring himself to share his fellow rabbits' enthusiasm. It wasn't much to ask for, but it didn't seem worthy of rocking the boat for. He didn't think the humans, fickle as they are, were going to pay much attention to correspondence from rabbits, no matter how united. He didn't believe for one second that Keith was going to allow himself to be ignored. He had a queasy feeling of foreboding about how this was going to play out.

Bobby's worries came to fruition when, five weeks later, and with no acknowledgement from either the King or Prime Minister, Keith called another meeting."Fellow rabbits and dedicated members of EARS, thank you for joining me here today. I am disappointed, although not surprised, to share with you that our letter containing a very reasonable request for recognition has been ignored. They think if they ignore us, we will go away. They have gravely underestimated us. We must make our demands louder and make ourselves impossible to ignore. Have you seen how humans treated their own kind? They used to own the ones who had different coloured skin! The female of their species, when they simply asked to be treated equally and allowed the right to vote? In our country they imprisoned them, ridiculed them, force fed them, tortured them. Women died for asking for democracy to be open to all. They only gave them the vote when they were forced to. When the cost of ignoring them became too great. There are still countries where women are regarded as second class, or property. I say to you that Great Britain can be a trail blazer in this area of ethics too. History will note how it became the first country to recognise rabbits' rights. To achieve this, we need to up our game."Keith finally paused in his speech. The other rabbits were on the edge of their seats, the air quivering with the twitching of ears. Bobby felt sickness building in his stomach. He had known this would escalate. Why was Keith quoting women who had been imprisoned and tortured as role models? No matter how noble their goal, Bobby couldn't say he wanted to copy their methods. "We are going to have to fight for recognition. I will be leaving a sign-up sheet here on stage. We are asking for volunteers to join the first ever rabbit army. We will provide all equipment and training and will be leading the righteous fight for our recognition with guerrilla tactics. We may be small, but we are smart, determined, quick and better organised. We'll hit them before they even realise this has developed into a war. The humans vastly outnumber us, but their current army is tiny. We already know that some people are on our side and will be sharing our ignored letter with the press so the media can put added pressure on the leaders to respond. We are confident that the animal right's protestors will side with us rather than their own kind and that we can build on this support. We still need to bolster our own numbers though. Ladies and gentlemen, we need to demonstrate the accuracy of the derogatory phrase 'breeding like rabbits'. The more kits the better. The larger the family, the better. We will be using some of our funds to offer free portions of vegetables to all expectant and recent mothers, to ease the strain of providing for bigger broods."Keith stepped to the side of the stage as three other rabbits hurried on discretely to unveil a set of posters. There was one of a rabbit in a pressed blazer and top hat pointing directly at the reader with a large red slogan declaring 'Your burrow needs you!" Underneath in smaller but still clear writing was the line 'Fight for rabbits rights, be part of Executive for Advancing Rabbit Suffrage'.

There was one with an image of old Winston, they must have dug that photo out of the archives as he died years ago. He had been one of the first rabbit films stars, his big debut playing the white rabbit in *Alice in Wonderland*. He was in costume as his most famous character, looking with gravitas at his oversized pocket watch. The slogan read 'Time is running out for excuses. Rabbits deserve recognition now. Join Executive for Advancing Rabbit Suffrage'.

A third poster showed a group of rabbits in an egg decorating factory, a huge human leaning over them with an evil grin. The rabbits looked tired. The workshop was barren and filthy. It didn't look at all like Bobby's happy workshop full of creativity and chatting colleagues. 'Time for slavery to stop. End rabbit abuse. Recognition for our work - Executive for Advancing Rabbit Suffrage' was emblazoned across the poster in bright blue.

The final poster showed a mother in bed, cradling her newborns whilst her other children gathered round wide-eyed. 'Don't let your children be born into a world where they are not appreciated. Ensure they become part of history and join the rabbit army.' It was stamped across the poster in normal black font, as if it was simply a bus timetable announcement and not a call for mothers to have more children and send them to war. No one seemed appalled by the posters though. The group was on their feet, chanting support and surging forward to sign up. The rabbit army was about to be formed.

Over the coming weeks Bobby tried to keep his head down and get on with his decorating duties. Work was mad. They had all the usual demand for eggs as Easter approached and EARS needed additional decoy eggs for their planned Easter Uprising. Most of Bobby's colleagues were distracted too. If they weren't excused from duties for army duty or paternity leave, their attention spans were mere seconds. All they could talk about was EARS and the rebellion. Their egg work was sloppy. Chocolate came out of moulds bubbly instead of smooth, halves of eggs didn't align, empty eggs were caught by quality control going out of sweet treats in their centre. Decoration standards plummeted; they looked like children's drawings.

Keith was most distressed by this. Although delighted EARS had captured such attention and dedication, he didn't want to be demanding recognition for work when their work was quite frankly, shambolic. Bobby had avoided signing up by hamming up his old leg injury he had incurred whilst been pursued by a fox. Since he couldn't fight and his eggs were still coming out exquisite, Keith offered him a pay rise to oversee quality control. Although uneasy with EARS and their planned methods, Bobby revelled in his new role and the younger rabbits under his guidance began to take pride in their work, valuing it as part of the campaign. To make up for those who were off training a lot of new crafters were hired. Many of the new recruiters were females between maternity leave. They kept needing more time off as they were expecting, but they were quick learners with dainty paws and eyes for detail, so Bobby was more than happy to have them on board.

***

Finally, after months of ignoring requests, pleas, then warnings, EARS decided to launch their next stage of attack on the ignorant humans. Chapters had popped up all over the world and it was decided one of the American groups would launch first. Keith and his generals had been disappointed but pragmatic. If you wanted to launch with a bang and garner as much international attention as possible, the White House Easter egg hunt really was the best place.

The factories fell still, and silence descended over homes as the rabbit activists all gathered round their screens. TVs were all tuned to the channel live streaming the White House's Easter egg hunt and phones were open on news pages. This story was about to blow up, literally. Bobby was glued to the TV. There would be no going back after they committed this act of war. He wasn't directly involved but felt whatever transpired after this would impact them all. Keith was sat in the corner of the town hall which had rolled out the big screen for this event. Keith's eyes were darting between his phone and the screen, trying to gage information from them both – the anticipation radiating off him. Then the first egg bomb detonated.

There was a shower of silver as foil exploded and rained down on the now screaming crowd. Fires crackled on the over manicured lawn, with gooey chocolate melting and oozing away. Some of the eggs had scenes carved into them, so melting faces of chicks or disfigured chocolate rabbits could be made out before the flames claimed them. Men in suits had ushered the president and his family away and the attending media were lapping up the pandemonium. Then more booby-trapped eggs went off over the hysterical crowd, chocolate shards exploding everywhere with a good scattering of colourful sweets flying through the air like rainbow shrapnel. A flag unfurled amidst the chaos. A bright white banner with the words 'Recognition for Rabbits Labour - Executive for Advancing Rabbit Suffrage'. After seeing this the broadcast abruptly stopped.

Bobby sat there in shock. How had things got to this stage already? The general chatter in the room though was one of excitement. They had had a taste of rebellion and couldn't wait for their turn. Bobby found Keith in the crowd. He was very still and still looking at the screen despite it now being black. He had a smile on his face and his eyes were shining. It was clear he had only taken inspiration from such dramatic scenes and no hint of a warning. Bobby knew things were only going to get more violent.

Little did Bobby realise how soon he would be proved right. It was less than three weeks until Easter and he was huddled under a caravan at a travelling fair with other rabbits. Only members of EARS could hold jobs within the egg making and decorating industry now. So, Bobby has been forced to join to keep his job and to avoid being shunned by society. He had been hoping his historic injury would excuse him from most things, but after the

Prime Minister had made a public announcement labelling them as terrorists and saying they would refuse their eggs this year, Keith had needed all available bunnies for his escalation.

***

Petitions hadn't worked. Marches hadn't worked. Interviews with the media had garnered some support but none of it from people in power. Those who had chained themselves to supermarket entrances had been dragged away by the police. So, Keith had decided it was time for more serious protests. They were going all out, and Bobby had felt obliged to fall into line after seeing the treatment the rabbits who rejected EARS methodology had received. Pelted with turnips. Booed. Banned from social clubs. So, he was here in the dark, squatted under a caravan with about a dozen or so other rabbits – who had varying levels of enthusiasm for the upcoming protest.

Bobby crouched low and peeped out at the fairground. It was evening and although the sky was dark everything was brightly lit with thousands of twinkling lights. Garishly bright bulbs flashed from each ride, floodlights on stands stood surrounding the grounds and all the food stalls were lit up with varying-coloured LEDs. It was so noisy it was almost overwhelming for a rabbit's sensitive ears and Bobby had folded his in to block out some of the sound. Worse than all the clanging bells, whizzing machines and awful blaring music was the squeal of children as they were thrown about on rides and won tacky prizes worth less than the cost of playing. This abhorrence on the senses was also where the Prime Minister and his family were visiting tonight – along with lots of journalists and hundreds of cameras.

Bobby was given his basket of bomb filled eggs and set about doing what Easter bunnies do best, delivering eggs to secret places without being seen. Bobby tried to put his near storage units or vehicles so they would cause a lot of physical and financial damage but were away from where crowds were congregating. He had a feeling his comrades would not be doing the same.

There was a delayed reaction between the explosions with flames erupting and people panicking. There were a few seconds where people thought it was just one of the carnival games being overly loud, or a ride with over-the-top effects. Reality sunk in and the screams started as panicked people scattered – fleeing towards the car park. The cries of joy turned to wails of terror as people scrambled to get off rides and attendants battled to stop the rides and release the safety mechanisms that were now trapping people. Bobby caught glances from his low vantage point of some of the other rabbits zipping around, throwing grenades that had been painted to look like mini eggs. Their explosions caused the ground to shake and rides to rock in their foundations.

The Prime Minister was whisked away by serious looking men in suits and earpieces, his daughters clinging to him in the chaos. A banner claiming the carnage as that of EARS fluttered from the midway point on a faded helter-skelter whose mats had all been abandoned at the base.

The haunted house the ghost train trundled through was on fire, the ghoulish painting looking even more frightening as their features melted. Hook a duck had been totally destroyed and the spilt water soaking into the ground made escape that way slippery. Bobby watched shrieking people lose their footing and stumble on the unexpected wet as they trampled the scattered rubber ducks. The ducks' yellow bodies were now covered in mud, scuff marks and footprints as their painted eyes looked out blankly at the carnage.

The most horrifying sight that captivated Bobby though was the Ferris wheel which was slowly turning – and on fire. The music had stopped, and the reams of colourful lights had gone out, but the buckets people sat in continued to slowly go round, blazing brightly against the night sky. Smoke was beginning to obstruct the view of most things and the shrieks of burning metal buckling under the flames was drowning out the shots of the remaining fair goers who had not yet escaped. Bobby could hear the wail of the approaching sirens which was agony on his sensitive ears. His eyes were running from the smoke affliction and the nearby flames made his fur feel suffocatingly hot. All these obstructions, distractions and bombardment of the senses was not enough to stop Bobby noticing that in some of the carriages on the Ferris wheel there were still some people inside.

***

The humans had responded swiftly, and it had not been with a declaration of love and support for the rabbits and all they do over Easter. They had been branded terrorists. Classed as dangerous enemies of the state. A shaken Prime Minister had announced how close he had come to death, the carnage he and his family had been forced to witness at the fair and expressed his condolences to the families of those who had perished. The government would not be working with the rabbits in any capacity going forward. Easter could of course still be celebrated, but the focus would be on hot cross buns as the sweet treats. Their new allies were the chicks who were delighted to be receiving a paid contract to supply said hot cross buns, with rumours of a second contract for Easter bonnets in the pipeline. The chicks would be paid in their first year when the rabbits had never received a penny. Keith was livid, the epitome of hopping mad. Murmurs circulated wondering if they had gone too far. Rabbits were worried about redundancy as supermarkets emptied their shelves of eggs which were now banned.

EARS urged them all to carry on producing eggs, confident they would be able to not only use them, but sell them soon. The government had proved they had money for such things by their public, flashy gesture to the chicks. Some rabbits who disagreed with the path EARS was now taking and had been in the egg making/distributing business for generations began to trade Easter eggs on the black market with humans who also disagreed with their leaders and wanted a traditional Easter. Bobby kept working and producing his finest eggs with the best decorations and never asked what would become of them when various rabbits collected their orders. Ask no questions and you can plead genuine ignorance subsequently.

Sensing a shift in opinion amongst the ranks, Keith recruited from outside of rabbits to swell numbers with angry and dedicated members. Santa's elves were now on strike. Outraged that Santa and even the reindeer received such praise and recognition, despite them being the ones who slaved away year-round in the toy factory. Keith's passionate speeches about unrecognised labour had struck a chord with many. They travelled down from the North Pole to join EARS. Their work ethic and factory skills meant they could quickly turn their hand to egg making. Their anger also meant they then poisoned them and put IEDs in some. Part of the conditions of the coalition was they could also target Amazon, who had been undercutting the elves for years. Keith readily agreed, delighted to offer this in exchange for support from his new allies. Bobby did not like working alongside his new colleagues. The elves were bitter and grumbled a lot. They only cheered up when they were plotting bloody massacres, which they did with great glee. They also drank a lot. Keith had bought them sherry as a welcome gift to reflect all the free drinks Santa was left out on his delivery rounds and never brought back to share. The elves took to it with vigour and apparently were susceptible to addiction. Their work got sloppy, and one or two devices exploded in the factory itself instead of once delivered to their targets. Bobby took on late shifts when they tended not to work as they were either too merry, or already passed out.

Easter was fast approaching and neither side showed any sign of willingness to negotiate. They burrowed deeper in their trenches and flung mud at each other as the next battle was fought via the media. With accusations of modern slavery and terrorism thrown at each other, the war of words was nasty as they battled for public support. Neither side could rely on 100% support from their own kind. Groups of humans felt it was slavery, or animal cruelty, or akin to factory farming. Many rabbits felt they had lost the moral high ground when EARS tactics had turned violent, and lives had been claimed. They were devastated that their Easter eggs, of which they had always been so proud, had been turned into a symbol of war. Something children were now warned to avoid eggs, instead of encouraged to seek out. Then, fearing a serious Easter uprising by an ever-vitriolic EARS, the Prime Minister upped the ante. He called in the exterminators.

****

It was an ordinary day in the burrows. Tensions were high, harsh words were being exchanged between previous friends, parents were fretting about the number of children they had had and were wondering how they ever thought it was a good idea. Rival rebel camps whispered plots amongst themselves. Then there was a tremble above ground. With rabbits heightened senses and their complex intruder alert rigging, word spread like wildfire throughout the burrow that something was up. A few mothers grabbed their children and bolted, their nerves tauter than piano wires and not wanting to wait to see what actually developed.

Bobby had tucked himself into his bedroom with a book, the blatant propaganda for either side made magazines unreadable for him now. So, he escaped into his books when he needed some space from the conflict his kind had become so embroiled in. He felt the vibrations move through his walls and ripple over his ceiling, a sprinkling of dirt raining down onto his pristine bed. Something big was coming. Bobby got off the bed and put the book down, keeping his ears on high alert. He made his way to the door, rubbing his leg and wishing today wasn't a day it was playing up. He opened the door onto the warren of corridors and saw some other rabbits had done the same, all looking to each other for explanation. Then all hell broke loose.

The ground gave way like an earthquake in parts as huge men encased in terrifying suits with all-encompassing helmets thrust massive hoses down into the heart of the burrows. Rabbits screamed, dropped to all fours for maximum speed and bolted. Bobby saw flashes of bob tails all around him as his neighbours ran towards their nearest exit through the dust plumes the crumbing ceiling was creating. Bobby followed them, fear gripping his heart tightly and his leg screaming at the excursion, but he had to run to live. He didn't know what those hoses were. Were the humans going to try and drown them and ruin the eggs stored in the underground labyrinth? He didn't want to stick around and find out.

As he neared an exit, he heard shots ringing out and more screams from rabbits. Sensing he was about to charge into even greater danger, he skidded to a halt at a burrow entrance and peeked out. Huge men loomed with shotguns. They were gunning down those who fled the burrows. The rabbits had been flushed out to a massacre. The bullets were tearing through rabbits, leaving their limp, furry bodies, streaked with red, a look of horrific realisation frozen on their now still marble eyes. The men were smirking as they lined up their shots, firing round after round at anything furry that moved. They were gunning down men, women and children – all treated equally - with utter disdain. The crack of gunshots was deafening, and Bobby couldn't tell what were original shots and what were echoes ringing out. The screams were growing less as more rabbits were cut down. Bobby saw a distraught mother cradling the corpse of one of her children, smeared in his blood as she rocked him and willed him back to life. Her prayers were cut short as a bullet tore through her head. Bobby turned away and vomited. He already knew he would never be able to get that sight out of his memories.

More rabbits were galloping towards him, and Bobby stood in their path – waving his paws and shouting that it was a trap and gunmen were waiting. Some didn't appear to hear due to the ringing in their ears. Others tried to stop but were swept up in the fleeing crowd and carried to their death. A handful skidded to a halt to see what Bobby was ranting about and saw the awaiting carnage for themselves. Then the noise got worse.

Bobby dropped to his knees, cradling his bleeding ears as explosions began to ring out. Was PTSD making him relive the fairground? He huddled against a wall and looked out to see what fresh hell had been unleashed.

The elves had been woken up by the racket and, tipsy and angry, had turned their morning tipples into Molotov cocktails. They were screaming something, their little faces flushed, but the ringing in Bobby's ears was too great to make it out. From the twisted expressions of rage on their faces though, he could only imagine the hate they were spewing. Their aim wasn't too bad either. Some men had fled but Bobby could see at least two who were engulfed in flames, frantically running round before their colleagues forced them to the ground that was littered with rabbit bodies and tried to roll the flames out. Bobby could smell burning flesh – both rabbit and human. Some people stood at the top of the hill filming it all but making no move to help either side.

Bobby retreated back into the burrow, wanting no part in the atrocities happening outside. The ringing in his ears subsided enough for him to hear a distinct and heavy hiss. His brain couldn't process what it meant at first. Then realisation hit him like a sucker punch to the gut. The hoses didn't contain water but gas. They weren't going to flush them out or drown them, they had turned their homes into a gas chamber. Bobby didn't have time to process the full horror of this before a choking sensation engulfed him. He felt strong hands grab his shoulders just as unconsciousness claimed him.

****

Bobby came to on a ship, feeling the rhythm of the ocean rocking him as he roused. He looked about to see a huddle of subdued rabbits and elves sat around. Some bruised, battered or bloodied. All sat with a haunted look in their eyes.

"Where am I?" He asked the nearest rabbit.

"Rescue ship. We've been offered asylum, so the survivors are off to Easter Island to regroup," the rabbit next to him answered grimly. "We lived, we're the lucky ones apparently." It was delivered between gritted teeth, and he never glanced at Bobby whilst saying it. Just ground the words out between very deliberate bites on a limp carrot. Bobby didn't feel lucky, and he had a feeling his fellow asylum seeker didn't either. He gratefully accepted a bottle of water, hoping it would alleviate the burning in his throat, and settled down for a long ride. He was unsure if he would ever see his home again. Or if he would want to considering what memories it now held.

***

After the relief of being alive dimmed to acknowledgement of the grim reality they were living through, tensions began to erupt between the Easter Island residents.

"They massacred families in their homes, we have to retaliate and make them realise they went too far! They committed war crimes!"

"They did that after we bombed a children's fairground, we started it! We can hardly claim the moral high ground."

"So you're saying what they did was acceptable?"

"None of what either side has been doing has been even remotely acceptable for months!"

"I lost nine children only days ago!" One wept, interrupting the arguing pair.

"Don't worry, we'll avenge them."

"I don't want them avenged. I want other mothers to be spared this pain. This war has to stop. EARS was meant to be about a petition for God's sake. How did it descend into this bloodbath?"

"The humans weren't listening to reason. We had to step up the campaign otherwise we would have looked weak."

"Better weak than dead!" Another bereaved parent shouted from the outskirts of the crowd.

The angry voices were too much for Bobby who edged away from the rabble and hoped the fight would remain verbal. He saw they had brought some Easter eggs with them on the ship. As a decorator it pained him to see such beauty in such a state. Most were broken, all were at least chipped. Sweets spilled out like guts on the battlefield. Colours had run or smeared together. Carefully stencilled designs had been obliterated. Dents were in previously perfectly formed curves. Ragged edges dripped in the sun as carefully crafted masterpieces melted away.

The elves, hungover by now, piped up,

"The heads on this island hold mystical powers."

"Mystical how?" Asked one of the rabbits, who had part of their ear missing and the remnants of singed whiskers. "They supercharge the supernatural. Make ghosts more powerful, psychics have clearer visions. Things like that."

The elf who was speaking was sporting a black eye and shrugged as he delivered this. As if he were doing something as normal as reading out a shopping list.

"How does that help us?" One confused rabbit called out.

"If we use a Ouija board amongst the heads, we can recruit powerful demons to the EARS army. See how the humans who caused so much death like being haunted until they lose their minds. Or their lives."

As he smiled, he revealed a tooth had been knocked out in the last battle. Bobby was incredulous. How could this get any more ridiculous, or dangerous? Things really had gone too far.

"What are we going to do with the eggs?" Bobby called out.

The crowd turned to face him, a shared look of confusion. No one expected that as the first question to the introduction of a possible demon alliance.

"Pardon?"Keith pushed his way to the front, his white fur filthy and his waistcoat in tatters.

"What are we going to do about the eggs?" Bobby calmly repeated, keeping his voice neutral so as not to aggravate his burnt throat.

"You care about eggs at a time like this?" Keith asked disbelievingly."I thought this was all about our eggs. Are we going to stop making them?"

A dark brown rabbit with a white belly pushed through, grey tinges to his fur and whiskers, one ear drooping more than the other,

"How dare you! We have been making and decorating eggs for thousands of years. It is our craft. Our raison d'etre! Why would we abandon our history and lose generations worth of skills and tradition? That's practically blasphemy!"

Another rabbit, presumably his wife, put a hand on his arm to calm him.

"We don't like chocolate," Bobby answered. "Pardon?" The man cocked his droopy ear at him."We don't like chocolate," Bobby repeated, "We can't eat it. So, either we stop making them or find a home for them. This started because we felt our eggs and work were not appreciated. So, sod them. Let's not make eggs to receive praise from all people, or give them to supermarkets, or hide them around the homes of presidents and palaces. Let's make eggs because we love to do so and then take our baskets and hide them where they will be appreciated. Around children's hospitals, near foster care homes, on estates where there isn't enough spare money for treats or desserts. In countries where chocolate isn't easy to come by and is still something magical. Instead of going to war with people who don't appreciate us, let's just stop supplying them and use our skills to craft eggs for those who will love them as much as we do. Let's not try to be a business and demand recognition from ungrateful brats. Let's be a charity."There was silence as this idea was pondered. Even the militants could voice no objections. A new way of life had just been born.

***

The Prime Minister and a whole horde of other MPs were forced to step down after footage of the gassing and shooting made the news. It was deemed a gross overreaction, abhorrently cruel and a violation of a swathe of laws. He avoided prison time but was left with a huge fine and a reputation in tatters. The chicks cancelled their partnership after finding their new partners untrustworthy. Apologies were offered. Monuments were built. Most families were unable to get Easter eggs that year – although it probably did them good to go without and stop taking their presence for granted.

The rabbits rebuilt. Bobby got a new workshop and was promoted to head up a large team. Some of the eggs they produced were so fancy, so intricate, such pieces of amazing beauty, they went on display in art galleries and museums instead of being eaten. People queued to see them, and Keith was delighted their work was recognised and praised worldwide. The Easter bunnies and their skills were held in high esteem. Bobby was most happy with the simple but tasty eggs that went to those in need. He would often hang around and hide himself after hiding the eggs to watch the joy on children's faces as they found and ate their Easter eggs.

So, if you ever take part in an Easter egg hunt and you yourself are a good person, a grateful person with kind intentions, then enjoy your eggs. If the answer isn't a definite yes with regards to your good character, then proceed with caution. As instead of a sweet treat, you may get your hand blown off, or a stomach full of poison. Appreciate the hard-working bunnies.

Bastille Day Mon Amour!
By *Alistair Rey*

As one o'clock rolled around, George was willing to admit he had had it. He sat slumped on the couch sullenly watching the afternoon ballgame. Only the third inning, and already the Royals were being mercilessly slaughtered. He wouldn't have minded so much were it not for Claire continuously darting between the bedroom and bathroom, each time donning a more expensive dress. With every circuit, she would march into the living room and position herself directly in front of the television set.

"What do you think of this one?" she asked, standing up straight.

"Fabulous," George droned, craning his neck to catch a glimpse of the game behind her.

"You said that about the last one."

"That's because you have an exquisite wardrobe."

"You don't think the sundress seems more appropriate?"

"Sure."

Claire knit her brow. "Is that what you're wearing?"

George looked down at his short-sleeved linen shirt and khaki chinos.

"What's wrong with it?"

"Honey, don't you think something *a little* more formal might be better?"

It's a barbecue for Christ's sake! he wanted to scream.

"It's business casual," he replied, although to be honest he had no clue what passed for business casual.

Claire gave a doleful wag of her head before retreating to the mirror and adjusting her necklace.

George got it. Claire wanted to put on a good show for her boss. Since taking the job at Sterling & Lanning all Claire seemed capable of talking about was work. Topics like "projected corporate growth" and "executive culture" were now regular fixtures of their dinnertime conversation. Of course, that was if Claire made it home for dinner at all these days. On numerous occasions George would be in the process of broiling salmon steaks or whipping up a Caesar salad when the phone would ring. Before he could even get in a "hello?" Claire would inundate him with a litany of excuses as to why she wouldn't be home at the usual hour. There was always a client portfolio that needed finishing up, an account that had to be finalized before morning. Claire was working herself ragged trying to impress her new employers, suffering unpaid overtime like a good corporate martyr.

George bristled whenever the names Lawrence Sterling and Gloria Lanning came up—and they always did. Two pioneering entrepreneurs who had founded a company "for business, by business," whatever that meant. Claire was impressed by Sterling's "smart and visionary" approach to finance. She found Lanning's "wealth and executive style" worthy of emulation. It all sounded like something lifted straight out of a company pamphlet. It was obvious Claire was drinking a bit too much of the corporate Kool-Aid. If only he could get her to see it.

Claire's phone began to buzz on the table.

"Abbie's calling," he said, reading the name off the screen.

"Uh-huh."

"Aren't you going to answer it?"

"I'll call her back," she said, eyes fixed on her reflection in the mirror.

George shrugged and let the call go to voicemail.

"Everyone is going to be at Gloria's," she reminded him, not for the first time that morning. "It would be nice to have a husband who looks presentable."

"It's just a barbecue."

"It's a Bastille Day celebration," Claire corrected.

"Right. Bastille Day," with a role of his eyes. "Who celebrates Bastille Day? They're not even French. Doesn't it seem, I don't know, kind of *pretentious*?"

Claire frowned in the mirror.

"Honey, I know you don't like rubbing elbows with business savvy people, but it would be nice to introduce my husband to my colleagues without . . ."

Without *what*? George wanted to know. Claire didn't elaborate.

"Why couldn't they just throw a Fourth of July get together like normal people?"

"Because the Cannings already had a gathering scheduled on that day, remember?"

How could he forget? He had spent the afternoon hunched in a lawn chair sipping banana daiquiris while

Claire and the rest of her colleagues cavorted around the yard laughing and making small talk. People gave their opinions on the new exhibition at the Kemper Museum or the financial impact of the recent crypto crash, subjects George had absolutely zero knowledge of. It was like listening to people speak in a foreign language. He could barely hide his relief when Claire tapped him on the shoulder suggesting it was time to go.

"I don't recall Gloria Lanning making an appearance at that party," George said, fully aware he was on the verge of picking a fight with his wife he couldn't possibly expect to win.

"Gloria's a very busy woman," she replied, as if this was common knowledge. "She was named top female executive last year by Forbes Magazine. *Forbes*, George. Don't you realize what that means?"

"That doesn't explain why she can't come to party," he said, unimpressed. "Jeez. I mean these rich types are so full of it. Celebrating another country's Independence Day. Like, what is that supposed to prove? That you're worldly?"

If Claire was still listening, she gave no indication of it. Her attention was on the mirror where she was leaning in close to inspect her lipstick like a girl about to head out on a first date.

On the television, the announcers were relating the latest act of the massacre taking place at Kauffmann Stadium.

"Ready?" Claire asked.

George switched off the television, sparing himself any undue heartache.

"Ready."

#

It *was* just a barbecue, after all.

Driving through the front gates, George cringed, realizing how foolish his retorts must have sounded. Cruising up the treelined drive, he spotted limos and BMWs parked on the grass. George had never felt so self-conscious about driving a Prius before. Up ahead, he could make out a large circular drive with a gothic porte-cochère staffed by a team of valets. Studying the arriving guests, he immediately understood what Claire had meant about wearing something more formal. The men exiting vehicles and turning over keys were all dressed in pressed white shirts and sports coats.

Claire's ringtone began to chime.

"Ugh," she mumbled looking down at the screen.

"Abbie again?"

Claire nodded. "She's going through one of her dramatic breakups. I can't deal with this now. Not today."

"Don't stress babe," George said, trying to be encouraging.

Claire made a face.

"Pull over here," she said as the house came into view. "There's a nice spot right there."

"But they have valet parking," he protested.

"It's a nice day out. We can walk up to the house."

"Who walks up to the house?"

"We do," Claire said in a flat voice.

George shrugged and eased the car over to the side of the drive. He wasn't in the mood to argue. If she wanted to walk the final hundred yards to the house to spare herself the indignity of arriving in an ordinary fuel-efficient car, so be it.

Making their way to the porte-cochère on foot, George took note of the valets milling about the entrance. They all wore the same peculiar uniform: a stark black coat and tight-fitting pants topped with a tri-corner hat. He had never seen anything like it. There was something almost clerical about the costume.

When it came to the house, the word monumental seemed an understatement. Lines of mullioned windows thronged a neo-classical entryway. Letting his eyes drift up to the second story, George spotted a series of balustrades adorned with palms and exotic plants. Gargoyles crouched in the corners, peering down at the arriving guests with expressions of pure dread that George could sympathize with.

Claire threaded her arm through the crook of his elbow and led him up the front steps.

"Don't gawk," she whispered in his ear with the tone of a remonstrative parent.

With Claire in the lead, they passed through the doors of the porte-cochère into a foyer attended by servants dressed in the same austere black. The reception area was packed with guests. At the center of the room stood a fountain with an intricately carved marble statue of a man bound in chains. A steady stream of water gurgled at the base where the inscription "Everywhere Man Exists In Chains" was chiseled in stone.

George was trying to make out the meaning of the inscription when a well-dressed man cradling a tumbler in one hand approached.

"Claire! I was beginning to think you wouldn't make it," he said warmly, leaning in to plant a polite kiss on her cheek.

"Wouldn't miss it for the world. The house is absolutely gorgeous." Her voice sounded light and fluttery. So un-Claire.

"Isn't it?"

It was difficult to gauge the man's age. His youthful face was offset by a coiffe of salty grey locks. Dignified, but certainly not old, George thought. In his facial expressions and gestures, he detected that debonair attitude so natural to successful men. George didn't need an introduction to know this was Lawrence Sterling.

"Gloria does have a certain panache," he said, taking a long sip from his glass.

"It's like a fairy tale."

George cleared his throat. "Kind of gloomy," he remarked, angling his head toward the statue.

"Oh, Larry, this is my husband," Claire said, almost as an afterthought.

"George, is it?"

He nodded.

Sterling looked up at the statue with a wry face. "Gloria has a taste for, should we say, the dramatic." He flashed a smile at Claire, hinting at some kind of inside joke between the two of them. "Look at the ridiculous getups she's got these waiters in. It's her idea of a joke, and a bad one at that."

"Oh?"

"Gloria has a head for business when it counts, sure," Sterling prattled on, "but *only* when it counts. Otherwise, it's all theatre. Spectacle. Know what I mean?"

George nodded, not having the faintest clue what he was getting on about. He did seem to be talking quite liberally about his business partner, leading George to suspect that the tumbler full of scotch he was holding was not his first of the day.

"And she celebrates a French holiday because . . .?"

Sterling's thin-lipped smile broadened.

"This? It's payback for the Deutsche Bank fiasco last month."

"Knock it off," Claire said, swatting at Sterling playfully.

"What? It's true. Losing the Deutsche Bank account? That deal was handed to us on a silver platter until Gloria came in with all her demands for a green budget. Ten cents on every dollar invested put into renewable energy? Of course, they told her where she could put that deal!"

"Come on," Claire said with a nervous look around the room. Thankfully nobody was in earshot.

"It couldn't have gone worse had she tried to sabotage it." Sterling raised one eyebrow. "It's still not smoothed over with the shareholders yet. She thinks she'll appease them with this little soirée, but I can tell you it won't work. When things go south everyone calls for blood. Sure, she can put on this spectacle, but she still has to face the board next week and it won't be pretty. But you don't get a writeup in Forbes by being modest, am I right?"

Claire placed a hand on his arm, throwing Sterling a cautious glance. Then, turning to George diplomatically, "Honey, do you think you could go get us some drinks from the bar?"

George was all too happy to get away. He had little interest in company gossip.

Without a word, he wove his way through the crowd in the direction of the buffet. The table was laden with a bountiful spread of pâté, assorted canapés, and soufflés packed into small porcelain ramekins. Shuffling past the food area, a woman dressed in the same black outfit took his drink order.

"It seems we have a *declassé* aristocrat in our midst," came a voice behind him.

George pivoted on one foot to find a tall woman; arms crossed in a judgmental pose. She was dressed in the black costume worn by the servants except on her head sat a red Phrygian cap, its conical shape flaccid and drooping over one ear. A small tricolor cockade was pinned to her breast.

"Huh?" George huffed.

"Your clothing, dear," she said, extending one hand and touching the sleeve of his crinkled linen shirt. Her mouth twisted into what appeared to be the beginning of a smile.

"I'm a guest. I didn't know it was formal." A lame excuse if he had ever heard one.

"Don't worry dear, you make an exquisite *sans-culotte*."

"A *what*?"

"A commoner. A worker, dear."

"Gee, thanks."

"No, no, dear. You misunderstand. It's a compliment. The *sans-culotte* are the heroes of Bastille Day. They stand above all this swine," as she passed a hand over the reception room. "Today is your day."

"Uh-huh," was all George could think to say. "And what about the people dressed in black? Are they commoners too?"

The woman responded with a funny laugh. "Sort of. They are the Jacobin, the voice and will of the *sans-culotte*. The ones who embody the virtue of the common people."

"Virtue?"

"Of course, dear. That's what Bastille Day is all about. Virtue."

"I thought it was about cutting off people's heads."

Again, that funny laugh. "That is merely the people's vengeance on its enemies. But even that is guided by virtue."

George gave a puzzled expression, indicating he was following very little of what the woman was saying.

"This is what Americans fail to grasp," the woman continued. "July Fourth is about freedom. But what is the value of freedom without virtuous citizens? A free individual can do whatever they like—print their opinion and vote, yes, but also exploit, dominate, and murder. Virtue is the thing that ensures freedom acts in the interest of the good. It also ensures vengeance is just."

The woman seemed proud of her brief history lesson.

"Right," George said, nodding. "So, a rich woman who heads a multi-million-dollar corporation is celebrating the virtue of the common people with an extravagant party? Do I have that right? It seems kind of disingenuous."

At this, the woman gave a pained smile.

"Maybe to unassuming eyes. But beware a wolf in sheep's clothing."

George had no idea what the woman meant.

As if sensing this, she leaned in close, her eyes appearing to drift in the direction of Claire and Sterling. "Just remember to ask yourself, will *your* vengeance be virtuous?"

George saw his drinks waiting on the bar.

"I'll do that," he said, picking up the two glasses and wanting nothing more than to melt back into the crowd.

"There you are," Claire said as he approached. She had been laughing at something, her hand on Sterling's arm in that practiced way of faux intimacy taught at business seminars.

"Hope I didn't miss anything interesting," as he transferred one of the gin and tonics to Claire's unengaged hand.

"No, nothing. Just some insider talk, that's all."

"Think I'll go freshen up my drink," Sterling said, flashing his charming grin.

Claire nodded and gave a long sigh.

"So, what's the rumor mill reporting?" George asked once they were alone, mainly just to keep up the conversation.

"Huh?" Claire seemed lost in thought. "Oh, nothing. Just talking about the Deutsche Bank mishap."

"Must have been pretty funny."

"Funny?" as she creased her brow. "More like alarming."

"That so?"

"Yes. People are talking about stripping Gloria Lanning of her partnership because—

but you're not interested in this."

She was right. He wasn't.

"But it does mean a new partnership opportunity might be opening up soon."

"So, all those long hours might be paying off is what you're saying." He tried to manage a smile, but for some reason his lips wouldn't cooperate.

"Listen dear," as she handed him her small Gucci purse. "I'm going to freshen up in the ladies' room. Do you mind?"

George stood about awkwardly in the corner watching small herds of guests migrate from one end of the room to the other. *Swine*, the woman had called them, and for a moment he could see it. There was something animalistic in the way they gambolled about in packs gossiping and chortling. Strip off the designer dresses and Hugo Boss blazers, and what was left? Certainly nothing George could relate to.

Claire's bag began to vibrate.

On the illuminated screen was an incoming text message from Abbie: *Everything Okay?*

A-Okay, he typed back, hoping Abbie would take the hint.

The reply that came back ten seconds later was nothing short of shattering.

OK. Gloria is def out. UR number 1. Discuss at my place Thurs?

He picked up the phone and stared at it, a sinking feeling entering his chest.

Against his better judgment he tapped the call button and waited.

"Claire?" a man's voice answer.

He instinctively scanned the room, already knowing what he would see. At the bar in the far corner was Sterling, a drink clutched in one hand and a cell phone pressed to his ear in the other.

"Claire?" the voice asked. "You there?"

#

It was the longest fifteen minutes of his life.

By the time Claire returned, the room had just about stopped spinning. She adjusted the neckline of her dress and smiled at him.

"How are you liking the party?" she asked.

He looked to the floor and bit his lip.

"Abbie called while you were in the bathroom."

"Oh?" as she reached for her purse.

"You should probably call her back."

"I can't be bothered with her now."

"I think you can."

"It can wait."

"No. It can't."

She paused and for the first time he saw a look of apprehension flicker across her face. "It's nothing, George, really."

"You should call her."

"Why would I—"

But she never finished the thought.

From out of nowhere a bell chimed. Conversations halted mid-sentence as guests began looking about the room with confused expressions. At the far end of the reception room people were being ushered through a door by the servants in black. Without a word, Claire took his hand and joined the stream of people shuffling toward the doorway scoured in pale afternoon sunlight.

Outside, guests were assembling in a large, English-style garden. George blinked in the afternoon sunlight. Over the tops of heads, a large structure was coming into view. It took him a moment to realize he was staring at a life-size guillotine made of papier mâché. The contraption was positioned on a large platform with tricolor bunting coiled along the edge. Servants fanned out on both sides of the guillotine in a solemn procession, their faces concealed by ballroom masks. At the center stood the woman donning the Phrygian cap, her arms spread wide like a priestess calling her congregation to prayer.

Murmuring voices circulated through the garden as faces turned upward, fixing their sights on the stage. George caught a glimpse of Sterling elbowing his way through the crowd and felt a sudden rage well up inside him.

"Call Abbie," he whispered, reaching for her purse.

"Not here," she hissed, slapping his hand away. "Do you understand me? Not here."

The last guests were filing into the garden. On stage, the woman lowered her arms and an expectant silence fell over the crowd.

"Who among us can lay claim to virtue?" the woman began in a thundering voice as she paced back and forth on the stage. "*Who*?"

The crowd remained mute.

"What's going on?" Claire mouthed to Sterling.

"No idea," he mouthed back.

George felt his hands start to tremble. He curled his fingers into fists, the knuckles growing white and bloodless.

"No one? Not *one*?" the woman on the platform continued. She placed her hands on her hips and sneered. "Much as I suspected. And yet *you* see fit to judge. To judge others. To judge *me*! Parasites!"

Sterling cast a look around the crowd, his face apoplectic. He was no doubt thinking of all the stockholders and partners in attendance, people who would definitely not appreciate being called parasites to their face. He clenched his jaw with the dawning realization of what was about to take place. Gloria Lanning was intent on having her final say. Not in front of a board and not behind closed doors. But in front of everyone, taking the entire company down with her in one massive conflagration. Sterling's suave demeanour was melting away by the second, replaced with the terrified look of a man about to face a head-on collision.

"You gather here today to celebrate human virtue. Yet none of you—not one!—is worthy of it. History teaches us what such a degraded aristocracy rightly deserves: the people's wrath, and nothing more!"

"Okay, Gloria, very funny," Sterling interrupted in a thin voice, clapping his hands. "Very amusing. But I think it's time we all went back inside everyone."

Gloria paused, a smile creeping across her lips. She stared down at her business partner with cold, gleaming eyes.

"Okay, everyone," Sterling continued, waving people in the direction of the door. "I think we've gotten the gist of this. Really, Gloria, very nice touch. *Very* theatrical. I think we get the point."

Nobody seemed to be listening. All eyes remained on the stage where Gloria was pacing back and forth like a panther about to spring.

"I think we've found our first redeemer of the day," she replied, unphased. "Will you allow yourself to come up here, dear? Will you allow yourself to be a martyr to virtue?"

She gestured to the guillotine, daring him to step onto the stage.

Sterling glared at her. "Gloria, I'm not doing that. I'm not playing into this little game of yours. Enough is enough."

He scanned the crowd with eager eyes, trying to encourage someone—anyone—to back him up. But nobody spoke. Heads bowed and eyes looked away, leaving Sterling speechless.

Out of nowhere, a rapid drum tattoo punctuated the silence. George turned his head in the direction of the noise and for the first time noticed that the servants in black were stationed along the perimeter of the garden like military columns. They had crept in while everyone's attention had been fixed on the stage, surrounding them. In their hands were cudgels studded with nails and long pikes carved out of wood. As the martial drumbeat started up, they began to advance on the crowd, boxing it in.

"Gloria, this isn't funny!" Sterling screamed, panic flushing his face.

People exchanged confused looks as the crowd began to pitch and sway. A sudden burst of screams rang out. George heard the thrust of pikes rip through flesh as the crowd dissolved into a chaos of jostling bodies and anguished cries. The black clad servants were rampaging through the crowd, hunting down anyone they could lay their hands on.

George stood immobile and watched the carnage unfold around him. Where was Claire? He feverishly searched the crowd seeing only a blur of atrocities. People being impaled. People pushed to the ground and bludgeoned. People being decapitated, their heads hoisted aloft on pikes. He heard the sound of cleavers hacking into wet meat, the shattering blows of cudgels splintering skulls. In the dirt at his feet, he noticed a discarded mask streaked with gore. He picked it up and gazed at it with horror. He could hear the drums pounding out their death march, filling the air with their frenzied rhythm above the screams.

Again, he looked about, trying to locate Claire in the crowd. She was nowhere.

A voice called out his name. Sterling was squirming to his feet, trying to find a way out of the crowd. Behind him, Gloria stood at the front of the stage, her arms folded over her chest, a malicious smile spreading ear to ear.

What was it she had said to him? Will *your* vengeance be virtuous?

George looked down at the mask in his hand.

Sterling was waving his arms, calling out to him over the screams. He could hear the pounding drums synchronizing with the beating of his heart, cold and precise. Everything seemed to be happening in slow motion. George lifting the mask to his face, wrapping his finger around the handle of an abandoned truncheon. The squelching sound of his feet through the blood-soaked grass. Sterling's eyes growing wide at the realization of what was about to occur.

How easily the violence of virtue became the virtue of violence.

Would his vengeance be virtuous?

Yes, he whispered as he raised the cudgel above his head, anticipating the blunt force of wood against bone. Yes, it would.

A Kindness
By Joseph Buckley

When Morris kicked the gas pedal to the floor, his station wagon juked into the icy left lane then began drifting instead of passing the more responsible winter driver like he had attempted. Panicked, Morris cranked the wheel, sending the station wagon into a tailspin. Inside the car, a shiny, plastic tiara whacked him in the shoulder, and food wrappers and picture books went flying. The snowy world outside the windows spun into a blurry white.

Morris had lost control, though it's debatable he ever had any. He kept yanking at the wheel to prevent his fate, which, luckily for him, took the shape of a monstrous snow drift off the shoulder on county road 72. A quiet eruption of snow clouded the otherwise somnolent, winter landscape. Flurries from the crash swirled through the air like some twisted version of a snow globe and Morris' crashed car was the centerpiece.

Still buckled in, Morris sat shaking and sweating so hard he was sure he'd already died. He had yet to fully grasp what had just happened. Certainly didn't realize he'd ignored the repeating yellow arrows urging him to use caution for the sharp turn ahead.

Once he plucked his white-knuckled hands from the wheel, he made it outside to assess the damage. By some miracle, he'd escaped what appeared to be any setbacks beyond the inconvenience of his car being stuck. Except Morris didn't see it that way. Why would he? It wasn't like he'd almost died racing up a random backcountry highway. No. This was the unfair hand the world continually dealt him.

The thing is, Morris never planned well. And sure enough, this holiday season was no exception. Not only was it most likely that old Buck would be out of Christmas trees, but surveying how badly his car was stuck in the snow pile, it was more likely he wouldn't even get there before Buck closed up shop for the day. But this wasn't his fault either. It was the fault of Buck's increased business. The fault of everyone else wanting a Christmas tree too.

Morris peered through the rear windows of his rusted vehicle. Fog breaths bloomed on the glass. Inside was Emma's scooter which she had retired after a crash into the bushes; a few wrapped gifts for her; anti-freeze; jumper cables and one of those scraper things for ice. He shoved the gifts and toys aside with a clatter. And with the brush end of the scraper tried to brush his car out of its newfound snow-garage. He quickly felt like a fool.

Add to that his fingers going numb. Same for the toes. It's not like Morris was any type of outdoorsman. He was a bartender. He wore sneakers to procure a Christmas tree, after all. Morris threw the snowy brush back among the back-seat detritus. At the least, the car still ran. Same for the heat which he then cranked to the max, seated back in the driver's seat until he could figure something else out.

No signal on his phone. It wouldn't have mattered anyway. By the time a tow got there, Buck's would be closed. Who else would even bail him out of such a predicament? His ex-wife Elise?

Not a chance.

The whole point was to get the tree for Christmas weekend. Prove to Elise how responsible he really could be. It was Friday. He was to pick up Emma the following morning. There was no way he would be reduced to buying one of those tacky plastic trees. There had to be a way. The radio chanted cheerful holiday songs like it knew how much of a schmuck he felt like. He smashed it off.

"The holidays have a way of sneaking up on you," was his go-to line for the locals at the bar he tended downtown. He thought how ironic it was that his perfunctory ice-breaker was now his fate, literally stuck in snow. There were a couple of days left until Christmas and here he was trapped on the side of the frozen highway, in complete solitude; the snowfall thickening.

All of a sudden a few friendly honks of a car horn interrupted his episode of self-pity. Bright headlights lit up the interior of his car as if he was about to be beamed up to some mothership. A large pickup then drew beside his car, pulled to a stop just in front of his car. A strange sense of deja vu came over Morris. He'd seen that truck somewhere before. Weird, it wasn't like he had any interest in trucks. Hell, he didn't even own a car until they had Emma many years ago.

And then a horrible knot grew in his stomach like some tiny fist had grabbed hold of his organs, and twisted them in opposite directions. It was the same truck he'd just passed. He remembered the mud flaps with an angry, dual pistol-wielding cowboy on them. He threw the car in reverse. Floored it. The tires squealed, spewed snow behind them but made no forward progress.

The pickup rumbled idly. Dirt and snow caked across the side panels. Brown exhaust spewed from the tailpipe. A burly man jumped down from the driver's side. He stomped back toward Morris dressed in coveralls and snow boots. Steam poured forth from somewhere within his dark beard like a cartoon bull. Morris locked his door. The man stopped at the driver-side window and with his massive hands made a motion to roll it down. All Morris could do was stare ahead, shaking his head *no*.

The man then knocked on the window so loud Morris wondered how it hadn't shattered.

"Hey, bud. Need a tow?" He grunted.

"No, I'm okay," Morris replied, still not looking to his side, trying to shoosh the man away with his hands.

The man disappeared into the snowfall and reappeared holding straps which Morris knew to be the devices by which he would be murdered. *Make it quick, please make it quick.* Morris thought to himself, eyes clenched shut. He heard the man's muffled voice through the window:

"Tie it up at the axles."

He opened his eyes, and the man was miming how to loop the straps. Morris' fear thawed out a little. Maybe the stranger really did just want to help out. So, he jumped out of the station wagon. Yet, close to the stranger, he was overcome by a mysterious aroma. It was like dead leaves that had grown wet and musty, moldy. He did his best to ignore it, act normal, and slid underneath the car to secure the straps, shivering in just a denim jacket.

"All right, I'll gun 'er and you steer out back onto the road." He looked at Morris dubiously. "Just hold it steady, okay?"

Morris' station wagon popped back onto the road before he had a chance to forget his instructions.

"Wow. Incredible. How the hell did you do that so fast? Look, can I repay you in some way?" Morris handed the man back his straps.

"No, no. Just gotta be careful out here in these parts." The stranger winked.

"Right. I just got ahead of myself. Sorry about driving like a maniac and all. It's just I'm trying to get to Buck's before he closes. I ruined my daughter's Christmas last year with the divorce. And I just have to give her a magical Christmas this year. And something has got to go right for once. And…" He laughed nervously. "Sorry, I'm a little strung out from the accident."

"Buck's closed. Sold out."

"Shit. Really?"

The man stared through Morris like the question had been answered long before Morris had ever gone and wedged his car into the side of a snowy field.

"My god. Of course, another frickin' failure. Geez man, it's always something." Morris kicked the door of his station wagon.

"Whoa…If you're really desperate for a tree, I know a guy. Just a little past Buck's in fact." He raised his arm to motion down the road and when he did Morris thought, for the briefest moment, the man's arm resembled a tree branch. But quickly dismissed this hallucination; chalked it up to after-effects of the crash.

"About a dozen or so miles past is a cut-off to your right. It's not really marked. But on the opposite side of the road is a lone pine tree. It should be plowed enough that even your car can make it back there."

"Geez. I don't know. I should probably just try to make it back home. Emma will be sad, but I don't want to fly into another snowbank." Morris laughed nervously.

The man had already made his way back to his truck.

"Hey wait! I didn't even get your name." Morris called out but the man shook his head.

Standing on the running board he looked back to Morris. And something strange happened with Morris' sight. Like the man had flickered among the snowfall. Disappearing then reappearing in the same place a moment later. With a click of the door and grumble of the engine the man had pulled away into the near white-out conditions. Morris couldn't make any sense of the curiosity other than it being a trick of the light or snow.

Morris' first thought was to turn back for home, he had a six-pack in the fridge already. But as soon as he got back in the car the Christmas queued up again. And he couldn't quite explain what had pushed him to trust the man's suggestion, driving his under-prepared self further into the snow globe, but he'd finally struck into some luck and just had to see it out.

Surprisingly, the stranger was right. The scraggly top of a lone pine tree peaked out from the snow on the shoulder of the highway. And it wasn't until Morris drove but a foot or two away that the road even became visible. It was all white, blended without a seam. A secret hidden in plain sight. He took the turn and driving at no more than a crawl, the station wagon managed to squeak along the crispy, cold snow.

Everything seemed peculiar to Morris since the accident. Like the kind stranger who, for all Morris presumed, couldn't be from his version of the world. It was like when he crashed the car he slipped into an alternate reality. Then this snowy road which felt like he'd been driving down for hours without reaching the forest's edge. Yet the forest had appeared only a few blocks out when he first turned. Through the car mirrors he confirmed the ground moving but that wall of green never drew closer. Brilliant, white snow stifled everything in sight, flattened depth, tamped down the weeds and trees, and in this way felt slightly unreal to Morris like he was in heaven.

Though his doubts finally concluded when a trailer came into view. Except once he pulled up, the trailer was empty, looked long since abandoned. The twiggy remnants of a pine wreath hung from the center of its door. Strings of dead Christmas lights drooped from the roof, doorframe, and window frame. Even the surrounding pine boughs had stretched out over the top and sides of the flimsy structure as if it would soon be reclaimed by the pine forest. Tall mounds of snow buried the whole thing, especially the doorstep. Yet, somehow, the entire road leading up there was packed down, and appeared regularly maintained.

A sudden knock rapped at the car window. Morris shrieked. Outside the window the man who'd helped him earlier stood, snowflakes dotting his beard. Morris opened the door and jumped out into the windy field.

"Hey, wait a minute. This is your place?" He lightly smacked the man's shoulder which strangely felt wooden. "Why didn't you just tell me?"

"Sorry?" The man seemed confused.

"Huh?" Morris replied.

"Sorry. I don't know who you are." The man offered.

"I was the guy stuck in the snowbank back down 72 a few miles. Remember? You just towed me out. Saved my ass!"

"Wasn't me."

The man shrugged and looked to Morris like he'd grown a second head. Morris' relief quickly flipped to concern.

"What the hell…well you look exactly like that person. Like…I mean…exactly." Morris wanted to mention the clothes and the smell, both of which were identical. Even the eerily distant tone of his voice sounded the same.

"Anyway, you told me…er, he told me to come here for a Christmas tree?"

"Yep." He replied absently.

The man's wiry eyebrows furrowed, looking Morris over: jeans, sneakers, jean jacket, no gloves.

"It's in those woods over there." He pointed to the frosted white forest all of which appeared swollen and sagging with accumulated snow.

Like all it would take was one more flake and the whole thing would collapse.

"Not much I can do. I've gotta get a great tree for my daughter." Morris blew into his cupped hands and slapped them together. "It doesn't matter. I'll warm right back up once we throw it on the roof and I'm back in the car."

Morris opened the trunk and dug through the stranded belongings. He found some old socks which he pulled over his sneakers, and a pair of pink gloves with feathered cuffs — Emma's. And only covered the top half of his hands but the extra layer already seemed to help. The cold already having proved its dominance as soon as he stepped out of his car. He noticed the man holding a hacksaw in his hand. And Morris thought for a moment what would happen if this man suddenly turned on him. He certainly had no method of recourse. He didn't even know where he was. He'd be hacked meat in a matter of minutes.

But these concerns mattered little in comparison to Morris' desire for the tree. He had no choice but to trust the man. Except he had acted so strangely when Morris recognized him. And further exacerbating his anxiety, he hadn't seen the man's truck anywhere around the trailer. Or any other car for that matter. Morris wondered if the man arose from the earth like a golem. He shuddered, turned his eye away from the creepy trailer and entered into the forest with the stranger.

A lonely silence fell over the men. The small tinklings of the winter forest, their footsteps, and the sounds of their breath were amplified. Almost like it all happened in his head. The smell of fresh pine overwhelmed Morris in a stunningly magical way. He felt like a child again. Like he was indeed within one of the picture books he read to his daughter.

"Hey, I never got your name. I'm Jack. Jack Morris."

"A little further ahead is a small hill and below that a thicket of trees you'll never see anywhere else." He replied as if he had never heard Morris.

Eager, Morris quickened his pace up the slight slope then lost his footing, fell to his knees.

"Little slippery out here, huh?" Morris tried to joke away his embarrassment only to realize the man was no longer in front of him.

"Hey wait up!"

He ran up the slope dodging below low branches, slipping and sliding until he reached the top. Below, he saw a ring of open, white space surrounding the small grove of trees like they were indeed different from the other trees in that forest. And there among the exclusive grouping of trees, he spotted the man.

Morris couldn't believe his eyes. The trees really were perfect looking. Like they'd been photographed for magazines or used on the cover of Christmas movies. Their beauty melted away the painful cold in his knees and hands. He was overwhelmed by the emotional resonance the forest conjured.

"Hey!" Morris called out. "I'm coming down. Wait up. Let me pick it!"

The man had already bent over, began sawing at a tree. Or at least it appeared to Morris that way. Except once he made it down into the glade, the man had disappeared again.

"Hello?! Where did you go? Hellooo?" He called as loud as he could. Turned round. Then round the other way. His eyes darted across the trees and snow frantically. It couldn't be true. It wasn't physically possible. He was probably just behind one of the trees. Everything did look the same in a puzzling way.

"Hey!" He shouted again.

Morris' paranoia deepened when he noticed there weren't any saw marks in the bark of the tree. It was untouched. There weren't any footprints either. But that couldn't be. If he had been in this grove of trees his feet would've certainly made marks. Unless he hadn't ever been down there. Morris then considered that perhaps he never did see the man sawing at a tree down here and hadn't seen him since their journey out.

His thoughts spun faster. Morris wondered how much he'd imagined and how much had actually happened. He wanted to get out of those woods. An unsettling feeling crept over him. Like the trees were conspiring against him. Conspiring with that man.

Morris had to resolve his situation soon. The sun had little light left to give before dying off. He trudged through the snow, back up the slope. Figured that maybe from the top he would have a better vantage point and see that the man was just behind a tree or somewhere else obvious. His stomach growled loudly. He remembered how he hadn't eaten since breakfast.

That was it!

He was just out of sorts from exhaustion. Nothing catastrophically wrong.

Standing back atop the crest of the hill, he saw something move across the ground. A deer? A bear? Something tall and brown certainly. But it vanished into the homogeneous scenery. Trees. It was only more and more trees. Then again. Another flash of movement that disappeared before Morris could make sense of it. Suddenly the man walked out from behind one of the trees. As if he'd been there the whole time just poking around the trees, trying to find the right one.

"Hey man! What the hell is going on? How did you get back here? Or you were down there, right?" Morris realized he was screaming. "Look, can you just wait for me? I can hardly feel anything in my body anymore. I think I've got frostbite…like everywhere."

Though he couldn't see the man's face. His back was turned to Morris.

"Hey! Hello!" Morris pressed up toward him.

And when Morris ran around the side of the man, he saw something impossible. He was screaming at a pine tree. He swore that was the man standing there, could even smell that musty scent. It was like some type of hallucination. Somehow the man was a tree. Or the tree had played a trick with the light?

"This damned forest!"

Morris kicked the tree; punched the snow; when a glint of light caught his eye down below — the sawblade. The man must've left it behind. What luck.

Morris more or less fell back down the slope, picked up the saw and set to hacking at the first tree in his sight. In a panicked rage, he felled the tree, almost cutting himself with each frantic pass of the saw. And hoisting the tree trunk to his shoulder he saw footprints once again. They trailed from where Morris stood, out the opposite end of the small glade. The deeper, darker end. But how was that possible? How could they appear and reappear?

Morris considered how he couldn't just leave him out there alone. Even if this was territory the man probably knew well. If nothing else, Morris' curiosity urged him to follow the markings. He had to find the man to confirm his existence if nothing else.

So, dragging *his* tree behind him Morris followed the prints. Alone, the forest had grown so eerily quiet like the whole earth had been paused. The air so cold that it had a highly defined quality. It was cutting. Sharp as a knife's edge. It was almost as if Morris could see the tree's finest details. Though the longer he peered into the trees, the less certain he grew. Faces appeared within the tree bark; they watched him. Morris kept his eyes glued to the snow below him until the prints grew faint. Looking up, he saw they faded deep into the forest.

"Hey!" His breath steamed. "Hey man! You out there? You okay?"

Hoo. Hoo. Back here.

A faraway voice called out.

"Where?" Morris begged.

His heartbeats and labored breaths were all he could hear. The forest silence weighed on him heavy as a lead vest. This voice did nothing to comfort him.

Hoo. Over here. Hoo.

Somehow the voice came from a different position.

"Hey, I can't see you. There's barely an inch of sunlight left, man. Come to me. I'll keep shouting."

Right behind you.

This time the voice must've been an inch from Morris' ear. He turned snap quick to see nothing but more trees. But then an even greater tragedy revealed itself to Morris. The tree dragging behind him had brushed away his own footprints. Only shallow, tree markings remained which were hardly distinguished amid the blustering snow.

"What the hell? What do you want from me?" The sound of Morris' screams couldn't compete with the thickening snow.

The sun was gone. Gaps between the trees had darkened highlighting the endless, snow-plated trees. Like hundreds of guards ready to block Morris' escape. Morris followed whatever landmarks or snow prints he could — none existed. Every direction he turned were more trees, more snow. The hill encircled him. Morris' feet had long since gone numb. His pink-gloved hands, locked on the sappy trunk of the tree, felt like distant memories.

"Why is this happening?" He blubbered to himself. "Hellloooo! Hey!"

On the verge of collapse. Desperate to stay optimistic. Stay aware and awake. Morris hummed a tune. Something about a Christmas tree he'd heard on the radio. Damned if he could remember lyrics at a time like that.

Amid this desultory shuffling about, footprints drew back into his view. Though he had long since trusted his eyes. Two pairs of tracks dotted the snow. It must've been the route they'd taken into the woods. Morris willed his body along the trail unsure if his legs carried him any longer or he was merely moving in his mind. He could only continue. The differences between dream and reality had slipped away so long ago. The forest, for all its magical splendor, had yet to show kindness. Its depths refused to relent.

Each falling snowflake clung to his frozen frame further dampening his clothing. It being dark, Morris didn't know if he'd turned around at some point. He had fallen so many times. Was so wet. So numb. He could no longer make sense of the footsteps. Which way they went.

He was out of breath.

Out of energy.

Out of mind.

Morris slowly froze in place. His brain unable to communicate clearly to the limbs of his body. A crunch of bootsteps sounded behind Morris as if they were inches away.

"H-h-help. I'm h-here." He spoke, stuttering with cold.

Suddenly, the man appeared in front of him.

"I, I got a tree." Morris thought he smiled but couldn't feel his face. "Emma is…Emma…"

But there was no tree in his hand. Only the man stood there. Frozen solid, Morris hadn't noticed. He only saw a vision of Emma's smiling face and a warm crackling fireplace with the most beautiful, green, Christmas tree beside them.

And the snow fell. Piling high on the frozen stiff Morris, until the pink gloves were all that distinguished him from the other wondrous trees.

Welcome to the Chip
By James Fritz

A disco ball spun over the gymnasium. The Monster Mash belted out over the loudspeakers. A hundred costumed high schoolers jerked to the beat. An apple bobbing tub sat next to a long table covered with candy and jugs of cider.

Don and Mikaela danced at the edge of the crowd. Their smiles seemed glued to their faces. They didn't break eye contact for the entire song.

"Nice costume," Mikaela said. "I never would've guessed that you'd dress up as a praying mantis."

Don spun around. He wore a green one-piece with wings and antennae. Claws ran down the legs and arms.

"They're badass," Don said. "They can camouflage themselves and keep really still to lure their prey in."

Don stepped back and squatted down. His head darted around before settling on Mikaela.

"And once you get in their sights, they pounce on you!"

Don shot forward and grabbed Mikaela by the shoulders. She threw her hands up. Her witch's hat fell off her head.

"You caught me," she said.

Don laughed as he planted kisses along her neck. She sighed. Her hands pressed into his back. He lapped up her floral perfume.

"And the females don't take any shit either," he said. "Sometimes after they have sex, they eat their partners."

She laughed. He kissed her on the lips. She responded. He palmed her green-painted cheeks.

Don couldn't believe that somebody as beautiful as Mikaela would ever fall for him. It wasn't that he considered himself unattractive. He didn't have anything going for him. He wasn't an honors student or a virtuoso musician or a superstar athlete. He had few friends. Most of the school didn't know him.

And yet, there he was. Making out with a girl that liked him.

"Well, I guess the freaks come out on Halloween! Get a room, Don!"

Don flipped the bird at Fingers. His best friend was dressed as a nun. A black dress bulged around his wide chest. A habit came down past his shoulders.

"I don't think there's a nun in the world with legs as hairy as yours," Don said.

"I'm not so sure about that," Fingers said. "Once you haven't seen a dick in decades, you stop caring how you look down there."

His date, Jill, wore a black and white striped shirt with black pants and a black beret. Her face was painted chalk-white.

"What are you dressed up as?" Don asked.

She didn't answer. She placed her hands out in front of her as if she were trapped inside an invisible cube. The walls of the cube pressed in on her. She scrunched her body together in a heap on the floor.

"Holy shit!" Don said. "You should become a contortionist when you grow up."

She straightened herself out and dusted her clothing off.

"Why don't we get out of here?" Fingers said. "There's this Chinese place that's still open. Do I have any takers?"

Don shrugged his shoulders. "Sounds good. I'll drive."

The group walked out of the gymnasium. Every spot in the parking lot was full. Jack-o-lanterns flickered along the sidewalk.

"I'm not sure we'll be able to get out of here," Mikaela said. "Don and I ran over a dozen traffic cones on the way in here."

"It's all because of that stupid fine arts center they're building," Don said. "Apparently, some rich old alumnus willed $28 million to Marianist High School! They say it's the biggest donation to a high school ever. And every cent is supposed to go into that building. They're calling it *The Chip* in honor of him."

"Guess you can't take it with you," Fingers said.

They piled into Don's car and drove out of the parking lot. Cones snaked around the road. Fingers whistled in astonishment as they drove by the construction site.

"Wow," he said. "It's like something you'd find on an Ivy League campus."

"Hold on," Mikaela said, "I want to see it."

She got out and walked towards the building. Don put the car in park. The rest of the group followed her.

"It's enormous!" she said. "My entire high school could fit inside."

The group stared at the skeletal husk of the building. A rotunda jutted out of the side. Plywood covered up gaping holes in the walls where the windows were supposed to go. White stone columns rose up in front of the entrance. Fresh red bricks lined the walls.

"I wonder what it'd be like to go inside," Mikaela said, "before anybody else has a chance."

"Why don't we give it a shot?" Fingers said. "I'm sure there's a way in."

They walked around the building towards the rotunda. A truck was parked in front of a loading dock. Fingers heaved himself up and pulled on a metal grating covering the entrance. It rolled up to the ceiling. Somebody had left it unlocked. The inside of the building looked pitch black.

"All aboard!" he said.

The rest of the group hoisted themselves onto the concrete platform. Fingers took out his cellphone, turned on its flashlight, and shined it inside.

"Let's see what $28 million gets you," he said.

The group walked in. Their footsteps echoed off of the bare concrete floors. Exposed piping ran along the walls. Wooden planks, carpet rolls, and construction equipment cluttered the hallway. The smell of drying paint made Don hold his nose.

"This is so freaky," Mikaela said. "Once you strip everything away, this is what the building looks like."

The group walked down the hallway. They took a right turn and entered the main lobby. The pieces of plywood rattled against the wind blowing from outside. A staircase without a railing led up to the second level. Squares of marble covered about half of the floor.

"YEE-HAW!" Fingers shouted. His voice echoed through the lobby.

"FUCK!" Mikaela followed suit. Her voice bounced off of the walls as it grew dimmer and dimmer.

They looked at Don. He grinned as he brought his hands to his mouth.

"COCK!"

The three didn't stop. Four letter words filled the air. As soon as one voice died away, another added to it. Their shouts blended together in an acoustic soup.

"Well," Don said, "it is the fine arts center. We were just making music." His throat started to feel scratchy.

They walked into the rotunda. A construction lift was fully extended. Where a domed ceiling should have been, the rotunda opened out onto the sky.

"Hope it doesn't rain in the next few days," Don said. "Imagine the water damage!"

Fingers sized up the lift. He rubbed his chin in contemplation. He then wedged his hands in between the x-shaped frame of the lift. It creaked under his weight as he pulled himself up.

"Dude! What the fuck are you doing?" Don shouted.

"Climbing up," Fingers said. "I want to see what it looks like from the top."

Don's heart thumped in his chest. Panic seized him. For a moment, the wheels of the lift came off the ground. Fingers was going to pull it down on top of himself.

"FINGERS! GET DOWN HERE! YOU'RE GOING TO TIP OVER!"

He didn't listen. He climbed higher and higher. For somebody as big as Fingers, he ascended with unexpected quickness. The lift groaned in protest but stayed up. Don sighed in relief as Fingers pulled himself into the metal cage at the top.

"Victory!" Fingers said. He patted himself on the back. "Guess what? It looks the exact same up here as it did down there!"

"No shit," Don said.

Fingers pulled a lever on the side of the lift. The frame collapsed itself. The cage descended to the ground. He jumped out of the lift.

"You never say *No* to anything," Don said.

"Yep!" Fingers said. "Life's too short for *No*."

The group walked through the lobby and into the finished theater. The velvet chairs had a musty odor. A red carpet ran down the aisles. The stage was covered by a towering curtain.

"Okay, you guys are completely spoiled," Mikaela said. "This theater is like a freaking concert hall."

"I guess they'll have the all-school assemblies in here from now on," Don said, "not to mention the-"

His voice caught in his throat. Something moved on the ground. A chirping sound made the color drain from his face.

"Oh my God…"

It was a praying mantis. A living, breathing, hulking praying mantis. It was as if somebody had dropped it in a vat of radioactive goo that caused it to grow ten times in size. It was as long as a ruler.

"HOLY SHIT!" Don shouted.

The mantis shot towards him. It swiped its claws at him and tore into his chest. His costume ripped open. Don stumbled backward and almost lost his footing.

Mikaela screamed and flung herself behind him. It made another go for him. He raised his foot and brought it down on one of the mantis's claws.

CRUNCH

Every single hair on Don's body stood up. The mantis squirmed in pain on the floor. Liquid oozed out of it and onto the red carpet.

"GET IT OFF!" Fingers shouted. "GET IT OFF GET IT OFF GET IT OFF!"

A mantis clung to his face. Its limbs were wrapped around his head. Fingers grasped its claws as it tried to swipe at him.

"FINGERS!"

Don rushed over and took hold of the mantis. Its fluttering wings cut into his hands like the blades on a fan. Blood ran from the cuts. He kept his grip and pulled. Its limbs came free of Fingers's face. He spiked it on the ground and crushed its torso.

"Fingers, are you okay?"

Scratches covered his face, but that was it. The nun's habit leaned to one side on his head. His eyes bulged in shock.

"What the fuck was that?" he said. "That thing was huge!"

Don couldn't think of an answer. No bug in the world was supposed to grow that big. Was somebody playing a prank on them?

"Shit!" Mikaela said. "There are more behind the curtain!"

The curtain waved as if a breeze was blowing against it. At least seven more praying mantises emerged from underneath it.

"RUN!" Don shouted.

The group sprinted down the aisle. Don crushed Mikaela's hand in his. The mantises flew through the air in pursuit.

Once outside the theater, Don grabbed the wooden double doors and slammed them shut. An instant later, the insects' bodies pattered against them. Fingers took a paint bucket from the lobby and used it to prop the doors closed.

"That was insane!" Mikaela said. "Those bugs were gigantic!"

"Well, call me a wuss, but I've had enough of the Chip for one night," Fingers said. "Let's get the fuck out of here."

They hurried through the rotunda back to the loading dock. Finger's cellphone flashlight went out for a few seconds before coming back on.

"Think it's time for you to get a new phone," Don said.

"*This is new*," Fingers said. "Maybe it's defective or something."

He fiddled with some settings, but the light kept flickering. The group walked down the hallway towards the loading dock.

"Uh, guys… didn't we leave the grating up when we came in?" Mikaela asked. "Because it's down now."

Don's stomach churned with bile. The door had been pulled down from the ceiling. Jill's hands flew to her mouth, but she remained quiet. He wondered what it would take for her to break character and actually say something. A horde of killer praying mantises hadn't done the job.

"Holy shit…" Fingers said.

The group sprinted towards the grating. Fingers set his phone against the wall. The light continued to flicker. He grasped the bottom of the grating and heaved. It didn't give.

"Don, help me out! This fucking thing's stuck!"

"Hold on," Don said, "it's a million degrees in this suit."

He tore the zipper down on the back of his costume and ripped it off his body. His blue jeans and white t-shirt were drenched.

He went over and helped Fingers.

"On the count of three… one… two… three!"

They pulled up on the grating. It didn't move an inch.

"Fucking hell!" Fingers said. Veins bulged on his neck.

"Somebody must have locked it!" Don said.

They heaved three more times. The grating remained in place. Don wheezed from the exertion. Fingers collapsed onto the floor.

"That bitch isn't going anywhere," he said. He threw his nun's habit off. His hair was covered in sweat.

"Okay… there's got to be another way out of here," Mikaela said. "We've just got to find it. This can't be the only-"

The light from Fingers's cellphone went out completely, leaving the group in darkness. Don blinked several times just to be sure. The light stayed off. Immediately, he pulled his phone out of his pocket. The screen flickered to life before it too went dead.

"No. No no no no no… come on you fucking thing…"

The phone didn't come back on. He threw it on the ground.

"Mikaela, is your-"

"Guys," Mikaela said, *we have a problem.*"

She held up her phone. It was on, but there were no apps to open. Instead, the screen displayed four blood-red words.

WelCoME tO tHe CHiP!!!

Everybody stared at the screen. Jill's mouth hung open in fright.

"Is this a joke, Mikaela?" Fingers said. "Because if it is, nobody's laughing."

"I can't get rid of the words," Mikaela said. "My phone's acting on its own."

Don's stomach felt as if it were being filled with a pitcher of ice-cold water. His hands shook. They were trapped. The Chip was the praying mantis, and they were the prey.

"Shit... shit shit shit..." Fingers said. He ran his hands through his hair like a tic.

"Guys," Don said, "we've got to find another way out of here. If you see something weird, just run. Run until you can't go any further. Everybody needs to stick together. Understand?"

The rest of the group nodded.

"You think we're going to make it?" Fingers said.

"Doesn't matter what I think," Don said. "We have to move. Or we die right here."

He led the way down the hall towards the rotunda. His heart went back and forth in his chest like a pinball. He could barely make out the construction equipment on the floor. They had no source of light. He crept on the balls of his feet...

"SHIT!" Fingers yelled. He recoiled and tripped over a carpet roll. "Something just touched me!"

"Sorry," Mikaela said, "that was me."

Don felt an urge to punch Fingers in the face.

"Hush up!" he said.

They went back to the lobby. Don tugged at a piece of plywood covering up a hole where a window was to be installed. Just like the grating at the loading dock, it didn't budge. Splinters lodged in his hand. He kicked the plywood and almost broke his toes. The piece had to have been an inch thick.

"Son of a bitch!"

He surveyed the lobby. Except for the doors to the theater, nothing had been installed yet. There was a hallway on the other side of the lobby that they hadn't explored, along with the entire second floor. He led the group across. Mikaela clung to his side.

"Babe, I'm really scared," Mikaela said.

"Me too," Don said. "Me too."

They walked around to the other side of the lobby. Barren classrooms lined the hallway. Don walked inside one of them. It looked like some sort of concrete bomb shelter. Fingers grasped his rosary like a stress ball. His head darted around at the slightest noise.

"After this," he said, "I'm going to church. I'm never sinning again for the rest of my life."

Ah ha ha ha…

Don felt the circulation being cut off in his hand. Mikaela's nails punctured his flesh.

"What the fuck is that?" he whispered.

"Oh, my fucking God dude," Fingers said, "somebody's laughing."

The laughter grew louder. It sounded like a woman's voice.

"Wait… why does that laugh sound so familiar?" Don asked.

Ha ha ha! Ah ha ha ha!

"Because we've all heard it before," Mikaela said. "I'm dressed up as her."

Don had seen the Wizard of Oz as a child. Whenever the Wicked Witch of the West came on, he ran screaming and crying out of the room. The nightmares of him imprisoned inside the witch's castle were unrelenting. Now he remembered why he was so terrified. The witch's laughs grew into a scream.

HA HA HA! AH HA HA HA HAAA!

"RUN!" Fingers shouted.

The group raced out of the classroom right as a fireball shot past them. One of the sleeves of Fingers's black dress burst into flames. He patted it with his hand.

"HELP! PUT IT OUT!"

Mikaela smacked at the flame with her witch's hat. The embers died. A burning smell filled the air.

"Well, four greedy children! Running around where they're not supposed to!"

Somebody - or something - stood at the end of the hall. Another fireball danced in her hand, illuminating her features. Warts covered her face. Her nails were so long they curled in on themselves. She grasped a broomstick in her other hand. A black gown fell to her ankles. Mikaela was a pale imitation. The witch at the end of the hall was the genuine article.

"Ring around the rosie! Where's the fire hosie!"

She threw another fireball at them like a pitcher. The group ducked. The fireball sailed over them and hit one of the pieces of plywood. It burst into flames.

"UPSTAIRS!" Fingers shouted. "COME ON!"

Don tasted blood in his chest. He sprinted across the lobby and leaped up the stairs three at a time. Another fireball soared over his head and hit the wall in front of him.

"HELP!" Mikaela screamed. "I'M STUCK!"

Don whipped around. It was as if one of the stairs had disappeared. Mikaela had fallen through the staircase. She held on like she was dangling off the side of a cliff. Don jumped down an entire flight and landed next to her. Taking her arm, he wrenched her up onto her feet. Her witch's hat fell off and toppled into the empty space. He practically threw her up the stairs as a fireball exploded right where she had been caught moments before.

"Come on!" Fingers said. "We've got to hide!"

They made it onto the landing and sprinted along a row of instrument lockers. Fingers threw one of them open and motioned inside.

"In here!" he said. "This must be for the percussion equipment! We'll all fit!"

He crouched down and forced himself in. Jill and Mikaela followed after him. Don saw the light from a fireball as the witch made her way up the stairs.

"Everybody shut the fuck up," he said as he got in and pulled the door shut.

It seemed impossible that Jill hadn't said a word the entire night. Either she was scared speechless, or she was intent on not breaking character as a mime. She zipped her lips and threw away the key.

The stench of sweat and body odor was contained inside the locker. Don plugged his nose and breathed in through his mouth. Fingers felt like he was on the verge of heat stroke from wearing the nun's dress.

"Come out, come out, wherever you are! Naughty children, playing where they're not allowed!"

Light from the fireball seeped in through the cracks in the locker. The witch tapped her broomstick on the ground like a walking stick.

TAP... TAP... TAP...

Don's heart banged against his ribs. There was nothing they could do. If the witch found them, they'd be burned alive. Mikaela hugged her feet. He put an arm around her. She leaned her head against his shoulders.

TAP... TAP... TAP... TAP...

The witch stood outside the locker. The fireball crackled in her hand.

"Where did they go? Little kids must be punished! Burned to a crisp!"

TAP... TAP... TAP... TAP...

Don held his breath. Time came to a halt.

The taps of the broomstick grew fainter. The light from the fireball dimmed. The witch walked past the locker. Nobody moved. The group waited.

Finally, after counting to a thousand, Don pushed the locker open. The hinges creaked. He stuck his head out. No witch.

"Okay, the witch is dead," he said.

His joints screamed at him as he emerged from the locker. He knew he would never be visiting a haunted house for the rest of his life. Once you'd experienced the real thing, that was more than enough.

"I think I'm going to drop out of Marianist," Don said. "I'm not coming within ten miles of this place ever again."

"We need to get the fuck out of here right now," Fingers said. "That witch was real. And those fireballs were real, too." He gave his arm a pat where the fireball had burned through his dress.

"Where else can we go?" Don asked. "The bottom floor's all boarded up!"

"Maybe we can get to the roof," Mikaela said. "Then we can steal that witch's broom and fly away or something."

They moved in a pack down the hallway. The lockers went on forever. Practice rooms lined the adjacent wall. Don's neck ached from turning around and looking over his shoulder so many times.

"Babe, when we were coming up the stairs earlier, I… I just fell through," Mikaela said. "I couldn't feel anything beneath me. It was like I was hanging off of the Grand Canyon."

"This place is like a fun house," Don said. "Except there's nothing fun about it."

They came to the end of the hallway. An opening in the wall led to a concrete stairwell.

"Oh my God, we made it," Mikaela said. "We're safe."

The group bounded up the stairs. All they had to do was get on the roof, bar the door, and wait till morning for somebody to get them down.

"Fuck, we'll have quite the story to tell," Fingers said. "We should write a book about this or something."

The minutes passed, and they hadn't made it to the roof. Their breathing grew labored. Mikaela paused after the twelfth flight.

"Everybody stop moving," she said. "We've been going up these stairs forever. When are we going to reach the top?"

Don's mouth opened in recognition. They weren't going anywhere. He looked up. It was as if somebody had placed two mirrors in front of each other. The stairs went on forever.

"Oh, come on," he said, "you've got to be kidding me. How the fuck do we get out of here?"

"We have to go back," Fingers said. "This is pointless. We're going in circles."

Don pounded his fist against the wall. The Chip wasn't letting them go. *Is there really no way out? Are we stranded here forever? Are we going to die in here?*

They only had to go down one flight to get back to the second floor.

"You know," Fingers said, "I've been thinking about this. First, we get attacked by a horde of praying mantises in the theater, and then we run into the ghost of Margaret fucking Hamilton. That leaves me and Jill. You think we'll encounter some undead nun or mime next?"

Before anybody could answer, something fell through the space between the railings and clattered onto the floor of the stairwell. Fingers bent over and picked it up.

"What the hell is…"

He paused. His body froze in shock. He stared at the object in his hand.

"Is that a… *rosary*?" Don asked.

Fingers nodded. Two more fell onto the floor.

"Where are they coming from?" Mikaela asked.

Nobody answered. The trickle of rosaries turned into a torrent. In seconds, the entire floor was covered. The beads started to accumulate like snow. Don threw the door open.

"Let's get out of here!" he said.

The group rushed out of the stairwell and shut the door. Rosaries piled against it. The door panel started to groan. Splinters broke off of it as the door came loose.

"COME ON!" Fingers shouted.

They took off running down the hallway past the instrument lockers. The door burst off its hinges with a deafening boom. A tidal wave of rosaries barreled towards them.

"Son of a bitch!" Don said. "They're coming up from the bottom floor, too!"

The rosaries came up to the balcony like a wave of water. He couldn't see the lift underneath. He knew there were more pleasant ways to die than being crushed under a mountain of plastic beads. Pretty soon, the entire building would be inundated.

Fingers threw open the door to the band room. There was nowhere else to go.

"GUYS! GET IN HERE!"

It took all four of them to shove it closed against the barrage. They saw the wave rise higher and higher through the glass pane on the door.

In addition to the theater, the band room was the only finished room. Chairs were set in circular rows. Each chair had a music stand in front of it. A platform for the conductor sat at the front of the room. The grand piano on the side of the room had a woody smell to it.

"That's it," Mikaela said. "We're dead. There's no way out of here unless we jump out the window."

Jill shook her head. She pointed to a vent in the ceiling and motioned like she was climbing a ladder.

Fingers threw his hands up. "Worth a shot."

The group scampered around and stacked up all the chairs in the room. The tower slanted as it reached to the ceiling. Don saw cracks form in the glass pane on the door.

"Okay, that's the last of them!" he said. "Fingers, you first."

Just like with the lift in the rotunda, Fingers scurried up the pile of chairs. It wobbled as he stood on tiptoe and pulled on the vent. The cover screeched as he tore it off of the ceiling and threw it on the ground. He hopped off the stack of chairs and wedged himself in the vent.

"Guys, there's plenty of room! This should work!" he said.

At that same moment, the glass pane on the door burst. Shards of glass shot through the air like bullets. Rosaries poured in like a leak in a dam.

"Jesus!" Mikaela said.

Don gave her a boost as she climbed up. Only now did he notice that she was wearing ruby slippers. One of them fell off of her feet as she made it to the top. Fingers pulled her up into the vent. Jill followed behind.

"Okay!" Fingers said. "You're the last one!"

The stack of chairs teetered as the rosaries closed in around it. Don felt like he was trying to balance on top of a surfboard in the ocean. His hands felt slick against the plastic chairs. He was halfway up. His white t-shirt was soaked through with sweat.

Suddenly, the tower wobbled. Don felt the chairs leave the ground. The rosaries were lifting them up.

"COME ON! YOU'RE ALMOST THERE!" Fingers said. He thrust his hand out.

Don made it to the top of the chairs. The stack gave out from under him right as he grabbed Fingers's hand. He dangled over the rising wave of beads.

"HELP ME UP!" Don shouted.

Jill and Mikaela reached down and grabbed his other hand. They pulled him up into the vent. Seconds later, the wave of beads rose to the ceiling.

The vent couldn't have been more than three feet high. It smelled as if a skunk had let loose inside it. An opening in the vent led up to what was presumably the roof. Nobody could see the top of it.

Don was out of breath. His limbs vibrated. He couldn't close his hands into fists.

"Fuck, that was close," he said.

"I guess everybody at Marianist is making it to heaven now because of all those rosaries," Mikaela said.

They rested for a few minutes before Fingers stepped inside the opening. He placed his hands out in front of him and pushed against the vent with his back. The friction allowed him to climb up like a crab.

"This is like fucking Chuck E. Cheese with the tubes that you crawl through," Fingers said. "Only this one's for grownups, and you can get yourself killed."

Each step he took sounded like a clap of thunder. Don nervously rubbed his hands together as he waited for Fingers to lose his grip and tumble back onto the floor of the vent.

But he kept going.

"I feel wind!" he said. "There's a tunnel up here! This must lead to the roof!"

Fingers pulled himself up into the tunnel and disappeared from view. His voice echoed inside the vent.

"This is it!" he said. "Come on up!"

Don grimaced. Every single muscle in his body was spent. His arms hung limply at his sides as he pushed himself against the vent with his feet and shimmied up. His shirt rode up his back the farther he climbed.

"Come on," Fingers said, "here you go." He stuck his hand out and pulled Don up into the tunnel. Light filtered in from the outside. Don's heart leapt. He could see the roof. His knees ached as he scampered to the end of the tunnel and toppled out.

"Thank God," Don said. The sky looked the same as it did in the rotunda. He gulped in the cool night air. Moments later, Jill fell out of the vent, followed by Mikaela.

"Well," Fingers said, "I think Mr. Chips n' Salsa would have been better off willing $28 million to his kids."

Everybody except for Jill erupted in laughter.

"Hey guys," Mikaela said, "there's a fire escape right here. It goes down to the ground."

"Don't mind if we do," Fingers said.

Don couldn't believe their luck. They'd made it out of the Chip unscathed. All they had to do now was go home and let somebody else worry about cleaning up the rosaries.

"Jill," Fingers said, "come on. It's okay. This fire escape's safe."

She didn't move. She stayed on the roof. Terror blanketed her face. She pounded her hand against the air. Don's heart sank to the ground. He noticed how empty his stomach felt.

"Shit shit shit…" he said. "She's stuck!"

He crossed the roof and ran into an invisible barrier. His nose burst into pain. A rivulet of blood dripped from his face. The barrier felt like a sheet of thick plexiglass. It wobbled slightly when hit but had no give.

"No, you can't be fucking serious," Don said. "You can't do this to us!"

The group pounded on the barrier like children banging on the glass at a zoo. It didn't even crack. Jill ran in all directions but couldn't go more than a few feet. She was trapped inside of an invisible, square-shaped structure. Just like a real mime.

"DON'T WORRY!" Fingers shouted. "WE'LL BREAK YOU OUT!"

Fingers stepped back a few paces and charged into the barrier. He collided and bounced off of it with a THUMP.

"How in the…" Fingers said.

The barrier started to compact itself. It closed in against Jill's outstretched hands. No matter how hard she pushed, the barrier squeezed in further and further.

"NO!" Don shouted. "MAKE IT STOP!"

Jill stood hunchbacked as the barrier pressed down from above. Seconds later, her feet gave out. The cube couldn't have been more than a yard across. She knelt on the ground.

"HERE!" Fingers shouted. He held a construction drill in his hand. "STAND BACK!"

He pressed the drill bit against the barrier and turned it on. The drill whirred to life. Sparks flew off of the barrier as the bit spun against it.

It remained undamaged.

"FUCKING DAMN IT!" Fingers said. He threw the drill across the roof.

That was when Jill uttered her first noise of the night. A scream. A blood-curdling, shrieking, wrenching scream that tore the molecules in the air apart. A scream uttered by somebody that knew she was about to die.

The barrier continued its onslaught. Jill's bones started to crack. Her scream crescendoed. Goosebumps broke out on Don's flesh. A splatter of blood shot up and painted the inside of the cube, making it partially visible.

A particularly loud crack made Jill's screaming stop. The streams of blood multiplied, turning the cube a ghastly shade of scarlet. It continued to shrink until it became as small as a shoe box.

Then as small as a cigarette pack.

Then…

POP!

The cube disappeared. Don stared at the spot on the roof where it had been. A sour odor filled the air as his bladder loosened. A wet spot mushroomed on his pants.

"She…" Don said, "she's… *she's gone*."

Blood stains remained on the roof, but that was it. Jill had been crushed into nothingness. It was as if she had never existed.

"Oh… my… fucking… God…" Fingers said. "Look."

He pointed at a tiny spec on the ground that was no bigger than a piece of lint. When Don realized what it was, his stomach lurched.

"*That's her*," Fingers said, more out of sheer amazement than terror. His mouth hung open.

Mikaela gasped. Don had no time to react as a torrent of vomit ripped against his throat and shot onto the roof. He wrenched again and again and again until he had nothing left.

"No way," he said. "That's so disgusting."

"Guys," Mikaela said, "we have to get out of here. Right fucking now."

"That's her," Fingers said. He still pointed at the spec. "Can you believe it? There she is. She's like a ladybug now.

"Fingers," Don said as he grabbed his best friend's shoulders, "she's gone! We need to go!"

The blank expression in Fingers's eyes told him that he had lost his best friend. The Chip had wrestled his sanity away from him. The praying mantises, the witch, the fireballs, the rosaries... Jill. Each acted as a cudgel against his prior grasp of reality.

Don let go of his friend. He and Mikaela made for the fire escape. Their feet clanked against the stairs. They sprinted across the grass on the side of the building and got into their car.

Neither said anything as they drove away, but they knew that their prior lives were over. They were seen leaving the dance with Fingers and Jill, and for all they knew, somebody saw their car outside of the Chip. The police would be looking for them, and they wouldn't have any good answers to give.

A single option was open to them. Flee. Get away from everything. Live life on the run. Or be tried for a murder they didn't commit.

Don dropped Mikaela off at her house to pack her things before rushing home and doing the same. An hour later, they were gone before their families had even woken up.

Four different families called the police when their children didn't return home from the dance. It took them no time to find Fingers. After days of questioning, two different psychologists declared him insane and committed him to a mental hospital. The police conducted a statewide manhunt for Don, Mikaela, and Jill. None of them were ever seen again.

The Dark at the End of the Year
By Hillary Dodge

Petger's grandmother had warned them not to go out into the forest. It was the last week of the year, a time of darkness and death.

Neighbors were covering their mirrors and shuttering their windows. Dogs, usually left to roam, were tied fast in their yards to prevent them from disappearing. Mist hung heavily, even late into the day. It was not a time for going into the forest, the old woman warned, tapping a shrunken finger against her creased brow to ward off evil.

But Josef, his young stomach full of fire, didn't believe in the old ways.

"We'll be back before she knows we've gone," he reasoned with his younger half-brother.

Petger's forehead creased in worry. "But Baba told us not to," he whined.

"Don't you want meat, Petger?" Josef asked.

Petger scowled. Of course, he wanted meat. He was just as tired of the year-end porridge and stale bread as was his older brother. He shrugged. "I guess."

Early the following morning while the grandmother slept, they crept out of the house, dreaming of the bloody venison and steaming fowl they would bring back. Out into the gray forest they crept, bows slung over trembling shoulders. The air was still, crystallized like bad memories. But the boys ignored the ill feel to the air and continued on their way.

#

Deep in the forest where the piled snow would remain well into spring, they encountered the first dead stag at the edge of a frozen stream, its head smashed through the crust and lost to view. A shard of antler stuck out from the mounded snow like a dead tree. The gurgling water beneath the surface sounded almost as if the animal were gasping, though its body was frozen solid.

"Perhaps it was getting a drink?" asked Petger, shuffling from foot to foot and rubbing his arms against the chill.

"Deer don't use their heads as hammers to break the ice," said Josef.

"Then why did it do it?" The familiar whine was back in Petger's voice.

"How should I know? I'm not interested in frozen stags. I want to take a fresh one. Let's move on."

#

Nestled under a bent tree, they found the second stag. It was curled upon itself, face buried in the fur of its back.

"How can it twist like that?" asked Petger.

"It can't and that is why it is dead." Responded his older brother.

"But what did it?"

Josef scanned their surroundings. The sky was a dull, heavy gray and the air was colder than he would have liked. "You and your questions. How should I know the answer to that?"

Josef yanked his woolen wrap from under the collar of his coat, intending to pull it over his chin. As he did, a pale golden chain swung free from under his shirt.

Petger gasped. "You're not supposed to have that!" he cried.

Josef hurriedly grabbed at the chain, slid his fingers along its length to ensure the locket was still in place, and tucked it back out of sight.

"Don't you worry about that. We need to keep moving."

#

Flies buzzed over the corpse of the third stag. Its eyes had become nests of squirming white bodies and its stomach ripples of bloated skin. The smell was overpowering and made their eyes water as they bent over the dead animal, looking for a cause to its end. Nothing obvious. No wound, no mangy hide that hinted at disease within.

It was as if the deer had dropped dead. One minute standing majestic, king of the ancient forest. And the next, fallen, servant to timeless death.

"It has been dead many days," observed Petger, squatting beside the head. "But what made it die?"

"Disease, old age, a broken heart. Unless you think it might be the forest itself, why are you so concerned about this, Little Petger?" Josef teased.

"I am not little! And Baba told us not to go into the forest."

Josef cracked a mean smile. "Compared to me, you are. And I don't care what that old woman said."

"My father was taller than yours. Baba says that'll make me taller than you someday."

Joseph's laughter was harsh and cruel. "Why should I care? You're smaller than me now."

"Why do you always do that?" exploded Petger.

Josef shrugged his shoulders, turning away. "I don't know what you mean."

"It's because of how Baba treats you, isn't it? You're angry that she prefers me."

"I don't care what she prefers. She's a greedy old woman!" shouted Joseph with sudden venom. He reached into his shirt, pulled out the locket, and shook it in Petger's face. "This is rightfully mine. Mother gave it to me, not her. Your Baba only wants to sell it."

Petger sniffled, the fight gone out of him. "You wish me dead, like this stag."

Petger knelt in the snow next to the dead stag. He pulled off his mitten with his teeth and reached out to stroke the brittle fur.

"Don't do that!" cried Josef, wrenching him away from the dead animal.

"Why?" asked Petger, tears springing into his eyes.

"It is a dead thing. We do not touch the dead at the end of the year."

Petger pulled out of his brother's grasp. "We also do not go out into the forest. But here we are." He glared defiantly at his older brother who said nothing. Then, with a tentative step, he moved towards the dead stag, bent over it, and touched its fur.

Josef turned his back on Petger and watched the forest, his anger cooled by his brother's accusation.

All bird song ceased as if a door had been closed on it. The gentle breeze stilled, and the swirling brown leaves dropped to the ground as if weighted with stone.

Petger scrambled away from the corpse and came to his brother's side. The forest darkened.

"I think we should go home." Said Petger quietly.

Josef nodded and, without another word, they set off through the forest the way they had come.

#

Grandmother was waiting for them at the door when they returned. Wrinkled hands twisting her apron, she cried out when they came around the bend in the road.

"Where have you been, you naughty boys?"

"We have been in the woods," said Josef.

Grandmother's face clouded. "Did you eat anything?" She seized Josef's chin roughly with her gnarled fingers and tilted his head back to look in his mouth.

He shook her off. "We did not eat anything, Baba."

"Don't call me that." She snapped. "Did you touch anything?"

The boys were silent. The old woman took Petger's hand in her own and turned it over to examine his palm.

She gasped and one hand flew to her mouth. "You are marked!" she cried, voice shrill.

She pulled Petger into her bosom and held him in a tight embrace. She put her cheek down on the top of his head and moaned.

"What does that mean, Baba?" Asked Petger, eyes wide. "How am I marked?"

She shook her head and pressed the boy closer, tears gathering and spilling from the corner of her eyes.

"Why are you so upset?" Asked Josef, fear edging into his voice.

The old woman looked over her grandson's head toward Josef who stood some distance away, her eyes full of disgust. "You disobeyed me. This is your doing."

"It was only a dead deer."

"It was more than a dead deer, boy. There are reasons we do not go into the forest at the end of the year." Her words were sharp through clenched teeth.

At last, she gently pushed Petger away and wiped at her eyes. She leveled a glare at Josef. "It is likely he will not live to see the morning sun."

Josef knew the old woman to be mean, but she had never directed her anger at Petger before.

Petger gasped and shook his head. "That can't be, Baba. I am fine!"

Grandmother shook her head sadly, arms cradling her bosom. "There is one thing you can try."

Josef stepped closer, heart thundering in his chest. "Tell us! We will do it. We will do anything."

Grandmother looked hard at Josef, seeming to consider.

"Stay here," she warned." You cannot cross any living man's threshold until the light of the new year's sun."

The porch shuddered with the passage of her steps as she disappeared inside their tumbledown cottage. The brothers waited in silence as the sun dipped and lost its edge to the forested horizon. Petger sniffed and rubbed at his eyes while Josef tried his best to ignore the burning cold of the chain at his neck.

Grandmother returned, carrying fur parkas and a crust of stale bread. She passed the bread to Josef but did not meet his eyes. "Do not use this until you get there. It is to keep the ravens away. Petger must not look at them directly. You must not let them close, and they must not touch Petger. This is your task alone."

"But what do we do?" pleaded Petger.

Grandmother turned and cupped Petger's rosy cheeks in her dry palms. "Only a spirit of great power can protect you. Go into the forest beyond the west bank of the river. Follow the old road that turns away from the mountain. Find the old church and dig beneath its southwest corner. Under the foundation stones, you will find very old bones. Take one and put it in your pocket or tuck it under your clothes. Do not leave the church grounds until the sun is well into the sky once more. And you," she turned to Josef and narrowed her eyes. "If you truly love Petger, you will not disobey me. Don't you lay a finger on that bone."

"And that will save me?" asked Petger.

Grandmother said nothing for a very long time. "I do not know. But the Church Grim is your only hope."

#

The tops of the trees blazed with the light of the dying sun. The sky above was bruised and heavy with lowering clouds. The wind had picked up again and pushed at the two brothers, making them wince and bear forward.

"What is a Church Grim?" asked Petger, panting to keep up with his brother.

"It is only a silly story."

"Tell me."

"It is nothing. An old ritual. An animal buried alive under the foundation. It is said to create the spirit that protects the place."

"But it's true, isn't it?"

Josef shrugged, but any traces of frustration at his brother's questions had long departed. "How should I know?"

#

The winds died as they entered the woods. It was darker than seemed possible. Ravens peppered the trees above the brothers as they turned onto the disused road. Here and there a fluttering of wings, a squawk of discontent. Josef picked up the pace and Petger ran to keep up.

In the silent forest, they could hear the birds hopping and settling in the trees above them.

"Use the bread!" gasped Petger.

"Not yet," grunted Josef.

They came to a broken wall at the edge of the road. Brown grasses fringed the blackened stones. Josef stepped over the crumbled wall and into the old church. Except where the rafters stuck out at angles like shattered ribs, the church was open to the sky and the murmuring ravens in the trees overhead.

"What happened here?" asked Petger.

"A fire. A long time ago."

"I don't see how this place can help me. It feels…bad."

Josef was shuffling around in the piles of dead leaves, kicking at the collected mounds of snow, settled in the spots with the most cover.

"Start looking. We must find the bones."

Josef circled the ruined church, paying close attention to the places where the walls met at angles. The light of the moon suffused through the clouds in fits and starts, alternately casting the weathered stones in shadow and light. At last, under the brilliance of a space in the clouds, he came to the southwest corner.

"Here!" he called.

Petger joined him at the gaping hole beneath the foundation stone. It was large enough for a man to squirm through and the blackness beyond hinted at a widening of the space just beneath the stone.

"I think you must go alone," said Josef, his forehead creased with emotion.

Petger shook his head. "I can't," he whispered. "I'm afraid."

The ravens were shifting in the branches above. A black feather fluttered down to the ground beside the hole. A raven dropped from its perch and swooped to the dry grasses not four paces away. Josef reached into his jacket and tore a piece of bread to toss to the bird. It pecked at the crust and hopped back into the shadows under a nearby tree.

"There is no more time. The ravens won't hold back now that they've seen we have bread. You must go. Now!" Josef pushed his younger brother towards the hole.

Petger got down on his stomach and shimmied into the hole.

"It's dark in here!" he called out. "I'm afraid."

Josef crouched near the hole, tossing out bits of bread to the birds, doing his best to avoid their beady stares. They hopped closer and closer, their talons scrabbling at the dirt.

"Be brave, brother!" he called out.

"How am I to find the bones? I cannot see!" whimpered Petger's voice from the darkness.

"Feel around with your hands. You will know a bone when you touch it."

Josef quickly ran out of bread. The ravens had circled him, their wings brushing at his back and arms. He blocked the hole with his crouched form and tucked his chin in towards his chest, eyes squeezed shut.

A weight settled on his back and claws pierced the parka on his back. A beak tore at his hair. Squawking filled the air until he could no longer hear his voice as he called out encouragement to his brother.

The birds continued their assault and Josef cried out in pain and fear. But he would not move from his place above the hole.

At last, Petger thrust his arm out of the hole. In his small fist was clutched a jawbone with a single stained incisor.

The ravens immediately scattered and returned to the trees.

#

The brothers retreated to an alcove tucked into the crumbling wall of the church. It was shielded on one side by weathered stone and on the other by a bent sapling with peeling bark. The ravens kept well away now that they had the bone.

"What is it from?" asked Petger, examining the jawbone closely.

"Perhaps a lamb or goat?" Josef was careful not to touch it.

"Can we go home now?" Petger's face was smudged with dirt. "I don't like it here."

"Baba said to stay until we see the sun," said Josef.

"Why doesn't she let you call her that? And why didn't she come with us?" asked Petger.

Josef chewed his lip before answering. "Because she's old. It wouldn't be safe for her."

"It isn't safe for us." Petger whispered, watching the woods.

Josef said nothing.

The ravens paced the branches high above the church. The brothers flinched at their shadows as they swooped from branch to branch. But the birds did not come closer.

"I'm hungry," Petger began to cry. "Don't you have any more bread?"

Josef shook his head. "The birds took it all. We must be brave. It is hours yet until the sun."

Petger fell asleep against Josef's shoulder, jawbone clutched tightly in his fist.

#

Josef startled awake. He could not guess how long he had been asleep because the stars in the sky above the whispering trees were not the ones he was accustomed to seeing and the moon was absent. His brother slumbered deeply, curled by his side.

Something had woken him.

Above his head, the branches were bare. He looked around at the shapes and shadows of the old church and saw them. The ravens clustered silently in a loose circle around the boys. Their beady eyes caught and rejected the starlight, giving off enough glint to give away their presence in the deepest shadows. Their heads cocked and turned in unison, following Josef's gaze as he looked around him.

Something tugged deep in his chest, and he realized that it was the same feeling that had brought him out of his sleep. It felt as though the air was slowly seeping out of the space he occupied. He felt dizzy and weak. He staggered to his feet, trying to pull Petger with him. His brother lay limp on the ground and would not move. But he was breathing evenly so Josef left his side and stumbled towards the church wall in search of fresh air. The ravens moved with him, spreading their circle wider to keep him inside.

A tall shape shifted in the shadows just beyond the church, beyond the sagging wooden crosses that marked the burial yard. Josef steadied himself against a stone, trying to catch his breath, while squinting into the shadows. The shape had vanished.

The ravens hopped closer, tightening the circle around him with a black flutter of wings. Josef sputtered, coughing as his chest tightened. The air felt so thin. He spotted the shape again, closer to the edge of the burial yard, standing just behind a stone plinth. Glassy eyes stared back at him.

Josef sucked at the air and the ravens threw back their heads and opened their beaks in shrill, grating screams that pierced the night like the howls of abandoned infants. Josef threw up his hands and clamped them tight over his ears. But he could still feel the screams, grating deep in the bones of his ribs.

Dizzy, Josef felt himself sink down onto the lichen-crusted stones of the tumbled church walls. A great wind lashed at the trees and something large passed overhead, blocking the feeble starlight. The ravens surrounding him went still and silent. He looked up, his breath hissing through constricted passages as he tried to suck in a mouthful of air.

An enormous bird hung suspended in the space between the treetops. Josef could see the stars through holes in its moldering wings. A flash of white protruded from the tips of its wings and a plate of stained bone showed clearly through a rent in its breast. Josef's head began to pound. The air he managed to suck in was not enough. His vision blurred.

He dragged at his collar, trying to shake loose his coat so he could catch a breath. A crumb of bread rolled from his pocket and caught the attention of the ravens. They cawed and hopped, and their large master sunk lower.

Josef gasped for air that was no longer passing into his lungs. Bright lights danced at the edge of his vision. The trees warped in his vision, stretching and blurring to deepen the shadows around him, and seeming to embrace the giant bird that was descending towards him without any movement of its outstretched wings.

Josef rolled off the wall and onto his back in the dirt, spittle dribbling down his chin, heart racing, and head hammering. He struggled, looking toward the burial yard again. He thought he saw the tall shape, a black blot moving closer across the dappled landscape of weeds. But his vision was so weak that he couldn't be sure of any details.

He felt the giant bird as it settled over his straining body. In the pounding blackness that was closing around him, Josef heard a rustling of dry leaves. He tilted his head back to search for his little brother through the curtain of feathers. He only needed a glimpse—splash of color, or a mounded shape against dark stone to tell him that Petger was still resting, unharmed.

A hooved foot stepped into his cloudy field of vision and there was a sudden thrashing noise above him. Josef rolled his head painfully to look up at the dark bird, chest heaving and bucking, but the bird was suddenly gone, the weight lifted from his chest, and he saw only stars above him. A towering narrow shape moved into view.

It had the head of a goat with sightless glassy eyes. It was all he could focus on with his failing strength. The body beneath was just a blur, drawn-out and cloaked. The goatman opened his mouth and a sound like the shattering of glass spilled from between his elongated teeth.

Immediately Josef found his breath and he filled his lungs with a desperate, gasping breath.

Before he could gain his bearings, the goatman bent over him and took hold of him by his collar. He dragged him across the dirt to where his younger brother was sleeping. Then the goatman bent low again and took Josef's hand, wrapping it around the other end of the jawbone inside Petger's fist.

The goatman's milky eyes seemed to regard Josef who was struggling to sit up. He put a hooved appendage on the brother's chest, bidding him remain where he lay. And then, with a dry rustle, he was gone.

#

Josef held onto the bone for the remainder of the night and the ravens made no further effort to approach and neither did their master reappear. As the sky began to lighten, the ravens took off in a chaotic cloud, feathers scattering and cries echoing mournfully.

Petger awoke to the sound and sat up. He looked curiously down at the jawbone in his hand. "But Baba said you mustn't touch it."

Josef released the bone but could not meet his brother's eyes. "Baba was…wrong."

"Is it over? Am I safe now?" Petger looked eager, not seeming to care anymore about the bone.

Josef nodded and steadied his voice. "It is. You are."

"Can we go home now?"

His older brother considered this question for some time before responding. He lifted the locket at his breast so Petger could see it. "That is not our home anymore. We must find someplace new. This will help."

"But why?" cried Petger.

"It is what the Church Grim told us to do. He came to us last night. You don't remember because you were asleep."

"Why didn't you wake me so I could see him?" Petger pouted.

"Because" Josef lied, "You had to be asleep so that he could protect you."

"But Baba will think we died. We should tell her we are alive."

"She will know." Said Josef. "When we get to the next village, we will send her a loaf of bread and this feather." The older brother plucked a night black feather from the ground and showed it to his younger brother before tucking it into his pocket for safe keeping.

Replacement
By Joshua Peddicord

Plastic cups were strewn about the table and floor. A damp spot on the carpet smelled strongly of spilled beer. The golden streamers danced with the bass of the music that drowned out most partygoer's conversations. Twenty-one-year-old Evan Gillis had been attending his first New Year's Eve party since reaching the age where he could legally drink. Evan's best friend of the past four years, Alex Paytah, had capitalized on one of the biggest party nights of the entire calendar year by gathering all their friends to ring in the new year at his house for this massive celebration. Alex had gone all out too, with black- and gold-colored decorations being put up all over the house, a ton of alcohol which included a keg, and pizza boxes that littered the dining room table. Guests stumbled around both inside and outside of the house in various levels of drunkenness.

The party was in full swing by this point as the midnight hour grew ever closer, bringing with it a new year and a new beginning. The alcohol in Evan's system helped to ease some of his anxiety, ripping him far outside of his comfort zone, resulting in a few new friends as well as a few phone numbers. He and many of the other guests piled outside to congratulate the Earth on another year with a show of various different fireworks that Alex had hoarded. A group gathered around Alex as he and a few others brought fireworks out of the massive stockpile he'd accumulated. According to Alex it wasn't even all the ones he had. Other party goers mingled around the keg trying to outdrink one another. Firecrackers were thrown by a particularly rowdy set of gentlemen towards two ladies, startling them and causing them to spill their beer out of fright. The loud pops of the firecrackers weren't heard by most guests, however, since the noise was drowned out by all the excited yelling of the party as the show was about to start. It was nearly midnight with less than a minute to go.

Ten. Nine. Eight. Seven. Six. Five. Four. Three. Two. One. On cue Alex lit the first firework as the gathered crowd yelled out "Happy New Year" as loud as they could. Alex took a step back from the lit fuse that seemed to linger just a little too long until the first rockets went up with a loud thud, whistling while they traveled into the atmosphere and ending in a smattering of purple in the night sky. Evan handed Alex one of the others and it ventured up even further, ending in a bright white pom-pom shape in all its beautiful visage before its subsequent crackle back down to earth. Noisemakers could be heard from the crowd as they watched the display that Alex, Evan, and a few other friends created. They sent numerous other fireworks of various sizes and colors into the sky for the next seven minutes. Car alarms across the block expressed their discontent through rapid honking that may just as well have been a whisper when compared to the explosions erupting from the sky and the excited shouts of encouragement, not just from Alex's party, but from New Year's Eve celebrations held by his neighbors.

Alex called for Evan to go get the rest of the fireworks from the garage, but before Evan could even begin moving, Alex dropped to the ground. Several people paused their conversations and looked over but none of them bothered to help in any way. They only wanted to see what was going on and what would transpire next. Evan nudged Alex's shoulder with the palm of his hand but got no response in return. It quickly became clear that Alex wasn't just playing some cruel joke. Evan knelt beside him, checking his breathing and pulse but there was nothing to detect. He shouted for someone to call emergency services to come help his friend but despite this, Evan knew that his friend was already gone. He cradled his body, staining his shirt with blood until the EMTs arrived on the scene.

As Alex's body was taken away in the ambulance, an entire party was left in a state of both grief and shock with more questions than answers, a sentiment shared by the police that arrived shortly thereafter. Nobody's stories were believed with the police badgering and pestering an already shaken up group of people. Alex dropped suddenly and without warning, but this answer didn't seem to be what they wanted. Evan tried to answer as best as he could but broke down a little bit, still devastated at the loss of his best friend. He thought about everything Alex wanted to accomplish in life; to become a doctor, to get married, to have a family, but all of that was ripped away in an instant. It was hard to even comprehend the situation and emotions ran even higher as the word of Alex's passing spread, making local news. The police eventually revealed the case was ruled a homicide and that Alex had died due to a gunshot wound to the head. Confusion spread as nobody could recall even seeing anybody with a firearm at the party and especially not anyone that would want to harm Alex, a young man that was relatively well liked.

Later all of the guests would find out exactly what happened that night on New Year's Eve. The shot that killed Alex Paytah came from a stray bullet that returned to earth, landing directly into Alex's skull. He was dead before he even hit the ground since the bullet killed him instantly on impact. Sixty-two-year-old John Cramer from a few houses away from Alex's home where he'd held the party was the culprit, unintentionally killing the young man via celebratory gunfire when he shot his AR15 style rifle into the air to celebrate the New Year. John ended up being charged with manslaughter as well as reckless endangerment and the lives of everyone at that party were forever changed. Evan in particular found it incredibly difficult to cope with the fact his best friend had lost his life as a result of a drunk man's poor decision making and pure bad luck right before his eyes.

*****

New Year's Eve rolled around just as it always did. It was exactly one year to the day from the very same night that Evan lost his friend in some freak accident. He spent the entire night so far isolated in his bedroom surrounded by food wrappers and empty cans of orange soda, eager to forget the events of the previous year that still traumatized him. He was intent on being a shut-in for the entire duration of this holiday, not being able to bare the celebratory noises of drunks yelling outside and the sounds of fireworks making him sick to his stomach. He rather intended on spending his night with eyes bloodshot from being fixated on his computer monitor. The bright blue glow of the screen provided the only illumination in the darkness of the room.

Over the past year, Evan's online interests became much more morbid and macabre, acting as a form of escapism to help him cope with what had happened to him. He spent most of his time on true crime forums and forums for the supernatural and paranormal. Thinking about other's much worse life experiences somehow provided him with a bit of comfort like a baby's blanket. These things had become interests of his nevertheless, and this was despite him not believing in anything that couldn't easily be explained by either science or simple logic but yet he still found it so fascinating. Evan was determined to get his mind off the holiday, clicking from link to link, thread to thread, intent on finding something interesting. What that was however, he did not know. In the span of just a few minutes, he read about a variety of topics from mass murderers, missing children, ghosts, demons, and dozens of conspiracy theories. He couldn't help but laugh, wondering to himself what type of person would believe such wild theories.

A little over an hour passed as Evan spent his time on different threads and forums, forgetting all about the grief this holiday caused him, making this night no different than countless others. During his browsing session Evan noticed something that caught his eye, a thread simply titled "DO NOT OPEN" in bold and all in caps. With his interest fully piqued, Evan opened it anyway. The only thing contained within it was an unrecognizable link. Evan hesitated for a moment, pondering whether or not it was worth clicking on since it could be host to any number of malicious viruses that could ruin his computer. He bookmarked the page and returned to endlessly venturing down the rabbit hole, reading about all kinds of freak encounters with strange people, skinwalkers, forest creatures, and other cryptids, all the while exhaling out of his nose at how silly this all was to him. He couldn't escape, however, from those words that repeated in his head. DO NOT OPEN.

Eventually, Evan's curiosity got the best of him. He reopened the thread and sat at his chair just staring at that link, contemplating what he was about to do. He felt nervous staring at it, his hands became clammy, and he started to perspire. A sense of dread overcame him and from his sleep deprived state, the blue text that made up the link almost started to distort the longer he looked at it. Breathing a deep sigh, he eventually highlighted the text as his cursor hovered over it and then clicked. The screen of his computer was completely black, which caused him to panic at the thought of his computer now being riddled with viruses. The only thing visible was his own reflection staring back at him from his monitor. Clicking around seemed to be a fruitless endeavor as not even trying to close the window with keyboard shortcuts seemed to do anything at all.

After several minutes of desperately trying to do anything, Evan decided that it would be best to cut his losses and just go to bed. As he got up and laid down in his bed, he heard an all too familiar voice call his name. He shot up and looked around the room, discovering it had come from his computer. That voice, it was one he could have recognized absolutely anywhere. It was Alex's voice. He sat back down in his chair at his desk and saw something on his computer that wasn't there before. The small, distant silhouette of a man on his computer screen. Evan clicked around trying to pause or close it, assuming that it was a video or GIF that started playing, but once again it was pointless as nothing on the screen changed, nothing except the man who had grown slightly closer. He was still relatively small and distant, far from the screen but seemed to be walking towards the screen at a steady, yet sluggish pace. If this was a virus, Evan couldn't begin to imagine what the point of this was.

As the man got closer, the room started to come into focus. No longer was it just pure blackness. Evan squinted his eyes, beginning to make out what looked like a long hallway. Water dripped down from the ceiling at a steady pace leaving a pool of water on the ground. Outside of the water and a faint mechanical hum that provided a bit of ambience, it was quiet. A chill shot up Evan's spine. As the man grew closer, his features became visible. At first, he thought the man was fully nude, but he quickly realized it wasn't the case. What he initially thought was a tall man, wasn't a man at all. The humanoid creature had long arms that hung much lower than they should, disproportionate to the rest of its body. This creature's wrinkled skin that covered its body was a pale, sickly almost green coloration. Its neck was much longer than usual, presumably to support its long bulbous head. It crept ever closer with its face, or lack thereof, becoming clear. It lacked ears, a nose, or even eyes, instead sporting a wide mouth that almost appeared to be grinning in the middle of the smooth canvas that made up its face.

Evan was glued to his computer chair, unable to get up and frozen with fear. He found it impossible to even look away. The faint sound of fireworks could be heard, not from outside but emanating from the computer, from somewhere behind the creature. The voice of Evan's late friend Alex was heard occasionally saying his name whenever the creature opened its mouth to reveal several rows of jagged teeth, and yet it still didn't appear to be speaking. Somehow it was able to produce these sounds, these same noises that occurred exactly one year ago on that fateful night. Evan snapped out of his hypnotic state, but was still unable to get up from his chair. The creature before him was close now, so close in fact that he could somehow smell it. The putrid scent of decay burned his nostrils and was almost vomit inducing. Evan tried to turn the monitor off, but the creature only seemed to be inching closer, with the sound of fireworks, cheering, and even subtle gunfire becoming slightly louder the closer it got. Unplugging the computer itself from the wall also seemed to do nothing to stop it. Evan was paralyzed, unable to get up, unable to run, stuck to this chair as a monstrous figure stopped and stared at him. Despite having no eyes it still seemed to be staring right through him and looking at it was as if he was staring right into Hell itself.

The creature reached both of its long arms out and resumed its stride, rendering Evan unable to scream or even speak despite all of his efforts to do so. Claws began to protrude from the computer, and he felt the cold wetness of the creature's touch as it began to wrap long bony fingers around Evan's throat, progressively tightening its grip. Evan struggled to breathe and scratched and clawed at the monster's arms as it flexed the muscles in its hand, getting tighter and tighter and pulling him in towards him. Evan's head was spinning and he had to desperately fight the feeling of losing consciousness until, as if in an instant, he was yanked right through his computer screen. He fell down hard into a hallway that until just a brief moment ago was just pixels and lines of code. He found himself in the same hallway the creature had been in. The ground was damp and covered in about a centimeter of a liquid that resembled water but had a yellow tint to it and produced a sour smell, like rotting garbage. He got up and saw pure darkness at one end of the hallway, and a very distant light at the other. He looked around to see no sign of the very same creature that brought him here and that he'd encountered previously. His breath steadied again but all of it had to be through his mouth to prevent vomiting from the smell of the liquid that covered the hallway. He didn't know where he was, but at least he was safe, for now at least. He ventured towards the direction of the faint light off in the distance, hearing Alex calling his name. The closer he got, the more clearly he was able to hear the sounds of fireworks.

Ice Boy
By Christina Delia

The night he died was like the scene in that movie *It's A Wonderful Life* when the little brother fell through the ice, only someone DIDN'T save him. December 25 had been his birthday, and it was also the anniversary of his death. No one seemed to care. He was consistently overshadowed by the baby Jesus lying in the manger cooing and saving souls.

I had read that Ingrid Bergman and William Shakespeare had died on their birthdays, but they had actually done something with their lives. They weren't twelve-year-old forsaken bastard boys whose drunken parents had sent them out to play hide and seek on a cracked frozen lake.

Harrison and I had moved to Lake Andrew because my aunt had left me her summer house when she died. We had nowhere else to go. The house was really more of a run-down shack that I had no idea how to take care of. Living in the city, I'd never even mowed a lawn. Now we had inherited nine acres of overgrown property. I was terrified of Harrison getting ticks, because ticks would lead to Lyme disease. This was what I thought of the country. Yet the city was filled with sex offenders and other criminals, plus the ghosts of every woman I had ever been prior to moving here.

I wanted to do right by my son.

The lake my aunt's property (how could I call it mine when I didn't know how to care for it?) overlooked had been the lake where Ice Boy had perished. I only discovered this because when I stopped into town that first day in September to buy bread and eggs for Harrison's French toast, I was greeted by a chatty shopkeeper who kept insisting I sample the "artisanal cheese plate" he had set out for his customers. It looked picked over, nothing fancy; just shiny plastic-textured globs stabbed through and through with splintery toothpicks.

"I'm Will and this is a camembert," he'd declared to me, with his chest puffed out proudly from behind his yellowed apron.

It wasn't. "Thank you," I said, chewing quickly, swallowing hard and nodding politely. If there's one thing I know from living in the city, it's an artisanal cheese plate. I used to date a chef. Hell, I almost married him. I would have been lousy with camembert. I would have had a sex life. We would have laughed while eating cheese in bed, and bonding over comments like, *"This camembert is almost as good as what we just did!"*

"Your house overlooks Ice Lake, right?" Will offered me the cheese plate again, and I shook my head. He smiled, probably thinking I was watching my figure, and not that his cheese tasted like *artisanal* garbage.

"Is that what it's called? I didn't know the name of the lake," I said, feeling itchy. Small town small talk made me feel as though I was breaking out in hives. "*Leave me alone, Cheese Man*," I thought.

Will smiled and said, "Wow lady, they sure fleeced you!"

"I beg your pardon?" I said, the words sounding strange coming out of my mouth. I had never used that expression before, but this moment seemed made for it.

"The lake is Lake Hope, but we call it Ice Lake on account of the boy who drowned in it on Christmas Day."

"A boy *drowned on Christmas Day*?" Instantly, I thought of Harrison, and how I was afraid of him getting ticks, and now *this*? I had named him Harrison because I had been watching that movie "The Fugitive" when I'd gone into labor.

"It was a long time ago."

The rest of the shopping trip was a blur. I asked him where the challah bread was, and he asked me if I was Jewish. I said no, I just wanted to make my son French toast, and I've found that challah is the best bread for French toast. He said, "You have a son?" and looked hard at my naked ring finger, the way people often do.

I said, "Yes, I do."

"If you're not Jewish, you can take your son to the Christmas Festival. It'll be happening right behind your house. Starts Christmas Eve and goes through to New Year's Day. Ice skating on the lake, first year since you-know-who went you-know-where…they never found the body. Dredged the lake with taxpayer money. Real nice, huh?"

I wanted to tell him that none of this conversation was "real nice." I wanted to tell him he was rude and prejudiced to assume that Jewish people couldn't attend a Christmas festival, and *will you stop looking at my ring finger like that! I'm a single mother, that doesn't make me lesser than you!* I wanted to throw his faux camemblechh right back up onto him, and make his apron even more discolored.

Only I said nothing. I walked away and found a bakery that sold challah loaves. I'm not a coward, I'm just a single mother who doesn't like confrontation because I've been at the bad end of confrontations with men who exude energy similar to this guy, and that's why we moved from the city.

You can't run scared all your life. Sometimes you have to lock your door, hug your son and stay in your new house scared, too.

Which is what I did: I stayed scared in my new-to-me house with my son; both of which I didn't feel I exactly deserved. I would leave to bring Harrison to school. After the weird encounter in town, I found it easier to just order a lot of our groceries. If I did go into town, I didn't make eye contact with anyone.

I didn't want to meet any new people. The majority of the people I'd already met in life had affected me negatively.

Over dinner I'd ask Harrison if he liked school, and he'd say, "I like it enough", which I think was more for my benefit. He'd toss cheddar goldfish crackers into his soup, and I'd picture Ice Boy dying helplessly and hopelessly, right in our backyard.

Anything that submerged into liquid made me think of Ice Boy: Marshmallows in cocoa, my nightly Sleepytime tea bag in hot water, me in the claw foot bathtub.

When watching an Annette Funicello and Frankie Avalon beach party movie, my chest hurt at witnessing their recklessness. How could they merrily dance so close to danger? The waves like underworld demon tongues, and these bright-eyed fools cheerily disregarding the potential for an undertow.

It was almost October now, and the house that didn't feel like mine was practically falling down around us. When the shed nearly caved in on Harrison, I decided enough was enough and called in a handyman.

His name was Brett, and he knocked loudly on my front door. When I cautiously let him in, he sauntered around the house in a way I had never: confidently, as though he owned the place. He picked up a book of poetry from my coffee table.

"You read this shit?" he asked, flipping through the book, before casually dropping it back onto my scuffed table. "Why does this guy write in all lowercase letters? Big famous poet and he never used a proofreader?"

I opened my mouth, but nothing came out. Yes, Brett was confident, and he smelled like pine needles, even though it was only October. I was lonely. Reluctantly celibate; and Brett had wide blue eyes that pierced and appraised me.

Did I want to be pierced and appraised?

It was going to be a very cold winter.

"Would you like some coffee?" I asked him, and he followed me into the kitchen. We talked about the work ahead, and his fees. He kept a thick orange pencil behind his left ear. He had a bushy brown beard that was starting to gray, and a tool belt.

I wanted him to take off his tool belt.

I wanted him to make love to me.

On his third trip to my house, that's exactly what he did. We collapsed onto my creaky bed, and he pushed himself into me atop the flannel rosebud sheets I'd slept alone on for too long.

The sex wasn't as good as I'd envisioned it in my head, but it was something. We were moving and sweating, and he was grunting. This was my sexual consolation prize. It was the at home board game version of sex instead of the big money moaning and the fabulous prizes hot climax. There wasn't any kissing or cuddling afterwards, but I'd never gotten that from any sexual partner, and didn't need it. The act itself was fine. This wasn't some romantic relationship.

Yet Brett said it was. Possibly I was so hurt and guarded that I wouldn't know the right one when I met him. That's how Brett explained it to me, and it made sense.

One thing Brett clued me in on during our weeks together was the Ice Boy. I wanted to know everything about the little kid who had died in the lake behind my house, starting with, what was his name?

"Fred? Clarkie…somethin' like that. You know, most people called him Little Shit," Brett laughed.

"Why?"

Brett leaned back in my kitchen chair, and then took a swig from his beer can. "Now here's the truth: nobody liked Ice Boy. He was a nosy bastard, always snooping around people's windowsills, trying to get a glimpse of their college aged daughters in their bras and matching panty sets. When he had a paper route, he'd steal magazines. Like just up and pull them out of mailboxes."

"That doesn't seem so bad," I considered, and Brett glowered at me with his blue dagger eyes and crushed his beer can like a bully in an Eighties movie.

"No? Men don't blame the paperboy when their skin mags go missing. Men blame the mailman. Ed Tramontine got punched square in the jaw, and he hadn't stolen anything-"

"Who got punched?" We both looked up to see Harrison come inside from playing soccer in the backyard. I had told him to stay away from the lake, and was grateful to have a kid who listened.

Brett glared at Harrison as if he had interrupted, and I fully expected the next words to come out of his mouth to be, *"Children should be seen and not heard."* Suddenly it was like he did a complete turnaround, and the annoyance in his face shifted to a full-blown friendly smile.

"Hi Little Buddy! What're you up to?"

Harrison stared. "Just kicking a soccer ball," he said.

Brett pushed his chair back, scratching the floor. "Well, how about you and me throw a catch one of these days?" He ruffled Harrison's hair in a way that I myself had always hated as a child.

"I guess," Harrison said.

The flicker of irritation blazed across Brett's face again, settling into an angry mask. "This is your fault. No wonder you're interested in hearing about Ice Boy, when you got your own rude kid. Maybe worry more about teaching your boy some manners than an old dead corpse at the bottom of the lake."

"Corpse?" Harrison looked afraid.

"Dammit, Brett!" I stood up and went over to Harrison. "I think you should leave. You're drunk-" I didn't think it was appropriate for him to be drinking so early, but knew even this early on into whatever-we-were that he wasn't going to listen to me.

"That's right, I am drunk! So, I'll just drive my car home and maybe get a DUI, or crash it! You'd like that, huh? You bitch!" He threw the wooden chair he had previously been sitting in across my small kitchen, and it hit the wall loudly. Then he stormed out.

"Mom?" I hugged Harrison a little longer, realizing that I was shaking, too. Then I told him to watch cartoons while I fixed him some leftover chicken casserole for dinner. I didn't feel like eating. I felt like throwing up.

As I heated up Harrison's dinner, I inwardly chastised myself for dating at all. I should have known better by now. These dating attempts felt psychically like suicide attempts; nothing but self-loathing and regret afterwards.

Brett had shown himself to be the exact type I kept attracting: men who lectured me about being a single mom, as though I was wearing a scarlet letter or a "kick me" sign. Men who presented themselves chivalrously, and acted like they heroically wanted to save Harrison and me, but all it turned into was control.

Sometimes it was nice to have a man around the house. Sometimes I felt so lonely. But often I was lonelier *with* a man around. Ever since I'd started dating Brett, I hadn't laughed in weeks; not real laughter, anyway. Canned, hollow, wooden, Pavlovian Dog-type laugh track laughter, sure.

"Harrison! It's time for dinner!" I called, a sob getting caught in my throat. It was important to me never to cry in front of my son. I wanted him to see me as strong.

Harrison came into the kitchen and pushed his casserole around on his plate and into his mouth enough to satisfy my motherly concerns. He drank a glass of milk and asked to be excused. I nodded, and when he was out of earshot, I collapsed onto the floor next to the fridge, shook with sorrow, and tearfully blew my nose into a red and white polka-dotted dish towel.

I had thought that it would be important to have a man around to toss a football with Harrison. Yet men like Brett made me feel like I was Charlie Brown: endlessly attempting to reach a football I could never attain. They dangled promises: marriages and vacations and stability, but then they snatched it all away, because I wasn't good enough.

Wasn't I? The faceoff was not between me and any man, but between the worn down version of me now and the healthier me I once was.

Could I get her back? Feel strong again?

I ignored Brett's calls for a week, but I had hired him to work on the house, and I didn't know how to get out of it. I thought perhaps it was better to let him finish the job and then part ways as amicably as possible. It was my own fault for getting involved with someone who I had a working relationship with, so I decided to just pay the piper, literally and figuratively. I made Brett coffee the way he approved of it (one cream, two sugars), and he scrubbed, sanded and refinished my hardwood floors until they actually looked like hardwood floors.

"Looks great," I said to him, unsure of what to say. The floors were great. Him? Not great at all.

"The trick to keeping them looking like new is Bona," he informed me. "You'll buy Bona from now on."

I nodded. For some reason, I fell in line with men like this, maybe from years of conditioning, or a deficiency in my own personality; I wasn't sure.

"There are about three years of work that need to go into this place," Brett said. "You get a discount because you're sleeping with me."

"I'm not."

"You did."

"Not anymore."

Brett laughed. "Think so? You will be." I felt a shameful stirring in my nether regions. Yes, I was attracted to him, but he also repelled me.

"I saw them setting up for the holiday festival–"

"Holiday festival? No one can say Christmas, anymore? The birth of our Lord and Savior–" Brett balled his big, calloused hands into tight fists, then slammed the right one down on my kitchen table. Last week I saw him smash his fist through my bedroom wall. *"A small price to pay for a beautiful home"*, my interior monologue rationalized nonsensically. Brett was equal parts creator and destroyer, but we had a business agreement and when it was over, he'd be gone.

"I thought you were an Atheist," I said quietly. When Brett got all menacing like this, he scared me.

"Did you hear about Will?" Brett said.

"Will?"

"The shopkeeper in town. He's dead. You'll never guess where he drowned–"

"Drowned?" I remembered the talkative shopkeeper. A look of horror must have crossed my face, because Brett looked delighted.

"What are you, a parrot?"

"Not the lake," I said. "It wouldn't make sense. They'd have canceled the festival for sure–"

"Boy, you really must hate Christmas! All you talk about is canceling the festival! The festival is the only thing going on in this cow turd town, so deal with it. No, he didn't die in your precious lake. He drowned in his own toilet. Isn't that hilarious?"

"Are you serious? That's mortifying." It was also extremely strange. "Was he drunk? Did he pass out and hit his head?"

"I have no idea, but get this: there was another death in town yesterday, too. Mandy Jensen, the lifeguard at the town pool."

"I didn't think the pool would be open now–"

Brett sighed impatiently. "It isn't, dumbass! They're saying she committed suicide."

"Poor girl."

"Yeah, whatever, except who drowns themselves in a bathtub *full of ice*?"

I felt sick. I thought back on dreams I'd had of Ice Boy rising up through my formerly tepid bath water. It couldn't be… it wasn't. He wasn't some Boogeyman Freddy Krueger grotesque villain. He was just a drowned child.

"You know what I think?" Brett continued. "Somehow Mandy owed money to some mobsters or drug dealers, and they decided to shuck out her organs to sell on the Black Market–"

"Was she missing her organs?"

Brett kicked my refrigerator, leaving a visible dent. "See how mad you make me? Why do you question what I say? You think you're so much smarter than I am? So superior?"

I talked Brett down as best as I could. I decided to go into town that day to get away from Brett, do a little last minute Christmas shopping for Harrison (he had updated his list at the zero hour), and eavesdrop. Even though I generally tried to avoid the townspeople, I was certainly curious to hear news regarding these odd deaths.

Clara's Cozy Café had a "buy one egg sandwich get a free cup of candy cane coffee" deal, which sold me. Clara set my order on the table. She was wearing a Santa hat and a scowl.

"Wasn't this supposed to be candy cane coffee?"

At this, Clara rolled her eyes, and then pulled a candy cane from her apron pocket. She unwrapped it with exaggerated annoyance, and plopped it into my mug, splashing a puddle of coffee onto the table.

"Crisis averted," she announced.

"Is there an issue?"

"I heard through the grapevine that you have a problem with the Christmas festival. Tough reindeer pellets, toots! You have a problem with Christmas, you got a problem with me!" with that, she flounced off.

My face flushed red as her hat, and I wondered what else Brett had been telling people about me? It must've been him; I didn't know anyone else in town. I started contemplating why anyone in this town would bother partaking in a holiday festival, given that they were such an icy lot. Perhaps they all wanted to dance on Ice Boy's watery grave.

It reminded me of a town I'd read about called Texarkana where multiple murders had taken place during the 1940s. The serial killer was never brought to justice. What made this case even more unnerving is that each year people gathered in the park where victims had died to watch a slasher film based on the killings. It seemed wrong, politically incorrect, bad karma…much like this holiday festival.

My eye caught the brown coffee puddle on the table. Perhaps it was the way the fluorescent café light reflected, but for an instant, I thought I saw a little boy's face peering back up at me.

"They're dead! They're all dead!" A woman rushed into the café, eyes as wide as her open screaming mouth. Customers and diner staff gathered around her, but I just sat and listened, waiting for them to say it was a drowning.

It was. Local fishermen had drowned in the nearby bay when their boat had capsized. I didn't stay to hear the rest, because it didn't matter. Tears and shouting and more screaming. This town was cursed.

It continued the next three days leading up to Christmas, this holly jolly plague. Perfectly alert and seemingly healthy adults: police officers, firemen, surfers. The local veterinarian died with his face in a basin of water in his office break room. None of it made sense.

On December 24, I was wrapping Harrison's one present. I wished I could have afforded him more, because he certainly deserved it, but the home repairs had proven costlier than I had originally anticipated.

Harrison's gift was *the* hot toy of the season: a robot that could record voices and play them back in several styles, the most annoying voice style being a toss-up between "Ren Faire" and "Auto-Tune."

I heard tapping against the window, and saw that it had started hailing. Why *wouldn't* the skies rain ice on the anniversary of Ice Boy's untimely demise? Because they had never found his body, Brett had told me that some townspeople speculated that he had run away, or been kidnapped. They were lying to themselves. Most everybody whose property surrounded the lake had heard *something* that Christmas Day.

Faint screaming is screaming still.

I looked at the TV. *Miracle on 34th Street* was on. The screen showed a pint-sized Natalie Wood skeptically pulling on Santa Claus's beard. Years later, she would drown in her own dark, watery grave.

Everything reminded me of Ice Boy. Ebenezer Scrooge had his Christmas Spirits, and maybe I had mine, too. I had tried to outrun my fragmented past, but like Ice Boy I was pulled down into the depths.

One of these men I had dated was going to kill me. I felt it. Possibly Brett… probably Brett.

I wondered why a town-wide festival would be held on Christmas Day at all? Especially given the history of the town. It felt mean-spirited.

"*Texarkana*," I thought.

"I'm still cold," said a voice. It was coming out of Harrison's Christmas robot. I dropped it as though it had stabbed me.

"Brett! This isn't funny!" I shouted.

The robot kept moving around on the table. It began shrieking; only the shrieks were Auto-Tuned. I covered my ears with my trembling hands and sank to the ground. I hadn't prayed in years, but *O Heavenly Father, O Holy Mother, O Some Entity Somewhere!*

The robot stopped shrieking and for a moment, there was silence. I sat in a sweaty stupor. Was I in shock? I had been in shock before.

"Yes, but have you ever fallen through the ice? Not yet!"

"Shut up! Please stop!" I yelled.

"I'm still bitter cold. Prithee cometh receiveth me." The robot spoke in a child's hiss, but in Ren-Faire lingo. I hesitated for a moment, but then flipped it open. No batteries.

"The festivities are gearin' up," said a voice, and I screamed. It was Brett (so there was reason to scream.)

"You hear about the Rogers couple? Found dead on top of each other in their bathtub. Probably the most action they'd gotten in a long time!" Brett roared at his own joke.

"A murder-suicide?" I asked cautiously.

"You serious? They drowned. And who could drown *themselves* in a bathtub full of ice? It's Christmas Eve, for chrissakes! At LEAST off yourself and your old lady in the garage with the car running, where the fumes make you drift off nice and cozy!"

"You're disgusting," I said.

Brett slapped my face, *hard.* I didn't flinch. I wanted him out of my home and off of my property.

"Go to hell."

"Maybe your boy will get there first. He's down at the festival, caroling with your icy friend," Brett sneered.

Harrison. I took off running as fast as I could in house slippers.

I stumbled through the snow, like George Bailey did in *It's A Wonderful Life*. There was no angel to save me, except for Harrison; my angel, my everything. "*O please God*", I wept as I ran; a mix of tears, ice and cold stinging my eyes. Snow was seeping through my slippers and onto my toes, and I didn't care if they turned blue and fell off. "*Please God, save my son from the lake.*"

A banner read "*Lake Hope Christmas Day Festival*", even though it was Christmas Eve. Ice skaters skated happily on the same lake where Ice Boy drowned years ago.

The popcorn was popping, the chestnuts were roasting, and people were stuffing their faces full of these from red and green paper sacks. They rubbed their mittened hands together, either in delight or to combat the cold.

There was no sign of Harrison anywhere. I didn't see his orange ski jacket. I thought I was so clever buying it for him, so he stuck out like a bright thumb, just in case he ever got lost.

Carolers began singing "O Come All Ye Faithful."

Where was my son?

A majorette troupe with "The O Tannenbaum-ettes" airbrushed onto their jackets twirled red and green (and blue for the Jewish townspeople) streamer festooned batons to the beat of "The Little Drummer Boy."

"*Rum pum pum pum!*"

What looked to be a hastily crafted mascot cousin of Frosty the Snowman skated dead center in the middle of the lake. "*Presenting Icy the Iceman!*" a beaming announcer exclaimed.

Icy the Iceman? It felt like they were taunting him. I saw Clara from the cafe sporting a sparkly reindeer antler headband, downing eggnog and seemingly drunk off of her ass.

"Look who it is! Hello Miss Grinch!" She pointed at me, and her group laughed.

"Harrison!" I screamed as loudly as I could, looking desperately everywhere. I felt a hand on my shoulder.

"You know what Ice Boy was doing on the lake that day? Jerking off! He was a little freak!"

"Get off of me, Brett!" I tried to shake him off, but he was stronger.

"The town's better off with him rotting on the bottom of the lake! But if you'd like to join him–"

"Go to hell!"

"You know there are dead people connected to every lake, right? Accidents happen in bodies of water! Good riddance, Ice Boy! I spit in your watery grave!" Brett stood on the edge of the lake and spat into it for effect.

"Ladies and Gentlemen, the Christmas Countdown has begun!" A big clock showed a countdown to Christmas Day. An a cappella group began singing Vanilla Ice's "Ice Ice Baby."

"You know what they're counting down to, right? The anniversary of his death," Brett laughed.

"Ice Ice Baby!" the crowd chanted.

They were celebrating his death!

It was ghoulish. It was Texarkana!

"Harrison!" I screamed his name until my throat burned.

Icy the Iceman doffed his top hat. The carolers began singing "God Rest Ye Merry Gentlemen."

Finally, I spotted Harrison! He was standing on the edge of Lake Hope, with another boy. When they turned around, I saw that the boy had no flesh on his face, just bones, and two wide icicles jammed into his eyeholes.

The lake began to crack.

The screams, the broken ice, the carolers whose voices had been filled with song moments ago were now gasping for air. I saw Clara go down into the lake, her eyes filled with hatred for me.

So be it.

The ghoulish specter that was once Ice Boy began pulling my son by his orange jacket down into the lake. I grabbed for Harrison, and in doing so, I snapped off one of Ice Boy's bony fingers. It made a sound like a sugar cookie breaking in two. He didn't like that.

"Don't take my son!" I pleaded. "Take him!" I pointed to Brett, who looked surprised.

Maybe it was because I seemed maternal and nurturing, but Ice Boy did as I instructed him. He pulled screaming Brett down into the icy waters, where they both belonged. Brett thrashed until he plummeted under, silent for once. I sat holding Harrison in my lap, watching the town drown.

The addition of Brett seemed to do the trick. The lake gurgled, and then was still.

This year, we sat at the lakefront and witnessed a lovely Frank Capra-esque town fall victim to a decades-old curse, devised by a pre-pubescent alleged pervert with a penchant for the JCPenney bra catalog, back before the Internet made cleavage accessible to the wet dreaming masses.

The clock had struck midnight. It was Christmas, after all. Harrison and I were saved, wrapped in blankets. I thought about Brett at the bottom of the lake. Ice Boy had someone to keep him company now. I thought about Jesus in the manger with his Mother Mary, and I clutched my son tighter.

Three medics from Holy Trinity Hospital approached us. They didn't have gold, frankincense or myrrh, but they had piping hot chocolate that burned the insides of our mouths and our tongues.

As a mom, you try to do your best, and then a dead Ice Boy rises from the lake to get revenge and ruin Christmas. We'd moved to this Norman Rockwellian hamlet to escape society's frigid insanities, so this irony wasn't lost on me. What will my son say about me in the future? I believe he'll say, "Mom tried." I protected Harrison, and it felt good; like the old me, but wiser. We were okay now, and there were mini marshmallows floating through the cocoa, aimlessly as icebergs.

The Wild Hunt
By Rami Ungar

Tatum wheeled herself into her little sister Mia's room. Carefully, she picked up the sleeping four-year-old out of her bed and laid her in her lap. Mia stirred and cracked open her eyes. "Tay-Tay?" said Mia, rubbing her eyelashes with a fist. "What's going on?"

"Shush!" Tatum nearly smacked herself bringing her finger to her lips. She whipped her head around the tiny room, really a converted storage space, listening. There were no sounds from the living room other than their father's drunken snores. Sighing with relief, Tatum whispered to Mia, "We're leaving."

"Leaving?" Mia asked, her voice low. "Why?"

Because I overheard our bastard of a father on the phone this morning talking about selling you off, Tatum thought, the terror and panic wrapped around her heart like an iron vice. *And I have no idea if Dad's planning to sell you to some family who don't have a daughter of their own, or if men are going to do to you what they've done to me, but I'm not letting anyone touch you or take you away from me.*

She racked her brain for something she could say out loud. After a moment, she replied, "Remember learning about Santa Claus on TV?"

A big smile filled Mia's face and she nodded her head enthusiastically. Ever since Thanksgiving, the TV had been airing Christmas movies and commercials almost non-stop. And since Mia learned about the world mostly from TV, she'd gotten the full education about Santa Claus and his one-night trip around the world. Excited about a possible pile of presents in the morning, she'd gone to bed early tonight, Christmas Eve, without a fuss. An unexpected benefit of this was that their father had begun his annual Christmas Eve drinking binge a couple hours early, leading to him passing out much quicker than expected and giving Tatum a little more time to prepare.

"Well," Tatum continued, "I know the best spot to watch him when he passes by, and this year, I'm going to show you!"

Mia gasped excitedly. Then her face fell in horror. "But don't we have to be asleep when Santa comes? What if he gets mad and decides we're naughty because we went out to see him?"

"He didn't mind last year," said Tatum quickly. "We just have to be quiet when we go see him. If we make noise, we might scare the reindeer and he won't stop by our home. Understand?"

Mia nodded her head again, her smile returning. Tatum smiled back. She adored her little sister's smile. It was the only light in her miserable world.

"Okay." Tatum grabbed the thick comforter from Mia's bed and draped it over them. "You go back to sleep, and I'll take us to see Santa. When I see him flying by, I'll wake you up. Got it?"

"What about Daddy?"

Tatum glanced back in the direction of the living room. She couldn't see him, but she could hear Dad's snores as clearly as she could hear her own breathing.

"Daddy's too tired to go with us," she said. Then she added with a slight edge of anger, "And he's usually on the naughty list, so I don't think Santa would like Daddy going out to see him."

"Oh. Okay."

Thankful that Mia wasn't going to question their father being on the naughty list, Tatum tucked her tighter into the comforter and maneuvered her wheelchair out of the tiny room. "Now, you go back to sleep," she whispered, "and when you wake up, you'll see Santa and all the reindeer. Do you remember the reindeer's names?"

"Mm-hmm. Rudolph, and Prancer, and Donner, and…"

But as Mia settled in under the blanket against Tatum's body, she closed her eyes and slipped into sleep. Tatum watched her sister doze for a moment, then pulled the blanket over her head and wheeled them into the living room. Her father was still snoring on the couch, his legs sprawled over one side. On the TV, James Stewart was finding just how much his town had changed after he had been taken out of existence.

Carefully, Tatum wheeled them past the couch and to the front door. There was a terrifying moment when the carpeted floor underneath the chair creaked loudly, but Chris only snorted and turned over in his sleep. Tatum let out a breath she hadn't known she was holding in and rolled up to the front door. Carefully, she slid back all four locks on the door and twisted the knob. It opened soundlessly, revealing a world of white beyond.

For a second, Tatum hesitated. She hadn't left this house in nearly three years, kept here by the monster snoring on the couch behind her. Doubt assailed her heart, whispering to her to stop this stupid stunt and close the door. Close it, go back inside, and endure everything Dad had put them through for the past three years.

But then she felt Mia turn towards her under the blanket, and she remembered why she had decided to run away, finally, after all these years and all the torture and abuse, in the first place. Steeling herself, Tatum pushed them over the threshold and into the white expanse. Thankfully, there was no step to maneuver over, or they both might have gone tumbling into the snow. Instead, the wheels sank into the snow with a barely audible crunch.

Closing the door behind her, Tatum wheeled them towards the road. She shivered as the cold assaulted her face, hands, and feet. She was only wearing ragged pajamas and slippers, and while underneath the comforter she and Mia were cocooned in warmth, farther down she could feel ice working its way into her bones. Not for the first time, Tatum wished that when she'd been paralyzed, she'd lost sensation in her lower body.

She also wished she had a winter coat, gloves and boots to wear, but she hadn't been allowed outside in three years, so Dad wouldn't have bought winter gear for her under any circumstances. And given that she'd heard him negotiating for Mia over the phone just that morning, there hadn't been any time to get something else to keep her and Mia warm. No, she would just have to go and hope she found someone to help them before he woke and realized they'd left.

As they reached the road, Tatum looked first one way and to the other. To her left were the lights of a distant town. To her right was a wilderness over which dark, foreboding clouds hovered. Even as she watched, Tatum saw the clouds were approaching rapidly. A snowstorm was on its way.

Silently, she cursed and began wheeling towards town. She hoped Christmas really was the time for miracles and goodwill towards all men. Right now, she could use both in spades.

By the time she reached town, however, the snowstorm was already over the town, and the winds that arrived with it howled like ghosts as they threw snow onto the blanket and into Tatum's hair. Her feet and lower legs were numb, as were her cheeks and hands, and even the heat trapped under the comforter was finding ways out. Teeth gritted and eyelids scrunched, Tatum forced the wheelchair through the thickening snow, intent on finding someplace that would give her and Mia shelter.

But it appeared no place was open. All the buildings were dark, all the cars sat empty and parked on the streets. Even the Christmas lights that should have lit up the building exteriors and trees like beacons were nowhere in sight! She cursed, wishing that it wasn't snowing so damn hard right now. Then maybe someone would notice them and offer help.

If only, she thought, scowling. *But then again, you know what good "if only" does. If only that idiot in the truck hadn't tried to run a red light and hit me and Mom while we were on our way to my ballet recital all those years ago. If only Mom had lived, and I hadn't lost my legs. If only we didn't have to live with Dad afterwards, even though he and mom were finally getting divorced after all those terrible years together. If only he hadn't blown all the money we got from the settlement on gambling and then moved us out here to escape the people he owed money to. If only Santa was real, and he actually gave a damn. Then maybe he would give us the gift of rescue and take us somewhere else.*

Tatum sighed. Ruminating like this and getting angry wouldn't do either of them any good. The only thing that would help them right now would be to find someone who would take them away from their father for good.

She kept pushing through the snow, even as it stuck to the snowflakes that had already fallen and formed walls eager to slow her progress. Tatum didn't allow herself to be stopped, however, even as her slippers became soaked, and the numbness clawed its way up her legs. Every time she considered giving up, she thought of Mia depending on her to get them somewhere safe, and she found a new reserve of energy to get her through her ordeal.

Finally, after what felt like an eternity, Tatum spotted light in the darkness. Wheeling closer, she saw a squat building through which light was spilling through a glass front. A sign next to the glass windows read SHERIFF'S OFFICE.

Relief and joy soared through Tatum's body and soul. Surely, a sheriff and the police who worked under him would help them. They took oaths to protect people, after all. At least, they did on TV. She grabbed the icy-cold wheels on either side of her and pushed them a bit closer to the station.

Over the wind, Tatum heard several dogs barking.

She paused mid-wheel, her head cocked into the wind. Had she just been imagining—no, there it was again! Many dogs barking, howling, baying, and yapping all at once. Was there a dog pound near here or something? Or were there a bunch of dogs out in this storm? If it was the latter, she felt for them. Still, she had other priorities. The dogs would just have to fend for themselves tonight.

She pushed her wheels forward again, ignoring the noise that seemed to be getting steadily closer.

The sound of horse whinnies mixed in with the dogs' yelling. They sounded very close.

She stopped again, looking around her. She thought she had misheard, but there it was. Multiple horses were whinnying and nickering and screaming alongside the dogs. And…were there people yelling?

My mind is playing tricks on me, Tatum thought. *Maybe cold makes you crazy. I better get us inside before I find out the hard way.*

Quickly, she began pushing again. In just the few seconds she'd stopped to listen, the snow had grown that much harder to work through. Even so, she continued turning the wheels, determined to get to that sheriff's station. *The wind is just making noise that sounds like people and animals*, she told herself. *People used to think thunder and lightning were gods being mad at us, after all. Who's to say I can't think there are voices and animals in the wind?*

Even as she told herself all that, she could still hear the dogs, horses, and people. If she listened closely, she could hear the pounding of thousands of hooves. And for some reason, they sent a chill up her spine that had nothing to do with the blizzard around them.

"Tay-Tay, are we there yet?"

The sounds on the wind were pushed completely from her mind as she heard the little voice from under the blanket.

"A-Almost," she replied, shivering. She cleared her throat. "I mean, we're almost there. Just go back to sleep."

"I can't," Mia replied, poking her head out of the blanket. "It's too cold. And I can hear doggies and horsies."

I guess I'm not the only one the wind is messing with tonight. "Look, we'll be somewhere warm soon, okay? So, just huddle under the blanket, and I'll—!"

She stopped midsentence as a figure emerged from the sheriff's station. Someone was there, a sheriff or a deputy. Tatum's heart soared and she lifted her hand halfway up to wave to him. She stopped as the man turned in her direction, her joy replaced with sheer terror. She wasn't sure the man who'd just emerged from the station could see them, but she could see him clearly. And his face. And she recognized him.

A lot of bad things had happened after Dad had uprooted his daughters from their home and moved them into that old shack they'd called home the past four years. At first, the bad things had been small. He'd told Tatum that she would no longer go to school so she could look after Mia, then a baby. Then he'd forbidden either of them from going outside. And she'd accepted her new role and the restrictions, because she was scared their father would hurt them if she disobeyed him, and because she partly blamed herself for their mother's death. Yes, it was the idiot in the truck's fault, but hadn't Mom been driving them to *her* ballet recital?

And for a while, that was the worst of it. Every day, Tatum would watch and care for Mia, and Chris would spend most of his time in the basement. What he did down there, she didn't know, but sometimes from the window she saw people driving up to the house and stepping into the basement from an outside cellar door. They would often come out carrying boxes they hadn't had when they walked in, so she assumed her father was selling them something that he could only sell out of a basement.

But then after a few months of this, things got worse. One night, while Mia was sleeping in the tiny room she shared with Tatum, Dad had woken her up and told her she would be sleeping in his room from now on. That very first night, he did the thing to her parents did when they wanted to make a baby. And she cried, because she was scared her father wanted to have babies with her and because it hurt when he went inside her. He then beat her and warned her she wouldn't ever move again if she kept crying.

From that night, Tatum refused to shed any tears. And most nights, when Dad wasn't dead drunk, he did the baby-making thing to her. But she didn't cry. She even did things he liked and pretended she liked them too, because he didn't beat her when she pretended. And he still bought her and Mia food. Sometimes, he even bought them new clothes, especially if Tatum cooked his favorite foods and pleased him in bed. And that was enough for her. They were surviving and Mia was happy.

But then one night, some of her father's customers started visiting the bedroom. And while Dad stayed in the living room, the men would have their way with her. Afterwards, Tatum would see cash changing hands, the men would leave, and he would sleep on the couch while she retreated deep inside herself, wishing for death.

The man who had stepped out of the sheriff's station was one of her most frequent visitors. She knew his face as well as she knew his cheap cologne and the tattoos on his arms he liked her to touch before he put himself inside her.

If Tatum had been alone, she might have stayed there, stock still, until the man noticed her and either killed her or ensured she went back to her father. But the weight of

Mia squirming on her lap reminded her why she had come out this way, so she gripped the wheels of her chair tight. Somehow, she managed to spin them around and take off the way they'd come before turning into an alleyway and propelling them towards the other end.

"Tay-Tay?" Mia whimpered.

"Sorry, Mia," said Tatum, huffing and puffing. "There—there was…a bad man back there." She stopped, panted, then continued, "He would have taken us home and we wouldn't get to see Santa. But look, I'm going to find us a new way there, okay?" Her breath back, she began pushing again, not even bothering to look down at her sister. "Just leave it to me, okay? I'll take care of you." Tears sprang to her eyes. "I promise, I'll always take care of you. So just please go back to sleep, and—!"

"Tatum!"

Mia shot out of the blanket and slapped Tatum's cheeks with both hands. By now, Tatum's cheeks were way too numb to feel them, but she heard her sister say her name. Not Tay-Tay, which she'd been calling her older sister since she'd learned to talk, but her real name. She never did that.

Tatum stopped pushing and looked down at Mia. There was a determined frown on her face that she'd never seen on a little girl before, let alone from her own sister. It was like Mia had decided to do something, no matter how bad or scary it might be, and nothing could deter her from it.

"Tatum," she said, "I know we're not going to see Santa! I know we're running away from home!"

Tatum was stunned. "Y-You knew?"

Mia nodded. "Everybody knows you're not supposed to see Santa," she said with the assuredness that only four-year-olds have. "If you do, you don't get presents!

So, we're running away because Daddy and his friends always hurt you. Right? We're finally running away from him and going someplace nice!"

Tatum's chest hitched and she began to cry. "He was going to take you away from me," she said. "I heard him on the phone." She hugged her sister tight. "Yeah, we're going somewhere nice! Because I won't let anyone take you away from me!"

Mia cried as well. "I don't ever want to go away from you, either! I love you, Tay-Tay! I love you lots and lots!"

"I-I love you too, Mia. I love you more than life itself."

"Well," said a gruff voice, "isn't this a touching display?"

Both girls screamed and looked behind them. There stood the man from the sheriff's station, a wicked, toothy grin on his face. "And your dad didn't call me but two minutes ago to let me know you two decided to fly the coop."

Inside Tatum's gut, a dark stone of despair formed, sapping away her will to fight. They'd been caught. Their bid to escape was over.

A few minutes later, they were drying off and warming up in the sheriff's station, decorated with a Christmas tree and cheerful ribbons on the wall, but neither Tatum nor Mia felt any warmer or cheerier. Besides the deputy, who only sipped coffee and grinned cruelly at them, they were the only ones in the station. Tatum wondered why that was, and found she didn't care. All she knew was, nothing had changed. The deputy had already called Dad and told him to come get them at the station. They were about to go right back into hell, only it would soon be much, much worse.

"You know, your daddy has been talking about getting rid of your younger sister for a while now," the deputy, whose nametag read Gates, revealed. He sidled up to the wheelchair and bent down so that he and Tatum were eye level. "Says she's nothing but another mouth to feed. At least he gets plenty out of you." He chuckled. "Though after tonight, I don't think you'll be giving him much of anything for a while, good or bad. Hey, maybe he'll sell you to me. I wouldn't mind moving far away from here and making an honest woman of you. Would you like that, sweetie?"

Tatum didn't respond. She only held Mia close and let the tears fall down her cheeks. It didn't seem like he was expecting an answer, however, because he stood, walked towards the window, and continued to sip his coffee.

A few minutes later, a familiar four-door black truck pulled up outside, parking at an angle as it skidded through the snow. When their father stepped inside the station, flakes of snow melting in his hair, his face was red, and his fists were clenching and unclenching.

Both girls shuddered and held each other tighter. Both of them, especially Tatum, had thought of their father as a monster before. He'd been a lazy, no-good, violent man who had drank and abused his wife to the day she died, and then abused his older daughter the same. But now, nearly steaming with anger, he appeared more like a marauding beast than anything that could be made for a horror film or a dark fairy tale.

"Do you bitches know how much trouble you're in!" he roared. Both girls flinched and Mia whimpered softly. "And why did you have to pick tonight of all nights to run away? Don't you know there's a fucking blizzard outside!"

"Cool your jets, Chris," said Gates, putting down his coffee and taking hold of Tatum's chair by the wheels.

"You can give 'em hell once you get 'em back home. Just don't do anything that would require a cleanup crew, okay? I'm not sheriff yet, after all."

"Sure." Chris spat. He grabbed the wheelchair from the other side. "Whatever. Can you help me get them in the car?"

Together, they lifted the chair and carried it outside to the truck, setting them down by the back driver's side door. They didn't resist, too afraid to try anything.

At least, until their father tried to lift Mia out of Tatum's arms. Then, like a lightning bolt, Tatum pushed herself up, grabbed Mia, and pulled her back into her embrace. Both men stared at her like she'd gone crazy, and their dad muttered, "What the fuck?"

"No." Tatum squeezed Mia close as the little girl wrapped her arms around her older sister's shoulders.

Dad's eyes narrowed. "No?"

"No!" Tatum insisted, an anger she didn't know she was capable of feeling taking hold of her. "Don't you dare fucking touch her!"

Dad's lips pulled back in a snarl and his arm shot forward, grabbing the collar of Mia's nightdress. "Don't you tell me 'no', you little slut!"

He yanked Mia out of Tatum's arms and lifted her into the air. Tatum screamed and reached for Mia, but a punch from their father's free fist sent her flying out of her chair and into the snow. Something warm gushed from her nose and turned the snow around her face red.

Gingerly, Tatum lifted herself out of the snow, wiping the blood from her nose away with the back of her arm. She looked up at her father just in time to see him smack Mia full across the face with the back of his hand.

A guttural roar escaped Tatum's throat and she somehow managed to launch herself at her father, wrapping her arms around his legs while biting his thigh.

Dad cried out and let go of Mia, who fell to the ground and scrambled to Tatum. Dad then kicked them both away into the snow before stalking towards where they lay, his fists clenching and unclenching again.

Tatum lifted herself up onto her elbows, her face and stomach now throbbing with pain. Despite that, she managed to gather Mia to her, comforting her sister as best she could. Already, the blood Tatum had spilled was gone or disappearing under the thickening snow. A few feet away, Dad and Deputy Gates were arguing, probably about better places to take out his anger at his daughters instead of in front of a sheriff's station during a blizzard.

Tatum glanced skyward. *Why won't anybody help us?* Whether it was a question or a prayer, she wasn't sure. All she knew was that she and Mia would probably be dead or in agony very soon, and she hoped it was dead. Anything was better than continuing to live under their father's boot once they got home.

Above their heads, several horses whinnied.

Chris and Deputy Gates stopped arguing, looking around in astonishment. Tatum looked as well. She'd completely forgotten about hearing animals and people on the winds earlier, and when the two men had carried her and Mia outside, the only sounds had been the wind howling and the snow crunching underfoot. Now the howls of dogs were rising from all directions, as were the pounding of hooves. And they were getting louder with every passing second.

In the snow, Mia crushed herself against Tatum's chest. "I'm scared," she whispered, shivering in a way that had nothing to do with the cold.

"I know, I know," Tatum replied. She then admitted what, under other circumstances, she would never have admitted to her little sister: "I'm scared too."

A few feet away, both men were still looking around, and Tatum heard Gates say, "They sound like they're right on top of us." Their dad opened his mouth to reply.

Suddenly, the air was rent with a metallic crash. Tatum and Mia screamed, staring up in horror and awe at their father's truck, which was now crushed under the massive hooves of a giant, white horse. On its back was a figure wrapped in a dark brown cloak and hood fastened with a black-and-gold brooch. The figure slid off the horse, its cloak whirling around it to reveal a black dress and a pale, emaciated frame, though a pair of breasts still rose under the fabric covering the chest. The figure's face was completely hidden by the hood, for which Tatum was grateful. If she were to see the figure's face, she was sure it would be more terrifying than the woman herself.

Dad and Gates backed away from the truck, their faces a portrait of terror. Gates's mouth was moving, and Tatum thought she heard him say, "...I looked, and behold, a pale horse, and he who sat on it had the name Death, and the forces of Hell were following with him."

A voice spoke from the hood, deep, raspy, and somehow as clear as a bell over the screaming winds. "Dost thou think thyself men for hurting children? Dost thou think thyselves strong?"

The men flinched at the sound of the woman's voice, and one of them even yelped, though Tatum wasn't sure which. From within her cloak, the woman drew a long, black staff and pointed it at the men. "I shall grant thee to the count of ten and one score," she said. "After, the hunt shall begin."

As the woman finished speaking, dozens of dogs appeared around them, all white and tipped with red on their ears and tails. The dogs growled, barked, and whined, baring teeth that looked more like fangs. The men shouted in surprise, while Tatum and Mia screamed as they found themselves surrounded by the white hounds. The dogs, however, didn't seem to notice the girls, their attention directed at Chris and Deputy Gates.

"One," called the woman. The dogs parted, leaving a path of escape for the two men. "Two!"

Chris and Gates didn't wait for her to say three. Instead, they sprinted through the knee-high snow, past the dogs and away from the sheriff's station, disappearing into the gloom and swirling snow. The hounds turned to watch, but none of them chased after the retreating men.

Several seconds passed, during which the cloaked woman continued to count. At the same time, several more figures appeared around the sheriff's station, in the streets and on top of vehicles and rooftops. Some were on horseback, while others ran on two or four or even twenty feet. Some looked like they were running or galloping down invisible paths from the sky above to the earth below, while others seemed to pop into existence between blinks of the eye.

Nearly all of them looked like creatures out of nightmares. Tatum spotted knights in spiky armor wielding all manner of weapons, flames leaping from eye sockets and gaps in their armor; translucent spirits, many of whom appeared to be teenagers and children, flitting among the knights and horses like dancers; and monsters with multiple arms, spikes and horns, forked tails and batlike wings. She wondered if Gates had been right when he mentioned the forces of Hell following Death. After all, who else could the cloaked figure be?

The woman shouted "Thirty!" And like that, the dogs began running at once after Gates and their dad, barking and howling loudly. The monsters and the riders on horseback followed the dogs, their shouts and war cries louder than the dogs' own cacophony. Tatum closed her eyes and curled her and Mia into a ball, sure they would be trampled by the chasing throng.

Nothing happened. The thunder of hooves and feet passed by them, but only the falling snow touched them.

Then, to her surprise, Tatum heard a girlish giggle.

Opening her eyes, Tatum saw Mia laughing as one of the dogs licked her face. Four others surrounded them, all wagging their tails and panting as if they hadn't been threatening to attack a moment ago.

But who were they threatening to attack? Dad and Deputy Gates, not us. In fact, I think they've ignored us up till now.

As Mia laughed and hugged the dog, which was still licking her, Tatum raised a cautious hand. One of the other dogs stepped forward and licked her fingers, its tongue warm against her cold skin. And as it continued to lick her, she felt the warmth transfer to her fingers and spread throughout her body. In mere seconds, she felt like she was wearing a warm sweater and was lying by a roaring fireplace, rather than sitting in the middle of a blizzard wearing the thinnest of clothes.

At that moment, the cloaked woman spoke. "Bring them with us."

The dogs vanished and two black horses appeared on either side of the girls, their riders dismounting. The riders, who looked anything but human, scooped up Tatum and Mia into their arms. Somehow, Tatum sensed that fighting back wouldn't do any good here. However, as the other rider returned to its horse with Mia in its arms, she screamed and reached for her sister. Mia reached as well, tears falling down her cheeks as she tried to climb over the rider's shoulder.

"Let her have her babe," said the cloaked figure, mounting her horse. "Mother and child should not be separated after a harrowing ordeal."

The rider nodded, stepped away from its horse, and handed Mia off to Tatum, who wrapped her arms protectively around her sister. Meanwhile, the first rider, who seemed unperturbed by holding two girls in its arms, mounted its own horse and deposited both girls in its lap. Tatum reached out to keep herself from falling off, but for some reason, her body stuck to the horse's bare back as if she were sitting on flat earth. She stared around them in wonder as the rider cracked the horse's reins and the horse began to trot. A moment later, the second rider, several dogs, and many others fell into step behind the cloaked figure, who led them away from the sheriff's station, Dad's crushed truck, and Tatum's wheelchair, which was fast becoming buried in snow. Somehow, Tatum knew she wouldn't see that chair ever again.

The crowd of riders, dogs and other creatures walked through the town, and while many of them made noise that could be heard above the wind, Tatum noticed no lights turning on in windows or faces peeking out of windows. Did the people inside the buildings not hear them outside?

"No," said the rider on whose horse they rode, startling Tatum. She had no idea it could talk, let alone read minds. "They hear us. They just choose not to look outside. They know, in their deepest of hearts, that to see this would be to spell their own doom."

Mia, meanwhile, ignored the rider and was looking around them in amazement. "Tay-Tay! It's a parade! It's like we're in a parade!"

"Yeah," said Tatum, glancing around as well. "It really is."

The cloaked figure led them to what a snow-covered sign declared a public park, now nothing more than a wasteland of white. In the center of the park, the crowd of dogs, riders and creatures formed a half-circle in the snow, the cloaked figure in the exact middle of the half-circle. A moment later, the sound of thundering hooves and yelling dogs reached them, followed a minute later by the ones who had chased after Dad and Deputy Gates. They formed and created another half-circle which merged with their half-circle, creating a full one with nothing inside. Then two riders broke from the circle and dragged two bruised, bloody figures through the snow behind them. It was Dad and Deputy Gates.

The two riders deposited them in the middle of the space and retreated back into the circle. Meanwhile, the cloaked figure's horse trotted forward, stopping just a few feet from the two prone forms. Both men looked pleadingly up at her, their faces cut and black and blue.

"P-Please!" Dad begged. "D-Don't hurt us anymore. We didn't do anything to deserve this."

"Y-Yeah!" Gates added. "It w-was just a couple of runaways. N-N-Nothing m-m-more. D-Don't kill us for that!"

The figure reached up and pulled back her hood. The men on the ground cried out in horror, while Mia turned into Tatum's belly with covered eyes. Tatum herself wanted to close her eyes, but instead kept her gaze focused on the cloaked woman's face. No, not face; faces. Three skulls with wild, white hair clinging to the craniums emerged from a single neck, glowing blue and with little blue flames in their sockets.

The cloaked figure pointed at the men on the ground. Her three jaws moved in unison, three voices speaking as one as they said, "Kill them."

This time, Tatum was able to look away as several dozen hounds rushed to the two men in the snow. However, she could not shut out the screams and rending of flesh, too busy covering Mia's ears from the noise.

After a while, the slaughter ended, and Tatum felt the horse moving away from the scene. Even so, she did not dare open her eyes until the horse they were riding stopped and a new voice said, "Let me see them."

The rider slipped off the horse, then picked Tatum and Mia up and placed them carefully in the snow. Tatum's eyes flew open. The cloaked figure stood before them, but she had changed: her body was plump, her black dress was green and looked brand new, and she only had one head, with the face of a kind, old woman with long, braided hair and warm eyes.

Both girls stared up at her in wonder, mouths hanging open. Finally, Tatum asked, "Who are you?"

The old woman gave them a friendly smile, and Tatum found herself smiling back. "I have many names," said the old woman. "As leader of my hunting party, I am The Cloaked One. As the punisher of evildoers committing crimes during storms, I am Lady Hekla the Terrible. And as the guardian of children, I am Grandmother Frost."

To this, Tatum didn't know what to say. Mia, however, asked, "Are you Santa Claus, too?"

The old woman laughed. "I might be. More people see me and my crew around this time of year, so we may have influenced the myth. In a way, child, yes, I am Santa."

Before Tatum could stop her, Mia had jumped out of her arms and was running to embrace the old woman's legs. "Thank you, Santa!" Mia shouted. "You saved us."

The old woman laughed and patted Mia's head. Sitting in the snow, Tatum felt compelled to say something. She coughed and murmured, "T-Thank you, ma'am. You really did save our lives."

The old woman smiled at her, and Tatum suddenly felt self-conscious. Here she was, sitting in the snow in her pajamas and slippers, and unable to properly thank this woman for saving her life.

Then the old woman said, "You did everything you could to protect your daughter, my dear. I only made sure your efforts weren't in vain. That, and the men who hurt you didn't go unpunished."

"Mia's not my—!" Tatum paused, thought for a moment, then said, "I mean, yes ma'am. Thank you, ma'am."

"Tay-Tay's my mommy!" Mia leaped into Tatum's arms and snuggled against her. Tatum laughed, kissing her sister-daughter's head.

"And now," said the old woman, drawing the girls' attention back to her, "I bestow upon you a gift. For all you've done for your child, I give you your legs back."

Suddenly, Tatum felt a tingling sensation in her lower half, starting from her hips and going all the way down to her toes. With the tingling came something she hadn't felt in nearly four years: strength. The strength to move.

Tatum let go of Mia and slowly, gingerly, tried to stand. At first it was as if her legs were made of jelly and she nearly fell face-first into the snow. But then she steadied and was able to stand. Mia gasped, staring up at her with wide eyes. Tatum glanced down at her own legs, unsure if she was really seeing what she was seeing. She took a tentative step forward. Her foot slid into the snow, but she did not stumble or fall. She took another step. Then another. A few more steps, she was running, her legs moving as easily through the packed snow as if she were running through grass on a summer's day. Then she was leaping, and then she was dancing, dancing like she used to dance in her ballet recitals. She even did a pirouette, and it was as smooth as the ones she'd done when she'd been eleven and took dance lessons three times a week.

A fresh wave of tears sprang to her eyes, and she mouthed, "Thank you," to the old woman. Then she began to laugh. She couldn't help it. She was happier than she'd been in years.

"Tay-Tay!"

Tatum turned and almost fell as she caught Mia, who practically flew into her arms as she leapt up to hug her, her pajamas placed with a thick fur coat, hat, muffler and boots. She resembled a doll of a little Russian girl Tatum used to own when she was Mia's age. "Tay-Tay! You were so cool! Can you teach me to dance like that?"

Still crying and laughing, she held Mia in her arms, standing proud and tall for the first time in years. "Sure thing. Whatever you want. But first we—"

"But first you must ride with us." The old woman had reappeared beside them, except now her hood was back up, she wore riding clothes instead of a dress, and yellow eyes glowed out from the darkness of her hood.

Both girls stopped laughing and the tears ceased to fall. "I-I'm sorry?" Tatum asked.

"Your legs were a reward for your love of your daughter," said the old woman. "And I killed your father and that brute of a man on principle. But now that you have seen us, you must ride with us for all eternity. Either that, or you must die. Thus is the law of the Wild Hunt."

The old woman fell silent, and Tatum realized she was waiting for an answer. She glanced at Mia, whose eyes were big and fearful again. And like that, the answer was there. Turning back to the old woman, she nodded and said, "Alright, we'll ride with you."

The old woman's face was still shrouded in darkness, but Tatum thought she sensed a smile under that hood. "Excellent. You shall join in our hunts. Though when we next make camp, I would like to see you dance. It has been many years since I've seen a maiden dance like that, and I'd rather not wait so long again."

As the old woman spoke, Tatum's clothes changed, her pajamas becoming a leather jacket and pants, while her slippers became thick winter boots. At the same time, a spear tipped with silver bound itself with a leather sash to her back, while a dagger bound itself to a belt around her waist.

Astonished, Tatum opened her mouth to ask a question, but the old woman had already returned to her horse and remounted. She then snapped her fingers, and a black horse with a white mane, tail and eyes emerged from the crowd, stopping in front of the girls. It lowered its head to them, and Tatum realized this would be their horse while they rode with the Wild Hunt.

Carefully, she sat Mia in the saddle and then, still in awe of her newly returned legs, leapt into it too. On her own horse, the old woman snapped the reins and yelled, "Hiyah!" The white horse sprang forward and galloped into the sky with a loud whinny. Behind it, the many riders, spirits, dogs and monsters followed after, rising into the air as easily as if they were climbing a footpath on a hill.

Tatum and Mia cried out as their own horse sprinted into the air, but did not fall out of the saddle, as if an invisible force were holding them to their seats. Remembering what it had been like when they'd ridden with the inhuman rider, both girls looked down and watched as the park and the surrounding town became miniscule underneath them. Soon, they were flying through the thick and chilly clouds and then into a field of moonlit mist that stretched as far as the eye could see. The girls gazed around them in wonder, their mouths hanging open as the mob of horses and creatures flew over the landscape.

From far in the front, the old woman's voice carried back to them, as clear as if she were riding right next to the girls. "Onward! Around the world and to worlds those on Earth rarely walk upon! Let the Wild Hunt ride for all time!"

The hundreds of riders, horses, dogs, ghosts and creatures yelled in agreement. Tatum and Mia lent their own voices to the shout, though Tatum was less enthusiastic than Mia. The spear on her back and the dagger on her hip were reminders of what the old woman had said. Those who saw the Wild Hunt either joined or died. That included bad men like their father and the deputy, but it also included good people too, innocents who may be just in the wrong place at the wrong time. In those instances, Tatum might have to be the one to kill them, might even be forced to so she could keep her and Mia's place in the Wild Hunt.

If that happened, would she be able to kill someone? And could she live with the answer either way?

Mia turned in the saddle and hugged Tatum around the stomach. "Best Christmas ever," she whispered. "Thank you, Mommy."

Tatum pushed thoughts of murder away and hugged her sister-daughter. "You're welcome," she replied, kissing her head. "Merry Christmas, Mia."

"Merry Christmas to you too!"

Unearthly music rose throughout the flying procession, and Mia closed her eyes with a smile, quickly drifting off to sleep. Tatum, however, stayed awake for a long, long time, thinking of hunting and killing people and wondering if she could. Unconsciously, she reached up and pulled the spear off her back. It thrummed with power, and she knew her answer. If it was to keep her and Mia safe and happy, she'd kill. She'd kill a thousand people if she had to.

After all, she was a mother. And motherhood came with all sorts of responsibilities.

The Feast of Saint Lucy
By Serena Daniels

St. Lucia, or St. Lucy as she is more commonly known, was born Lucia of Syracuse around 283. She was born into parents who were wealthy and of nobility, her father was Roman and her mother, who was named Eutychia, was Greek. Her early life was upended when her father died when she was only five years old. When she became of marriageable age, Eutychia, who was suffering from an unknown bleeding disorder and was concerned about her future, arranged for Lucy to marry a young man from a rich pagan family.

However, unknown to her mother, Lucy had different plans for her future; she had already promised to God that she would remain chaste and had hopes of dividing her dowry among the poor. In order to keep her vow, Lucy came up with a plan; she persuaded her mother to come with her on a pilgrimage to Catania, to visit the shrine of another saint, Agatha of Sicily. Her mother was eventually convinced, while there, St. Agatha appeared to her in a dream and told her that because her faith was so strong, her mother was now cured and that she would be the glory of Syracuse as Agatha herself was of Catania.

Upon her mother's recovery, Lucy this time persuaded her mother to take a great amount of her riches and distribute them among the poor, including her dowry. However, when word reached her betrothed about her generosity, he paid a visit to Paschasius, the Governor of Syracuse and revealed her Christianity (Christians were being persecuted by the Roman Empire at this time).

Paschasius had her brought before him and ordered her to burn a sacrifice to the emperor's image to prove her loyalty to the Empire, upon her refusal, he sentenced her to a brothel for defilement. However, when the guards were attempting to take her away, she couldn't be moved, even after they had attached a team of oxen to her. Then he ordered that she be burned, but the bundles of wood that surrounded her refused to light. Then her eyes were gouged out, but were replaced by the Holy Spirit. Her life was finally ended by a sword to her throat.

She has since become a patron saint of many things, among which are of the blind, those with eye illnesses, ophthalmologists, throat infections and writers. She is sometimes depicted with eyes on a stick, but she is most often depicted holding onto a plate with a pair of eyes on it.

Her feast day is on December 13th.

#

It was from engrained routine that caused Rebecca Archer to wake up at half past six in the morning. She didn't even need to check her phone to know the time, it had been time to get up this early for as long as she could remember. At least when it came to this time of year…

'Can't sleep in today,' she didn't know why she had to remind herself of this fact, but even after all these years it was hard to resist the urge to sleep in. She stretched her back a little as she pulled the covers off, she needed be dressed quickly before it was time for everyone else to get up.

She didn't dress in her formal wear though, she didn't want to get it dirty, always remembering her mother's gentle scolding the first time she did that, managing to scrounge up a spare outfit, Ragna's old one to be more precise, as simply cleaning it would have taken too long. She never made that mistake again, especially when she realized just how dirty baking could be.

What she called her "baking outfit", consisted of just a plain white T-shirt and a pair of jeans that had seen better days; she used to use an apron, but as she got better at baking and stopped leaving big messes on the counter and on herself, she abandoned the apron and just put on something plain that she could just toss into the laundry whenever.

"Alright, let's get going," she muttered as she rubbed the sleep out of her eyes before she opened and closed her door softly, it wasn't time for everyone else to wake up yet, not even her mom had to wake up now anymore, not since she was old enough to do all of the morning preparations herself. It almost made her want to hurry up and have her own daughter…

'Slow down there, you're barely an adult.' It was true, at twenty she was barely into college, just beginning the next phase of her life, and she was barely taking over the family duties as it was.

Still, she couldn't help but spare an envious side glance at the still closed bedroom door of her younger sister and another one at her younger brother's. She wished that she could trade places with Aggie, if only to have the ability to sleep in every morning, even if it was an extra few days out of the year.

She eventually reached the kitchen, but stopped as she realized that she didn't have all of the ingredients yet, she had been too busy talking with Max to get the stuff when she was supposed to. But she didn't need to panic, she was lucky that the nearby grocery store carried everything she needed and that they were open this early.

The only problem was that big snowstorm that had hit during the night, she dreaded seeing how much it had piled up overnight, but she had to go nonetheless. After all, St. Lucy's feast day was the most important day of the year for her mother's family…and her dad was more than happy to go along with their traditions.

She could not afford to screw this up.

She quickly ran to the front and changed into her winter clothing before she took a breath and grabbed her purse and left.

#

'I think all my extremities are going to fall off,' she thought as she almost fell through the door upon returning. A quick glance at the hall clock told her that she'd been gone for over an hour and knew that within half an hour the women would start waking up and expecting things to be running like clockwork, she had no time to waste!

'I guess I'm gonna have to put on my apron!' She decided as she ran as fast as she could to the kitchen while carrying her bags. She was thankful that the house

was well maintained and that they didn't have walls or floors that creaked so there was little chance that her family was aware of her absence or her late start. She knew that she would only get scolded like a child if nothing was in the oven by the time they came to check on her, so she had no other choice then to prep everything faster than she'd ever have before.

Once she passed the kitchen threshold, she turned the part of her brain that put her into automatic mode on and shut the rest off. Her mind was blank as she quickly began to bring out the equipment from the cupboard after throwing on her apron, she needed to quickly get to work on the recipe that took the longest, and she had to chuck it in the fridge as soon as she could in consideration the minimal time required.

It always irked her that their saffron Christmas bread could be left in the fridge for up to twenty-four hours, but her mother's family tradition insisted that it be at least the minimum of two hours, yet no more than three or four because of the timing that everyone got up. It would be so much easier on her if she could at least leave it overnight…

'Maybe I'll change that once I'm old enough to be in charge of the family,' she contemplated as she shut the fridge door. *'But I can't afford to dwell on it now, I got to get the ginger cookies ready.'*

Being Swedish, her mother's family strictly carried on the traditions that came with Saint Lucy's feast day, like dressing the oldest daughter in a white dress with stockings and a crimson sash and have a wreath for a crown with white candles and having the duty of waking up all family members to serve them coffee and some kind of sweet bread. In her family's case it was usually the traditional saffron buns, but sometimes they would be switched with something else. And it all had to be at dawn, although considering where they lived the family elders allowed it to slide to be no later than nine in the morning…for the younger members, since the oldest members weren't exactly spring chickens.

She immediately went to work on the treat that had to be in the oven, and judging from the time, her mom was going to be up soon. Luckily the ginger cookies didn't take long to prep or bake so she still had time to start preparing the coffee while they were in the oven.

She was grinding the beans as she heard footsteps coming into the kitchen behind her.

"Isn't this a surprise?!" She heard her mother say as she finished to move onto the next step.

"What is?" She asked somewhat knowing the answer already.

"You not having the coffee or biscuits ready yet," Ragna Frisk-Archer replied as she stepped further into the kitchen. "I haven't seen that happen in forever!" Rebecca said nothing as she concentrated on pouring the hot water in just the correct way, she'd long since lost count of the amount of times her great aunt had hit her knuckles after being served what she'd had considered to be "an inferior brewing process"; yes, Great-aunt Agnes was a cranky old woman, traits that luckily didn't pass onto her namesake.

Rebecca had always assumed it was because she never got laid and hoped that her younger sister would have better luck, like the rest of the women in the family.

"Is there a particular reason for this delay?" Ragna asked as she walked around to sit at the island she was working on; Rebecca had to truly repress her smirk at where the dirty line of thoughts had taken her. She continued to not say anything as she finished pouring, was still wordless as she pushed the cup over to Ragna before going over to retrieve the cream from the fridge, as the sugar was already at her mother's elbow.

There was nothing more than Rebecca wanted at that moment to avoid the gaze of her mom's piercing blue eyes.

"Is it because you forgot certain things last night?" Ragna's voice was casual as she added her extras. "Because of a certain man?" She took a sip, nothing about her demeanor changed, while Rebecca's tensed up, unable to deny it.

"I won't say anything," Ragna waved a hand. "You think you're the first in our family to have done something like this? The night before our first Saint Lucy feast, your dad and I had stayed up all night and ended up in a hotel…" Rebecca winced, she didn't need to hear something like this now.

"Anyway, while I remembered to get the supplies in the afternoon, I had to rush home at seven just to attempt to begin the saffron bread…I was just lucky that Aunt Agnes had a cold that year and had confined herself to her room, because she definitely wouldn't have been as understanding as your grandma was." Ragna took another sip.

"Too bad she seemed as healthy as ever last night," Rebecca muttered as she peeked into the oven to check on the cookies' status.

"Like I keep telling your father, she'll die someday," Ragna said casually. An average person would have flinched at hearing a parent say such a thing, but Rebecca was used to this kind of talk from her mother, and it wasn't like she could deny that she had similar feelings. She also wasn't surprised that her father was annoyed enough to pester her mom about it, she never had to ask, she'd overheard a conversation about it.

'Yeah, what dad had really hoped out of this relationship was just the five of us.' "These look like they're on the verge of burning…" she said aloud before she reached over to grab the oven mitts and cooling racks.

"It's just something to keep in mind for the future…" Ragna replied, almost amused at how flimsy her daughter's attempts to ignore her. "Anyway, what time will your friends be arriving?"

"Max said that they were going to be leaving around ten and hopes to be here by one," Rebecca replied as she moved the cookies onto the rack. *'Unless Alicia keeps changing her mind about what color eyeshadow to wear,'* she tramped down the annoyance that came with the thought, even if it was true.

"It's so nice that it's your turn to bring guests to the feast this year!" Ragna said chirpily. "It's been such a long time since either your father or I had a break for that!"

"Yeah, cause dad's a real social butterfly." She muttered as she put the empty baking sheet in the sink to wash for the saffron bread. "I thought you enjoyed bringing people home?"

"Of course, I love talking to people! If I didn't, I wouldn't have met your father!" Ragna said before draining the rest of her coffee. Rebecca knew without needing to turn around that she was eyeballing the cookies, but was following her common sense of not reaching for something that was still that hot.

"It's just that this reminds me of how much time has passed," Ragna's voice turned wistful. "You're a woman now, with friends and a relationship. Before I know it, it will be Aggie's turn, and then C.J.'s. Then it will be my grandkids…"

"Please don't," Rebecca said as the sink finished filling up and turned around to let it soak for a moment, and she saw her mother pick up a cookie and take a bite, the latter's eyes were closed in bliss.

"I will never get tired of eating these," Ragna said after she swallowed. "Nothing about this family recipe has changed in many years, it reminds me so much of my childhood in Stockholm."

"You've said that every year since I've been learning to do this by myself." Rebecca pointed out.

"Because I'm so proud of you for helping to uphold our traditions," Ragna replied. "I still remember how reluctant my parents and aunt were about leaving Sweden with your father to America, how concerned they were about you children; but I never doubted for a moment that you would make us proud."

"We'll soon see," A croaky voice muttered from the doorway and both women nearly jumped as they turned to the voice. Rebecca held back a groan as she took her cue to begin to make another handmade cup of coffee.

"Good morning, Aunt Agnes!" Ragna said chirpily with a frozen smile as she rose from her chair in greeting. Rebecca could hear the ancient woman's footsteps hobble over to the chair that her mom had vacated, she put her presence out of her mind as she concentrated on making the coffee, even as she heard the chair scraping and the sound of a cookie being bit into.

"At least the biscuits are as passable as they always have been," Agnes groused. "Still, its taste feels kind of rushed and not made with as much care…" Rebecca was saved from forming a reply by some noise coming from the hallway outside.

"You ran into me first!" Her sister Aggie was heard saying.

"I did not!" Her brother C.J. indignantly replied.

Rebecca could only sigh as she looked at the kitchen clock and saw that it was almost nine already, meaning that it was only a matter of time that her dad and grandparents would be up to congregate for their morning treats.

But first, she went to the fridge to retrieve orange juice for her siblings, keeping her mental fingers crossed that she would be able to maintain her sanity until Max and the others got there. Despite being used to it all, the excitement of seeing her boyfriend after so many days of being back home and only phone calls between them was quickly welling up.

'Just need to pretend it's an average day,' she thought as she pulled out the carton and went about her morning on autopilot.

#

'For fuck's sake!' Max inwardly yelled as he looked at his phone clock to see that it was almost eleven and none of the women were ready yet.

"What the hell is taking them so long?" He heard Bobby whine from the passenger side. "We've been here almost an hour and a half now!"

"I'll call and ask," Max snapped just the dorm doors opened and he saw them appear.

"Finally!" Bobby shouted as the trio sauntered their way to the car and entered the backseat, barely getting their seatbelts on before Max pulled away.

"Hey!" Alicia shouted. "What gives?!"

"We were supposed to leave at ten, I even arrived a half an hour early and called you to remind you of that!" Max replied sourly.

"Chill out Max," Chloe said. "We just wanted to look our best!"

"Couldn't you have figured it all out that last night so you wouldn't have had to take as long?!" Max was in no mood for excuses. "Now we just might be late!"

"Why's he so uptight about this?" Diane asked turning to Bobby.

"He's meeting her family for the first time," Bobby explained. "I don't know why he even wants to bother anyway."

"What's that supposed to mean?" Max gritted out as he tightened his hands on the steering wheel if only to keep himself from reaching over and strangling his so-called friend.

"I'm just saying that it just seems a little mean that you're getting her hopes up like this," Bobby said casually, much to Max's confusion. He sighed before continuing. "Max, how long are you going to keep up the pretense of being in a relationship with her?"

"What pretense?" Max asked irritably, hoping that Bobby would get the hint and shut up, but of course he didn't.

"You seriously don't like her right? I mean she is a little weird…" Bobby continued and a quick glance in the mirror told Max that none of the women were going to jump in and refute his statement. Alicia not doing so didn't surprise him, considering the advances that she'd made toward him lately, but the others disappointed him.

"I'm not in the mood to deal with anyone's shit right now!" Max suddenly yelled. "Let's just be quiet!" No one dared to disobey him, so the drive remained silent.

#

"Nice digs!" Bobby breathed as they arrived at the Archer mansion. "Now I see why you're with her!"

'Damn it Bobby!' "Just keep your mouth shut while we're inside," Max said with exasperation. "If your antics get us kicked out, I will kill you!"

"Fine mom," Bobby replied with a roll of his eyes. No one wanted to test his patience, his voice certainly sounded like he would kill them if they stepped out of line. It could wait until they left. Max had barely raised his fist to knock when the door suddenly flew open and Rebecca's smiling face greeted them.

'She must have been waiting by the door,' Max thought. Part of him was annoyed that this meant that they really must have made her wait, but he also felt warmth from the fact that she was so eager to see him, no them, that she waited by the door. Not wanting to ruin the mood, he plastered on a half-genuine smile for her.

"Becky!" He exclaimed before he pulled her into a hug, his anger was somewhat disappearing as she returned it and buried her face into his neck and feeling the cold get to him when she separates from him.

#

Rebecca had been checking her watch every five minutes after the clock in the hall had chimed that it was one o'clock. Her mother must have sensed her agitation as she turned her attention away from separating her fighting siblings.

"Rebecca, why don't you go and greet our guests when they arrive?!" She managed to shout over the cacophony.

"Okay!" She shouted back and took her leave without hesitation. However, her irritation returned the longer she waited for them to show up and she knew who the ones at fault were.

'I just hope that Max doesn't crash the car on purpose out of frustration,' she sighed. The fact that he even had a temper at all was something that he kept well hidden. She certainly had been startled the first time it came out, when Max had all but drop-kicked a guy that had groped her ass during a campus party.

Startled, but not scared, when he'd finished, he'd simply grabbed her arm, gently, and escorted her out of the party. No, she knew he would never hurt her, if anything his reactions reminded her of her father.

Unfortunately, the more time that passed, the more she became concerned that that scenario had indeed come true, or that they got stuck in the snow or got lost. Her phone clock indicated that it was five minutes to two that she finally saw Max's familiar black Corolla, which contrasted quite well against all the white outside. She witnessed everyone emerge and saw Bobby's lips move and Max get upset and say something back, no doubt Bobby had said something stupid.

'I guess I'll greet them now,' she decided, placing her hand on the doorknob as she saw them come up the walkway. Feeling cheeky, she pulled open the door as soon as she saw Max about to knock and greeted him warmly.

'Wow, he really must have had a hard time with them! I think I'm in danger of having my ribs crushed!' She gently extricated herself from his embrace and put on her usual fake smile.

"Hi guys!" She ran over and gave each of them a brief hug. "What took you so long? I was so worried!" She could practically feel the glare that Max was aiming at them, and she pretended not to notice their flinches.

"Traffic!" Alicia managed to get out. "There are just so many people on the road today!" Rebecca didn't believe her, but knew that she had to let it go.

"It is the Christmas holidays," she said pleasantly. "Come on, let's get inside before you lose your chance for some cookies." She beamed before she headed back to Max and grabbed his arm to pull him inside.

#

"That smells good!" Max said as he did indeed smell the heavy scent of ginger in the air.

"Thanks!" Rebecca said as she removed her boots. "I made them myself; my mom's family is Swedish and it's the tradition over there."

"How?" Chloe asked from her position in the rear.

"I'm the oldest daughter, I've been doing it since I've been able to hold a mixing spoon," she explained as she removed her last boot. "The family is to be woken up to handmade coffee and baked goods, while wearing this…" She stood up straight and opened her arms wide. It was only then that Max finally noticed that it was only her boots that she came out in, no jacket.

"You must be freezing!" Max said as he struggled with his jacket, wanting to go over to her.

"It's not a big deal!" She said with a laugh. "I'm used to it! It comes from having two younger siblings that like to play truth or dare!" She didn't elaborate as she practically flew down the long hallway and through an open arch on the side.

"Wow," Alicia breathed. "I would put a bullet in my head before I would willingly wear something like that." Max pinched his face.

"I think she looks cute," he said. *She really does look good in white.*' It was a beautiful dress, all white with a red sash, with those silky looking white stockings and the impressive candle filled crown on her head. It wasn't long before everyone saw her come running back, a large plate being held in her hands.

"I managed to snag some," she said breathily as she stopped in front of them and put it in front of them. "Sorry if it's not enough, I'll just make some more for you guys another time!" They each grabbed a cookie from the plate and began eating.

"These are great!" Max said enthusiastically. *'Never get anything this good at my house!'*

The others only made noises of agreement as they finished theirs, Rebecca excitedly bounced a little in place with a huge smile.

"Just follow me guys!" She said before she turned and started walking again. For Max, each step made him more nervous. She'd complained in the past about her Great-Aunt Agnes, who she'd described as a "cranky old bag" and occasionally about her dad and his overprotectiveness.

Max could only breathe slowly as she led them to the living room.

#

Max held back his groans of aggravation as he caught Bobby eyeballing Becky's mom, and he knew exactly what he was thinking too.

'That's one hot milf,' Max felt his skin crawl just thinking about it. Mrs. Archer was a perfectly nice lady, beautiful with a slight Swedish accent, it would be easy to picture her as an older version of Becky. A quick glance out of the corner of his eye proved to him that he wasn't the only who noticed Bobby being inappropriate, and it was the last man that he wanted to piss off.

'Aw man!' He shifted his eyes away from Mr. Archer's steely gaze and swept over the rest of Becky's

family. Great-Aunt Agnes was just as Becky had described her, full of sour and spite; but her grandparents, Olaf and Saga, were seemingly down to earth people and her siblings were just like any other kids, apparently it was much to Agnes' chagrin.

'I wish she was beside me,' he thought ruefully as he sipped the coffee that she had prepared. He could swear that it tasted better than usual, it…comforted him, he certainly wouldn't expect this kind of special treatment at his house. But Becky was helping her grandmother with dinner preparations, leaving him with a slight feeling of envy as his attention turned back to her parents who were huddled up together as everyone talked.

#

"Your friends seem to be…the perfect guests." Grandma Saga told her granddaughter.

"They are, aren't they?" Rebecca replied as she began to form the meatballs.

"And your first boyfriend!" Saga gushed as she heaved the pot onto the stove. "I've hoped since the day that you were born that I would live to see you carry on our traditions like this!"

"Grandma, I've been carrying on the traditions since I was old enough to do so," she said as she took a look at the clock before she carried the tray of meatballs to the fridge.

"You know what I mean dear!" Saga said as she combined the orange juice, sticks of cinnamon, sugar and the orange quarters that had already been prepped with cranberries and cloves.

"I'm just a little concerned about how this is going to end," she said as she made her way over and took the potatoes from their cupboard.

"It will work itself out dear," Saga said turning the heat on. "It did for your mother and for me when we brought our men home, if you are anything like us, you picked a good man that will be a benefit for our family."

'But it didn't work out for Aunt Agnes,' she thought ruefully as she tried to concentrate on cutting the potatoes with losing a fingertip. "Yeah well, it isn't up to me, is it?" She pointed out, her grandmother's face became pensive.

"No, it isn't dear, it's up to *her*."

#

As everyone finally sat down to dinner, Rebecca couldn't help but think back on her college life and how it had led up to this point.

At first, despite the bravado that she had shown to her family, she had been a nervous wreck at being so far from home just to go to her dream school and being away from their (for the most part) comforting embrace.

Meeting Max during that freshman orientation had eased her somewhat, only tolerated Bobby's presence because of Max and becoming friends with Alicia, Chloe and Diane helped ease her homesickness, but not for the reason that one might think. And it was for that reason that she even invited them over for this year's St. Lucy feast, giving them the impression that it was tradition. That wasn't a lie exactly, her feast was celebrated this way…except for what was to come during dinnertime, that was something that her family kept under tight wraps, and only prospective partners would discover just how deep the tradition ran…if they got through dinner.

'Hopefully grandmother is right, and it will work out, like her and mother,' Rebecca couldn't help but reach a hand to her neck and discreetly rub the St. Lucy

medallion that she was wearing for the occasion. Unlike other people, she knew that praying to the saint was useless, rather she was praying for a positive outcome in general.

For the first time in her life, the smell of their traditional feast turned her stomach. Now that everything was served and everyone was seated, Diane asked the inevitable question:

"What's this for?" She had picked up a cloth that everyone had on their plates.

#

Max had felt the air change as soon as they had all entered the dining room and he didn't like it. As good as the spread looked, and smelled, the hairs that stood up on the back of his neck refused to relax. He felt robotic as he and the other guests were directed to sit at chairs that had water glasses, the seats that went to Becky and her siblings also had water in front of them, but the rest of the family had glasses of reddish liquid in them.

"It's mulled wine," Becky had whispered, as if sensing his curiosity, before she'd had to separate from him to join her family on the side of the table opposite them, much to his disappointment.

'I guess they aren't sure if any of us are old enough to drink,' he just shrugged it off; but what he couldn't shrug off was that terrible feeling that this might be his last meal, and the cloth on his plate, which turned out to be a blindfold, didn't help matters.

#

The so-called 'game', which Max had his doubts about, consisted of them being left in different rooms and waiting to be found by the family. There were only two rules, one was to stay in their chosen room and the other was to never remove their blindfold until someone did it for them, the winner was the one who took the longest to be found.

'Pretty big risk they're taking, letting people wander around their place like this,' Max noted as he tried to find a place to stay in. He suddenly found himself in a certain wing, and he managed to avoid staring at how nicely decorated the hall was.

'Are these for guests, or is this the family bedrooms?' His palms began to sweat a little at the possibility of intruding into a room that was that private. His steps forward were careful, as he looked for anything that could indicate who occupied which room, it was to his relief that the last three doors had indications that they belonged to Becky and her siblings. The last door, closest to the window, had a painting of a begonia hanging on it, and he knew that this had to be her room.

"My grandmother is a talented painter," she once told him. *"Many people came to buy her work in Stockholm, but she stopped when they moved here. But she picked it back up again after I was born and started selling again when she came out of the dinosaur era and discovered the joys of online galleries. The first painting that she did was of a begonia plant, I proudly have it hanging on the front of my bedroom door."*

"Are begonias even native to Sweden?" He'd asked.

"I know that there's a plant called a 'Swedish Begonia', but that's native to countries south of the equator." She'd replied. *"When I asked her why, she only laughed and said that its meaning is supposedly special to our family, whatever that meant."*

Part of him regretted not looking up the begonias' meaning now.

'I'm sure she won't mind if I hide in her room, right?' He hoped as he slowly turned the knob and opened the door and entered. He took a moment to look around and appreciate her room before he put on his blindfold. After what felt like a short time, he heard the door open and close. He felt a hand touch his cheek, a feminine one, and he almost leaned into the touch...until he smelt that cloying perfume.

"Alicia," he hissed lowly. "What the fuck do you think you're doing?"

"Aww c'mon Max," he heard her purr. "We're all alone and when opportunity knocks..."

"I let this go the last time because you were drunk," he told her coldly. "Now, you have no such excuse. When have I ever given you a hint that I was even the slightest bit interested in you?"

"Who doesn't want me?" She replied and tried to reach for him again, but he sensed the air movement and ducked away again.

"Alicia," his tone was firm. "I'm warning you, if you don't turn around and leave right now, I might make a mess in the room."

"Sounds promising," she said, and he felt her body come close to his and he had just moved away again when the first scream was heard. They both froze as another sounded, then another, until the number reached everyone but the two of them.

'What the hell?' He wondered as he carefully moved away from her. His glance around the room earlier had given him a rough idea of where the obstacles were and he pressed his advantage by carefully moving, hopefully away from her, and didn't stop until he reached the corner of the room that was between her bed and the window.

There was no sound, save for Alicia's heavy breathing, Max managed to stay quiet by biting into the flesh of the back of his hand. Suddenly, the air in the room changed, despite the screaming and Alicia's antics, it had been still, but now…he wasn't quite sure how to describe it, only that there was something bad that had now come into the room without the door opening.

'One…two…three…' he had no idea why he decided to count the seconds, but it kept his mind occupied as he seemingly waited for…something. After ten seconds had passed, he heard Alicia speak.

"What the-" she was suddenly cut off by her own scream of pain; causing Max to flinch but still didn't make a sound, even after he felt a cold draft come towards him.

'Just stay still!' He commanded himself even after he began to feel what felt like icy fingers run along his blindfold, almost curiously studying him. After what felt like eternity, the fingers removed themselves and every strange sensation suddenly vanished from the room, like the very air sucked it out. With much trepidation, he didn't untie the blindfold, but pushed it up his head enough for him to see that Alicia was just lying on the floor haphazardly.

Against his will, his feet took him towards her; despite the darkness of the room, he could see that there were dark stains on the floor in front of her, her blindfold on it. Avoiding the mess, he eventually saw her face, he could only guess that her eyes were wide open…considering that they were gone.

'I should be horrified and scared…but I'm just relieved. I guess I should wait and see what happens next.' He walked back over to his corner and pulled the blindfold back down and only continued to stay there and wait.

#

"Perhaps your young man has indeed been spared," Great Aunt Agnes croaked from her seat in the living room.

"Nevertheless, the feast was still a success," Grandmother Saga said calmly. "Surely, she can now perform many miracles this year."

"It wasn't as difficult as my first gathering," Agnes begrudgingly admitted. "Rebecca…you have done well."

"I am glad you believe that," Rebecca said primly as she tramped down the glow she felt from her praise.

"I guess all that's left is to see if he's going to help with the cleanup," her father grumbled.

The Man Who Hated Halloween
By B.K. Crafton

It was late October when the wind began to really pick up and the brownish leaves started to shed upon the well-maintained lawn of one, George Mainyard, that the pleasant old man decided to do what he had the last two years prior. He cursed himself for putting it off this long, but when you are pushing seventy and the twilight of your best years are sinking in the far horizon of what had barely amounted to a dip in the chasmic bowl of life compared to the many things you wanted to achieve, then things don't always get done when you plan on them getting done.

And spare me all that well-worn rigamarole of age just being a number, he thought. Age *is* everything. It's why the rickety joints in his knees moaned their distress on each occasion he got off the couch, and it's why it now, to this day, felt like a drunkard's morning after when he hadn't gone out the night before. Yes, it was true with age came wisdom, but it also came with a complement of ills, aches, and, above all else, that dark, insidious feeling of uncertainty. How much longer did he have until the grim reaper acknowledged him and laid its cold, bright, skeletal hand on his shoulder? He didn't know, which is why George needed to get his old bones in high gear. There was much work to be done.

George Mainyard opened the door to the basement, withered boots on creaking steps, making his way down. As a young boy he could remember being too frightened to dare tread in such dark spaces on his lonesome. His older brother, Howard saw to that, by sharing with him awful tales about monsters and a ghostly madman waiting to sweep him off the stairs and swallow young George into the darkness. Ready to pierce him with a pickaxe, slice him open using a rusty straight razor, and decorate the basement walls with his wet, juicy insides.

"He'll hit ya with the pickaxe a few times, and then finish ya off with his rusty razor blade!" he chimed while giving the air a terrible slashing motion.

And the way Howard said it, it felt all the more real. His matter of fact and straight-line diction bore no semblance to good-natured goading or mere teasing to get a rise from him. No, the monster waiting in that dank pit *was* real and ready to gnaw on his guts for disturbing it, and worse, a crazy man *was* waiting there too. His trusty pickaxe in hand and ready to tear apart little boy flesh with his other sinister implement. But it was nonsense; a wealth of years had passed since his sibling's awful tales and obnoxious hectoring. George had survived two bouts of pancreatic cancer, been married thrice, suffered through two back surgeries, one heart attack, and retired from his job at Blake Plastics, a respected senior advisor and a gentleman.

Yet…he never would have fessed up to it, but Howard Mainyard's words had left an indelible impression that never quite healed. The effect of his brother's words far outpacing and outliving the lips which spoke them so, so many years ago.

Born four years apart, they were never close, and once Howard turned eighteen, he enlisted in the army, just in time for the First World War. The unlucky fool died overseas on his initial tour of duty.

"The bastards killed him! They took my boy…took him right away, oh Martha, why?"

Their dad, Howard Senior, began to weep right after the Western Union carrier with the little policeman-style cap handed him the notice, and their mother followed suit. The sight sickened him. Good riddance, teenage George mused. Maybe now I'll get some of their elusive love and stop hearing the effusive praise for the obvious favorite. However, to this day, he'd never say such disrespectful things out loud, and George would have liked to believe it was due to respect for his parents, but it ran deeper, as deep as his own blood.

Issuing these kinds of bare emotions out loud might bring Howard Mainyard back, not back from the grave though, after all dead is dead, but it could serve as a catalyst of sorts and bring him really back into his mind. Stirring up more memories—the type of thankfully faded memories which could grow within and crawl underneath the folds of his consciousness and nest there while haunting his sleep.

George realized that there was a stark difference between when you yourself were the one responsible for dredging up these images, giving them the all-too-essential first gasp of breath they required and when they had been imposed by some other source. *Stop it old man.* There was no reason to give his brother the satisfaction of chasing an old ghost, and no further reason to put off what needed to be done.

It took a minute for his eyes to adjust, and he still had trouble finding the light switch when they finally did. He groped along the walls, found the plastic lever and pushed up. The basement flooded with light. What he sought was next to the old Maytag washer and dryer set: two rows of boxes stacked three high and written in bold black lettering, HALLOWEEN DECORATIONS.

George bent down, easy does it, and felt a pop in his right knee. Despite the pain, he lifted a box from the first stack. Carrying the damn things upstairs was never not a problem, and this year it was a much bigger chore. Hopefully, this would be the last time he had to bother with the painful but salient ritual. And if all went according to plan, it would be.

He spent a good hour loading and then unloading these special wares, taking a small break to tip a cold one and eat a small lunch. The rat cheese, saltines and cold cuts gave him the boost of energy necessary to finish the task. He stripped off the masking tape, opened each box, and then stood back to admire their seasonal contents. In his living room now stood six cardboard receptacles full of holiday fear, and the kiddies loved every bit of it. A lot of money paid to make his the most inviting house on the block. Each year he added more stuff—there could never be enough. In the end it would be worth the financial expenditures, not a single doubt.

"Step right up you little monsters," George grinned.

And they were monsters. Oh, they weren't the fanged, red-eyed beasties hiding under the bed, raised strictly from fiction and fantasy, and the masks they wore might have been cute indeed, but George *knew* the naked truth. Truths even their gullible parents didn't see, and those who did acknowledge those inklings shrugged it off as

"Just kids being kids." George knew better, knew more than they could ever know, in fact.

Yes, facts that couldn't be denied, and facts he wasn't foolish enough to share with anyone else. If he did, they'd say that he was a weird conspiracy theorist, perhaps, or even plain crazy, and George was neither. No, he kept his mouth shut and played dumb to lull the monsters and their imprudent parents into a false sense of security. Remain silent and feign a smile; people never suspect the kind old man who didn't cause a stir when the little hooligans trampled his rose bushes and "accidentally" busted out the side window of his house. So nonsensical, only it wasn't some baseball that happened to get away from the batter. It was a goddamn rock.

"We are so sorry, let us pay for it Mr. Mainyard."

"They didn't mean it, kids will be kids," the parents would say or some other variation excluding their little ones from taking on any form of accountability.

He'd heard the same song over and over, ad nauseam. His replies never deviated, and he never believed the artificial sincerity of their supposed apologies.

"Pay for what, an accident? No real harm done, like you said, just kids being kids," he lied.

Why, what kind of neighbor would he be if he allowed them to dole out their hard-earned money over a simple mistake? Not a very good one, he continued the pandering. It's nice to have youngsters around, neighborhood's been too quiet for too long. He put on a good charade, but inside he raged.

The damn nerve! How naive of them to think slates could be so easily wiped clean with an apology and a petty financial exchange. Concepts such as effort and honest-to-goodness toil were foreign notions to this new breed of parentage and people. Gardening and lawn care were not tireless endeavors. What an insult to believe he could be bought off. What did he really expect, though? This was nineteen eighty–five not nineteen fifty–five, back when ideals like respect, morals, work ethic, and personal accountability were the standards expected of a fruitful lifestyle and not the nihilistic, morally bankrupt hedonism of today. Oh, what a world to be cleansed! Dirty, dirty world!

His precious Netherton was part of that world; the small rural town he'd called home for so many years had gone from a slice of heaven into a big basket of hell in a handcart. A decline that came by way of vacuum because there were no stages of infancy. No tell-tale signs Netherton was soon to be a cesspool. One day it was like a strange hand passed over and the God-fearing town he cherished had adopted a new hideous identity.

God Fearing.

Bizarre choice of words considering his general irreligious stance on most any topic broaching that particular subject. But, he'd never be too stubborn as to not admit things were better when people held such base fears, no matter how silly, of an omnipresent force which ruled over all close to their hearts and their souls closer to the edge of that perfect ideation of heaven.

Just because one didn't pray or make Sunday trips to so-called houses of God didn't mean they couldn't sense, nor see the outright evil in front of them. Demons were real. They needn't originate from biblical fantasy and spiritual gobbledygook as some sort of tangible proof. It was what the word represented that was important. Evil. Evil was real and so were demons, and so were the oblivious responsible. Big-shit city dwellers that were tired of the crowds, tired of the constant hustle and bustle of the neon jungles they created and wanted more than a taste of Netherton's small-town charm. Not content to destroy their own habitats, they felt the need to spread the sickness.

And spread they would, like locusts attaching themselves to a healthy crop. Every empty house and newly renovated property they could purchase they did, all the while bringing their repugnant and self-indulgent lifestyles with them. Children followed shortly thereafter, which at first caused no alarm, however, once the babies began to mature, the troubles really started. They were just little things, but they had an enormous impact on George. Leaving their big wheels, bicycles, and other playthings in the middle of the streets and sidewalks. Sports contests without proper equipment or strict adult supervision, which explained rocks being substituted for baseballs, and a myriad of other dumb made up-games that resorted in various types of property damage.

All that being said, Halloween was the absolute worst, no doubt about it. The miniature hellraisers went far beyond the normal mishaps and petty vandalism associated with the act of kids being kids. Toilet papering trees, bombing houses with eggs, soaping windows, and even knocking over mailboxes—these were small samples of the terror they inflicted on his beloved neighborhood, and what purpose did it serve? They weren't given their fair share of treats? No, as always, George knew better. He saw things most couldn't or refused in perfect clarity. The harsh, unyielding truth was they did it for fun, taking great pleasures over their devilish exploits.

October 31st became an invitation to cause real trouble, and these brats were happy to oblige. Why should anyone expect anything better or be the least bit surprised? The parents had seemingly lost all control; those who didn't ignore each incident or granted them the shallowest justifications for their actions. What was to happen when the monsters grew up to their full potential? The answer was plain as day: they'd graduate from "harmless" pranks and immature mischief into darker criminal activities. Drug usage and dealing, home invasions, and muggings becoming the norm. Soon the entire block on Farris Road would fulfill its disgusting promise and transform into a crime-ridden slum. The parents, again bound by nepotism, would, of course, continue the trend of making excuses for their precious dears.

But that could only become a certainty if they were given the chance to blossom, if he could well…cut the root beforehand, then his quaint little neighborhood, indeed all of Netherton, had a slim chance to be saved. He just needed a solution, and George discovered it ironically sewn into the very fabric of the holiday that the kiddies revered the most: Halloween itself.

The answer materialized two years ago. It was a typical Monday; George was running his normal beginning of the week errands. A stopover at First National Bank, and his weekly grocery shopping at the Right Stop Food Mart before returning home to settle for the night. He was stuck in aisle five, trying to make the life-altering decision of having to choose between creamy or crunchy peanut butter, when he heard a commotion.

A youngster's high-pitched screech resounded through the spacious store. George rolled his shopping cart towards the repeated yowling, keeping his distance. A peek into the next aisle revealed a kid crying as if he had taken forty lashes, while his poor, suffering mother held tight to a candy bar, shaking it and admonishing him for throwing such an exaggerated fit. The answer came in a flash, it was so simple, he'd incorporate a trick into the very treats themselves. The ultimate prank!

Not right away, though. He had to establish a few things first.

Luckily, he'd never been the cantankerous old geezer which made a ruckus or fussed about a loose ball or frisbee landing in his yard. No, he'd keep his cool and hand them back to the offender. He would dress as a clown for children's birthdays or visit them at hospitals if they needed cheering up, and he even volunteered his services as good ol' jolly Saint Nick at United First Methodist. Generous acts, all free of charge, that went a long way to create trust from the parents and children alike. Anything to come across as the perfect neighbor and a good Samaritan, and anything to hide his true intentions.

Admittedly, such unabashed generosity was an odd personality shift for the rather introverted, though kind, old man. The townspeople, to his relief, said and suspected nothing. These tikes weren't the only ones capable of putting on a good disguise.

Poor health choices pushed his back against the wall, and he knew time was growing shorter, but he had no choice except to play the long game here.

George began phase one.

His benign one-story ranch home became something more during the past two Octobers. The vacant square (though well-manicured lawn) became littered with Styrofoam tombstones and prop skeleton arms bursting out of the ground. The house itself was bedecked with spooky lighting, countless props, paper cutouts, full-bodied skeletons and homemade ghosts fashioned out of actual bed sheets hanging from the big elm tree that stood resolutely in the middle of the yard, and all the additional

Halloween trimmings one could hope for. No expense was spared.

He also had to admit feeling a tad silly when bringing these morbid purchases to the counter at Ray's Drugs each year and had to field a few questions concerning the items while fishing out his billfold.

His mask answered for him.

"Oh, you know, I just want to give these kids a real Halloween. Something they'll always remember." The lips moved, but were disingenuous at their core.

Ray, who might as well have lived at his place of business, gave him a genial smile and said it was a great thing to do for the children. George agreed and went about his way.

Phase two meant giving the brats not only the most enjoyable experience when they visited his house, but the best Halloween loot as well. All the finest and expensive candies dished out in huge plastic novelty bowls shaped like Frankenstein and Dracula heads. Handfuls of glorious sweets were permitted to outstretched, and grubby paws, as opposed to the one or two measly pieces being dispensed by the other residents on Farris Road.

"Plenty to go around, take all you like!" said the benevolent old man.

And for the past two years they did.

George peered at the boxes stacked in the living room, a thin smile extended to each sagged end. *Something they'll always remember.* Yes indeedy, and very soon.

The smile wasn't completely sincere; there was always the moral conflict to account for, wasn't there? After all, these were just children, no matter how you arranged or rearranged, for lack of a better word, the indisputable facts. Highly unlikely they realized what they were or what they would grow into if allowed to thrive. The eyes, though, or what was behind them, eroded any sense of responsibility or compassion. Beneath the innocent sparkle lay something different.

Something…malevolent.

George recognized the deception straight away, how could he not? For the eyes projecting their sinister aspirations were of his brother, because that's what each child was, pint-sized Howards and like his long-perished sibling, they too needed to be dealt with before it was too late. But unlike Howard, he didn't need to wait for fate to intervene. George himself would be the righteous hand to serve atonement.

Righteous hands.

Working hands.

Devil's hands?

No, helping hands.

There was not much time, so it was imperative he pick up the slack. Three days, tops, and he still hadn't even carved the Jack O' Lantern. Wisely, he had already bought the candy. Enough. The longer a person sat around thinking about what had to be done, the longer it would take for it to get done. He took his dishes to the sink, gave them a light rinse, dried his tired hands, then rolled up his flannel sleeves. It was time, no point putting it off for another minute.

Four and a half hours later, George Mainyard stood facing his front yard, exhausted on spaghetti legs and leaning against the mailbox for support. His pain-afflicted body reminded him of the reason behind the procrastination to begin with. Nevertheless, that didn't stop his self-admiration and looking at the house in estimable aplomb.

"Might as well be made of gingerbread," he remarked, gulping down the remainder of the warmed-over can of beer in his hand.

The October chill began to bite. George wiped the collected sweat from his brow and began to gather the empty boxes off the lawn. A young man who happened to be taking a jog offered to help. George politely declined and sent him on his way. Where was this noble charity earlier? Hell, where were any good Samaritans like himself during the strenuous process? He encountered only a couple pushing a stroller who gave him a timid wave as they passed and nothing else. Not that he would have accepted their aid, but still…

With his work finished for the day, George stowed the boxes in the corner of the living room, took off his boots, turned down the lights, and headed to his bedroom. Not bothering to change into his pajamas, he collapsed into bed.

Eyes shut, yet sleep did not come as normal. A single question sprouted from the fertile ground of his mind. Like an otherworldly earworm burrowing deep, his inner self began to vocalize.

Was saving Netherton really the goal, George?

He answered quickly, as if he were expecting this sudden intrusion.

Yes, why else would he formulate such a convoluted plan if not? Terrible events were set to unfold, and he was going to be the one solely responsible. A cross worth bearing though, no matter the weight, and on Halloween no less, a delicious irony he'd take great delight tasting. Sweet, like the candies he'd be handing out later.

"Come on, George, do you really believe that? We both know damn well there is something more going on here. Admit it."

He shot up from his bed. George's ears perked and his eyes darted back and forth, trying to perceive if what he heard was real.

"I think we both know what this is really about, don't we, Georgie?"

That *voice,* unmistakable, undeniable and hideously authentic. Howard Mainyard, once far and forgotten and silenced, now spoke to him. His presence felt barely ten feet away even though he was supposed to be six feet under. As if he'd been residing in the dark corner the whole time waiting to announce himself. Dark corner of his room and a darker corner in George's brain.

No!

This isn't happening, couldn't be happening—only it was, and the worst thing about it was that it came from the outside and not the inside. Not a manifestation conjured by a wayward mind in need of sleep, but an actualization whose presence couldn't be dismissed. Howard continued to babble. George had no intention of listening to his dead sibling's squawking. He clenched his eyes shut, put a pillow over his face, and started to press down on the soft clump. Pushing his thoughts into a void and trying to tune Howard out by sheer force of will. His temples pulsated and his teeth locked into a defiant sneer as he insisted on the voice's arrant removal.

A short while later, the voice of Howard and its assertions finally retreated. The quiet returned, and so did Geroge's grip on his sanity, and that's all it had been—a lapse, a brief and convincing intrusion forged by his own emotional guilt. It'd be quite abnormal if he didn't harbor such feelings, would it not? After all, he was about to perpetrate a very despicable, horrible act on poor, hapless children, and to a greater extent, their parents as well. Even with this acknowledgement, he remained one hundred percent committed to the odious deed.

A monster for certain if he didn't express proper form challenging this obvious moral dilemma. But he wasn't the monster; they were, and he must never be so naive as to forget or think otherwise.

"Has to be this way, one day left," he said before calming down and slipping back into his sheets for a good night's sleep.

George swore he heard a sound from the corner, but it faded out before his mind could access the actual source of the disturbance. Nothing there. Nothing there at all.

He awoke bright and early as always and began what had become a meticulous routine—or tried, for the specter of last night's episode tugged at him. George made his coffee a bit stronger and put a smidge more butter on his toast than usual. He had trouble reading the articles in the Netherton Herald when he fetched it off the porch stoop.

He switched the television onto the morning news and raised the volume higher than normal, then eased into his battered recliner. A reporter stood outside trying to get a grip on his microphone, a strong wind blew his wavy brown hair to and fro, giving the intrepid trench coat wearing man pause. Behind him was Mahlia Park, a nice local plot of land constructed for children and adults alike with plenty of swings, slides, walking trails, a giant playset for the kiddies and picnic areas.

Another gust of wind pushed through, then the reporter broke into his scripted spiel.

George stared at the television intently, picking up very little.

Howard Mainyard was endeavoring to make contact.

"So, remember to bring out the little ones. Mahlia Park is going to have all kinds of spooky Halloween activities, including an appearance by the Headless Horseman himself. You heard that right, the Headless Horseman made famous from the story The Legend of Sleepy Hollow will be—" A bigger gust of wind punched through. The reporter lost his happy thoughts for a moment; being a true professional, he soldiered on as if nothing occurred. "He will be showing up at Mahlia Park on steed and all to make this a Halloween your little trick-or-treaters will never forget. Not only that, but there will also be prizes, giveaways, a costume contest, and even a tractor ride. Don't forget, that's Mahlia Park located at—"

He turned off the television. George stepped onto his porch, needing some air. Fresh intakes as the morning sun beamed into his heavy-lidded eyes. The silence, save for his neighbor Scott Davis's dog Taz barking was palpable. He drank every ounce in; this the way it used to be (would still be) before the monsters arrived. Now the once serene block was inundated with the annoying and frustrating sound of children's play. The high rabble of young voices, and their racket cutting through the peace and tranquility that had been commonplace when he first planted roots.

Oh, how he longed for those days. George closed the door and opened his mind. He was aware that he wasn't the only one to have these particular thoughts. Many conversations were had and overheard with like-minded associates and the inhabitants of Farris Road, all hitting the same reverberant note. George, ever the amateur thespian, took the opposite stance if asked, not wanting to be exposed. Still, he wondered why the task had to fall on his elderly shoulders—not that he had any issue or dared to shirk the great responsibility bestowed on him, but it did seem a trifle unfair for a lone individual to have to bear the full brunt of this dire undertaking.

Naturally, he knew the reasoning: each man and woman to the last were all talk. They possessed no desire or the belly to take action. The spineless jellyfish were content to wallow in these miseries, whatever the price they'd eventually be forced to pay. And had a single one become aware of his plans; they would turn on him with less than a heartbeat's notice.

Hence, he kept his dark secrets, and after the big change happened, they could all keep their neighborhood. Was it fair? No, but that wasn't for either here nor there. George was more concerned with the next forty–eight hours than tussling over the idea of what was morally just and what wasn't.

The rest of the day was an uneventful one. He tried carving a pumpkin; the effort was solid, but the results were slipshod at best. He almost sliced his trembling hand during the process, as his once reliable digits capable of steel grip upon a time ago, were now ancient and turned against him, similar to how the rest of his geriatric frame had done. A bitter pill to swallow, one of many when heading towards the golden years and have no way to refuse its journey.

He finished the face of the Jack O' Lantern, as George Mainyard was never the type to leave a project undone, no matter how trivial it might seem, and sat it back on the porch unsatisfied. The grin was not jagged enough, and the triangles he'd cut for the eyes not even enough, but he'd be damned if he would spend another drop of exertion to rectify these slight imperfections. Just hollowing out the oversized gourd and scooping out the seeds and orange slime proved to be a real physical chore. One he hadn't counted on, leaving him drained.

Afterwards, he ate a small dinner of mashed potatoes and a leftover piece of fried chicken, watched some TV, and was astounded to look at the clock on the wall and see that it spelled that his normal bedtime had been surpassed by an hour. As the sun fell from its perch and surrendered its eminence to nightfall, George changed into his pajamas, took a piss, tossed his dentures into a glass of water, and slid into the king-sized comforter.

Turning off the lamp, the room was soon enveloped by darkness. He had no trouble sleeping. His final images before dimming out were the neighborhood children that he spied earlier as he hid behind the anonymity of his living room drapes. They trooped merrily along, some alone, the rest in pairs, and would stop at the entry to his driveway and point in uncontainable zeal with respect to the fun house he'd created for their enjoyment and ultimate elimination. Fully settled and comfortable, he waited for Howard's reanimated voice to emerge from the corner of his room like before, but no, nothing. His sleep was dreamless, and the night was silent.

George awoke four hours later than intended, and through blurred vision could see the red numerals on the alarm clock. The morning had passed, and it was closer to the afternoon.

Damn it! Damn it all to hell!

He rushed out of bed—well, as fast as his old bones afforded him. Much work was still at hand; the preparation alone would be taking a substantial chunk from his stratagem if he didn't hustle. He skipped lunch, for the kiddies would be letting out of school soon, and every minute he deemed valuable. George marched into the basement; the steps creaked, but the accompanying old childhood terrors and Howard's enforcement pertaining to those fears were a thousand miles away. Pulling the chain attached to the hanging fixture, the naked bulb opened the cloak of darkness.

He sat at his work bench, where a giant plastic punch bowl, (he'd misplaced the iconic monster heads), one glass container, and multiple bags of name-brand candy occupied the majority of space. A single medical syringe sat underneath a dry washcloth. He tore open a bag and poured it onto the wooden table, as a diabetic seeing the colorful candy laid out like loose puzzle pieces made him physically wince.

George picked up the syringe and stared at it for a moment before bringing close to him the glass container filled with a most deadly concoction. A right mixture he hoped, as a man blind to science and its many compounds there was no proper way to judge whether or not it would be a success. He took the syringe and jabbed it into the poisonous liquid, drawing a small amount that he deduced would be suitable, then brought a single piece of candy and the needle to unison. He folded a loose seam and peeled back the wrapper, securing the candy and injected the needle, carefully pressing the plunger until the full dose had been administered.

One down, many, many more pieces to go, he sighed. He worried his fingers might kink as the operation continued, but to his astonishment not so much as quiver. This devil's toil was being done in the most heavenly conditions. Not too long did he labor on the notion though, and he could only be thankful for its possible rare happenchance.

He advanced through the grueling, repetitive procedure until each bag was emptied and the oversized plastic bowl was filled to capacity. Not all the sweets were loaded with the lethal blend; there were various tarts, bubblegum, *Tootsie Rolls* and other assorted Halloween delights as well.

The task was finished, so George returned upstairs, rinsed the glass, and disposed of the syringe. He then went back downstairs to retrieve the bowl, halfway to the bottom, the basement door swung shut behind him. That wasn't so unusual. The door was old and heavy. *Just another thing to fix*, he thought, giving the matter no further consideration.

George gleamed at the colorful bounty with a malformed sense of pride and picked up the bowl, which was a bit heavier than one would think. The candies moved from side to side as he lifted the bowl for transport. He pulled on the chain, cutting off the light. Unbeknownst to George, the subtle jostling led to some of the candies accidentally spilling out onto the concrete floor. One step forward, with his treasure in tow and ready to ascend the stairs, George went crashing down in an instant. He smacked the back of his head against the ground, and a Stygian mouth swallowed him whole.

He came through an undefinable time later, still clothed in pajama bottoms and a plain white T-shirt. His head throbbed and hurt like the devil's own; it felt like he was laying on a sheet of ice, a bitter chill running up each arm. His eyes became accustomed to their surroundings, and it didn't take him long to put together his location. A small prism of light filtered onto his prone form. George stared upward and tried to turn his head, but to no avail. A dread rose within him, ugly and sincere. A single word emerged in a similar anxious tone.

Paralyzed?

No, couldn't be.

He moved his toes and found only the absolute numbness in his lower extremities as the whole truth that now settled over him. Panic had the opportunity, but George's mind stayed close to the rails of rational thought.

I'm in my basement. I remember trying to carry the bowl upstairs and somehow lost my footing.

The back of his head throbbed, causing him to grimace, and he again attempted to move. Nothing doing. A shaft of light shone onto him like a body outline traced at a crime scene; the source was from Scott Davis's porch, which meant it wasn't *too* late at night yet. His next-door neighbor never turned in for the night until the lights had been extinguished, and he never called it a night before ten o'clock or later.

Ah, a chance, perhaps even a great chance, that there were still trick-or-treaters making the rounds, and since he'd made his house the most desirable on not only the entire block but undoubtedly Netherton as a whole, this boded well for him. He could see the costumed little creeps and their parents stationed at the door, ringing the doorbell and wondering where the kind old geezer could possibly be.

Yes, this was feasible, no need for alarm. Just take a breath and wait…and wait he did. No way to judge with any real accuracy, but a solid guess would have him angling around twenty minutes, maybe a bit longer. Be patient and block out the pain. Any second the doorbell will sound, and I'll be able to yell for help, he told himself. But wait a minute, a cold line hooked into his mind and was ready to pull this hopeful scenario from the previous calm waters.

Would he be able to? Laying on his back and immobile, might that hinder his ability to churn out a cry for help? Only one way he'd find out. George opened his mouth, took a deep breath and forced a strong bellow that bounced off the basement walls, its echo resonated ever so briefly. Satisfied, George smiled. Then he remembered and the smile drooped to a worried O formation. The basement door was closed, wasn't it? No matter how many scores of trick-or-treaters paid a visit, George could scream himself hoarse, and they wouldn't be able to hear.

But you better believe I'm gonna shout myself mad if I hear that bell or knock at the door.

He made another go at rising off the cold concrete, but with the exception of some stubborn and slight movement from his arms and neck George remained stationary. It was a start, though, and right now he needed something—anything likened to encouragement.

He could see that various candies lay on his chest.

The forbidden candy.

A way out? Best not to think about it. Keep a level head and wait for that all- important sound.

Just be patient. Just have to wait.

Damn it, why did he have to divorce Barb? She might have been his third wife, but she would also have been the first to help him out of this awful predicament. And she never needed to know what he was doing, after all, George wasn't under any sort of obligation or anything to tell her his business. Not that she would have asked or cared, which was one of the main issues that led to the divorce—communication or lack thereof—well, that and the fact he'd become an overbearing asshole.

He could admit it now. At least it'd been an easy separation; he got the house while she got the car and damn near everything else, including her precious freedom. Freedom, she claimed he'd kept locked up in a gilded cage. So dramatic. She nagged him about how he was nothing more than an "Old buzzard that couldn't accept change." He replied that he had no problem with supposed change, by going from a married man to a bachelor. What a zinger; after divvying up their meager assets, she never talked to him again. That was fine with him, however, her assertions alluding to his inability to accept gradual changes never faded.

The unflinching truth George tried keeping at bay inched closer and closer as each year came and went, but his dear ex-wife hadn't been entirely right with her smug accusations. It wasn't so much he couldn't change; he just couldn't agree to these particular changes. It'd happened too fast; the world was rushing when it should have been realizing.

Realizing what they had already lost and what more they were bound to lose if life continued steaming ahead without impediment. Technology, for instance, the advances had happened so quickly that people didn't have the mental latitude to ponder if the new items, ideas, gizmos and gadgets would cause more harm than good when it was all said and done. As long as it meant instant gratification, the mindless hordes marched to technology's artificial and persistent drumbeat.

Not George: he was too smart and much too careful for that. Let the rats march in lockstep and dance for the corporate pied pipers all the way to the edge of the cliff, and then jump to their inevitable destruction. He'd sit and watch from afar, unaffected by its sweet, saccharine allure, whilst his friends and unsuspecting neighbors welcomed the shiny new toys.

No worries, because he'd stand watch over the trusting lemmings. George the wise old owl had to do it for their own good. Time, however, was running short, and this final act to ensure the poor souls of Netherton had an opportunity at survival was in dire jeopardy. All of it owed to some loose candy escaping out of the big plastic bowl and onto the concrete floor. What rotten luck, and such irony. Nothing sweet about it, though. Just bitter.

He went to move again, nothing doing, not so much a twitch of progress. The frustration was building as each minute ticked by. Damn it, where were the little bastards? There didn't need to be a whole gaggle of them or anything. A single trick-or-treater would do the job, and just one chubby digit pressing on the doorbell. Why, he could even see them on the porch, and with better clarity.

The boy or girl, as George made no distinctions, dressed up in shabby clothes and a flimsy hockey mask like that Jason guy who prowled the late-night features on the TV or the strange character wearing the striped sweater and metal fingernails. Quite a few of those types showed up at the door last Halloween, and he imagined this year would be no different. Pillowcases and multicolored bags clutched in their grubby mitts, ready for the bounty of goodies sure to come from a house so inviting. Mom or dad off to the side, grinning happily and enjoying their child's or children's October excursions. Big white smiles, but he wondered if those pearls would be as bright if they were made aware of the actual meaning behind Halloween.

These would-be parents were obviously fabrications delved from the thicket of his imagination, but what they represented was all too real. He was confident the real parents who allowed their children to celebrate such an odious "holiday" were oblivious of its true origins. Not George, though, for he could claim to be not only a cultured man but a well-studied gentleman as well. It started by first peeling back the most deceptive layer, the very name itself. The real name of the holiday, if you prefer to call it that, was not Halloween, but All Hallows' Eve (All Saints Eve if that was your pleasure, most certainly not Geroge's), and it had nothing to do with kids parading door to door in outrageous costumes and asking for candy by way of threat.

The truest origin lay in the Celtic festival of Samhain; during this ominous gathering, the souls of those who died would return home, and the spirits of the recently deceased began their journey to the otherworld. Massive bonfires were lit on the steep hilltops across the old country to frighten away the wayward and evil specters, and you can guarantee with this kind of bizarre fountainhead, the so-called harmless holiday pranks and wearing of masks was hiding something not so innocent and altogether more horrendous.

"I hate Halloween," George expelled in a guttural breath.

His blunt anger twisted into a sharp panic once the glow from his neighbor's porch went out. The single spirit of light was extinguished, and the room was captured by total darkness. George's mind and calming sense of self began to break apart like a crystal glass that'd been shattered on the ground. Cold, unfettered reality grabbed him and started squeezing. How long until someone noticed that he was missing? How long could he realistically hope to survive without food, water, or critical aid? No, we must not despair. The capacity was there, but George reminded himself not to panic. Stay calm and stay regular. It was the only way of getting through this.

That was perfectly sensible, and he had to adopt what logical thinking could provide him right now. If he refused, the situation would get worse in a hurry. His stomach growled. He ignored it. The uneven requirement of finding sleep in such a cold and uncomfortable environment weighed upon him. He fought the urge, but a short time later he was in its numbing embrace.

George awoke to the sound of a man's voice, faint and a few feet above him. He was still half asleep but recognized its source and the urgent course of action necessary.

"Help! For God's sake, help me!" he yelled, ignoring his general distaste for religion and insistent pain, hoping his next-door neighbor would hear his invigorated pleas.

The voice paused.

Did he hear him?

No, Scott Davis had only ceased because he was waiting for a reply, and said voice continued once he got the desired response. Then the screen door shut, footfalls padded on the driveway, a car door swung open then shut, and an engine rumbled leaving the driveway and motored down the street, no doubt belching puffs of exhaust in its wake.

George lay there helpless, helpless, and so very hungry. His belly recoiled, demanding to be fed. George had no suitable answer and tried ignoring its not very humble beseeching, but his hunger clawed at him unrelenting. He began to harken back to meals in which he'd taken part and those special meals that were his favorites. It wasn't conducive to be recollecting about these things of course, but it couldn't be helped.

Hearty meatloaf, mashed potatoes drizzled in gravy and green beans with hammock, including the neglected gristle he usually tossed into the trash. He promised to never spurn the fibrous chunks of meat again should he find a way to wrangle himself out of this hell of a mess. Oh, that Barb, boy could she cook. Corn on the cob drenched in rich golden butter; steak too—oh yes, steak. A nice grade A cut like a T-bone cooked medium rare. Visions of food danced like that old Christmas poem.

"And a nice, big baked potato," he said aloud, a thin trail of drool dribbling from the corner of his mouth.

He decided right there on the spot to eat like a king once this was over. George often considered himself a rather frugal man regarding the amount of money he spent on food, but he would be making an exception after they (whoever the heck that was) found him alive. A meal fit for a king, maybe even an entire kingdom. He uttered a delirious laugh.

"How about a New York strip? Gotta have the macaroni and cheese in a separate bowl, you can't mix the flavors."

"That steak better have A1…oh Barb, where are you?' he whispered before nodding off.

He came to and discovered the basement was dark again, and Scott Travis's porch light had been cut off the same as the night before. How could he have possibly slept for so long? George cursed himself, knowing the window for being saved had again closed. He attempted awakening his limbs and found shrill stabs of pain for the effort, except for his hands, they still functioned by some equitable measure.

He took a breath, moved his finger around on his chest, and felt the smooth rub of a candy wrapper.

The same candies that were going to solve Netherton's problems.

The same candies for the trick-or-treaters.

The same candy which now might be the only way out…

No, it wouldn't come to that, someone will notice he's missing, someone will come looking for him, right? The monotone hum of the house answered. Still, George knew someone would notice his absence, someone would come to his aid. He was sure of it.

Three days passed, or was it five? Hard to tell, as he'd been coming in and out of consciousness for the better part of what he could barely remember. Black patches and random visions that he was aware of but could not exactly recall, except for one.

He was eight years old, and Howard was twelve; they were with a few other kids, most of them older than he. One of the teens had bright orange hair, a noticeable gap in his teeth, and a cruel, derisive laugh. The reminisce was blurry, like a camera lens slightly smeared with

Vaseline, but he could see the massive shapes of trees and leafless, disfigured branches towering overhead. The kids gathered in a small circle, hovering around a big furry lump. Howard turned the motionless slab onto its side; the rest of the kids stood upright and acted dumbstruck with a mixture of awe and disgust.

George could see it was a dog of some kind of mixed breed (a nameless stray most likely) and that it had a large gaping hole punctured into its fur. The sunlight peered down, and the unhampered view reflected onto the gore seeping out, giving the wound an impossibly ugly sheen on the crimson coating. George wanted to run, to turn away, but Howard and the others linked their hands together and constructed a human wall, blocking his only exit.

"See George, I told you he was real, you can even see where the pickaxe got him! Look everybody, look at the baby crying!" Howard openly mocked.

But he did not look, not when the kids began their collective teasing and the teenager with the orange hair and gap in his teeth started to cruelly whoop. And not when Howard tripped George and started to shove his reluctant face towards what he was sure was his older sibling's handiwork, pushing him closer to the awaiting wet viscera…

That was just a snapshot from the past. The truth played as a different dynamic in the basement altogether. Sometimes George could see daylight outside the window, and others he'd be blanketed in absolute darkness. Time operated as periodic flashes, and this, combined with his insatiable hunger and throbbing pain, made it impractical to concentrate on preserving a genuine timeline.

Even worse, when the blackness fell over him, George could hear sounds from the corner. He didn't hear them the first night or the second night, but by the third night, George did notice something. A light tapping coming behind the wall, as if whatever it was had been trapped inside and wanted out. No, his mind was playing tricks on him; that was all.

"Yes, tricks. Tricks and no treats for ol' George, but somebody will come, and they'll have a piece of pumpkin pie for me. Golden brown crust too. Trick or treat, give me something good to eat," he chuckled and nodded off once again.

Another day (or was it two?) passed. It was hard to tell anymore; he didn't know for certain, but he *did* know the slight rapping in the wall had advanced to a heavy thumping. *Very heavy thumping.* He also knew his brother's voice. It casually taunted him, but with a filthy, gargled choking that was amused by George's pain and utter helplessness.

Still think you are going to be saved? the voice rasped.

George did not reply.

That sound is getting louder. Listen, it knows you're here. Know what it is?

George remained silent, trying to put a constraint on the rotting utterances like he had previously the other nights before.

Not this time, you can't shut me out and you can't stop what is about to happen. It's almost here, and it's ugly old boy, ugly and carrying a rusty razor blade and a big ol' pickaxe. It wants your wet, juicy insides.

The footfalls were drawing closer.

Wet. Juicy. Insides. The words were announced with a slow, intentional pause between them. His mind was playing more tricks, but the steps gained more sluggish traction. Plodding as though waterlogged, and a stench began to arise out of the void. Vile and potent, it burned

George's nose. He could feel his body quake, trying frantically to look to all sides, terrified to learn its origin.

Too late. No, not yet. If he could just reach the candies laying on his chest and tear open a piece of the tainted chocolate. Almost there. His hand was badly shaking, no longer under his control, but he was able to pinch the colorful wrapper. The slow, menacing slog of invisible footsteps drew closer. He brought the piece of candy to his teeth and clamped them shut on the end of the wrapper. He tried jerking his head to initiate the tear; but the shaking had grown steadily worse, and George was unable to grasp the covering to finish the meek but grave proposal.

His final thought was not one of a life flashing before his dull and somehow fulfilled existence. It was one of regret in not eating the tainted sweets when he had the opportunity, it might have spared him of the oncoming and familiar horror. However, George's main regret was not being able to save Netherton and his neighborhood from the advancing evil. Evil, which was only going to fatten and fester within the town's sick, beating heart.

There would be no saving it, and no one would ever know of his heroic efforts. George could have wept about his ultimate fate and misfortune, but he did not. Then the rancid odor disappeared, and the footsteps did too.

What the blue hell?

Silence. Pure silence.

He allowed himself a touch of nervous relief. It was all in his head. George Mainyard closed his eyes, and when he opened them, a necrosed face birthed from his nightmares greeted him. Scott Davis's porch light beamed in the basement, giving exquisite gruesome detail to Howard Mainyard's decayed patchwork.

"Oiche Shamhna Shona Daoibh," it croaked, the head of the pickaxe coming into full view.

He did his best to usher a final languid scream, but it died in his belly as Howard's corpse closed over him, its putrid smell the last sensation George would ever know…

A week later, the local authorities discovered the remains of George Mainyard. An iron-gray-haired detective chewing on a toothpick called to his youngish charge as George Mainyard, Netherton's would-be savior, was being zipped inside a body bag and loaded onto a stretcher.

"Did you already get a statement from the neighbor?"

The boyish officer stepped around the plastic bowl and numerous candies that surrounded the concrete floor.

"Yeah, the guy who called about the welfare check—Davis is his name—said he had been really busy lately and didn't notice or think anything was wrong at first. That is, until the mailman knocked on his door and asked him about Mr. Mainyard's bills and junk mail piling up."

The older detective shook his head and sighed.

"What did the coroner say?"

"Nothing definite, but he thinks it was most likely a heart attack. And get this, he thinks it was," he pulled out a miniature notepad, "triggered by terror," he scoffed.

"Huh?"

"Yeah, pretty absurd, right?" he said, but with a skittish titter.

"Hmm, why would he say that?" the veteran detective asked, hands on his hips, and surveying the scene.

"Did you get a chance to see his face?" the officer asked.

"Nope," he said, while continuing to work on the toothpick.

"Well, his face, I mean it looked like he was uh, maybe—"

"Scared to death?" the older detective asked, not really believing the coroner's possible ruling himself.

"Yeah," he replied uneasily.

The detective flipped his toothpick and looked at the various colored candies spread on the concrete and large plastic upturned bowl. Bending down, he made sure the rookie didn't see him and then snatched a few samples off the ground and pocketed them. The missus wouldn't be thrilled that he was ruining his diet, but what she didn't know couldn't hurt him.

"It's a real shame," he said raising up, "you can tell the old guy really loved Halloween."

The Last Earth Day
By Zé Burns

I never thought much of Earth Day. A dying holiday celebrated by aging hippies and idealistic youth. Then again, I was exactly what they were fighting against. I made a mistake. Or rather, I made many, but it was that one that sealed the deal. It cost me my wife, my daughters, my house, so much. That is why on April 22nd I climbed into my old beater Toyota and drove two towns over.

I pulled my car off the dirt road into an overgrown field where the other cars were parked. A small group congregated at the far end of the clearing. I reached into the glove box and took out an orange prescription vial. It was the last of my ex-wife's stash. I chewed the Klonopin to help it kick in sooner and stared at my disguise in the mirror.

The blond wig was askew atop my bald head. I applied a little more spirit gum to the fake moustache—my own facial hair too wispy to grow out. *They'll recognize me*, I thought. Even if I was two towns away. During the court case, my name and face had been plastered over the local news, my mugshot on the front page of the town gazette.

Relax. You're here to do good. They'll see that.

I opened the door of the Toyota and stepped out into a pleasant spring morning. My hand went instinctually for my Mercedes's fob, only to remember it was gone along with every other possession I cherished. And every person.

The group before me paid no mind as I approached. The website stated twelve volunteers, but here were only seven, and I thought I knew why. The news coverage about me vanished overnight when the first abduction took place. Then another. And another. A serial killer, some said, attacking hikers, joggers, and any unwary pedestrian who strayed into the nearby woods. In my mind, there was safety in numbers. Still, not everyone must have shared that opinion.

I was a couple yards away when a man turned toward me. He was the very stereotype I expected: a shaggy gray ponytail on top, Teva sandals with hiking socks below. The relaxed apathy of the Klonopin stunted the anxiety coursing through me.

"Hey! Welcome, welcome." He looked at his clipboard. "You must be Gregory."

I almost forgot my pseudonym. "Yeah, I'm here." My voice squeaked.

A few murmured hellos. Many of the volunteers seemed normal enough, but off to the side were three women in their late twenties, early thirties, trying to make a statement with their peculiar hairdos. They seemed to be together.

"Now that everyone's here," said the ponytailed man. "Let's say our names and an interesting fact about ourselves. I'll start. My name is Rick, and this is my forty-third-year planting trees on Earth Day."

God, I hated this.

Around the circle they went. All I wanted was to plant trees. I could care less about these people. Then it was my turn.

"My name is Gregory, uh, Johnson. And I, uh... I guess there's not much interesting about me."

This earned a few chuckles, but I noticed one of the young women staring at me. Numerous piercings covered her face while her lime green hair was sculpted into a fauxhawk. Her eyebrows lowered. That glare lingered as she introduced herself as 'Rachel', a member of an eco-rights group.

A breeze blew past, ruffling my wig. For a second, I thought I might lose it and instinctively held it down. Recognition dawned on her expression, and I knew I was screwed. I should just run to the car and drive away. Then I remembered why I was here. I wanted the world my daughters inherited to be unmarred by the mistakes of humankind. I had to start small. Lord knows I'd done enough damage.

With the horrible introductions concluded, Rick led us over to a parked truck with a trailer attached, full of saplings wrapped in burlap.

"Forty trees," he announced. "Now I know we're not all here, but let's see how much we can accomplish today."

We began unloading the trees. I felt Rachel's stare burning into the back of my head, but I was determined not to meet her gaze. With the first twenty saplings off the truck, Rick directed us to a stack of shovels.

As I reached down to pick one up, I heard a voice in my ear. "I know who you are, *Gregory*."

I turned to see the three young women looming over me.

"Pardon me?" I rasped.

"You're Roland Greenwald," said Rachel.

"Who?"

"Don't play dumb. You own the dry-cleaning chain that dumped hundreds of gallons of tetrachloroethylene into Gorsuch Creek."

"Listen—"

"No, *you* listen. I don't care if you're trying to alleviate your guilt or doing some PR stunt or what, but we don't want you here. Just do us all a favor and blow your brains out."

"Please, I just want to—"

"Is everything all right here?" came Rick's voice.

"This man is a criminal," said Rachel. "He caused the biggest environmental disaster in this county's history, maybe even the state."

"Well, if he's out here, then I can tell he's a changed man."

I could hug that obnoxious old hippie.

"It's either him or us," said Rachel, gesturing to her cadre.

"We're here to plant trees. If you really want to help the planet, you'll overlook your differences and grab a shovel."

The scowl lasted for a few seconds before she and her friends picked up their spades and stormed off.

Rick turned to me. "I thought you looked familiar."

I reached up and pulled off my wig and moustache and stuffed them in my pocket. They wouldn't do any good now.

"I admit that I'm disgusted with what you've done," Rick continued, "but I appreciate that you're here."

I gave him a close-lipped smile and grabbed my shovel. Wooden stakes indicated where to plant the trees. I chose one as far as possible from Rachel and her crew. As I pushed the shovel into the earth, a bubbly voice came over my shoulder. "Lovely day, isn't it?"

I turned to see a thickly built, middle-aged woman garbed in L.L. Bean, smiling at me.

"I'm Anne."

"Gregory, er, Roland."

She seemed oblivious to my change in disguise.

"The last two Earth Days it rained, you know. The forecast this morning said sunny skies, but I brought my slicker just in case. You never know with these spring days."

Anne droned on and on—one of those people that cannot abide silence. Still, it was far better than the vitriol I had experienced earlier. I deserved to be chewed out; I didn't blame Rachel for how she acted. But I also believed that I deserved a second chance. I pushed my shovel in, scooped, and dumped the soil behind me. The hole soon fit the width and depth Rick had prescribed. I took one last shovelful when I saw the squirmy legs of a centipede. I leapt back and smacked it with the spade. My heart did the quickstep in my chest.

"You all right?" Anne asked, interrupting her monologue.

"Damn centipedes. My brother used to put them on me when we were kids. I can't stand the things."

"Oh, they're harmless enough. At least the ones in this neck of the woods." She chuckled and resumed her palavering.

"Yeah." I risked a glance into the hole and didn't see it. In my mind, though, I could feel those little legs crawling all over me.

I massaged my brow for a moment and moved on to the next hole. Soil darkened my fingernails. The sore spots on my palms heralded blisters. I couldn't help but wonder what Cathy would think of this, averse to dirt as she was. My ex-wife loved the pampered lifestyle I gave her and when it was taken away, she couldn't leave fast enough. I caught myself. Here I was blaming her when it was all *my* fault. The couple's counselor had often accused me of that: blaming everyone but myself. A stench soon overwhelmed my thoughts of guilt.

It was the smell of decay, like passing a dead bird on the sidewalk swarming with flies. It emanated from the hole I was digging. A horrible thought entered my mind. Had I uncovered the serial killer's mass grave? No, this ground was firm, untouched. Something bubbled and I looked down.

A black viscous sludge rose from the hole, the source of the stench. It glistened in the sunlight. I took a few steps backwards only to trip and fall on my rump. Anne went over to help me up. Behind me, someone cackled. Rachel. From the corner of my eye, I saw her approach, her cadre in tow.

"What happened? You get a hangnail?"

"I... I... I..."

The black sludge shot upward, the smell overpowering. It formed the shape of a hand, eight feet from pinky to thumb, with thin gnarled fingers. Screams rang out from the volunteers. But before we could flee, the hand reached down and snatched Anne, Rachel, and me. The icy digits gripped us firmly, our bodies mashed together as we were pulled into the earth.

My mouth filled with soil as I screamed. I grasped for rocks, roots, anything to prevent me from being pulled downwards. I latched onto something with the tips of my fingers, only to have my nails ripped off.

Down we went. Through the cold dirt, I felt the warmth of the two women beside me as they flailed. We were soon hundreds of feet below the surface. Claustrophobia overwhelmed me as I struggled to breathe.

Then the soil disappeared beneath me, and I was falling. Green light illuminated a massive cavern the size of a football field. At the bottom, the black sludge formed a lake, impenetrable to the light. Twenty feet, fifteen, ten and we splashed into the pool. For a moment, I was submerged. That cold, malodorous liquid embraced me. Vomit escaped my mouth, only to have the sludge pour in. It tasted worse than it smelled. I thrashed until I reached the surface. Rachel emerged soon after and a few seconds later, Anne.

Other than the animated sludge, we were alone.

"Make for the shore," I cried, spitting out the vile liquid. The three of us swam, but it felt like moving through maple syrup. I saw the green light came from floating chartreuse flames encompassing the cavern.

Then something touched my leg.

"What was that?"

"What?" said Rachel.

"Something… something…"

I felt it again, like fingers brushing against my legs. It only caused me to swim faster.

Anne bobbed, struggling to stay above the surface. "Something's got me!"

I looked at the shore, just twenty feet away, then turned back to Anne.

"Fuck it," I muttered and swam over to her. An arm around her shoulder, I kept her head above the sludge, and with my strongest one-armed breaststroke, I extricated her from whatever held her.

The three of us were yards away from the edge of the pool when I saw them. Working their way through the earthen walls were long, crawling creatures. As they entered the green light, I saw with horror that they were centipedes, eight feet in length, a foot in width, their red bodies armored with chitin. My bowels clenched.

I would rather be pulled under and drown in the putrid sludge than get within a mile of those things. Four, then five, then six emerged from the wall. They crawled over each other, forming a mass of writhing legs. A whimper escaped my mouth. I just wanted to plant some trees. Was that too much to ask?

The centipedes stayed at the shoreline, their antennae twitching. I was so focused on them that it took me a moment to register the massive form rising from the pool. Clicking filled the air as the centipedes snapped their mandibles together. Higher and higher the form rose, assuming the shape of a figure swathed in black robes. But rather than any solid material, it seemed to be made of the sludge. A deep rumble reverberated through the cavern, shaking the very walls. I soon forgot the centipedes as I stared at this being. An aura emanated from it. Every fear I'd ever known compounded and entered my mind. Over the pounding of my heart in my ears, I heard Anne scream. The form reached its final height of twelve feet, floating atop the pool. Though its face was a mask of glistening sludge, I could feel it staring down at us. The temperature of the pool dropped twenty degrees. My muscles strained against the cold, my entire body shivering, yet I couldn't look away from its eyeless gaze.

Our labored breaths and frantic treading filled the cavern. Then it spoke.

From the one mouth came many voices, all with a bass that made my bones vibrate. It was a guttural language, full of sharp consonants. I shouldn't have understood it, yet the words came across as clear as English.

"The time has come. Our apotheosis is nigh. Bring the humans to us."

The centipedes clicked their mandibles and dove into the pool of sludge. From the wake, I could tell they were swimming toward us. I broke into a crawl stroke, hoping to escape them. Rachel quickly joined me. Meanwhile, Anne blubbered. A centipede rose from the liquid, clamped onto her neck, and pulled her toward the cloaked being. A few seconds later, despite her frantic splashing, they seized Rachel. She let out a tremendous scream before disappearing into the sludge.

I was almost to the opposite shore when I felt the mandibles lock around my ankle. It held tight but didn't do more than break the skin. Whatever our fate, they wanted us alive and unharmed… for now.

The centipede dragged me back, despite my thrashing limbs. A second one latched onto my other ankle. With no way to stay afloat, my head went under, and I swallowed another mouthful of sludge. I fought for air a moment more, then relented. My body sunk into the fetid liquid. What did I have to live for? My life above ground was ruined, my fate below ground well-earned. And then I thought of my youngest daughter, Victoria. Cathy rightfully distanced the kids from me. But Victoria? She had the best heart of any human being I'd ever met. Still called me Papa after all that. Still ran to greet me when I stopped by. And then there was my eldest, Giselle. She hated me for destroying our family. I couldn't blame her, didn't love her any less. She had a quick wit, wisdom beyond her years, so much potential. I wanted to watch them grow up and become the remarkable adults they were destined to be.

I was ripped from these thoughts as the centipedes pulled me from the pool and threw me against the wall of the cavern. Beside me were the exhausted forms of my companions. Anne shuddered while Rachel knotted her fists and clenched her teeth. Both shook from the cold. A single green flame floated above my head. But rather than heat, it gave off a chill.

The clicking mandibles caught my attention as the centipedes swarmed around us. They raised their U-shaped stingers. I backed up as far as I could against the wall of the cavern. The others did likewise.

"Do it," the many voices commanded.

With cobra-like speed, the stingers darted toward us. It penetrated my flesh above my left bicep. It felt as if I had been jabbed with a steak knife, but soon weightlessness overcame me, the pain diminishing. Fatigue washed over me. My arms slumped to either side. Through the haze of the sedating poison, I saw Rachel and Anne sway.

Sleep never came. Instead, it felt like I took an entire bottle of Klonopin—something I had regrettably done when Cathy left. Aware of my surroundings, but indifferent to them all. My head swung to the side, and for the first time, I saw an antechamber beside the cavern. It was stacked full of something. I fought to focus. It could be a way out. As my vision cleared, I saw it was a massive stack of limbs and torsos. There was no serial killer; there was only what dwelled down here. I realized that would be my fate. A mutilated corpse buried beneath the earth for no one to find, my daughters never knowing what happened to their father.

I just wanted to plant trees.

"Roland," I heard Rachel hiss.

I turned my head like it was a bag of sand.

Her eyelids lowered then raised. "We have… we have to get out of here."

I held back a remark about the obviousness of her statement. Now was not the time. "If those bugs can tunnel into here… we should be able to tunnel out."

She gestured at her ragdoll body. "How do you propose we do that?"

She was right. Hundreds of feet of dirt separated us from the surface. There was no way our sedated bulks could crawl that far. I looked at Anne, her jaw slack, her eyes glassed over. The woman was broken, and I was not far behind.

"Of all the people to die with," said Rachel.

"I'm not too happy about it either."

With that, I saw her smile, and I smiled back.

A clicking drew my attention. The centipedes chattered as the sludge-cloaked being floated across the surface to face us.

"Kneel before us, mortals."

We looked at each other.

"KNEEL!"

Anne went straight to her knees, clasping her hands in prayer, still swaying from the poison. Reluctantly, Rachel and I did the same.

"We are your gods now. You have been chosen for a great honor. Your pitiful mortal forms will serve a higher purpose."

"I believe in no god," said Rachel, struggling to stand.

"Your insolence amuses us. When you see what we will become, you will prostrate yourself before us and grovel for mercy. Our realm is not corporeal like this floating rock of yours. The form you see before you is an amalgam of dark energies and cannot stray far from their source. The most we can manifest is this liquid.

Therefore, we require your human bodies if we are to ascend."

"Fuck you," said Rachel. I couldn't help but admire her guts.

A growl came from the depths of the pool. Fat, gray bubbles rose to the surface.

"You no longer amuse us," it said. "Your blasphemy will be your downfall. Restrain her."

A pair of centipedes emerged from the dirt wall and wrapped their bodies around Rachel's form, pining her tight. As she struggled against the many legs, I realized that other than the gnarled hand that pulled us down, only the centipedes had handled us. It appeared this sludge-being had limited power in its current form.

It continued, "Unfortunately, your pathetic human bodies have so far been unable to contain our divine energy. There have been many attempts."

I glanced at the room of corpses. How many times had it given this speech? What perverted satisfaction did it provide?

"If you prove to be the right vessels, then this Earth of yours will be ours. We've learned that this point on your calendar is called Earth Day. A fitting name for your world's funeral.

"Now, bring us the weak one."

More centipedes poured from the walls. Behind them, I saw the myriad tunnels they had dug. I fought against the apathy, bracing myself for those crawling legs. But they passed me by. Instead, their mandibles grabbed Anne by her underarms and dragged her to the edge of the pool. Unrestrained as I was, I could have reached for her as I did earlier. But the presence of this dark being, this dark 'god', halted me in place. I hated myself, but what good could I do?

The centipedes held Anne down. A serpent made of the black sludge rose from the pool. It darted back and forth for a moment, before plunging down her throat. Her scream became a gurgle. In horror, I watched the liquid pour through her system. Anne shook violently, her face blanching, every limb straining.

Her skin fractured into cracks, a red glow beneath them, growing brighter and brighter until I had to squint my eyes. Then, as if her body could no longer contain the energies coursing through her, she burst. Her head and arms sloughed off the body, while her torso bisected. There was no blood, no offal. The light had cauterized her innards. These remains were dragged off to the corpse room by a pair of centipedes.

"As we assumed," said the dark being. "Now bring us the petulant one."

The centipedes holding Rachel pulled her forward. She fought back as well as she could in her state. "You fuckers, get off me!"

"This one has promise, has strength."

In the same place as Anne, Rachel was forced down. The black oily serpent rose once more and shot toward her mouth. She pressed her lips together, holding back the sludge. It pushed harder and harder until I heard the crack of teeth. I winced at the horrific noise.

Like Anne, she shook as it rent her body apart. I looked for the red cracks, signs that she would be torn to pieces, but she fought against it. Her body twitched violently as her knees lifted from the ground. At first, I thought she was standing, but as I watched, I realized she was levitating. Her flesh reddened, and the hairs of her green fauxhawk sloughed off her scalp. The bones in her arms and face pushed against her skin, stretching it until I thought it would tear. The cloaked sludge-being sunk beneath the surface, becoming part of the pool.

"Yes! Yes!" The words came from Rachel's mouth, but in the being's deep, many-throated voice. The perverted Rachel-Thing floated higher. Red light swirled through the cavern, snuffing out the green flames. Strands of sludge rose from the pool, winding around the levitating form like threads of black silk. A cocoon. I knew it wouldn't be a butterfly that emerged.

If ever there was a chance to escape, it was now.

I pulled myself up, fighting against the lead in my limbs. The cavern stretched far above. No egress there. Along the wall were multiple horizontal tunnels, but I doubted few if any travelled upward. The centipedes seemed occupied with their master. I imagined the creatures were dumb as their tiny counterparts, guided by their god's commands. I half-walked, half-crawled around the edge of the pool. If I was correct, the sludge could not attack me. Still, it felt as if a thousand eyes stared up at me from beneath.

The stench of the corpses overwhelmed the smell of the sludge as I entered the antechamber. High up on the wall was one of the holes left by a centipede. It travelled at a diagonal toward the surface. Rachel had dismissed the idea as impossible, but I had run out of possible. To reach it was another matter.

Knowing my time was limited, I hastened to the mound of gray limbs and torsos. *I must keep going. I must keep going.* My repulsion overwhelmed me, and I vomited once more, emptying the last of my stomach's contents. I wiped the bile from my lips and started to climb. The bodies had grown saggy with decay and my hand sunk into the abdomen of a headless corpse. I fought on.

I was a yard away from the hole when the clacking of the centipedes returned, sounding louder, closer. I reached the summit of the cadavers and dove through the hole, squirming through the dirt like a worm. Those centipedes would be on me in a second. This was their domain. I felt the hole continue to slope upward, a good sign. The claustrophobia returned in these dark confines, but I imagined myself on the porch of my old house, the cool morning air, the freshly cut grass. I wanted to see the sky again. I wanted to plant trees. I wanted to hug my daughters and tell them I love them. I had screwed up in life, chasing dollar signs while neglecting everything else. Was this my comeuppance?

The clacking mandibles grew closer. It seemed yards away. I didn't know how much time this cocoon, this 'apotheosis' would last. But I didn't want to be climbing through this tight, dark tunnel when it did.

Something sharp clamped onto my leg. The centipedes had found me. A couple hours ago, I squealed at the sight of a two-inch centipede. Now, I slammed my foot into the maw of one larger than me. I heard something crunch and I kicked again.

Another burrowed by my stomach. Those mandibles could eviscerate me if they had the chance. Adrenaline coursed through me, and strength returned to my limbs. I seized the creature by its two antennae and pulled in opposite directions. With a yank, I tore off the crown of its head. The creature trembled in its death throes before going still.

The other was still by my leg. With those chomping mandibles, I couldn't reach the antennae without losing my fingers. The longer I waited here, the sooner the rest would come. If I could just—

A stinger penetrated my calf. I stomped the creature back, and it retreated a few feet. Rather than a sedative effect, it felt like acid was shooting through my veins. This was a different poison. I didn't have the time or room to tie a tourniquet with my belt. To my relief, the poison halted just below my groin. The skin stretched, and by its stiffness, I could tell it was greatly swollen.

As the centipede reared to strike once more, I tried to kick it again, but my leg was useless. Its many limbs, each tipped with a spike, started to crawl up my body. It was going for my head. I squirmed as I fought back.

"Leave him." The Rachel-Thing's words resonated in my head. "Let him witness his demise."

In the darkness, I stared in the direction of the creature, waiting for its stinger to rear back, but it scurried back down the hole. For a moment, I rested there, my breathing rapid. Whatever divine intervention from whatever god that was, I wasn't going to take it for granted. I continued to crawl through the dark earth, pulling my swollen leg along. I just had to go up.

After what felt like hours, my fist burst out of the ground. I could feel the cool air above me, the smells of spring, yet I heard nothing. No volunteers, no birds, no insects, not even the breeze through the tree branches. It didn't matter. I was out of that subterranean nightmare.

My other arm reached out, and I extricated myself from the hole. I was caked in dirt. Tears forced their way into my eyes, and I blubbered there for a few minutes. My sobs turned to laughter. I was free.

Night had settled. How long had I been down there? Above, I caught a glimpse of the moon and the stars. They seemed dimmer, farther away. Impenetrable darkness obscured the surrounding woods. Not even the lights from the nearby town could be seen.

I felt about my pockets and chuckled, a tinge of madness in my tone. My car keys were still there. Though I could not see much, I wandered in search of my Toyota, my swollen leg dragging behind me.

My foot collided with something firm. I reached down and felt a pair of Teva sandals. Rick. I yanked my hand back before realizing I had crawled up a mountain of dead bodies not hours before. The flesh of his leg was cold. He had been dead for some time. What had happened to the rest of them? I shivered and it had nothing to do with the temperature.

I kept moving, my hands spread out before me. Surely, my car wasn't too far away…

The weak light of the stars and moon winked out, leaving me in utter blackness. The ground rumbled beneath me, and I fought to maintain my balance. Red beams of light burst from the earth. I could now see the field littered with corpses and unplanted trees.

Why had it killed them all? I wondered as I stared at the bodies bloated with centipede venom. It only needed one body.

Because it could, I realized. Human lives meant nothing to it. This was a being that could destroy worlds. We were less than insects. Less than the centipedes who served it.

The crimson light grew stronger. Mounds of earth shot upward, and something horrible emerged. The Rachel-Thing. Her arms spread wide as she levitated ten then twenty feet into the air. The heavens and distant surroundings remained black. I could hardly recognize the strong-willed woman. Her skin was crimson, glowing from within. Jagged protrusions of bone pierced through her now emaciated, naked body. But her *face*… I had to look away. Those bulging black orbs for eyes lingered in my mind. I felt them probing me, eating away at my remaining sanity.

"Your escape from our lair was futile," it said. "You cannot halt our hunger. We will consume this realm like so many others until your galaxy rests in our belly."

The hairs on my arms and legs stood on end. I continued to avert my gaze, yet all I could think of were those black orbs as they rotted me from the inside. From the corner of my eye, I could see the crimson light growing. My skin burned, and I collapsed to my knees. Agonizing bubbles of flesh sizzled across my skin.

The light became unbearable, even with my eyelids squeezed shut. What a world to leave my daughters…

As my body melted away, I could only think one thing:

I just wanted to plant trees.

Last Call for Candy
By Kevin M. Folliard

Leonard scoffed. "Trick-or-treating is kid stuff, Keith!"

"We *are* kids."

He shrugged. "I'm thirteen now. I'm going to Amy O'Connor's party tomorrow." He ran a comb through his gelled hair. He'd been wearing product and collared shirts since he'd started sitting at Amy's lunch table.

I tried to shrug off the sting that she'd invited Leonard to her Halloween party, but not me. "No big deal. We'll trick-or-treat in the afternoon, and you can go to the party later."

"I need time to get ready."

"How long does that take? Just wear your costume."

"It's a mature affair." He rolled his eyes. "Keith, if you grew up a little, people would like you."

I mumbled some insult. Brushed it off. But later that night, I cried into my pillow, surrounded by the comics, action figures, and dinosaur posters I was supposed to be outgrowing.

Outside, rain pelted my window. Thunder grumbled. I was the *only* kid not invited to that stupid party. But that wouldn't have mattered if things could go back to the way they were.

Leonard never used to care what other kids thought. Did some switch get flipped when he turned thirteen? He'd been obsessing over Amy since the start of seventh grade.

Even worse, Leonard told me not to come to the mall last weekend. *Amy will be there, and I don't want you trying to drag me into the toy store and the arcade.*

Nuts to Leonard. I'd have more fun on Halloween by myself.

I stared out my rain-splattered window. For as long as I could remember, my backyard and the woods behind my house had been our imaginative playground. We took our bikes down the nature trails and played explorer. We'd have pretend motorcycle races, with baseball cards flapping in the spokes, and set up obstacle courses.

"I wish I could be twelve forever," I said. "I could be my own best friend."

Lightning flickered, and a figure appeared, lingering at the edge of the woods. A man, with broad shoulders and a brick jaw. I couldn't make out his face through the drops of water. He pointed two fingers at his eyes, then pointed directly at me, as if to say *I see you.*

His eyes glowed like green lasers. I gasped. Exhaled. My breath fogged the glass, but by the time I wiped away the condensation, the man had vanished.

What was with those green eyes? *It's just some weirdo,* I told myself. *Just an optical illusion from flickering lightning.*

Childhood is just like that, I thought, *a flash of lightning.*

Rain pelted the rust-crusted swing set at the edge of the yard. I stared at trembling treetops and prayed for everything to stand still.

* * *

The next day, I cobbled a costume from a tattered sport coat, plastic hockey mask, and rubber machete. I slung my pillowcase over my shoulder and headed out.

Little kids raced along sidewalks dressed as ghosts, witches, fairy princesses, and superheroes. Their parents lingered at the ends of walkways. They rang doorbells on pumpkin-adorned porches, sing-songed "trick-or-treat!," and accepted candy from approved strangers.

I remembered how cool it felt the first time our parents let us trick-or-treat unsupervised. Leonard and I found the best houses with the best candy. We'd swap costume pieces and circle back for second helpings of full-sized candy bars and heaping handfuls. The ice cream store gave out single scoops to kids in costume. The burger joint gave out pouches of hot greasy fries.

We'd end up in Leonard's basement, fill our stomachs with junk, then watch a bloody horror flick on late night cable.

That was kid stuff to him now.

To everyone our age, it seemed.

I still wanted to pretend. To dream bigger than impressing some girl.

I drudged onward, house by house, trying to believe everything was normal. But my guts felt packed with sour balls. The scene around the neighborhood was achingly familiar. Like an overplayed song on the radio.

The air grew colder. Neighbors seemed less familiar. Even the candy selection felt different this year. The packaging was more colorful. The portions smaller. Maybe I was just getting older. How strange that I had only experienced twelve Halloweens in my lifetime. It felt like a thousand.

Maybe I *was* getting bored with this.

Maybe I *couldn't* be my own best friend.

I passed kids in unfamiliar costumes—an ice princess, some weird inflatable robot, and big blocky video-game masks. *I must be getting older,* I thought. *I don't know who half these characters are.*

I realized that I had been trick-or-treating unconsciously toward Leonard's house. *Maybe once he sees me, pillowcase half full of candy, he'll want to come out for a few hours? Maybe he'll even ditch the party.*

The sun was setting into a pool of orange clouds. I skipped houses and hurried down Leonard's street.

If he hasn't left yet, maybe he'll take pity and let me tag along. Who cares if I wasn't invited? I could borrow one of his dumb collared shirts and be his wing man.

I can prove I'm cool enough.

At first, I thought I had the wrong house. The green and white awning was unfamiliar. The bushes had been ripped out, replaced by black stones. But the house number was the same. Leonard's mom's plastic skeleton remained propped on the stoop, but were the bones always so yellow?

Guess Leonard's parents did some landscaping.

I rang the bell, slid my maniac mask down, and held out my pillowcase.

Leonard's dad opened the door.

"Trick-or-treat!"

His dad grimaced. He looked wrong somehow. Older. Fatter. And since when did Leonard's dad wear glasses?

"Is Leonard home? It's me, Keith." I pulled the mask up.

Leonard's dad froze. His face blanched.

"Everything okay? Did you run out of candy?"

"Keith, you have to rest." Tears spilled down the man's face. Hearing his voice, I was certain this wasn't Leonard's father. "You do this every year."

"What do you mean?" *Of course, I trick-or-treat every year. All kids do.*

The man opened the door and took a cautious step onto the porch. He stooped to my height. "Keith, you need to move on." He grabbed my wrists. "Listen."

I struggled. I felt sick, like icy licorice ropes were wriggling through my veins.

"It's me," the strange man said. "It's Leonard."

Déjà vu festered in my guts. This wasn't my twelfth or thirteenth or fourteenth Halloween. *And it's always Leonard who makes you remember,* a cold voice scraped in back of my head. *He always ruins this.*

I tried to pry my arms from the stranger's—from Leonard's—grip.

"I'm sorry I didn't go out with you that Halloween. If I'd been there. If there had been two of us, maybe you'd still be alive. Maybe we'd know who did it. I've tried so long to figure it out."

"No!" How many times had I been here? It was so hard to remember. So easy to forget.

Leonard sobbed. "Tell me his name, Keith, and I'll make it right, I swear."

"I'm *not* dead!"

You're dead, Leonard, that vicious voice sliced my mind. *You gave up on your childhood!*

"Keith, I've never gotten over what happened. I still live with my parents. Still see your face in my nightmares. And every year, you come, in this same costume." He choked on his words. "You have to move on. *We* have to move on."

"Never!" I bit Leonard's fingers. Blood pooled like chocolate melting in my mouth.

Leonard screamed and released me.

I ran.

Leonard called after me.

How could I have failed again? I had to remember next time.

He's not my best friend.

I am.

I'm my only friend!

But that wasn't true, was it?

Not anymore.

Before I knew it, I reached the end of my street. Unfamiliar houses formed a cul-de-sac of blocky white suburban homes. Where my house once stood, was now an unfamiliar monstrosity of stucco rectangles, with a strange chrome van in the driveway.

This was no longer my neighborhood. This was some alien world decades removed.

Only the woods remained the same. The same path carved the same trees where Leonard and I had explored on our bikes.

A sliver of yellow moon hooked the sky above trembling treetops. It was late now. Halloween was ending. No kids remained on the street except me.

Chill wind carried Ferris wheels of brown and orange leaves.

Then I saw him—the thing that kills me—that granted my wish. My dark reflection, built like a linebacker. The adult I would never be.

He emerged from the woods and marched the empty street. He wore my same Halloween outfit. He flipped his hockey mask over his shadowed face and pinned me with the green searchlights of his eyes.

"I envy you." His knife glimmered. "Eternal Halloween."

I tried to escape, but he snatched me by the collar, choked, and lifted me. My pillowcase turned to fog, and candy spilled onto the pavement. He squeezed my neck.

Pop rocks of pain burst up my spine as he knifed my lower back. Syrupy blood seeped down my pants.

"It's a perfect day, every year, but only if you bother to enjoy it," his voice scraped. "Only hurts for a minute, buddy, then we start again. Next time, do better. Remember to have more fun."

He held me—*I* held *myself*—in a frosty embrace.

The scythe of the moon blurred.

"Forget Leonard," we told ourselves. "We've got each other."

If A Tree Falls
By Ron McDougall

Paul was uncertain what he found more bothersome, the cold or the waiting. He stepped from side to side, trying to keep himself warm, the snow beneath him crunching with every shift of his feet. Curtis stood in front, jacket unzipped, hands bare, assessing the Douglas fir standing before them. Loosely gripping the bucksaw given to them at the entrance of the tree lot, Curtis circled the promising candidate, scrutinizing it from every angle, judging the fullness of its foliage, the uniformity of its shape.

"I like it," Paul said. He took a sip from his take-out coffee cup, thick woolen gloves wrapped around its sleeve. He gave a shiver. "Let's cut it down and get going."

Curtis shook his head. "Uh-uh. We can do better." He turned away, crossed his arms, and surveyed the lot in its entirety. They stood at the far corner on a rise overlooking the grid-like arrangement of Christmas trees, cultivated over several years and now at their optimum height for yuletide trimming. A handful of other couples and families strolled between the rows, slipping in and out of view, considering their options. Severed trunks randomly poked up from the ground, like partially hammered nails, where trees had already been felled.

Paul cleared his throat. "We've been out here for over an hour, Curtis, and I'm starting to lose the feeling in my fingers…and toes…and ears. We've seen every single tree they have…twice. I think this is as good as we're going to get."

"Yeah, it's good, but it's not perfect," declared Curtis. "Not for our first Christmas together."

Paul gave a chuckle. "I didn't peg you for a romantic."

Curtis gave a wink then turned and looked beyond the split rail fence encircling the lot. Nailed to every second post was the same sign: *Private Property: No Trespassing*. He stepped forward a few steps and leaned against the ineffectual barrier, scanning the field on the other side. The empty expanse was entirely snow covered, barring random clumps of soil breaking through the pristine surface. It was edged along the far side with an unending parade of trees of every shape, size, and color.

"Pretty desolate, eh?" said Paul, sharing the view. "Couldn't imagine living out here…nice to visit though."

Silently, Curtis continued gazing across the stretch of white, the glare of the reflected sunlight forcing him to narrow his eyes almost to the point of closure. And then he saw it, on the far side of the field, like a beacon summoning a vessel lost at sea: the *perfect* Christmas tree.

"There," he said, pointing. "That's the one."

"Where?"

"There," repeated Curtis, thrusting his arm forward. "Straight across."

Paul leaned against the fence and squinted, then he shook his head. "I don't know…they all look the same to me."

"So, we'll take a closer look, then," said Curtis already hopping over the fence.

"What the hell are you doing?" asked Paul plaintively, as though he was about to add, "now?"

"Come on," said Curtis, already fifteen paces ahead. He glanced about for anyone who might object to their encroachment while proceeding without pause.

Balancing his coffee cup so it wouldn't spill, Paul slowly climbed over the fence, after which he scanned the stretch ahead; Curtis was already to the midpoint of the field. Stepping in Curtis's footprints, Paul followed, the snow sometimes coming up to his knees and forcing him to stop and steady himself. *How the hell did Curtis get across so quickly?*

By the time Paul reached the opposite side of the field, Curtis had already cleared the shrubs and underbrush surrounding a well-proportioned and evenly filled-out blue spruce that stood about seven feet tall. Curtis stood next to it, gripping the trunk as if posing with a record-breaking deep-sea catch.

"Okay," said Paul. "It looks really good; I'll give you that. Better than anything in the lot, that's for sure, but–"

"No buts," insisted Curtis. He wagged his finger toward his prize. "This is the one." And before Paul could object any further, Curtis was already slicing into the tree with the bucksaw, the scent of freshly cut wood penetrating the air around them.

While Curtis made his way through the trunk, Paul nervously looked around their surroundings. He spied up and down along the edge of the field—he gave a start.

Someone was coming.

"Uh, Curtis…I think we have a problem."

Curtis gave one final thrust with the saw and the tree gently tipped over onto the ground with a hush, like a broom sweeping the floor. He looked up at Paul, and then to where Paul was staring.

Approaching them was a woman, bowlegged and walking with a waddle. She was accompanied by two dogs running back and forth across her path, leaping up and down through the snow. Every so often the woman picked a branch up off the ground and tossed it into the field, and then the dogs would race toward the makeshift toy and tussle with one another before the victor returned the branch to the woman. She would occasionally speak to the animals, telling them to "heel," that they were "good boys."

"Shit," said Paul. "What do we do now?"

"We could make a run for it."

"And get taken down by those dogs?"

"Bah…" Curtis gave a sniff. "Animals love me. I'm not too worried about—"

"Hallo!" the woman called to them with a wave.

Paul and Curtis looked at one another, then turned back to the woman. Paul tentatively returned her wave with his own.

"Bear with me, dear," said the woman, huffing and puffing. "Almost there."

Curtis smiled. "She sounds friendly enough." He brushed snow and sawdust off his pants. Paul took one final gulp from his coffee cup and slipped the empty container into his coat pocket.

The dogs reached them first and greeted both men with curious sniffs up and down their legs. Curtis held out his hand so they could get a good whiff while Paul turned away in case the animals jumped up on him. The woman arrived soon after, her face beet-red from walking in the cold, her peculiar gait explained by the snowshoes strapped onto her boots. She looked to be in her sixties, Paul thought, and seemed in pretty good shape given how well she kept up with her dogs. She tucked a loose strand of gray hair up under her toque. Paul caught himself staring at some nasty bruising around her right eye and swiftly glanced away.

"Afternoon," she said with a slight drawl. "Lovely day, isn't it?"

Curtis smiled and nodded. "It sure is."

"You out here picking up a Christmas tree?"

"Uh, yeah. We found this beaut' that's gonna look great in our place."

The woman surveyed the felled tree. "Hmm…it sure is a nice one. But you do realize you're on private property, don't you?"

"Oh, really?" said Curtis, feigning ignorance.

"Maybe you didn't notice the fence with all the *No Trespassing* signs. They can sometimes be hard to see, I suppose, especially on bright sunny days like today. You know…with the glare and all…"

Paul stifled a chuckle and glanced over at Curtis. *Talk your way out of this, buddy boy.*

The dogs continued to sniff around the men's feet.

"Okay, you got us," admitted Curtis, raising his arms in mock surrender, "but you have to admit, they don't have any trees on the lot half as nice as this one, and the last thing we want to do after driving all the way out here is go home with something less than stellar."

The woman gave a wry grin. She pulled a handkerchief from a pocket and wiped her nose. "I don't begrudge your good judgement, but still, you're trespassing on *my* land and chopping down *my* property."

Curtis folded his arms and stroked his chin. "Sure…sure…but how about this? We could pay you…*double* what we would have paid the lot. Surely it's worth that much to you, and after the other trees around it fill in and cover up the trunk, by the end of the summer you won't even remember it was there. How about that? In the spirit of Christmas…"

The woman gave a sharp whistle and the dogs immediately raced back to her and sat side by side in front on their haunches. She pulled out treats from her coat pocket and gave one to each of the animals. They devoured them with gusto.

Paul couldn't tell what the woman was thinking—her face was a blank slate—but she was thinking something. And then her face lit up, her eyes widening as if shocked by a scare. She spoke quickly after that, her words tumbling out like water pouring from a bucket. "Here's what we'll do. I won't take your money, but I'll barter with you. I do it all the time. There's a couple down the road…I plow their driveway and they give me some of their homemade wine. And there's this other neighbor— old fella who can barely stand up straight—I help him stack wood and he gives me rabbit meat pie. So, how 'bout it?

Curtis and Paul trade glances.

Carol confronted them with a broad smile. "In the spirit of Christmas…hm?"

Curtis smiled back. "Sure, that sounds great. I love to barter."

Paul turned toward Curtis, smirking. "You *love* to barter?"

"Sure! I do it all the time," he said without returning Paul's look. "What do you have in mind, um…" Curtis extended his hand toward the woman.

"Carol," the woman said before removing her glove and shaking Curtis's hand. Her own hand was covered with scratches and scrapes. "And these are my babies, Bodie and Milo." She gave each dog a scratch behind their ear.

"Pleased to meet you, Carol. I'm Curtis, and this mild-mannered gentleman is Paul."

Paul rolled his eyes and smiled as he shook hands with Carol. "Hi."

Curtis gestured to Carol's face. "I have to say, Carol, that's quite the shiner." Paul cringed at Curtis's brazenness. "I hope you got a few good licks in yourself."

Carol swiftly brought her hand up to her tarnished eye. "Oh, this…" She looked down at the ground, and then to her dogs. "It—I was leaning over just as Bodie was jumping up and our heads met somewhere in the middle. I'm afraid I caught the worst of it."

Curtis winced. "Ouch."

Carol forced a quick smile, then said, "My place is just back through those trees." Carol pointed vaguely in the direction from where she came. "Won't take any time at all."

"Oh," said Paul, "you want to do this bartering thing now?"

"What, I wait till the next time you're out this way? When will that be…when you pick up next year's Christmas tree?"

Paul gave a shrug. "Uh…"

"Don't worry, Carol," said Curtis. "We're on the clock as of this minute. You just lead the way."

Paul checked his phone. They'd been walking for close to thirty minutes now. "Um, Carol…we almost there? These boots aren't really meant for hiking."

Carol walked about ten strides in front, Bodie and Milo bouncing through the snow alongside. With snowshoes to keep her steady, she easily outpaced the two men. "Not much longer, dear," she said looking back. "Almost there."

Curtis and Paul exchanged looks, Paul rolling his eyes.

"Lovely country out here, Carol," Curtis called ahead. "You been here long?"

"A good thirty years and counting. Me and the husband run a dog kennel. We breed them and board them and groom them. A *one-stop doggy shop*, we like to call ourselves."

Curtis nodded his head. "How satisfying that must be for you and your husband."

"If I didn't have my dogs," Carol said, "I don't know how I'd survive."

"I hear ya, Carol." Curtis gave a wink to Paul. "I love animals too."

"It's just over this knoll up ahead," Carol added.

Paul sighed. "This is taking forever," he whispered to Curtis. "I changed my mind. Let's turn around and make a run for it."

"No, not now. I'm dying to see what she wants us to do. And anyway, I think you were right earlier; those dogs seem pretty tame, but I'll bet they'd rip our nut sacks off if she told them to."

Realizing how vulnerable they truly were, Paul gave a deep swallow. "Why did you have to ask about her black eye?" he said. "That was embarrassing."

"You were wondering, too, weren't you?"

"Well, yeah…but, I wasn't going to ask, and it obviously made her uncomfortable. I doubt she was even telling us the truth."

"So maybe she got into it with her husband. She looks like she can handle herself, and who doesn't get in a tussle once in a while anyway?"

"Maybe if you're twelve…not at her age. Unless you're trying to tell me you sneak out at night and go fight clubbing."

"Ha!" Curtis flashed a wink. "If you want to join me some night—get your brains knocked around—just say the word."

"How many fights did you get in when you were growing up?"

"Not many—a few every year, I think."

Paul huffed. "Not many? That sounds like a lot."

"I suspect more than one is a lot for you."

"I was the sort of kid who avoided trouble. I didn't look for it."

Curtis pressed a hand against his chest. "Hey, neither did I. But in my neighbourhood, if you didn't show you could handle yourself then you became a target. Having a black eye was a badge of honour…a signal to everyone else that you couldn't be pushed around."

Paul stopped abruptly; his foot caught in the snow. "Hold on," he said while grabbing Curtis's shoulder for balance. After a few yanks of his leg, the snow released its hold and they continued onward.

"Say, what sort of setup do you think Carol has?" asked Curtis. "I'll bet she lives in a compound surrounded by an electric fence with razor wire along the top, and she's got enough food and guns to wait out the apocalypse. Hm?"

"Maybe she's a cave dweller," Paul theorized with a smirk. "Or maybe she lives in a lean-to made of bones from all the animals she's killed—"

"—or all the people she's eaten," a wide-eyed Curtis blurted.

True to Carol's word, after climbing the knoll the group descended upon a small plot of land cleared of trees. But instead of a military compound or squalid hovel, it was occupied by a modest yet well-groomed cedar-shake cabin with similarly styled sheds flanking both sides. The entire property was surrounded by clusters of manicured shrubs, beyond which stood the forest. It was an idyllic setting, with pristine snowbanks curving around the cabin walls like a lover's embrace, richly colored cedar fencing bordering a cleared laneway, pine trees festooned with bright pillows of snow. There was even a wreath of holly adorning the front door.

"It's lovely," said Paul. "Like a snow globe."

Carol turned with a smile. "It's not much, but it's home."

"So," said Curtis, "what do you have in mind for us, Carol? Stack some wood? Clear some snow? Shovel some dog shit?—Excuse my language."

"No," Carol said quietly. "Nothing like that. Just…follow me."

Carol led the men toward one of the sheds. She placed the dogs each on a leash, then unlocked and opened the main door before leading them down a hallway. The group passed several vacant kennels, each one containing empty dishes and bedding.

"Not boarding any dogs right now?" asked Curtis.

Carol put her finger up to her mouth, urging them to be quiet. She wrapped the leashes tight around her hand. "Let's keep everything to a whisper now, please."

Curtis and Paul both nodded, then exchanged glances with one another. *What the hell*, Paul mouthed to Curtis.

They reached the end of the hallway and approached another door, this one bolted shut with a padlock. The dogs whined and pulled against their tethers. Carol tied them to a ring bolt fastened to the wall, then pulled a key from her pocket and unlocked the padlock. "When we go inside," she said quietly, "you're going to see some things you won't be used to seeing…things you've probably never seen before in your life. I only ask you to stay calm, and I'll explain everything to you."

Paul gave a nervous gulp. "What are you getting us into, Carol?"

"I'll open the door and go in first, and then you follow after me. Go to the right side just inside the door and stand up against the wall. Okay?"

Both men nodded.

Carol took several deep breaths, then opened the door and slipped inside. Curtis and Paul followed behind, doing as they were told. Carol immediately closed the door behind them and slid a bolt shut.

The space they entered was drenched in shadows. The walls were nothing but cinderblocks, the windows boarded up with sheets of plywood screwed into their frames. The only shred of light entered through holes drilled into the plywood. The resultant beams cast spotlights onto the opposite wall and the concrete floor. Across the floor was a mixture of straw and torn up blankets, with random clumps of fur strewn about. With a start, Paul noticed streaks of blood on both the floor and walls. He looked at Curtis, whose sudden pallor suggested he saw them too, and then at Carol. "What the hell is going on here, Carol?" he said loudly.

At that moment, a grunt echoed out from the darkest of corners. The two men froze and scanned back and forth across the room.

"Wait…what is that?" said Paul, spotting a form lurking in the shadows. Glancing over at Carol, he noticed tears running down her face. She pulled a flashlight from her jacket and flashed the beam into the corner. The form bolted away from the light and scrambled to the opposite side.

Curtis leaned forward and squinted. "Is that a…person?"

Without warning the form sprang out from the shadows and into the light. Paul and Curtis both pressed their backs against the wall—hard.

A man on all fours leapt straight for them with the speed of a predator. Then he stopped short and fell—a chain attached to his ankle and bolted to the wall on the far side of the room yanked on him, forcing his entire body down onto the floor.

"Don't worry," Carol said, her voice wavering. "He can't reach you."

The 'man' quickly regained his balance and lurched at the group again, stretching his arms out toward them, pivoting his head atop a straining neck to get a better look. The stench of shit and rot hit Paul and Curtis like a wave.

"What the fuck, Carol!" yelled Paul, covering his nose and sliding away along the wall. "What is this? Who is that?"

The man veered toward the sound of Paul's voice.

Carol sniffled. "My husband, Joseph. Something…something is wrong with him…I don't know what."

"Well, you bring in a doctor for something like this, Carol. Not two strangers you meet in the fucking woods."

"I can't call a doctor. He's—he's too far gone."

Curtis crouched down and took a good look at the man. From his body hung torn remnants of clothing, bloody and wet like the shedding antlers of a deer. He stood with a pronounced hunch; his back arched like a hyena. Smeared across his face was a mixture of dirt, blood, and sweat. His eyes were so red they appeared to be bleeding. He bared his teeth at them, blood red as well, the gums so receded they resembled fangs. Drool spilled out his mouth like a waterfall.

"He came home one day from a hike in the woods," explained Carol, "and he'd been bitten by an animal that snuck up behind him. He didn't get a good look at what it was—maybe a coyote…or a wolf. I cleaned up the wound as best I could, and it seemed to be healing fine. But then he started getting surly, bursting out in fits of rage at the smallest of things, which wasn't like him at all. He's a gentle soul…he really is. He loves animals even more than I do."

"Why didn't you take him to a doctor then?"

"I tried to, but he wouldn't go. He insisted he was fine. And then one morning…I found him…I found him in the kennels—" Her voice caught in her throat. "He'd killed all the dogs we had, all but Bodie and Milo, and was…eating them…with his bare hands. He had torn them apart with his teeth and was devouring them…raw."

Paul's heart dropped into his stomach. "Holy shit." He glanced down at Curtis, who was looking up at him equally aghast.

"I could have called a doctor after that, but…the shame of what he did, I knew he'd rather die than anyone else find out. I did manage to inject him with a sedative that knocked him out, and then I locked him in here, hoping he might get better. But he didn't—he only got worse."

Joseph paced back and forth on all fours, pulling against the chain as tight as it would go, swerving toward whoever's voice was speaking. The palms of his hands and soles of his feet were torn to shreds and left bloody prints everywhere he wandered.

"If we ever had a dog get this bad, get this sick, we would put it out of its misery." Tears flowed freely down Carol's face. "That's where we're at with Joseph. There's no hope of him coming back now."

Curtis's eyes widened, a look of realization washing over his face. He stood back up. "Fuck. And you want us to put him down."

Paul's mouth dropped open, speechless.

Carol nodded. "I—I can't do it. I want to, but I can't. He's the love of my life, but I could never be the cause of his death. I'd never be able to live with myself."

"Godammit, Carol," said Paul. "You call a vet when you put an animal down. In cases like this, there's got to be someone you can call."

Carol shook her head. "I can't risk it." She pulled out her handkerchief and wiped her eyes and nose. "We're not exactly a legitimate kennel, and drawing attention to our operation is not the best idea. We mostly deal with the locals anyway, and they couldn't care less if we're licensed or not…as long as we provide good service, which we do."

"You're worried about your goddamn Yelp reviews?"

"My animals are all I have," Carol said with a sob. "If I lose them, I'll have nothing to live for. At least before, Joseph and I had each other, but now I don't even have that. Please, I beg of you, help me do this…help me end his pain…our pain."

"And if we refuse?" suggested Paul. "What's stopping us from walking out that door, going back to our car and driving home? Aren't you even worried we'll call the police?"

Carol looked down at the floor. "I know what you must think of me, that I'm vile…a wretched, selfish person who should be locked up in jail." She looked back up, her eyes soggy with tears. "I'm well aware I haven't thought this through. I know I'm in over my head, in so many ways. I've put myself in the worst position possible, involving complete strangers with my problems. But that's why I hope you'll do this for me, because you have no connection, no interest at all in who I am or who my husband is. Who are we to you except some old couple living in the middle of nowhere?"

Carol gave her face another wipe.

Curtis scowled and ran his hand through his hair. "How did you think we would do it?" he asked. "How did you imagine we…put him down?"

Paul turned to Curtis. "You're not seriously considering this, are you? This is nuts. It's insane!"

"I'm only asking. That's all."

"This…is…murder."

"This is a *mercy* killing, Paul. Look at him. Have you ever seen anything like this before?"

"Of course, I haven't! I'm an accountant. Where would something like this fall under my job description?"

Carol stammered, "I…I have a gun—a rifle—you can use."

"Nothing like the sedative you gave him, only stronger?" asked Curtis. "Something a vet would give to an animal?"

"No, I don't have anything like that…just the gun…it's back out in the hall. But I can't be here when you do it. There's a slot in the door I'll slide the gun through from the outside. After you're done, I'll let you out then lock the door and never open it again."

Paul piped up, "Why don't you just lock the door and let him starve? We won't tell a soul…promise."

"I thought of that, but…I don't know how long that could take, and I just don't want him to suffer. He seems like he's in so much agony already."

Paul shook his head and mumbled to himself, "I can't fucking believe this…"

"Plus," Carol continued, "I can't take the risk that he might escape. He almost did once before. Can you imagine? What if that ever happened?"

Curtis turned back toward Joseph, who hadn't shown any sign of letting up his efforts to reach the group, sniffing the air like a bloodhound tracking its quarry, straining his body like an elastic band stretched to the point of snapping.

"Have either of you ever fired a gun before?" asked Carol.

Paul scoffed. "No."

"Yes," admitted Curtis.

"You have?" asked Paul "When?"

"High school. I had a friend…his dad was a hunter. Whenever we got bored, we'd sneak out with his gun and shoot at bottles and cans and hubcaps."

Paul stared at Curtis. "I can't believe this is the first I'm hearing of this."

Curtis shrugged. "I guess it just never came up. What can I say? I got into a lot of shit when I was younger. It'd take a lifetime to explain half of what my childhood was like."

"Well, I want nothing to do with this. This is insanity! Carol, I want you to let us out, right now."

Carol grabbed onto each man's jacket. Her entire body was trembling. "Please…I beg of you. I need you to do this…before I lose my nerve."

"This is not what I had in mind in terms of bartering, Carol," said Paul. "This is not even in the same universe as plowing a driveway or stacking some wood. No Christmas tree is worth—"

"We'll do it," said Curtis forcefully.

Paul swung his head toward Curtis.

Curtis looked him in the eyes. "*I'll* do it."

Paul gaped back, unbelieving.

"I'll get the rifle," Carol said while swiftly unlocking the door. She paused, turned back toward Joseph, and mouthed the words, *Forgive me*. She then made the sign of the cross and slipped out through the door. The bolt clicked shut on the outside.

Paul continued to stare at Curtis.

"What?" said Curtis. "Haven't you ever wanted to know what it's like to"—Curtis lowered his voice to a whisper—"*kill* a person without worrying about the consequences?"

"Uh…no. Not even once…ever."

Curtis shrugged. "Maybe you're just not being honest with yourself."

Paul gave a huff.

"You ever see a dead person before…outside of a funeral home or hospital?"

"No," Paul said flatly.

"I did, when I was about ten. I was taking a shortcut through an alley and tripped over a homeless person buried beneath a pile of garbage. At first, I thought he was asleep because he had a newspaper covering his face, but I figured out pretty quickly that wasn't the case—at all. I lifted off the newspaper and could hardly make out any facial features his head had been bashed in so badly."

Paul winced.

"The weird thing was, with the newspaper over his head he looked just like someone relaxing, like he was lying down on a couch at home. He even had his hands clasped together, resting on his chest. That image always stuck with me, and even then, I wondered what it would be like to take the life of another person…how it would feel…how it would affect you."

"I can't believe this shit," said Paul, backing away. "I'm dating a sociopath."

"Come on…it's not like that at all. I don't go around wanting to kill random people. But this whole situation…it just made me wonder like that homeless person made me wonder."

"Whatever…I'm out of here." Paul turned toward the door.

"Look…" Curtis gently placed his hand on the back of Paul's shoulder. "I'd really like you to stay, but…regardless whether I'm a sociopath or not, think about it from Carol's perspective. Her entire world has fallen apart, and in the most fucked-up way possible. She puts on a good face, but you know she's barely holding it together. Think of the peace we can give her. We can literally change her life for the better, right here and now, maybe even save her life."

Paul gave a snort.

"I'm not even bullshitting you; I truly believe it. I'd still be in my old neighborhood tripping over dead bodies—or worse—if my aunt didn't get me out of there when she did. She saved *my* life, so if you want, you can think of this as paying-it-forward or some other bullshit like that, but we have a chance to make a real, tangible difference in someone's life. How often does an opportunity like that come along?"

Following a moment's pause, Paul turned back around, a look of resignation across his face. He sighed. "Fuck."

The slot in the door slid open and the butt of a rifle appeared.

Curtis pulled the rifle through and checked it over, sliding open and shut the bolt handle. The action wasn't smooth, and Curtis repeated himself a couple more times to loosen it up. Then he held up the rifle in a shooting position, pointing it at the opposite wall, and looked down the barrel as if scoping out a target. He shifted the rifle's placement against his shoulder, then lowered it and said to Paul, "You don't have to watch."

"No shit," said Paul, already turned toward the wall, away from the impending carnage. He took a deep breath and held it in, waiting. He considered placing an anonymous phone call to the police when they got home, if for no other reason than to give this poor man a proper burial.

"You'll probably want to cover your ears too."

Paul dutifully covered his ears with his still-gloved hands, and gradually leaned forward until his forehead touched the wall. He closed his eyes and let the cinderblocks absorb his weight. If only they would—

The *crack* of the rifle ripped through Paul's body like a whip. His head throbbed like cannon fire, even with his ears covered, and his heart felt like it might burst from his chest it beat so violently. A soreness immediately engulfed his jaw—he was clenching his teeth like a vise.

He stretched open his jaw and lowered his hands from his ears.

Curtis was grunting, "Shit…shit…"

Paul opened his eyes and turned around. "What is it?"

Curtis was frantically opening the bolt handle to eject the spent shell and load another bullet. He quickly glanced up at Joseph.

His chain—broken in two.

Curtis hastily spoke. "He flinched just as I was pulling the trigger. The bullet—it ricocheted and hit the chain."

Curtis barely had the rifle ready for another shot when Joseph was on him, slamming into his chest and forcing him back against the wall. The rifle flew from Curtis's hands and slid across the room with a metallic skidding. The pair fell to the floor, Joseph on top, his mouth open wide, teeth bared like a viper ready to strike. Spittle and blood spattered across Curtis's face. He tried holding Joseph back, pressing up into his shoulders, but Joseph was still able to claw at Curtis with his hands, scratching his face and neck. Curtis's arms shook, ready to give way at any moment.

And then—relief. Joseph was off Curtis. He looked up. Paul and Joseph rolled into the corner of the room, Paul on top following through with a tackle. Joseph pushed him off with ease and leaped up from the floor. Paul scrambled away on his hands and knees, slipping on the loose debris strewn about, and just as he was finding his footing to stand up, Joseph grabbed his legs from behind and brought him back down onto his stomach. Paul looked back over his shoulder—Joseph was gnawing at his pant cuffs—then kicked his legs as if swimming out of the grip of a riptide. His eyes darted about the dim room, desperate, and then he saw it—the rifle.

Paul stretched out his arm to grab hold of the barrel. Joseph crawled up Paul's wriggling legs and onto his back. Just as Paul was feeling Joseph's hot breath on the back of his neck, drool trickling down the collar of his jacket, he clutched onto the warm steel and twisted his entire body around, swinging the rifle like a pendulum. He clocked Joseph in the head, stunning him momentarily. Paul slid out from beneath his attacker, sprang to his feet, then grabbed the barrel of the rifle with both hands and brought the butt down onto Joseph's head. Joseph collapsed onto the floor. Paul struck again and again, Joseph's skull giving way with each blow like a boot smashing through a frozen-over puddle. Only when Joseph's head was completely caved in and he was lying on the floor, motionless, did Paul cease with his onslaught.

Paul stood hunched over top Joseph's lifeless body. His chest was heaving, his arms trembling, his clothes wet with sweat and drool. He looked over at Curtis, still down on the floor, propping himself up on his elbows. Ruddy-faced, he stared back at Paul, eyes wide with…what—Horror? Shock? Arousal?

The gun slid out from Paul's slackening grip. It dropped to the concrete floor with a stabbing clatter.

Having refused Carol's offer to drive them to where they had parked their car, Paul and Curtis stumbled back along their trail of inverted footprints, as if traveling back in time. Curtis pressed handfuls of snow against his face where Joseph had scratched him. Spots of red trailed behind them on the ground, like breadcrumbs leading back to the scene of the crime. No one said a word. The only sound either man made was the crunch of their feet pressing into the snow.

They barely gave a moment's pause as they walked past the blue spruce, as if they had silently agreed to spurn the cursed object that had dragged them into Carol's orbit.

Treeless, they crossed the field toward the lot. The sun was setting, wisps of clouds streaking across the sinking sky. The snow-covered field shimmered with washes of pinks and purples, yet neither Paul nor Curtis looked up to acknowledge the splendor of the moment.

They climbed over the split rail fence and trudged back to the lot entrance. No one else was in sight anywhere.

After unlocking the car doors, Curtis slid into the driver's seat with a heavy sigh. He dabbed his face with a crumpled tissue found stuffed in the center console. Paul grabbed the passenger door handle—

He dropped to his knees, his legs suddenly like jelly. Without warning, the contents of his stomach spewed out his mouth and onto the ground, like a water balloon hitting its mark. Throat burning, eyes watering, Paul clutched the door handle while his body heaved and swayed; he was certain that letting go would mean guaranteed death in the most agonizing way imaginable.

And then, as quickly as it came, the vomiting ended.

Following several deep breaths, Paul gave his mouth a wipe with the sleeve of his coat then rubbed the tears from his eyes with the heel of his hand. Glancing about the soiled ground, he noticed his bootlaces untied. Upon pulling up his pant cuff—a sharp intake of breath.

A bitemark on his ankle.

Paul glanced through the car door window at Curtis— he was busy digging his keys out from his pocket—then quickly pulled the cuff back down, concealing the bite. He took another deep breath, opened the door, and climbed into the car. After putting on his seatbelt he leaned back in his seat and closed his eyes. Curtis remarked on something, but Paul didn't respond; he didn't even acknowledge him. He had nothing to say to Curtis. He was the reason this outing went south in so many horrible ways—ways it didn't have to—and there was nothing he could say to make it better. There was nothing Curtis could do to lessen the burden he would now have to carry around for the rest of his life.

Curtis started the car, then played around with the radio, searching for a station that came in clearly. Finding one, he hummed along to the song coming out through the speakers.

Paul was silently mortified. *How can you be so blasé over everything that just happened to us...to me?* he marveled. The more Paul thought on Curtis's apparent indifference the more it turned his stomach, so much he felt he might retch a second time. A surge of warmth crashed through his entire body and a layer of sweat suddenly coated his skin. He could even feel his gag reflexes kicking in, but this time he managed to keep everything at bay with a forceful swallow.

Paul opened his eyes and gave Curtis, now maneuvering the car out of the parking space, a side-eye glance. Paul avoided looking at Curtis's face—he didn't want to risk making eye contact. He didn't want Curtis to think everything was all right. Everything was *not* all right.

What is going on in your mind now anyway? Paul wondered. *More thoughts about killing? More secrets I'd be loath to know about? Well, 'Mystery Man,' if you can be a well of secrets then so can I.*

Paul rubbed his ankles against one another, curbing a sudden itch stemming from the bite.

I'll just have secrets my own, he resolved to himself, *and I guarantee, you won't have a fucking clue what hit you when they come to light.*

Long Forgotten Ghosts of All Hallows' Eve
By Andrew Murphy

I am not sure who will find this tome, let alone who will read it and consider it to be more than the ramblings of a man half-mad with fear.

Yet write it I must, in the hope that someone, somewhere, will understand what happened to me- what happened to us, and why it should have come as no surprise when it did.

I tell you this as best I can. To warn you. So that you may sympathize with my plight, as well as what is liable to have come my way if you are reading this and I am not there to corroborate it. But believe me when I say that every word of this account is true. Not a word nor a name has been changed to paint me or anyone else as better than we were.

It began when I was but a child, one who should have known better than he did, yet who still damned himself and others to a fate possibly worse than death...

I was ten years old when I saw my first ghost.

That is to say, in the time between my tenth and eleventh year, I came face-to-face with something which should have long since moved on from this world but instead lingered on for reasons unknown.

Even at such a young age, it was neither something I had ever expected nor in the years since have found myself overtaken by any urge to repeat. But I am getting ahead of myself. Looking back, it baffles me still how such a thing could have happened, let alone to someone like me.

Firstly, I wish to state that the events which shall unfold from here on out do not stem from some childlike imagination nor any prior interest in anything supernatural. Even as a boy I found myself more on the side of reason and was thus not one to be taken in by such superstitions. So please know I was no believer in ghosts or ghouls, for those things existed only in books and films, not in the real world.

Yet a spirit I did have the grave misfortune to encounter.

It was a little ways before All Hallows Eve- that joyous time of the year children were provided the opportunity to head into the streets after dark under the guise of creatures of all sorts, then return home with a supply of sweets and treats as to make the rest of the year pale in comparison. Alongside Christmas morning and the final moments before summer break came 'round, few other times of the year brought along with them the same sort of excitement.

As I said, it was just before that blessed day when the six- for there were only six of us in our class, being a split group, and unevenly so, of year sixes and sevens, the latter of whom numbered fourteen, were sitting 'round talking of Halloween. Of costumes and candy and all the things we were looking forward to when that night, at last, came 'round.

Now we were not a particularly close bunch outside the school, but inside, we had to be. It was us against them, and being six against fourteen meant sticking together was the wisest course. We played together during break and talked when we could about this or that as children do, all beneath the shadow of our older, antagonistic schoolmates.

So it was that, during a lull in our teacher's lesson, we found ourselves with the rare chance to sit 'round and talk of all things Halloween. And in doing so one of us, that being Thomas- who was, for all intents and purposes, our resident tough guy, came upon an idea.

"You know," Thomas muttered whilst staring out the window at a house across the street whose yard was festooned with a great many spooky decorations, "candy and costumes are all well and good, but you know what I reckon would be more fun?"

None of us knew, for we were not the sort who could read minds and thus hadn't the slightest clue what Thomas was thinking, so we sat in silence and waited for him to bless us with whatever idea had popped into his head. "I think," he continued, "that it'd be a bit of a lark to go out to the cemetery on Friday night."

Friday being Halloween of course.

I had only stepped foot in the local cemetery once in my life, for the funeral of a great uncle whom I'd met when I was an infant and thus possessed but the slightest bit of familial connection to. It was a rainy Sunday afternoon and we'd all stood there feeling miserable until the storm forced the proceedings to be rushed through, thus making the whole ordeal rather pointless. That had been my sole experience amongst the dead, and I was keen to keep it as such.

It also did not strike me that a cemetery would be the best place at night, least of all when you are only ten and even on Halloween your bedtime is nine 'o clock. I did not voice these concerns, however, for you see even amongst the six of us I was very much an outsider, for reasons I still cannot fully understand even twenty years on. We were all the same age, had grown up in the same neighbourhood and went to the same school- for it was a small town, yet I always had the sense that they saw me as somehow different from them.

That, or perhaps they simply thought I was a little off and kept me 'round out of sympathy. I did not know then, and I do not know now, but I tried my hardest to keep up appearances as much as possible lest I lose even the loose sort of friendship I had with them and be left to the wolves.

It was a survival thing you see.

Regardless, the idea was in the air now, and it slowly settled into our minds. I don't recall who spoke first, but I believe it was Maureen, the tomboy of our little group, who chose to throw her two cents in.

"You mean the one just down the road?" she asked, although it was a seemingly pointless question. There was only one cemetery in our sordid little burg, and I think even she- a troublemaker at times, knew it was highly unlikely any of our parents would be keen on us trying to go to one in the next town.

Thomas mulled this over, though he did not have the chance to confirm Maureen's suspicions before someone else chimed in. Jessie, whom I considered the brainiest of our group, and upon whom I must confess I had a bit of a crush on, perked up excitedly. "There's another one," she whispered, "about three blocks from my house. Behind the old church."

I thought about this for a moment, and slowly the picture formed in my mind. Small as our town was, it had managed for some time to have more than a single place of worship, although the old one had fallen into disrepair long before I was born. So old was it that its very name had been lost to history, and the only reason it still stood was that no one wished to knock it down and possibly disturb the graves which surrounded it.

And oh, there were graves there. Abandoned as the church itself may have been, the grounds upon which it sat had more than their share of permanent residents. And while they had not been tended to for generations, you could still see the headstones sticking out of the tall grass whenever you passed by.

It certainly seemed spooky enough for a late Halloween jaunt.

"That's the one I was thinking of," Thomas replied, though I don't believe he meant it. Rather, he had likely been referring to the one most of us had been to at least once for something or other, but now that a more fitting option had presented itself, he was quick to claim credit for it. "It's not too far from my house either."

Mulling it over, we all came to the same conclusion rather quickly- it was close to all of our houses. Most of us lived within walking distance of both the school and the old church, for the town had been built around such places of importance. Even I, who lived a few streets away from even the closest of our group, would not need to stray all that far from my trick-or-treating route to get there.

It certainly sounded like a plan, although I remained unconvinced, and luckily, I was not alone.

"I'm not too sure," inserted Alex, who tended to be quite a reasonable fellow and with whom I was probably the closest. "What would we even do there?"

A sensible question, and one it appeared that Thomas would not have an answer for it. Perhaps he had not expected any of us to show much interest when he'd first broached the subject. Now it was plain to see he was trying to find a good enough reason for us to set out upon such an excursion.

He never had the chance.

Katie, the only girl who had yet to speak up and who was in some respects the den mother of our bunch, decided to take charge as she often did. "That's easy," she concluded. "We'll look for ghosts."

I'm not sure who laughed first, myself or one of the others or if we all did at once. But I do know that before I knew it, we were all caught up in a fit of giggles that nearly caused the teacher to reprimand us. It was an unspoken agreement that none of us, even then, truly believed in spirits.

"Right," Thomas resumed as the laughter died. "We shall go to the old cemetery on Halloween night, and look for some ghosts. Who's with me?"

Katie raised her hand first, understandable as the idea had been hers to begin with. Maureen and Jessie followed suit, Alex joining in soon after. This left me as the only holdout but, not wanting to feel left out even if I was more than a little unsure if this was a good idea or not, put my hand up as well.

I think the rest of them were surprised by this, as I had not said a word the entire time, but if they were not one of them mentioned it. This was fine by me, for I felt that if they dared question me, I would likely have taken it back then and there.

With all hands on deck, we worked out the details until the final bell rang. Our plan, as it came to be, was exceedingly simple. We would already be out and about trick-or-treating, either with family or friends, so it was not as if we would need to sneak out. Though Thomas disagreed at first, we decided to inform our parents of what we were planning, if for no other reason than if the weather chose to turn, we would be alright. It had done so in the past, such as one Halloween in which a sudden blizzard struck not ten minutes into the evening's escapades. This way, we could count on someone coming to pick us up, as none of us had any desire to be caught up in a snowstorm nor torrential rain or any other cruel whim of nature.

In truth, that would be the least of our worries.

After trick-or-treating was over with, for none of us wished to miss out on the procuring of candy, we would meet outside the gates and go looking for ghosts. We would arrive no later than eight o'clock, for the sun would have just gone down and we would not get lost in the dark.

At the time, I doubted this excursion would last longer than ten minutes before we grew bored and headed for home, but still decided to go along with the plan so as not to lose face amongst my peers. The whole thing was so delightfully simple in its execution that now, with the benefit of hindsight, I can only sigh at how not a single one of us had foreseen just how wrong things would inevitably go.

Indeed, they did right from the start, before the night in question even arrived.

You see, one of the year sevens, a boy by the name of Lucas, had overheard our planning. Lucas had a bit of a nasty streak to him and during break the next day sauntered over to where we all stood playing and began to sow the seeds of doubt.

"So," he teased, "you lot are gonna go looking for ghosties are ya?"

Thomas looked over at the older boy. "We are," he replied. "What's it to ya?"

Lucas grinned, and his smile unsettled me more than any thoughts of ghosts could have at the time. "Bunch of sods like you is liable to scare yourselves silly. Go running out into the streets cryin' for yer mums after seeing your own shadows."

Then he started to chuckle, but Thomas was having none of it. "There won't be no cryin', 'cept maybe you when we come back to school and tells ya we found a ghost."

I do not believe for a moment that Thomas thought that any of us would find anything, but it was clear he did not wish to say so in front of his older tormentor and thus did what he thought was best.

Lucas didn't care, he simply continued to laugh as he shrugged his shoulders. "Course ya will. You'll walk right into class with dirty nappies and red eyes you will." Then he headed back to where the older boys spent their break, and Thomas turned 'round with a look of such anger plastered across his face I swore he was going to take it out on one of us.

Instead, he refrained, and took the insults thrown at us as a reason to push onward. "Tomorrow," he declared to the group of us, "we will find ourselves a ghost."

I think he believed that.

The scary part is he was right.

That is not to say that what happened next was his fault. The honest truth is blame lies at all our feet, even if Thomas was the one who set everything in motion. I have often heard it said that the world gives us back what we throw into it, and at that moment, Thomas seemingly dared the universe to send a spirit our way.

Those who say to be careful what you wish for speak the truth. I only wish I'd known just how true that old warning could possibly be.

Before we knew it, Friday night had arrived, bringing with it all the expected excitement of All Hallows Eve, as well as the newfound unease that went hand in hand with our plan.

Though no one else had said a word against it, I could tell as the school clock clicked by that second thoughts were not my burden alone.

Still, when the bell rang we reaffirmed our plans and split off, each heading home for dinner and homework and to get our costumes ready. I myself kept things simple and wore a skeleton shirt and mask my mother had picked up at the shops the day before. It wasn't much, but it did the job just fine.

As night fell and the streets started to fill with kids of all ages, carrying sacks just begging to be filled with treats, I headed out to join them, my father in tow for the first part of the evening's festivities. For a little while at least, things felt as they should- as normal a Halloween night as one could hope for.

If only it could have stayed that way.

We walked along our street and around the nearby blocks, passing other children from school including Maureen and Alex, both of whom nodded as we crossed paths. Neither of us said a word, for we knew in our hearts what was coming next.

Alas, before I knew it- and quicker than I would have liked, I'd filled up my bag and the hands on my watch were closing in on the appointed hour. My father, bless his heart, took my bag and mask with him back to the house, telling me to be careful and to be home as soon as possible, as well as reminding me that he would be 'round if the weather turned. I thanked him in earnest and headed off on my way, unsure of myself but knowing it was far too late to turn back now.

I was, as it turned out, the third person to arrive outside the cemetery gates. Jessie and Thomas were already there, as they lived the closest. If they were surprised that I'd shown up neither one said a word, simply welcomed me as we waited for the rest to arrive.

By five after eight, Alex, Maureen and Katie met us by the gate, each of us carrying a torch in case the lingering traces of twilight were not enough to make our way around by. Gazing through the rusted iron bars of the gate, we could see the wilting grass which even this late in the year threatened to swallow the tombstones, all of them in the shadow of the abandoned church which was certain to house a great many spirits just waiting to be awoken.

Thomas opened the gate carefully, its hinges crying out in the night after so many years of unuse. From a nearby tree, a murder of crows scattered to the sky at the sound, and if I believed in omens of any sort that would have been the first clue that our evening would not go as smoothly as we had planned.

The six of us pushed our way inside before Alex, who was the last one in, gently shut the gate. Our torches lit up, illuminating the bare branches and faded tombstones around us. Vacant cobwebs hung in the shattered windows of the church, adding to the already spooky atmosphere, and if I were being honest, the whole place certainly seemed fit for Halloween.

I'm not certain who it was that suggested we split up, but the idea was raised and agreed upon likely out of sheer desire to do something besides stand around. I'd seen enough scary movies by that age to know this was not the best idea, but as with my decision to join the others here, I went along with it so as not to appear cowardly.

Once the rest had chosen their paths, I made my way down a small trail which led between a mess of headstones, hoping not to lose sight of the gate which led us here nor the beams of everyone else's torches. Alas, it was not long before I managed to fail at both endeavours.

The thing is, cemeteries are, by their very nature, a frightening concept. Hallowed ground within which a community has interred their deceased, with only several feet of dirt separating you from a decaying corpse. Add in all the unkempt grass and shadows of both the trees and the church in which most if not all the dead were memorialized, and it would be hard for anyone not to feel just the slightest bit afraid.

I tell you this so you will understand what comes next. That you will not judge me for my actions. Remember that I was little more than a child, one who had found himself somewhere he had little interest in being, let alone at night and alone save for five schoolmates who were lord knows where in this great mess of a place.

Yet, unbeknownst to me or any of the rest, we were not nearly as alone as we thought.

You see, Lucas, our schoolmate and tormentor, had no desire to see us succeed in our endeavour. In fact, while he likely did not believe we would find anything of the ghostly variety, he wished to make sure if anyone was proven right in their predictions for the night's events, it would be him.

Not long after we had arrived and split up, he and a few of his mates had also congregated outside the cemetery gates. They were still in costume, however, although they were not looking to continue their trick-or-treating in such a place as this. No, their intention was to sneak inside and wait until the time was right, then scare the dickens out of us.

A simple enough plan yes, not unlike our own. Yet by its very nature, as well as his boasts and Thomas's own lingering in that strange either which surrounds and connects this world to the next, just as doomed to failure.

But at the time, I was blissfully unaware of all of this. To be honest, the only thing I was truly aware of was the sound of my own, shallow breaths in the dark and the crinkling of leaves beneath my shaking feet. Though my torch lit the area in front of me, it was not enough to assuage my growing unease at just where I was and why. Not that I truly expected to encounter a ghost or ghoul but even so, standing in a cemetery in the dark was not how I had planned to spend my time once trick-or-treating was over and done with.

There's just something about the darkness and the overbearing silence of the night that seems to intensify any and all unexpected noises. I couldn't hear any of my schoolmates, which told me they were likely further away from me than I thought, but I could hear something else.

What appeared to be footsteps that were not my own, pressing down on the freshly fallen leaves.

At first, I believed it to be one of the others, making their way back towards where I myself had stopped to catch my breath by the back of the old church. However, the lack of any torchlight accompanying the sound told me it was someone else entirely, which did little to temper my growing unease.

Still, I did not expect anything supernatural. The truth of the matter was I worried that a groundskeeper or local passerby had noticed our lights or seen one of us walking through the gate and was coming 'round to give us all a good talking to. That, or perhaps they had placed a call to the police, and they had come to arrest us for trespassing.

Thus, you can clearly see where it was that my fears resided at the time- more in the realm of reality than anywhere else. I had little desire to be dragged by the ear back home by some angry grown-up nor brought to the station by a member of the local constabulary.

It was because of this more than anything else that, rather than fear or surprise, I was instead elated when the source of the sound revealed itself to me by way of stepping into the path of my torchlight. I may have even uttered a small sigh of relief at the sight, for standing scarcely three feet away from me was neither officer of the law nor cross elder, but a girl whom I'd never seen before.

She appeared to be about my age, although it was difficult to discern at first glance. Her hair was golden brown like the fall leaves which rested silently beneath our feet, and her eyes as dark as the night sky above, though they were kind and at that moment kind was good enough for me. The fact that I did not recognize her did not strike me nearly as much as perhaps it should have, given this was a small town and we only had one school so I should have seen her in passing. Yet before I had the chance to consider this, she approached me, her lips held together in an uncertain smile as if she were more unsure of me than I should have been of her.

As she was the first person I'd come across since our group had split up, I think I was just happy to no longer be all alone out here. "Hi," I whispered, so as not to frighten her. She gave me a small nod but did not speak a word, which again, should have tipped me off that there was indeed something strange about all this. "Are you here alone?"

The girl nodded once more, which made me feel slightly better. Though it had only been me before her arrival, I had come with a group. The idea of being here all alone would never have crossed my mind. Indeed, it would have terrified me on principle alone.

Even so, I wondered if she had spotted the rest, for I hadn't as much as seen their torchlight nor heard their footsteps in some time and wondered where the lot of them may have wound up. "Have you seen any other kids about?"

She seemed to think on it for a moment, then nodded again. Though her lack of speaking seemed rather odd, I was aware that mutism was a thing, and even if it were not a disability such as that, she could just not have been the talkative type when strangers were about. Given how often I kept my own mouth shut, who was I to judge?

"Could you show me where? My friends and I split up and I think it's time I catch up with them."

I half expected that to be when the girl at last spoke or perhaps ran off into the night, but she did neither. Instead, she grabbed at my hand and lead me down the path from whence she'd come, her grip chillier than I'd expected even in the late October air.

We made our way past several tombstones and down other paths, the breadth of the old cemetery only then truly dawning on me. Most of us had only ever seen bits of it as we walked past or drove by with family, but the truth was it went further than I'd ever imagined.

Through the bare trees and up a small hill she pulled me until I could look down and see the majesty of the place firsthand. From my vantage point, I could see a great many things- the church in all its dilapidated glory, the gate from whence we had entered, and the torchlight of my five classmates.

But they were not the only people I noticed mucking about in the tall grass below.

Though they were far away, it was plain to see that this group making their way along the path which led deeper into the cemetery were older boys, and while I could not see their faces a part of me knew that one of them must be Lucas. He was the only person besides my classmates and our parents who knew we would be here tonight.

Young as I was, I quickly surmised their intent. They wanted to scare us and, given that the others were still going about on their own, would likely succeed. I needed to gather them together and then, perhaps, turn the tables on our would-be tormentor and his friends.

Beside me, the strange girl seemed puzzled, following my gaze down toward Lucas and his mates. "Those aren't my friends," I explained. "They're older boys. Probably looking to give us a scare... If I can get to my friends, perhaps we can scare them instead."

She nodded, giving me another small, tight-lipped smile, then grabbed my hand once more and pulled me down the hill towards the first beam of torchlight. As it was, I didn't have to do all that much. Whether by luck or a twist of fate, by the time I reached that first beam- which belong to Alex, his already intersecting with some of the others, Maureen's and Katie's to be exact.

The three of them saw me coming, though neither said a word about my mysterious companion. In truth, as I ran towards them, I felt her hand slip out from mine and, looking back, I noticed her standing in the path alone. Confused as I was, I knew I had to get to the others, and assumed she would catch up to us momentarily.

"Find anything?" Katie asked as I caught my breath, perhaps half-expecting me to say no as well as explain my rush to join them. Alex and Maureen shook their heads and before I could say a single word, Jessie and Thomas came along another path to join us. This was rather fortuitous, as once they joined the rest of the group, I managed to get the words out.

"I found something, but not a ghost. Some older kids are in the cemetery, and I think I know who they are." I relayed my suspicions, explaining what I'd noticed while atop the hill, but refrained from mentioning the girl, who strangely enough had not caught up with us. I brushed this off as her perhaps not being comfortable amongst strangers, even if a small part of me was beginning to ponder other possibilities best left unspoken.

With all of us back together and informed of things, we made our way in the opposite direction from where I'd seen Lucas and his mates coming from, to lay in wait ourselves to catch them in their act. We had little in the way of a plan but figured at worst, we could slip out unseen and thus rob them of their desired success.

As we moved along, with only Thomas's torchlight lit so as not to give up our location, I kept my eyes peeled not for our pursuers, but instead for the mysterious girl. She had to have gone somewhere, even if I hadn't a clue where.

The fact that neither Alex, Jessie nor Maureen had mentioned her even though she must have been visible beside me as I made my way towards them filled me with further unease, as well as a bit of guilt. She'd been so helpful, and I hadn't even managed to learn her name.

After a little bit, Thomas finally stopped, pointing out a crop of trees which stood between the nearby fence and the last row of tombstones. It would be here that we six would make our stand, whatever that may be. We made our way behind the trunks and waited, with Jessie noting the gate a little ways away in case things took a turn.

It took a few minutes for us to hear anything, and even then it was difficult to surmise just what it was. Had we been unaware that there were indeed others in the cemetery this night, it would have been rather easy to blame the sounds on a fox or raccoon, but we knew better. Lucas and his mates were closing in, and we readying ourselves to do to them what they'd planned on doing to us.

I would love nothing more than to tell you we succeeded. That the night's events concluded with our tormentor and his friends getting their comeuppance and the rest of us returning home without having found that which we sought yet triumphant all the same. This more than anything is what I wish to say occurred that fateful evening but, as I noted at the start, my intent is to tell things as they happened, and the truth of the matter was far different than the desired outcome.

We could see the beam of a torchlight coming up the path, and hear the whispers of the older boys who seemed to still be plotting their own scheme even now. We watched as they passed by the rows of tombstones we ourselves had only moments before walked by, and we waited with bated breath until they were close enough that we could leap out and frighten them off.

Alas, we never had the chance. Someone else beat us to the punch.

She appeared out of nowhere like she'd been standing in the path this whole time yet none of us had spotted her. Mere feet between the approaching boys and the trees behind which the rest of us waited behind. If that had been it, then perhaps I would not have been as frightened as I was. But it was plain to see, even from where we were standing, that Lucas's torchlight was shining right through her.

The strange girl was translucent, and though her feet rested upon the stone path, that did not seem to matter. All the older boys stopped in their tracks, unsure if this were a prank or something. I looked over at Thomas and the others, wondering if perhaps one of them had indeed set this all up, but the nervous expressions painted upon their faces told me all I needed to know.

We could do little more than watch as one of her spectral arms moved up, brushing away the hair which had fallen onto her face. And though she was not looking at us, something inside told me that it was not the same kind smile and dark eyes I'd first encountered that Lucas and his mates were now greeted by.

Screams filled the air, and within seconds the torch fell to the ground as the older boys turned white as sheets and ran as far from the girl as they could. And much as a part of me enjoyed the sight of it, the sudden realization of what it all meant robbed me of any possible mirth.

As did what happened next.

We watched in horror as Lucas rushed to escape the cemetery, pushing through the gate as if his life depended on it, and ran screaming into the street. Just as a car came screeching 'round the corner.

Now I had seen people hit by cars on the telly and in films, and though it always seemed ghastly even there, it was nothing compared to seeing it firsthand. The sound of his bones cracking from the impact of the car's hood, the sight of his body flipping over the roof and landing with a twisted thud upon the street.

Much as I wanted nothing more than to vomit, I restrained myself best as I could, turning away from the sight and landing my gaze upon my classmates, all of whom had bore witness to the same thing. None of us spoke a word, our mouths dry and our breath practically trapped in our lungs. Then, slowly, we looked back towards the girl, who stood there watching us, her eyes the same as they had been before, but her mouth... The smile she sported now was unlike anything I had ever seen. It was kind and cruel and fun and frightening all at once, and the chills it sent down my spine made those brought about by the cool autumn air pale in comparison

And yet, even that was not as bone-chilling as when she spoke.

Looking our way, her handiwork laying in the road as the driver of the car frantically tried to help while dealing with the frightened and distressed older boys, she opened her mouth and spoke four simple words. Words which would echo in my mind for years to come.

"Penny for a smile?"

Before any of us could say a word, someone ran up the path, torch in hand, and voice breaking whatever spell the spirit had begun to weave. It was Jessie's father, who had come to see if she and the rest of us had grown tired of our little adventure and who had noticed the accident. Upon making sure it wasn't his daughter or any of us laying there in the road, he rushed in to find us, driving off the ghostly girl who had brought all this upon us.

The six of us followed him out of the cemetery, our own parents and an ambulance arriving soon after. I did not look back for the girl, none of us did as far as I could tell. Yet something inside me told me that she was still there, watching, waiting. Waiting on a penny that was never coming. Payment for her services.

Lucas did not survive the accident.

The doctors claimed the impact of the car had killed him instantly, but I believed otherwise. I believe he was already dead by the time he reached the road, and the expression on his face as they loaded him into the ambulance all but confirmed my suspicions.

He had died of fright.

His friends were questioned, as were the six of us. They admitted they had gone in with the intent to frighten us, and we told of our plans to find a ghost. Not a single one amongst us mentioned the girl, either out of fear or perhaps knowing in our hearts that regardless of what we had all seen and heard, no one was liable to believe us.

The official story, as it came to be known, was that Lucas had suffered from an unexpected panic attack, caused by something in the old cemetery, which then led to his running out into the street. His parents did not agree with this one bit and tried to sue the driver to no avail. It was listed as an accident and nothing more, and most people just tried to forget it had ever happened.

School was closed for a few days after, and a counsellor came in to talk to all of us who had been there that night. She was nice, but we still kept our mouths shut. Much as a part of me wanted to tell her everything, to confide in someone the truth of the matter, I was far too frightened to do so.

Frightened that the girl would come for me if I dared speak a word.

After that, we all tried to keep on as we had before, but the six of us were never truly the same. We weren't as close as we had been, which wasn't say all that much really. It was as if the burden of that night drove a wedge into the already fragile ground between us, and we couldn't as much as acknowledge it out of fear of what may happen if we did.

When the year ended, my family moved away. They said it was for my father's work, but I knew the truth. They wanted to get as far away from that town and what had happened there as possible. And to be honest, I agreed with them. After all that, I had no desire to remain and hoped that eventually, the events of that horrid All Hallows Eve would fade away.

And for a time, they did.

It was several years later when, on as cool an Autumn evening as ever there was, several mates of mine and I found ourselves sitting 'round with steaming mugs of tea between us, and got to talking of strange things.

These were of a different breed and place than those whom I had known in my younger days, for our acquaintance was made long after those dreadful ones of which I have informed you. It was neither our custom nor planned in advance that we would meet up in such a way, but rather, the result of a peculiar series of events which conspired to bring us together once more.

Or to bring me ever closer to a fate I had long since driven from my mind.

There were, as it turned out, four of us present that night, myself being one of them of course. There was also Marty, whom I used to call my best mate when we were chums over at St. Margaret's, but who I regret I had lost contact with several years past.

Old Joe was also there, called as such for being two years our senior yet remaining amongst us, nonetheless. Not for any educational deficiency, but rather his fancying a young lady in our class, and wishing to spend as much time around her as was possible.

Lastly, but most importantly as it would turn out, was Smith. As quiet fellow as you could find, yet always good for a lark when we'd been lads, and who was recovering from a minor stay in the local hospital some weeks prior, though seemingly no worse for wear.

It had not been two hours earlier that our little group had become reacquainted after ten or so years apart by way of an impromptu reunion set up by an over-eager schoolmate of ours. One who seemed to think enough time had passed to warrant a coming together of people most of whom still ran into one another at the shops or at the pub.

That was certainly true for me. While I'd left home after my schooling days had come to an end and taken a few years travelling all about the back roads and countryside in search of something or other, I'd been back home and settled in long enough to have crossed paths with more of our erstwhile schoolmates than I'd have preferred.

Strangely enough, it is only now, looking back as I write this tale out, that I realize I was not in fact searching for something all those years. Rather, it would appear I was instead trying to escape something which I myself had forgotten was even chasing me.

Oh, but at the time it had seemed a great stroke of luck that my original plans for the evening had fallen through, and I'd decided to brave the chilly October air to see just who would bother to show up at this little get-together. I had scarcely noticed the date upon the calendar, for that once blessed day had lost much of its lustre as I grew older, and now it was just another day.

Even so, it proved fortuitous, for I had not seen the old gang since a month after Marty's wedding, three years after we'd finished up at St. Margaret's, and I was most pleased to be back in their company, though less so most of the others. It did not take long at all before one of us suggested we vacate the hotel in which we had found ourselves and find somewhere more suited to our tastes.

Once upon a time, that would have been the pub, but it seemed the lot of us had outgrown our youthful indulgences- myself having not touched the drink in years, although now I wish I had, and thus decided upon a small cafe a little way up the road. We settled in at a table and ordered cups of tea, as well as some biscuits- for Smith informed us he could not enjoy tea without biscuits these days, and began to revel in one another's company without the interruptions of those we had not seen, nor wanted to, for some time.

At first, we spoke of the usual things, where our paths had taken us since we'd last seen one another and such. I told of my foolhardy adventures along the back roads- and of nearly freezing my knickers off one dreadful evening. Rough is it had been, and it had, such things had more than laid the groundwork for my current livelihood, writing for the local rag.

Joe spoke of his 'career' as it was; selling office furniture out of a truck alongside a fellow old enough to be his granddad. He'd given up his pursuit of our classmate Lydia sometime after school had let out for good, though it was clear he still carried a bit of a torch for her, given how sullen he appeared when she did not turn up at the reunion.Smith related his tale of being out on the dole ever since he'd taken a tumble at the warehouse he worked in, and how horrid the stay in the hospital had been- especially the night in which some food disagreed with him so much he'd gone and broken the loo. We all had a good laugh at that.

Poor Marty told us of his divorce, scarcely five years into an unhappy marriage, and with a child to boot. Of how his ex, Amelia- whom none of us had ever cared for, claimed she'd been robbed of her youth by him, and how not once had he told her what he had lost due to one drunken mistake. Even so, their daughter, Joni, was the light of his life, so some good came from it after all.

It was pleasant enough conversation, noting that as much as we had grown and changed over the years, we were still the same blokes we'd been ten years back, and how nice it was that we could settle back into one another's company so quickly.

Yet, just as quickly, as if by the cruel whims of fate, our talk began to drift away from more jovial matters and towards stranger things indeed. It was not decided by any one of us, at least not consciously, and though I cannot recall who got the ball rolling in the first place, it was there that we wound up.

At first, it was upon nothing specific that we dwelled. Little tidbits, such as the spirit everyone used to claim haunted St. Margaret's. The one we all joked must have spent copious amounts of time in the ladies changing room given the noises they always claimed to hear. Or things I'd seen and heard whilst wandering the countryside, like the time I'd been convinced for a half-mile or so that a Black Dog was coming to claim my soul, before realizing it was nothing but a lost beagle and that I was rather drunk.

Marty tossed in a rather humidors quip about Amelia, who even in our school days had been an ardent believer in all things supernatural, much to my dismay. And how she claimed after birth that young Joni was the reincarnation of Churchill of all people. Marty blamed the epidural they'd had to pump into her but added he would wait until his daughter was of drinking age to confirm her suspicions.

Laughs abounded, for it was all in good fun, but something else seemed to be brewing alongside our tea. Something like fairy dust or angel feathers, a spiritual red flag of sorts. Rather fitting, given it was once again All Hallows Eve, when the door between worlds is open to shadowy things best left alone.

It was Smith who changed the tone of things, though part of me wishes to God he hadn't. His normally quiet green eyes took on a far more sombre look than I'd ever seen. Sipping from his steaming mug, he stared at the lot of us and sighed. "If it's ghosts you want to chat about, I've got a tale for ya."

The lot of us sat there as Smith began to tell of something he had heard whilst laid up in the hospital, from the man in the bed across from his own. A rambling sort of fellow, one who looked as if he'd either been in an accident or was planning out his mummy costume, so wrapped up he was.

Whatever the reason, it was what the man spoke of, in hushed whispers nearly every chance he got, which piqued ol' Smith's interest, and which he chose to share with us. Something about a bogey sort of thing which seemed to walk the streets of our fair city."It's an odd thing," he related, "for it did not sound to me as such a thing to take fright of, at least not right off the bat... Sent a chill down me back to be sure, like a fella was walking 'cross me grave, but seemed to scare this bloke all the way through."The man had been, as it was, out walking one evening, minding his own business, when, he saw it.

Out of the corner of his eye at first, then standing right in front of him. A woman.

"She had dark, chestnut eyes, nestled all hidden 'neath long auburn hair," Smith continued, "looked a bit lost just standing there on the side of the road. Then she was right beside him, and any thought he had of walking away slipped right out of his mind."

Old Joe perked up at that, joking adding that she likely asked if the lad wanted a quick shag before she showed him she was a bloke as well. He spoke from experience, a story we all recalled that he wished to forget, and which we all shared a laugh at before letting Smith get on with his tale.

"Nothing like that," he resumed as his smile faded away. "Said those eyes of hers, when they looked his way, was more like they were looking right through him. Then, in a voice warm as Spring morn' but cold as a witch's tit at the same time, she asked him a question. 'Penny for a smile'?"

A chill shot down my spine at those four words, one which had sod all to do with the weather. They struck a chord deep within my soul, one which had not been played in many a year. I nearly spilled my tea as I tried to set the cup straight, a sight which was more than enough to catch the attention of the others.

"You all right there?" Marty asked, half-concerned and half, I think, amused looking to have a go at me for my apparent fright at what sounded to them to be little more than the sort of tale you'd hear around a playground. And much as I wished to agree with them on that, something inside me refused. A memory.

"Fine. Go on then."

Smith shot me a look of his own, one that made me think even he didn't pay much mind to the yarn he was spinning. "Anyhow, bloke reached into his pocket, knowing he didn't have a thing in 'em but feeling like he had to try anyway. Just in case. And when he came up empty-handed, she still gave him a smile. One he said he'd never forget. Then she was gone." He took a fresh biscuit and broke it in two, swishing each piece 'round his mug before tossing 'em both back. The look in his eyes was still on the sombre side, but it could not hold a candle to the feeling growing in the pit of my stomach.

"Said he looked 'round, up and down the street but he couldn't find her. Tried to call the coppers- they told him to cut down on the drink and quit wasting their time. But he knew she was there, and knew she wasn't quite done with him. Not until he paid his due."

Sitting there, my mind trickled back to days gone by. Before I was acquainted with these lads. Before I called this city home. When my family had lived in the country, and I'd gone to school not far from a forgotten cemetery... I shook my head, convinced my imagination was getting the better of me and determined to hear the rest of Smith's tale.

"This bloke, he kept on looking. Eyes in the back of his head and all that. Convinced this girl, or whatever she was, would slide up beside him again one night... Then one day, some bird bumps into him on the sidewalk, and he's so scared it's her he runs straight into the middle of the road and gets nailed by a car."

Again, my mind jumped back, throwing memories at me of another violent encounter with a vehicle. One whose victim did not live to tell the tale. Thoughts mixed with the story, and I did not care for what was drummed up by their twisted dance.

Now it is not uncommon to hear such tales, for the world is filled with stories of ghosts and ghouls and tricks the night plays on the unsuspecting. It's easy to tell yourself that this is all they are, all they could ever be.

Because the truth is, if they are real, then one must ask questions they may not want answered.

Smith finally broke the silence after a moment, saying it was a hell of a story and one which had kept him entertained whilst in recovery. He shot a grin my way as he could plainly see it had given me a bit of a fright, then laughed like he always did. We joined in, even if I was not nearly as jolly as I'd been at the start. Something about that story was familiar to me, but I could not put my finger on what.

Our conversation such as it was mellowed out after that, and the clock ticked on 'til it was later than older fellows like us could stand to be out any longer. We all had lives waiting 'round for us when morning came, so we paid our tabs and collected our coats, agreeing we ought to do this again, on our own terms rather than waiting for another pointless reunion to be called.

Joe had brought his car and offered Marty a ride, and Smith planned to make his way over to the station so he could catch the last coach home. Both options were offered to me as well, but the cafe was close enough to my flat that I thanked them and wished them a good night and headed off on my way.

Before I split off though, I turned to Smith and asked, out of curiosity as well as unease, what the name of the bloke who told him the story was. I was not sure why it mattered, nor could I explain myself if he asked, but it seemed important. He thought it over for a moment or two, then his eyes lit up. "I think it was Alex something or other... Why do you ask?"

"No reason," I replied, trying in vain to hide my growing chills. "Thought it might make a good story is all." Then we shared one last laugh and parted, though I knew the tale he had told was not one I would ever write for the public. After all, it was one I had lived once, so many years ago.

Try as I might not to dwell on things, nor to think back to days gone by, the memories lingered at the fringes of my mind like scavengers waiting on the shoreline. At the time I could not recall them clearly, yet I knew in my heart that Smith's roommate's tale, as well as their name, was familiar to me, and not because I may have heard them in passing.

No, there was something else to it, as well as those four words I had heard in what I thought had been nothing more than a dream.

A dream about a brown-haired, dark-eyed girl who was not all that she seemed.

I walked along, trying to shake off the memories as best I could. Nary a half-dozen others were out and about, all either heading to or from the pubs, as well as a busker packing his gear away for the night. Had it been earlier, the streets would have been filled with children seeking candy and fun, but now they were mine and mine alone.

As were the memories which threatened to rise up and consume me.

Scarcely a block from my flat, the cool night air had calmed my nerves and I was ready for a good night's sleep to do the rest when I saw it. Out of the corner of my eye, just a little way up ahead. A young lady stopped at the corner, seemingly waiting on the light to change.

For the briefest of moments my heart jumped in my chest, but as the woman remained where she was it passed. It was likely she too was trying to get home just as I was, and so I steadied myself and continued forward, doing little more than sparing her a glance as I approached.

She looked about my age, with golden hair draped down over her back and her face in places. A face that, while hidden, still looked a little on the fetching side of things. Neither of us spoke

a word and, as the light changed, I prepared to leave her behind, along with my worries and Smith's spirited tale.

And then, a soft voice made its way to my ears. One I had not heard in a great many years, but one whose words had only just returned to my memory.

"Penny for a smile?"I dared not turn around. Dared not face her again. Instead, I ran, ran as far as my legs could carry me, and did not stop until the door to my flat was safely shut behind me, and I could release the breath which had been caught in my lungs the whole way.

And still, I knew I would never be safe enough.

It has been three days now, and I have neither slept nor brought myself to look out the window. Instead, I write these words down, the memories of my youth now as clear as day. I do so in the hope that I may expunge them from my soul and, should things take a turn as I am almost certain they will, that someone may understand.

As I do so, I wonder about poor Alex, laying there in his hospital bed. Did he succumb to his injuries, or did she come for him when he was no longer able to escape? Will she wait until he is free and continue to follow him until he has at long last paid the price?

And what of Thomas, or Maureen, or Katie or sweet Jessie? I had never thought to seek them out in the years since I'd left our old town and school behind, yet now I wonder and I worry that they too may have fallen prey to the machinations of something far beyond the scope of our world, let alone our understanding.

She has already come for me once, and had I not run, what then? Could I have paid her off with thirty pieces of silver just as the Romans did with Judas? Or would she not rest until she claimed my life in return for the one which she took that cold Halloween night so long ago?

I cannot say, and I am too frightened to ponder it further. Once I have finished here, I shall get my affairs in order as best I can and then, perhaps, head out once more into the world. To wait for her to finish what she started. And to get what she has waited all these years to obtain.

A penny for a smile.

Lord knows it is far less than our lives are worth.

Jupiter's Moons
By Josiah Santos

They knew how long their mission would take, and what being in space that long would do to their psyche. So, just to give the spacecraft Zeus a livelier feeling, they brought aboard decorations for every holiday.

"This is Giovanni Cassini aboard the Zeus! Houston, please respond!"

A few moments of silence were later followed by a small voice, mostly hidden by static. It was October 24th and the spaceship had been decorated in several Halloween-themed items all month long. Took them forever to decorate and Captain Cassini tried to argue that it was a waste of time. Necessary? Probably not. But a lighthearted tone had been felt throughout the crew since the decorations went up.

"Zeus? We're having trouble reading you, Zeus. It's been eleven days…we haven't been able to…why haven't you—" the voice said.

"I know, Houston! Our comms has been down ever since…look, one of my men has…I don't know what's happened to him! I just need help; please advise!" Giovanni slammed his fist against the wall impatiently. "Houston, I don't know how much longer comms will be up before it cuts out again! Houston, I'm lost here!"

Static and no response. Back at NASA, a man sat in his chair and sipped his cup of coffee while he heard Giovanni's broken voice. Most of the crew were laying facedown by now; some in one piece, most of them in multiple. None of them suspected that NASA had planted a bomb on their craft. However, this bomb took the form of one of their own.

"Cassini? We hear you; what's the situation with Clyde?" The man calmly asked.

Giovanni paused for a moment in shock. "I didn't tell you it was Clyde that's in trouble. How did you know that?" Giovanni felt a cold chill come over him.

Adams, a fellow astronaut standing next to Giovanni, slowly put his hand over the radio and switched it off.

"*They* chose us for this mission for a reason…put Clyde on our ship on purpose. Made sure our comms wasn't functioning when Jupiter's moons were surrounding this ship!" Adams' voice began to rise.

Giovanni slammed Adams against the wall and put a hand over Adams' mouth.

"You keep your voice down! He's still out there and we still don't have a plan!" Giovanni whispered.

Adams shoved him back.

"Accept it, Giovanni. NASA knows what's going on. This mission was just a front for the real reason we're here," Adams lowered his voice.

"Which is what? They can't just cover this up!"

"Come on, don't be stupid. Our radio mysteriously stops working the moment we start passing a few of Jupiter's moons…" Adams' voice trailed off like he realized something as he was talking.

He slumped against the wall and sat on the floor. He looked straight ahead at the plastic jack-o-lantern staring back at him on the floor. That smile it wore; it made Adams feel as though NASA was the pumpkin with the cruel smile, pleased that their plan had worked so perfectly, and now laughing at him for falling so easily into the trap. A low thumping noise was heard off in the distance. The thumping began to grow softer, and it seemed to stop after a few minutes. Adams felt his eyes begin to water and he put his head back on the wall and looked up at Giovanni with tears in his eyes.

"…it makes sense," Giovanni whispered, unable to make eye-contact with Adams. "We have one moon. Jupiter has seventy-nine. This mission was never about gathering information for habitable environments. This is a test."

Adams closed his eyes and tears streamed down his face. He opened them and the jack-o-lantern met his gaze again. It felt strange; looking at something that always reminded him of candy, horror movie marathons, and taking his kids trick-or-treating. Now it was a twisted joke; a reminder of the home he'd probably never see again. And that smile!

"We're going to die on this ship, aren't we? You know NASA will never let us come home," Adams asked.

Giovanni looked at the floor and thought for a minute. Then, he looked at Adams and smiled.

"What?" Adams asked.

"The airlock. I'm the only one with the authorization code to open the airlock!"

Adams looked confused, "so what? Even if we managed to get Clyde off this ship, what difference does it make? You really think NASA will let us live even if we made it back home?"

The thumping slowly returned, this time, growing louder until it began to make the walls in their room vibrate. Giovanni pulled out his wallet and took out a picture of his wife and kids, tossing it at Adams.

"We have a reason to *try*, Adams! Think of your own family! I'm not giving up on them just yet. Now…get up. If we're going to die out here, I'm going to die on my feet trying. Our families deserve that much."

Giovanni extended his hand and Adams nodded and took it. Giovanni pulled him to his feet and Adams wiped his eyes.

"First thing we need to agree on…if either of us dies in the process—" Giovanni began.

"— Don't turn the ship around. I know. Clyde can't make it back to earth one way or the other. Just one question," Adams asked as he picked up a crowbar.

"What's that?"

"Why don't we get as far away from Jupiter as we can. Then, do what we need to do?"

Giovanni shook his head, "you know we'd never make it. The moment we leave this room, we'll only have a few minutes before Clyde finds us. There's no way we'd be able to turn the ship around and get away from here without Clyde reaching us first. We have to blow him out of the airlock before anything else and unfortunately…" Giovanni looked out the window at the black void of space. It was beautiful and terrifying. Surrounded by the empty blackness would've been a tranquil scene. You could look out into space and see all the beauty and majesty of the Good Lord who created it.

The mystery and wonder of everything out there were something Giovanni and Adams had loved staring at and taking pictures of to bring back to their families. It had never looked more beautiful than the day they first launched into space. It was a view few human beings ever got to see, and it was all theirs. But now that blackness held seventy-nine moons that were surrounding the Zeus, ominously staring at them. "…unfortunately for us, we have seventy-nine reasons why this is a suicide mission."

Adams bent down and picked up Giovanni's picture of his family.

"Well, we have *one reason* why we're going to try. They deserve that much, right?" Adams made his best effort to smile.

Giovanni nodded, "that's right. So, let's get it done."

The thumping gradually fell silent after a few minutes.

"Now or never," Giovanni whispered.

Giovanni picked up a large wrench, a little over a foot long, the only thing in the room he could find. Adams gripped his crowbar and stood by the door. Giovanni looked at Adams as he reached for the doorknob.

"I never thanked you for saving me yesterday," Giovanni whispered.

"I should've saved more," Adams frowned.

"You did the best you could do. You nearly got yourself killed dragging me in this room."

"I would've traded places with any one of them, you know that, right?"

Giovanni nodded, "of course I do." He put his hand on the doorknob and began to turn the handle until they heard a soft click. "Ready?"

Adams nodded. Giovanni held up three fingers. Adams took a deep breath and held his crowbar like a baseball bat. Giovanni put one finger down; he closed his eyes and pictured his wife the day they got married.

Space was beautiful, but nothing on earth or in space could ever be more stunning than her. He put another finger down. Giovanni opened his eyes and gripped the wrench with white knuckles. He put the last finger down and swung the door open.

They both dove in the hallway; the metal and paint on the walls were torn apart by claw marks. Giovanni pointed to the left and they both quietly rushed down the hall, Giovanni in front. Once down the hall and before turning a corner, they put their backs to the wall as Giovanni peered around the corner. The mess hall was a complete massacre; littered with corpses, not a single body was fully intact. The plastic pumpkin lights that were previously hanging down from the ceiling were drooping down; one long strand of lights was hanging all the way down, touching the floor. No sign of Clyde. Giovanni silently motioned that the coast was clear. They continued into the mess hall, covering their noses and mouths due to the stench, and were careful to watch their footing for fear of stepping in blood and slipping.

Adams noticed the windows in the mess hall, next to one of the windows was a small poster of a poorly drawn ghost, drawn by one of the crew members, with the words, "Halloween Party on October 31st, 5pm! Be there or be scared!"

"Where else would we be? We're all on the same spaceship!" Adams had teased the crew member at the time.

That's when he saw it; large and wide, a giant window was displaying one of Jupiter's moons in full view. He silently cursed to himself and tapped Giovanni on the shoulder.

"I know…we can't let Clyde reach the mess hall. We'll be royally screwed," Giovanni confirmed.

The thumping seemed to grow more audible, and the silverware on the tables softly vibrated with each thump, making a gentle jingle noise as the force of the thumping moved them. Adams' first thought was that someone was ringing a tiny bell. Though, it only meant that Clyde was closer than they thought.

Giovanni continued out of the mess hall, and into another hallway, which led into a large meeting room. Giovanni cautiously turned the door handle, unsure if Clyde was in the meeting room or not. In any event, both men were ready if he was. Adams nodded and Giovanni opened the door halfway and quickly nodded, gesturing that the room was empty. Nearly empty. Giovanni quietly shut the door behind them and exhaled, realizing he was subconsciously holding his breath the whole time they were in the hallway. The meeting room looked like a gorilla had been searching the entire room for a banana, and upon entering the room, they were both immediately met with an awful smell coming from behind a desk in the corner.

The only thing they could see from where they were standing was a pair of legs sticking out from the side of the desk. Adams walked over to his right to get a better look and saw that the legs weren't attached to anything. The sight caused Adams to immediately turn and vomit noisily on the floor. Adams covered his mouth and stood motionless with Giovanni as they heard a low growl apparently coming from behind a wall. Giovanni was only a few feet away from Adams and held out his hand with his fingers spread out, motioning for Adams not to move. Adams tried to hold his nose but the rancid smell from behind the desk was unbearable. It was as if the disgusting odor was inside his nose and every time he breathed in, he smelled only the stench itself.

Unable to hold his breath any longer, he inhaled, and the stench entered his nostrils once more. The growl came again and was higher in pitch. The sound made both men jump. It wasn't coming from behind a wall. It was coming from upstairs. Adams flailed his arms, trying to get Giovanni to run away from him and he suddenly puked again, this time much louder. A large arm punched through the ceiling and they both jumped back, screaming. There were two doors in the meeting room. The door they came in, leading back into the hallway, which led back to the mess hall. And the other door which led directly into a lab room.

"Split up!" Giovanni shouted, pointing for Adams to go back through the door they came in.

The arm, which was covered in dark hair and possessed long, vicious-looking claws at the end of each finger, tore a chunk of the ceiling away. Then came the second arm, which began ripping another piece of the ceiling off.

"And go *where*?" Adams shouted.

"You go through the hall! I need to get something in the lab room!" Giovanni shouted back.

"Are you insane? We can't let Clyde reach the mess hall! If he goes after me, we're both done for!"

Faster and faster, the two hairy arms were tearing the ceiling apart, creating a much larger hole. A large snout came through the hole and the mouth opened to reveal bloody fangs as it howled.

Realizing Adams had a good point, Giovanni ran and grabbed Adams by the shirt and pulled him into the lab room, slamming the door behind them. Adams and Giovanni both hid in a large locker; they were crammed but there was nowhere else to hide. They listened closely as they could hear the thing tear all the way through the ceiling and crash down into the meeting room. They heard another furious howl and some chairs crashing against the walls. One flying chair managed to hit the door to the lab room so hard, it broke the door off the hinges, sending the door flying into the lab room. The thing caused the floor to feel like it was shaking as it entered the room. Each time its feet hit the ground after a step, there was a low rumble, slightly shaking all the lab equipment on the tables.

Peering through the slits in the locker, Adams could see the thing raise its snout in the air and loudly sniff the air. The head was massive and was covered in fur. The ears were large, about the length of an adult hand, and pointed like a bat. They shifted back and forth, listening for anything nearby. Its dark purple and soulless eyes scanned the room until they saw movement, then raised its large muscular arm, and swiped at the rat cage. The cage flew across the room and broke apart, releasing a few rats. Two black rats, frightened from the sudden destruction of their home, scurried across the floor and into the meeting room.

One white rat scampered by the thing's feet, causing the large thing to notice and swipe at the rat with its claws. The claws tore through the rat and sent it flying against a wall. The white rat squeaked in terror as it landed on the ground, two large gashes in its side began to bleed. The large thing then noticed the other black rats escaping into the meeting room and went to chase after them.

"We need to act fast," Giovanni whispered.

"What are you talking about? Why did you lead us here? I thought we were going to the airlock?" Adams whispered back as they both quietly snuck out of the locker, making sure to stay low and out of view of the big thing.

"There's some tranquilizers in here; we used them on the lab rats. If we can use them on Clyde, we can drag him to the airlock asleep instead of having him chase us there. You know he'll kill us before we ever got to it."

"Those sedatives were used on *rats*! Look at Clyde now! He's nearly three times the size of an adult!"

"Which is why we have to use every tranquilizer we have left! It should be enough to put him out long enough to drag him to the airlock before he wakes up."

Adams peered around a lab table and saw Clyde still chasing the rats in the meeting room, occasionally trying to step on them to no avail. The white rat's breathing was labored but it was still alive. Its tail faintly stirred as it tried to get up.

"What if you're wrong?"

Giovanni shook his head, "I won't be. Now hurry, help me look for them."

As quietly as they could, they moved around lab equipment and slowly opened drawers until they found six tranquilizers. Adams grabbed them all and carefully placed them in his pocket as they stood by the lab room doorway, waiting until Clyde had his back turned to them. From Clyde's elbows, down to his waist, was a large thin piece of cartilage that served as a wing. When Clyde raised his arms to swipe at the rats, the men could see just how large his wings were; something that was barely visible back when Clyde first started feeling ill.

"Had he grown them over the past few days? Even during yesterday's attack, I didn't see…bat wings under his arms. Maybe I just didn't see him clearly…I didn't get a good look at him," Giovanni thought to himself.

Just what NASA had created and turned Clyde into, Giovanni had no idea. But this wasn't the time to think about that. He got his wrench ready and held a finger to his lips as he slowly crept towards Clyde, now that

Clyde's back was to them. Adams had momentarily forgotten about the mutilated body in the corner, and now, coming from the lab, he could not only see the severed legs on the floor, but the rest of the body behind the desk. Too revolting for words, Adams gagged at the sight and felt himself ready to puke again. They were about ten feet away from Clyde and Adams knew if he let himself vomit now, Clyde could easily turn around and kill them both. Still, the gag reflex came again, and with a decision to make, Adams decided he wouldn't let Clyde have that chance. The urge to vomit was seconds away and Giovanni would never reach Clyde in time.

Adams gave Giovanni a look and he threw his crowbar with all his might. The crowbar whipped through the air and smacked Clyde in the back of his giant head, sending Clyde stumbling forwards and falling to the ground. Giovanni darted towards Clyde as Adams vomited on the floor. Giovanni swung his wrench, sending it slamming down on Clyde's head. Clyde let out a yelp like a dog when it gets its paw stepped on. Standing over a stunned Clyde on the floor, Giovanni then realized that Adams had the tranquilizers.

"Hurry! He's getting up!" Giovanni shouted.

Adams winced in pain and forced himself to run, taking out the tranquilizers from his pocket and handing them off to Giovanni. Giovanni uncapped each tranquilizer and injected Clyde as fast as he could. Clyde twitched and flailed on the ground as the first few tranquilizers were administered. Once the convulsions stopped, Clyde lay motionless on the ground and his long snout began to let out soft respires.

"We don't have much time. I'll help you drag him to the airlock, but then I need to run back to the control room to enter my authorization code to open it,"

Giovanni spoke quickly as they each took an arm and began to drag Clyde across the floor.

Clyde was monstrous and heavy. Each arm alone had to weigh fifty pounds. They struggled as they continued to pull him through the hallway. The white rat finally began to limp across the lab room floor as it made its way into the meeting room.

"Wait a minute! We have to drag him through the mess hall to get to the airlock! If he wakes up and sees that moon while we're—"

"He *won't* wake up! He won't, Adams! Keep it together and keep pulling. Time is against us."

Running on pure adrenaline and fear, Giovanni and Adams pulled with strength they never knew they had. Out of breath and their muscles beginning to ache, Adams suggested they stop for a few seconds to catch their breath. It was decided that they needed all the time they could spare. It felt like ten minutes, but, was only thirty seconds before they reached the mess hall. The moon was still clearly in view in front of the mess hall windows. Adams and Giovanni had never dreaded seeing the moon before this moment. It was like seeing the Grim Reaper standing right outside your bedroom window; and right now, he was using his scythe to scratch at their window, taunting them, letting them know they had only a few minutes left before he came inside to collect.

Clyde felt heavier, but Adams knew it was just fatigue setting in. The blood! Adams was so distracted by exhaustion that he forgot about the blood on the ground. The moment he heard the splash of his back foot hitting the puddle of blood, it was too late; he pulled Clyde, putting all his weight on his back foot, and his foot instantly slipped in the blood, causing him to fall on his back and smack his head against the tile floor. His arm bumped into one of the tables, causing some silverware and plates to fall off and hit the ground with a loud crash. Clyde began to stir.

Dazed and the back of his skull throbbing in excruciating pain, Adams groaned and struggled to move. Unable to carry Clyde's full weight by himself, Giovanni also fell to the ground. Clyde began to breathe faster, and his hands began to move; his claws scrapping the tile floor, resulting in an awful noise.

"Adams! Adams! Get up! Adams, get up!" Giovanni's voice sounded far away, and Adams looked around, still stunned.

He leaned forwards and touched the back of his head; he couldn't tell if he landed in someone else's blood or if that wet spot on his head was caused by his own bleeding. He looked over and saw Clyde's eyes slowly opening. The sight of that purple eye shocked him back into reality. He was lying on the ground. Giovanni was still yelling and trying to pull him up. Clyde's purple eye grew bigger…and brighter. The color in his eye changed into a dark red. Clyde had seen the moon and their time was up.

Adams shot up and rose to his feet with the help of Giovanni. Giovanni took his wrench and began smacking Clyde with it, but Clyde was faster. Giovanni was knocked back by Clyde's massive arm and Adams stumbled back as Clyde jumped up. Clyde's eyes were bulging and dark red, his muscles mass seemed to increase right before their eyes, and his howl filled the spacecraft as the fangs grew longer. Clyde was morphing into something bigger, and Giovanni knew they both couldn't get to the airlock and still have time for him to reach the control room. They had one shot at this.

"Get to the airlock! I'll go to the control room!" Giovanni shouted as they both took off down the hall, then went off in different directions.

"Hey! Over here! Come on! Over here, Clyde!" Adams shouted, causing Clyde to avert his attention to him instead of Giovanni.

Adams continued to shout as he ran full speed down the hall towards the airlock. Adams silently prayed that Giovanni would reach the control room before he made it to the airlock. Right on his heels, Clyde growled and lunged forwards to take a bite out of Adams, only managing to tear off a piece of Adams' shirt. The white rat continued to limp on its little paws, finally making it out of the meeting room and into the hallway.

Adams looked back to see that he had gained a good distance away from Clyde. However, Clyde raised his arms to spread his wings and leaped into the air, managing to glide through the hall and above Adams. Clyde then used his feet to grab onto Adams, digging his sharp claws into Adams' shoulders and picked him up, then tossed him forwards. Adams screamed as he hit the ground and skidded across the floor, landing on his stomach. Clyde landed on the ground and lowered his head, getting ready to pounce. That's when Adams looked up to see the airlock was only a few feet in front of him.

Adams quickly pushed himself up and noticed a green light illuminate above the airlock; Giovanni had reached the control room. Adams felt a sharp pain in his right leg as Clyde's fangs punctured his flesh and Adams was violently jerked back, sending him to the ground, face first. Adams was dragged backwards, and he felt himself being slammed against the wall. Adams knew that Giovanni could see what was happening through the cameras in the control room. The cameras also provided live audio of each room.

Spitting out blood, Adams shouted, "open it!"

In the control room, Giovanni cursed and pounded the monitor.

Clyde picked up Adams again, taking another bite and holding on, then tossed him to the ground in front of the airlock.

"O…op…open it! Op—" Adams gagged on blood as Clyde picked him up with his massive arms.

"I'm sorry," Giovanni uttered as he typed the authorization code.

The front door of the airlock opened into the small room. The back door in the airlock was the only thing standing between the vacuum of space and them. Adams was thrown to the ground once more and he crawled his way into the airlock, where Clyde followed. Clyde's claws, now twice as long, speared Adams through the stomach and lifted Adams up, so his face and Clyde's were now staring back at each other.

Adams spit out blood into Clyde's face, causing Clyde to flinch. Giovanni pressed the button, and the front door to the airlock closed, followed by the back door breaking the seal. The last thing Adams and Clyde heard was the sharp, high-pitched sound of the air being sucked out of the seal, and then total silence. Giovanni fell to his knees and shouted. In almost complete shock, Giovanni got up, went back to his room, and lay down on his bed. Then, he closed his eyes and let himself cry. The white rat arrived at the mess hall and began wildly squeaking at the sight of the moon before it. The rat's wounds began to close as its body violently convulsed.

It stood on its hind paws and let out a squeak, which quickly morphed into a low growl, then a clearer howl, as its body produced the otherworldly features Clyde was cursed with. The rat's white hair grew twice its length as the body widened and became muscular and large. Each of its paws grew to the size of a bulldog's and the tail of the rat elongated, whipping around and smacking against the tables, sending the silverware to the ground with a loud crash. The tail whipped the pumpkin lights that were hanging down from the ceiling and were ripped from the ceiling, causing a bright flash of electricity, and then total darkness. Giovanni's eyes shot open wide. The jaws rose in length and the teeth of the rat extended out so far that it quickly became impossible for the rat to close its mouth. The rat fell on all fours and began scurrying across the ground, scratching the floor with its claws and making a sharp scraping sound as it moved.

Upon hearing the howl, Giovanni sat up in bed and listened, remaining still. A soft scraping noise was very faint at first, but grew more audible, more distinct, louder and louder, until it stopped right outside Giovanni's door.

Pursued
By Bill Hatfield

ilk
Eggs
Shredded cheese
Ground beef
Christmas presents…

Dylan started to fuss in the shopping cart, prompting his mother to briefly put her grocery list down and dig into the cluttered purse sitting beside him, eventually finding a pacifier. The baby's frustrated moaning instantly lightened into a quiet babble when he saw his favorite lime green binky, and he happily accepted when she plopped it in his mouth.

Liza wanted to smile at her son's rapid mood swing, but the energy required to move the facial muscles just wasn't in her this evening. A distant pounding somewhere in the back of her forehead made its presence known, the promise of a migraine to come. Having taken the last of her ibuprofen that morning, there was no other option but to hope for the aching to stay muffled.

She pushed the cart forward toward a long row of refrigerators full of dairy products, stopping at the one that held gallon jugs of milk. Liza moved her finger along the cold, foggy glass door, trying to decide between whole or two percent. *What the hell, it's Christmas,* she thought, opening the door and grabbing the jug topped with a red lid. The yellow price tag on the rack where it had been sitting displayed the milk's price at $6.22. A lump formed in Liza's throat, but she nonetheless placed the jug in the cart and continued on toward the cheeses.

Go tell it on the mountain, an angelic female voice sang over the store's loudspeaker, *over the hills and everywhere, go tell it on the mountain that Jesus Christ is born.* "That's right!" a bombastic male voice proclaimed as the song faded out, "And you had better go tell it everywhere that Northspring Shopping Center is the place for all your holiday needs! There's no better way to show your loved ones how much you care than with the amazing gift products that can only be found…"

Liza tuned out the announcer's pre-recorded declaration as she reached for a bag of shredded mozzarella cheese, glancing at the price tag above it. "$4.70?!" she whispered out loud to herself. This was the generic brand, too, which was supposed to be cheaper than the name brand stuff. At this rate, she didn't know if she would be able to get Dylan the shirt and pants she had planned as his present, not to mention something for Aunt Audrey, whose name Liza had drawn for Secret Santa.

Isn't it just like the little whore? she imagined her aunt saying. *I suppose we should have expected someone who had a baby out of wedlock to not even bother getting presents for her own family.*

Her right hand gripped the cart handle tight as her left stroked her child's curly black hair. It was bad enough that she had to choose between food and gifts, but worse still, she knew she would be judged either way, damned if she did and damned if she didn't.

"$4.70," she muttered again, taking her hand off from Dylan's head and grabbing the mozzarella off the shelf.

"I know, right?"

"Huh?" Her head jerked to the left where the sudden noise had come from. In the space that had been empty just moments prior stood a man smiling sheepishly at her, his hands tucked inside the pockets of his black peacoat.

"The prices," he said, motioning with his eyes at the yellow tag. His dark hair was grown out and tickling at his neck, and it bounced with every movement of his head. "I'd almost rather buy a cow and cut out the middleman, but my apartment only has one bedroom."

Liza gave him a courtesy half-grin and mentally prepared herself for the conversation that she knew was about to happen. Whenever an unknown male approaches a female uninvited, it's for one reason only. She turned with her back to the cart not only to face him, but to provide a wall of protection for Dylan, and also to be near the can of pepper spray kept in her purse next to him.

"Ready for Christmas?" he asked without a single hitch in his rhythm, as if chit-chat with strangers was a regular thing for him.

"Ready as I'll ever be," she said, hoping the disinterested tone was clear enough. He wasn't outwardly threatening; the shaggy hair looked well-managed, more a stylish choice than an unkempt mess, and his red sweater and white scarf looked straight out of a Hallmark movie's wardrobe department. She conceded that he was even kind of cute. Then again, many said the same about Ted Bundy.

"I'm Wevlen," he said, flashing a million-dollar smile.

Liza raised an eyebrow. "I don't think I've ever heard that name before, what does it mean?"

He shrugged. "For my mom, it meant, 'Get your ass inside before I tear it up!'"

She laughed in spite of her suspicious nature, but it was a humorless laugh, an instinctual reaction with no emotion behind it.

Before either one could say anything else, Dylan started babbling and cooing behind her. She turned around and saw that the boy had spit his pacifier onto the floor and started on a rant that was, to him, vitally important.

"Hey, little buddy," the man named Wevlen said, craning his head to look over Liza's shoulder at the child, "you busy giving Mom a hard time?" Dylan continued his grandiose declarations at him while Liza blew off the pacifier and stuck it back in the purse. She discreetly took out the pepper spray and slid it inside her sleeve, taking note that Wevlen kept his hands in his pockets the entire time.

"Well, I guess we had better get going, Happy Holidays."

"Yeah, my boy was really talkative at that age, too."

Had he even heard her? "How old is he now?" she asked, resigned to the fact that she was stuck in this conversation for another few moments.

The light in Wevlen's eyes dimmed just the slightest, and the sharp edges of his smile briefly dulled. "Uh, he would have been twelve."

Liza's heart sank into her stomach, realizing what was being implied. "Oh, I'm so sorry."

He kept his eyes on Dylan, who had gone uncharacteristically quiet and was now staring at the man with his full attention. "I wasn't even there when it happened. I was overseas, fighting for a freedom that never came to pass."

She silently chastised herself for being so quick to judge someone who clearly just had a soft spot for children after losing his own. "That's awful, I can't even imagine."

"Yeah, all you can do is try to pick up the pieces and keep living." He turned his eyes toward her. "Listen, I hope I'm not being too forward, but are you seeing anyone?"

There it is, she thought, and the walls instantly went back up. "That's flattering," she said, trying to sound genuine, "but I'm really just focused on raising him right now." She motioned to Dylan, who was completely focused on him.

Wevlen nodded. "That's fine, I understand." He turned around and started to walk away. "Happy Holidays, Liza."

"You too," she said, grateful to finally be pushing the cart somewhere else. Before she had left the refrigerated section, though, she stopped, unable to remember when she had told Wevlen her name.

The idea of bringing your child along while Christmas shopping for them may seem counterintuitive to the whole point, but in Liza's case, there wasn't much she could do about it. No family was willing or able to help, and there was no way she could afford the overtime costs for daycare, so Dylan would just have to see what his gift was early. At least he was young enough that he probably wouldn't remember.

The baby & toddler section was a jungle of haphazardly placed clothes racks and ladies having deep conversations in the middle of the aisle. She expertly weaved through the congestion, muttering quick *scuse me's* to everyone she passed, until she managed to reach a rack holding shirts fitting her son.

"What do you think of this one?" she asked him, picking out a long-sleeved red-and-black checkered button down and holding it up for him to see. The only answer she received was when he blew a raspberry at her, so she took it as a negative and kept looking.

Finding a cute blue sweater with a snowman on the front, she held it up in front of her face, inspecting the fabric and design and deliberately avoiding the price tag. "Yeah, this will work," she said to herself, lowering it to place it in the cart. She caught the briefest glimpse of a black peacoat and a mop of long black hair before it disappeared behind a shelf of folded t-shirts. *No*, she thought, her heart jumping a small bit at the sight. *Surely not*.

Liza swallowed a lump that had formed in her throat and again fished out the pepper spray from the purse. She pushed the cart toward where the figure had been, wincing every time one of its wheels squeaked. She could feel the pumping of her heart all the way up in her temples, the blood running ice cold. *Why are you being like this?* a part of her wondered. This was a small store; for all she knew, he was just cutting through the clothes section to get to the automotive, or hell, it may not have even been him. There was no reason for her to be so nervous about a coincidence.

Nevertheless, once her legs started moving, she couldn't stop them. The shelf that whoever-it-was had disappeared behind was only ten or so feet away, yet every step was made as if in a sea of molasses, trying not to make a sound.

Dylan made a quick yelping noise, and when Liza looked down, she realized that she had been squeezing his arm. "Sorry, buddy," she whispered. Her other hand gripped the spray can so tightly that she almost worried it would burst. She slowly craned her head around the corner of the shelf, biting her tongue and trying not to hyperventilate.

Nothing but empty space. No one was there.

Along with the relief that rushed her system came a feeling of irritation at herself for acting so stupid. Was she really going to pepper spray someone if they had been standing behind the shelf? This Wevlen person hadn't done anything to warrant this kind of paranoia, where could it have been coming from? She made a silent promise to go to sleep early that night, simultaneously aware that she wouldn't keep it. Pushing the cart away, these thoughts kept her occupied to the point where she didn't hear the heavy footsteps following behind her to the front of the store.

Beep.

Thump.

Beep.

Thump.

Her heart thudded along to the beat of the self-checkout machine scanning the barcodes of each item she swiped through with its red laser. *Stress,* she told herself, answering a question deep in her subconscious that hadn't yet formed into a coherent thought. *It's just stress. Go home, have a glass of wine, and forget it.* She thought about trying to ease out of the sixty-plus hour workweeks once Christmas was over, then thought about rent & utilities and instantly nixed that plan.

She imagined how things might have gone down if Wevlen had been standing where she thought he was, and she had attacked him. Store employees would have pulled them apart, someone would take him away to deal with his burning eyes, and the cops would inevitably be called. They would most likely go to the security cameras, and what would they have seen? Some guy minding his own business until a crazy lady runs up and sprays his eyes.

Thank God that didn't happen, she thought, scanning the last item and pulling out her debit card, warped from constant use. The total was quite a bit more than she was expecting to pay, and the shaking in her hand caused her to miss the mark with the card twice before finally planting it into the slot. *Please,* she prayed as the machine looked up her information, *please go through.* The three seconds felt like three hours until a small green light blinked, and a message read *APPROVED, PLEASE REMOVE CARD.*

Liza blew a long, slow breath out of her mouth and took her card back. As she waited for the receipt to print out, she couldn't help but let the first true smile of the day form on her face. Work was over, shopping was done, and there was nothing left to do but go home and relax- well, the house needed straightening up, but that could wait until morning.

A quick rush of movement and a rustling noise forced her eyes involuntarily to the left.

Him. There was no mistaking it this time. The long hair and coat seemed almost signature at this point. He was in front of a small rack holding snack bags of chips, ostensibly trying to choose between ranch and nacho cheese flavors, but she instantly felt exposed, as if she had been hiding in a closet and he had burst through the door. He was following her.

Stop that, she snapped at herself. *It's just a coincidence. It's nothing but–*

She saw his eyes quickly dart away and his head turn from her. Was he watching her?

He shifted slightly, and in that brief moment, his right hand slid out of the coat pocket where it had been stuck the entire time. He quickly shoved it back in, but before it disappeared, Liza saw a glint of light reflecting from in between the fingers of his closed fist. He was holding something metallic. A quarter? A lighter?

A knife?

Not wasting another moment to find out, she briskly pushed the cart away from the self-checkout area and toward the exit, leaving the receipt and the gift card she had purchased for Aunt Audrey behind.

Dylan's head whipped forward at the sudden increase in speed, and he started to whine. "Shush babe," Liza begged in a sharp whisper, turning her own head around to see if they were being followed. Wevlen wasn't behind them, but he wasn't at the chip rack anymore either. The machines weren't tall enough for him to hide behind, and he couldn't have run down another aisle in the few seconds since she had started walking. It was like he had disappeared into thin air.

She was so distracted by this that she didn't even notice when she bumped the cart into something, and she probably would have kept going had the something not spoken to her.

"Oh!" said a female voice, and Liza spun around to see an older woman holding a plastic bag full of fresh vegetables. Her hair was a red and gray bob, and she wore a forest green rayon blouse with black leggings and flat black shoes.

"I am so sorry," Liza said, feeling a hot rush of embarrassment on her face, "I wasn't watching where I was going, are you okay?"

"I'm fine, honey," the lady answered, no hints of anger or pain in her voice, "I was off in my own little world and didn't see you coming. No harm done." She brushed at her hip Liza had run into. By now Dylan had started whining again, the jolt of the impact having disrupted his fragile equilibrium. "Aw, don't cry, sweetie," the woman told him, and unlike with Wevlen, Liza felt no apprehension watching her walk to him and gently squeeze his hand.

"He's had a long day," Liza said, taking a quick glance back to ensure that they weren't being watched.

"Looks like you have, too. Is everything okay?"

"Yeah, totally, just, you know, one of those… actually, no, everything's not okay." Why had she admitted this to a stranger? Was she that desperate to unload on someone? "There's this guy, and I think… I think he's been following me around the store."

The lady's eyes widened, and her face became deadly serious. "Where is he?"

"He's gone now– I think so, anyway. I've just had this weird feeling about him."

"You want me to walk you to your car?"

"Really? You wouldn't mind?"

"Of course not, us girls have to look out for each other. Plus, it would give me an excuse to spend some more time with this handsome fellow." She wiggled her fingers at Dylan, who giggled and drooled gleefully.

They walked out of the store, Liza occasionally taking a quick glance back just to be sure. The woman, whose name turned out to be Diana, was quite the chatterbox, going on about how her late husband had always been the shopper and she was still getting used to it, how her grandchildren were growing up so fast, and how she couldn't wait to get back to them. "Where are you from?" Liza asked her. It was nice to have someone who could naturally keep a conversation going without letting the air grow stale.

"Oh– you've probably never heard of it. It's a small town."

"Smaller than Northspring, Arkansas?"

"Point taken, but it is nice and hidden away. I like that. Never could stand living in front of the highway where any two-bit crazy could come right to your door. My late husband always said that any fool willingly living in a town bigger than a thousand people was just asking to get robbed. He was always paranoid like that."

"I know the type. If you don't mind me asking, what happened to him?"

Diana sighed, and for the first time took a few seconds to reply with a single word. "War."

"Oh my God, I'm so sorry. Persian Gulf?"

She didn't answer, and Liza thought it best not to pry any further. Thankfully, they were approaching her car. "Oh, this is me," she said, pointing to the dusty maroon Honda. "Thanks again for walking with me, that was so sweet of you."

"Think nothing of it, dear. You be careful with my boyfriend, now." She squeezed Dylan's hand, and the baby cooed at her. Diana walked away into the darkness, and Liza tossed her few meager groceries into the trunk of the car, got Dylan strapped into his car seat, and sat herself behind the steering wheel. She prayed for the engine to turn over and the vents to blow warm air, and when both prayers were answered, she pulled out of the parking lot and headed south for home, a pair of bright white headlights staying close behind her.

She didn't notice it at first. Dylan had nodded off in his seat, and she was preoccupied with the radio dial, turning it to the right in search of something other than static or Christmas music. *Dashing through the… Let Earth receive her… And a partridge in a pear…* She finally found a station playing one of the romantic ballad guys with acoustic guitars, John Mayer or Jason Mraz or someone.

A thin layer of fog began to gather in the winter air once she drove outside the town limits, not enough to obscure the road too badly, but she gently pressed on the brakes, nonetheless. The truck behind steadily gained on her, and she expected it to pass once the yellow line on the highway turned dotted, but the opportunity came and went, and it kept its place. *Great, a tail-rider,* she thought to herself, pushing the rearview mirror up so the LED headlights wouldn't blind her.

It was only twenty minutes from the store to her house, but this trip was feeling like an all-nighter, and Liza had to slap herself to keep out of highway hypnosis. Her son mumbled in his sleep, and she found herself wondering where his father was, and what he was doing. Not that she cared; she had lost any sympathy for that particular sperm donor even before Dylan had been born, when he tried denying that he had knocked her up while simultaneously practicing the job with half of the women in Northspring.

Was that same truck still behind her? She was now deep in the boondocks where she lived, and normally any vehicle would have turned onto some other road by now. She knew every person that lived around here, and there was nothing else for quite a while. Maybe their GPS had messed up and gotten them off the interstate too early?

Getting close to the turn down Muller Road that led to home, she reached for the blinker to push it down and indicate a left turn, but something in her gut made her decide against it. She instead simply pulled the steering wheel and guided the car onto the narrow dirt road. Without missing a beat, the truck turned as well, staying directly behind her.

Now Liza knew that something was up. Her house was the only one on Muller. There were no ponds to fish in or corners to park and light a joint. Why was this person following her? As much as she didn't want to admit it, there was only one answer that came to mind: she was being pursued.

Calm down, that's enough jumping to conclusions. Maybe they-

BANG!

The impact thrusted her forward, slamming her forehead into the steering wheel and jolting her back up just as quickly. In a sudden panic, she twisted the wheel one way, then the other, swerving the car in either direction in a desperate attempt to get back on track. Dirt flew by the windows and the tires screamed out. If Dylan's cries in the back seat hadn't brought her back to reality, she would have ended up slamming into a tree within seconds.

Liza gritted her teeth and pushed the brake down, trying to ignore the throbbing pain in her forehead as she gripped the wheel as tight as she could and held it steady while the car spun one hundred and eighty degrees into a ditch, then finally stopped.

The truck stood still about a hundred yards away, its front bumper twisted and a dent in the hood. From the way her tires had slung the dirt, she could tell that it had stopped right after hitting her. It stood there, engine idling, the driver making no attempt to flee or step out.

"It's okay, baby," Liza's trembling voice managed as Dylan screamed his little throat raw. She turned back and stroked his hand, using her other hand to reach for the phone in the cup holder without looking. Her fingers touched its cold plastic, but her shaking inadvertently pushed it over the edge and onto the passenger floorboard.

Shit. Shit. Shit. She ducked and grabbed it from the floor, trying not to make any visible sudden movements, lest they happened to have a gun and shot through her windshield. Yet, as she kept her head low and used one hand to dial 911 while using the other to keep her son's head ducked down, the truck sat motionless, headlights pointed at her car.

"911, what's your emergency?"

"A truck deliberately rear-ended me and sent me into the ditch, and now they're just sitting there, like they're waiting for something. My child is in the back seat, and I'm afraid to get out."

"Are you or the child hurt?"

"I don't think so. We're down Mul–"

A jolt of electricity shot through the phone and on her hand, the sudden burning sensation causing her to cry out and drop it. She bent down to pick it back up, but whipped her hand back when she discovered how hot it was to the touch. A smell of burnt plastic wafted up to her nose, and at the same moment, the lights on the dashboard all switched off and the engine died instantly, leaving them in near total darkness. *What the–*

The truck's door swung open with a loud creak, and Liza's heart nearly jumped out of her mouth. She could feel her lower lip trembling, and the adrenaline from the wreck was starting to wane, bringing the aching in her head and the back of her neck to a roaring crescendo. She just wanted to go home. She just wanted to get out of this mess and bring her son home safely.

Dylan. His crying had reduced to a low moaning, but the thought of whoever this was bringing harm to her child brought something else inside her to the forefront. The physical pain was still there, but this other sensation numbed it down to almost nothing, and she could feel her face heating up as she reached for the door handle, hands trembling, but not from fear.

"Mom will be right back," she told Dylan in a low, even tone she hardly recognized. She opened the door, the chill of the night instantly turning her breath frosty, and walked to the truck, its dark maroon paint job nearly invisible from a distance of more than a few feet.

"Hey, asshole!" Liza shouted at the driver's tinted window. "The cops are on their way, so you'd better take off running!"

A shadowy figure stepped out from the darkness. It was hard to make out any definite features, but once it spoke, Liza froze in place.

"Oh, did I bump into you, sweetie?" Diana asked in her sweet old lady tone as she came into view and stood face-to-face with her. "I guess that makes us even after you ran into me back at the store."

"You? What the–"

"Well, I couldn't let that handsome man get away from me so easily." At the same moment, Liza heard the back door of her car open and the sound of Dylan crying.

She instinctively whipped around and tried to take off running toward him, but Diana was one step ahead, grabbing her wrists and pulling her back. "Hold still," she said, somehow keeping up the sweet grandma facade, "struggling only makes it worse." As Liza tried desperately to slip loose, she felt Diana clamp something cold and metallic onto her wrists, then loosen her grip.

Liza immediately tried to get to her car again, but at the first step she took, a sharp electrical shock buzzed from the clamps on her wrists and traveled throughout her body, dropping her to the ground and sending her body into convulsions.

"I warned you," Diana said as Liza spat dirt out from her mouth and tried to stop shaking. She heard the woman's footsteps as she walked past her, toward her car, and heard her son just a few feet away. "It's about time you got here," Diana continued, but not to her, "I was getting sick of waiting."

"I'm here, lay off me," said another voice, one that Liza recognized immediately. "Wevlen," she moaned, craning her head up to see them, which sent another shockwave. She could just make them out in the headlights of Diana's truck. They had both changed into all-black outfits that made them look like burglars or secret agents, and they had what she could only guess were some kind of utility belts, with several black pouches circled around. Wevlen was holding Dylan, who was screaming harder than ever. Without thinking, she tried to move her legs to stand up, but the clamps blasted her back down.

"Go ahead," Diana told Wevlen, completely ignoring Liza's struggles on the ground. There was a long pause, with a soft but steady breeze being the only sound. "Well?" she snapped impatiently.

"It's just," Wevlen murmured, "do we have to–"

"Yes, we have to! It's the whole reason for all of this!"

"He's just a kid, Captain."

"I don't care, just do it. If you hurry, we can make it look like the wreck did it before the cops get here."

"Please," Liza begged, her voice strained with pain and desperation, "we didn't do anything to you!"

She heard footsteps approach her, then felt a hot blast of pain in her side as Diana kicked her, then another electric shock from the movement of her body.

"You have no idea what he did to us," she spat through gritted teeth in a voice much lower and angrier than before. "I'm gonna turn the juice up on her," she told Wevlen as she walked toward the truck.

When Diana passed her feet, Liza shot her leg out and kicked the old woman in the ankle. It resulted in another shock, but it also tripped Diana, who screamed more in anger than pain as she crumpled to the ground. Without wasting any time, Liza jumped off the ground and stood straight so that when the next shock came, it shot her body down right on top of her before she could get up.

"Get off me!" Diana shouted, and tried to shove Liza away, but it only activated the cuffs, which sent painful jolts through both of their bodies. It was excruciating, but Liza kept the shocks going, even when the air around her smelled of smoke and ozone and she felt as if she would pass out. "Stop!" the woman cried, "Stop it!" Liza could feel her skin burning, and Diana's pleas went from intelligible to desperate blubbering. Finally, she saw blue lights flashing and the yelp of a police siren, and she rolled off of her, gasping for breath and drifting between awake and unconscious.

"Freeze!" a voice screamed, "Put the kid down!"

"Okay, okay, I'm doing it," Wevlen said.

The last thing she heard before everything went dark was the muffled, far-away voice of a police officer running toward her. "Ma'am, can you hear…"

A few days after she was released from the hospital, Liza was trying (mostly without success) to feed Dylan some sweet potatoes in his highchair. "Come on buddy, they're full of carbs! Yummy, tasty carbs!" The baby stood firm in his protest, so she threw the fork down in mock-frustration and instead massaged the red rings around her wrists.

Apparently, the police had found some sort of key fob in Diana's truck that controlled the cuffs, and they were able to get them off of her. "Must be something from Japan," she had been told after she woke up.

There was a knock at the door, and she went to answer it, leaving Dylan to deal with the potatoes on his own terms. When she opened the door, she was pleasantly surprised to see Josh, the officer who had run to her as she passed out and had stayed by her side at the hospital until she woke up.

"Hey! We were just having lunch, you hungry?"

Josh looked over her shoulder and grinned. "Been a while since I had potatoes from a jar. Actually, I came to give you a little update. They talked."

Liza's mouth dropped open. Wevlen and Diana had been held at the police station for days, and neither of them had said a word until now. "What did they say?"

The officer looked down at his shoes, then back up at her. "That's the thing. Looks like we may be dealing with a couple of nutcases." Liza arched an eyebrow as he continued. "The guy was the one to spill the beans, if there are any beans to be spilled. He went on this whole spiel about how he and the old lady were soldiers from the future. Said there was a global war that had wiped out almost all life on Earth, and they had gone back in time to stop it from happening."

The shock and confusion must have shown on her face, because Josh let out a small laugh.

"Yeah, I know, I told him I'd seen that movie about a hundred times, but it gets even better. Apparently, they had traveled back in time to assassinate the dictator that's gonna start this whole war– and that dictator…" he pointed into the kitchen, and Liza turned her head around to look at Dylan as Josh continued, "...currently has orange mush all over his face."

They both stood in silence for several moments until he spoke up again. "I don't know what to make of it either, just thought you might like to know. Anyway, I'd better get going." He waved goodbye and walked toward his squad car, and Liza shut the door.

My God, she thought standing in the hallway, they really are crazy. An image of the electric handcuffs flashed in her mind, and she thought of how her phone had gone crazy, how her car had just suddenly died. Had Diana done that?

No. They're just making up nonsense. That has to be it. Nevertheless, a pit formed in her stomach as she looked over at Dylan in his chair, who met her gaze and began to laugh.

What Would Make Common Life Impossible

By Sergio 'ente per ente' PALUMBO
Edited by Michele DUTCHER

The lonely Natsuo looked at the sea in front of him and remembered an old Japanese idiom that went, more or less: *'If a fish is friendly toward water, water will be kind to the fish...'*. He turned his head downwards as another old saying popped into his mind, *'The flow of water and the future of human beings are both uncertain.'*

So, what was in the sea? What was his future going to be?

A proverb that would have better fitted his present situation was: *'Forgiving the unrepentant is like drawing pictures on water'*. As a painter of landscapes, he thought that such words were exactly what he preferred to tell himself now.

His wife was gone, well, she had moved away from that small island of Hachijō-kojima, Japan, leaving him alone. But the reasons for her actions were still uncertain, being entirely unknown to him. At times he thought about that, along with his present condition, and it all saddened him. Well, some sadness provided inspiration for new paintings, as he knew, but it also prevented him from releasing his full artistic gift at its best. What he saw before his eyes at this moment was just the sea, and not the thousand colors and shades that an incoming storm might bring to the sky, along with the different sensations that a partly cloudy day could give you while watching the varied scenes drawn from the sun above to the shoreline below. He recalled images that raced across the ground, and then, in different steps, found their way to the slopes of the volcanic mountain of that island.

Without water vapor there would be no clouds in the sky – no rain or snow – and no weather. In his field, without the right stimulation, art couldn't reach its full power. He was well aware of this.

If a man had no tea in him, as he had read in his father's books, he was incapable of understanding truth and how beautiful the surroundings themselves really might be. So, no, the young dark-haired man wasn't going to paint today, maybe not even tomorrow. The grip he still felt on his heart was so overwhelming that he could never do his job as he normally was capable of doing. This was not a good day to stare attentively at all the many local scenes while putting his thoughts, and art, on canvas. So, his next piece of art had to wait, and he didn't know if he ever would be able to start it, let alone complete it, in the next week.

What everyone else would just think of as the whole sea that shone calm and clear, and the air clearer, all the way to the far distance, had always held another greater meaning to him. This was what gave him inspiration, and what forced him to put his colors on the growing image that slowly appeared before his eyes as he sat on his chair near the shore, using his paintbrushes here and there.

On that day, the sun sank beneath the sea late in the evening, without him having ever had the will to do much, and the unhappiness he felt inside merged into the greyness of the coming night.

The night that brought along with it some strange perceptions of deeply unearthly things, and was filled with another form of reality, seemingly. Something that was hard to read, just as if it was not 'normal' either. More or less like those ill-defined—strange sounds in the darkness beyond the comforting glow of a lamp, or a shape, half-glimpsed in the dim light along the wooden fence of his lonely house.

These were things that had the power to touch the minds of anyone, and to fill a man like him with many worries.

*****

Oriented in the same northwest to southeast direction as Hachijōjima, the small island of Hachijō-kojima was surrounded by high cliffs and had as a summit a volcanic mountain with a height of 2,024 feet. Located in the Kuroshio Current, in the Philippine Sea approximately 178 miles south of Tokyo, the whole area had abundant sea life, and was popular with sports fishermen and divers. Here summers were warm, and winters better than elsewhere. Precipitation was present throughout the year, but decreased during winter.

This was where the 41-year-old Natsuo lived now.

During the Heian period, Minamoto no Tametomo was said to have been sent to Izu Ōshima after a failed rebellion, but per a semi-legendary story, he escaped to Hachijōjima, a volcanic island, too. That was where he had attempted to start an independent kingdom and where he built his castle on the more easily defended Hachijō-kojima situated nearby. Hachijō-kojima has been almost uninhabited since at least the Muromachi period.

As with neighboring Hachijōjima, in the past, the island was a place for convicts and where more serious delinquents were sent. Its use as a prison had come to an end in the Meiji period. The population had peaked at 513 residents at that time, but by 1955 it was of almost half a hundred people. In 1965, the remaining residents voted to abandon the island, citing lack of public services (including electricity and schools) and the island's inability to support more than a very simple subsistence lifestyle. There have been no residents of Hachijō-kojima since 1969, when the last group of 31 left the island.

Then, though strange it might be, somebody had come to live here again. It was a man, named Kazue Morosawa, and his wife, Chiyo, in the early 2000s. The husband was a painter who liked to paint on canvas the main mountain of the small island, and he depicted this scene with oils from almost every point of view. It was as if it was his obsession. The woman helped him by supplying his needs, day by day, until the moment they had a son, Natsuo. Unfortunately, the wife died after giving birth to the boy. The man managed to take her by boat to the nearest hospital on Hachijōjima island, though it was late because of some health problems the woman already had at that time. Because of her death, the husband was left with his son that he attended to for a year there before he decided to move back to the much smaller Hachijō-kojima island where his home was situated. In a way, it seems that the man didn't like places that were too crowded, and though Hachijōjima had only 7,500 people living there, this was deeply unsettling to him. After all, he had chosen the much smaller island of Hachijō-kojima to peacefully dwell for a reason, and there he had lived with his only son.

After going back home, the task of eking out a living wasn't easy, as he had to look after the young boy, but he gained the help of his brother who lived in Tokyo and allowed his paintings of that small island, with the strange colors he made use of, to become known, and bought, by wealthy people of Japan. This allowed the man to stay on Hachijō-kojima with his son, as he kept painting and selling his works of art taking every new canvas completed, just once per month, to the port of Aigae. At that city, his paintings would be shipped out later. Not that he enjoyed going to Aigae, though he knew that he had to, at least once every two months, because this was the only way to have his pictures shipped by airplane to the buyers who lived elsewhere.

He did this for about two decades, until one day, sadly, the boat he was on was wrecked and he was lost at sea with his last work of art. So, the son, who was already 21-years-old, decided to remain alone on the small island, as he wasn't used to living on a bigger island or in a city. The young man soon started following the steps of his dead parent, tending his little vegetable garden and the needs of his chickens/goats. He started painting the scenes of the island itself by slightly changing the views and the colors used by his father. At times, the lonely Natsuo kept painting all day long, and forgot about his lonely situation, as a matter of fact. His elderly uncle had come there one summer and tried to make him move away from the small island, but the boy didn't want to do that. So, the man had a look at the new great paintings he had made, in the steps of his father, and thought that he might be of help and make him sell his works of art the same as Kazue had done in his lifetime.

Great was the surprise of his father's brother when he not only got buyers for the boy's paintings, but also a young female artist who lived in Mitaka, located in suburban Tokyo, eventually decided to visit him. Call it love at first sight, but when the woman, named Kimi, got to Hachijō-kojima, simply said, she fell in love with the place, and the two started living together in the man's home, spending the hours by watching the amazing scenery and painting it. One year later they were married, happily living on that small island. This continued until the couple were in their forties.

But, as in everything, there was an end.

*****

Natsuo considered that, on some mornings, the dim light of the sun that was partly visible through the mist that covered most of the sea in the distance made it look ghostlike and unearthly. On other days, dark clouds and the series of rain showers that followed their path quickly changed the scenery for several hours, transforming the area in something entirely different. Then a contrast appeared between the first part of the day and a somewhat warm evening. So, where else might you see anything like that?

Also today, early in the morning, the young man had forced himself to continue painting the scenery that he loved so deeply, and this was the reason for him to go to the shore where he sat with his canvas and everything he needed. The usual painter's tools he made use of included oil paint, of course, with its thick consistency, paintbrushes, his artist's palette, and a cup of water.

Some people wouldn't properly have their canvas primed when using oil colors, so the oil itself would sink into the canvas, leaving dull patches on the surface of the whole painting. Of course, he didn't do that, because there was a really good reason to have a canvas primed before starting. The wet-on-wet technique involved applying a coat of liquid whitish in color to a canvas before starting an oil painting. At times, he also painted his canvas reddish first, as it allowed him to work on light colors and dark colors, so that was the main reason. Then, he painted in the background color first around whichever object he was painting. That way if the paint dried on the canvas, he could very easily blend into the dry background colors to re-wet those areas and continue.

That day, after laying out his supplies and immediately angling his canvas to paint comfortably, he had taken his paintbrush with tough bristles and had started with a toned background to add the needed quality. The previous day he had made use of his pencil to outline the scenery and its main features, and today it was the time to really start putting the right color on the canvas itself.

The impressions a viewer could get from Natsuo's works were a very strange mix between traditional Japanese's paintings by Fujishima Takeji – an Impressionist who was very famous in late 19th and early 20th-century - and Van Gogh's colors.

His collection of works of art had soon become known as **'291 views of Hachijō-kojima'**, though he had completed many more than 291 paintings if you considered also the daubs, which were the preparatory studies and such that he had started and never finished, as not all of his works satisfied him in the end. But his form of art was very appreciated, and highly valued by many, and so a considerable amount of money was placed into his account. Well, not that this mattered too much to him.

Luckily, internet by wi-fi worked there - well, not all the time - but it allowed him to post his new works, so they became widely known among fans of many countries other than Japan. He had a lot of patrons in Taiwan and South Korea who really loved what he painted of course.

The strong bond that had long linked him and his wife Kimi, had been cut unexpectedly because the woman had moved away one day, without giving too many explanations, deciding to stay elsewhere.

For many months the man wasn't capable of figuring out the woman's reasons for her actions, but he accepted her choice, and so he remained alone, again, on Hachijō-kojima. But in the following months, especially during these last days, his mind had become upset, and many were the bad thoughts he had. In his heart he wanted to know, he really needed to figure out, why his wife had left him. The man didn't think he had done anything to make her angry, though just one week before she moved away, he had seen for most of the day some darkened expression on her face, exactly as if something was worrying her or she was unhappy about staying there any longer. But Natsuo was sure he hadn't done anything bad nor had he behaved inappropriately. So, what had happened?

"Why did she leave me?" the young man kept asking himself, in his troubled mind, but couldn't find an explanation yet. *"How might I have ever been so unwise as to let go of her? How?"*

Was it possible that his wife had had enough of living only with her husband on that small island? This would have been strange as she well knew what to expect when they married and she had come to stay in this place. But anything could be the reason for what had happened. Really, he didn't know what to think about that, and he didn't stop thinking that maybe it was because of something he had done, or said. Or maybe she had left because of something he hadn't done, or hadn't told her.

Eventually, he had accepted what she had decided for herself. After all, he had been used to living a lonely life here since he was a child, and then he had been all alone after the death of his father. In reality, he missed his wife day by day, more deeply as time went by.

For example, he hadn't exactly found the will to paint this week given the many desolate thoughts he had and the sensation of loss he felt for the recollections of Kimi and the good days spent in the past on Hachijō-kojima. It had to be said that for some time he thought about trying something else, a gesture driven to distraction some people might think. He had discovered where his wife had moved to, thanks to the brother of his father that had given him news from distant Tokyo, and since the day he had been told about that, he hadn't stopped being pensive about what he could do, and when.

Now Natsuo knew where his woman had gone to stay, on the furthermost island of Aogashima, where there was a village located in Hachijō Subprefecture. So, why exactly was she there? *Was it due to another man?*

Now, about one year after she had moved away, he was going to make his move, which was something unusual, at least to him. And this was what almost made his mind overwhelmed. Taking his boat to get to that island wasn't something he would have ever done, under normal circumstances, as he had never travelled alone across the sea for days. He hadn't even gone beyond Hachijōjima, in reality!

So, this was the reason for him to be uncertain, and full of doubts, early in that morning. In fact, he stopped painting very quickly, left his tools where they were, and went for a walk along the shore. He really wasn't able to keep his distressed mind on his work today. He had to make a decision, and he knew that, maybe, tonight he would decide what to do.

As it was during the nights that those strange perceptions of deeply unearthly things filled his mind, and dreams. Things, as he had considered once, that had the real power to touch the minds of anyone, and to fill a man like him with many worries, usually.

*****

So, it was two days later that, in full desperation for his lost love, the man made up his mind. He thought, '*For once in your life, do it!*' - and got on his boat. Then, he moved to that distant island because he wanted to win her love back and bring her to Hachijō-kojima again. If she still loved him, maybe she would come back, maybe. He traveled to that place using his seacraft, and it took him several days before he got there, which proved to be difficult, as he wasn't as knowledgeable as his father had been about travelling by boat. But, of course, as he had almost always lived on an island, he knew how to manage a motorboat, and so he made it, mainly thanks to the good weather that allowed for a safe journey across the sea during the week.

It was almost the time of the famous holiday known as Toka Ebisu Festival, that was held in January, in Osaka where people prayed for good trade fortune in the year ahead. But Natsuo found more than he expected when he arrived, for sure. First of all, he knew that his father hadn't ever liked crowded places, and this was why he had stayed on the small island of Hachijō-kojima for most of his life, until he died at sea. The young man shared his views and, to make an example, he had only once been on the near Hachijōjima island. Commonly a motorboat came to the place where he dwelled to take his paintings that sold from time to time. However, when he got to Aogashima island, which was much smaller than Hachijōjima, and where only 200 people were supposed to be living, he found a much larger number of citizens in the area. And this greatly surprised him. How was it possible? Why there were so many people crowding onto that island, even being on the beaches and on the hills, night and day?

Some had on unusual and very showy ancient costumes, that he surely would never have known about if it wasn't thanks to his father's history books at home in Hachijō-kojima. Maybe it was because of some festival that was going on now, or due to some other ceremonies he hadn't heard anything about. But the strange circumstance was that, in groups, they had different clothes from varied historical periods, so, what was going on? Perhaps this was a multi-period re-enacting event, or something based on ceremonies from different centuries? Well, it was difficult to be certain, of course.

Then, with his mind full of such thoughts and many doubts, he arrived at the house where his former wife was reputed to live now. Actually, she was still his wife, as they had just gotten separated after she had moved away from Hachijō-kojima, and Natsuo had almost immediately spotted her. He was glad to see the long dark-haired head and her slim figure as he approached the garden outside the building he had been told about by his father's brother. She was there, as beautiful as he remembered her, standing on the meadow, and the place was full of colorful plants. The garden, actually, appeared a bit overgrown.

But when he addressed Kimi, what he got as a reply left him speechless. He could have never expected this.

"You shouldn't have come here, Natsuo," the woman said, looking at him as the young man approached. "There was a reason why I moved away from our home, a reason why I left you…"

"Why? Please tell me now…was it because of another man? Did you want to go to live with him? But why here? Why so far from our small island of Hachijō-kojima? Please, explain it to me!" the man begged her.

The woman looked at the upset Natsuo with what seemed to be loving eyes, and added, "Because I was ill, a deadly illness was going to have soon the better of me. A medic told me this one day when I got to the hospital on Hachijōjima. My bloodwork was loaded with tumor markers, and even if I had felt pain before, certainly this was something beyond even that. I did not have many months left so I moved away. No other man was involved, no one else replaced you in my heart, you can be sure of that."

"Oh, I see…but you should have told me about this!" Natsuo cried out. "I would have done my best to help you! Perhaps I can still help you now!"

"I'm sure you would have, but I didn't want to die on Hachijō-kojima. I didn't want my body to be buried there, and for good reason," Kimi said.

"Why did you go so far away from me? Why are you staying on Aogashima island?"

"This I'm going to tell you, my dear. What did you notice on this island once you got here?" the woman asked, staring at him.

"It's a beautiful small island, much bigger than that where our home is, but it's very crowded, really full of people. This surprised me."

"Yes, I knew of this. But the facts are different: only about 200 people live here. And I'm speaking of the living people," Kimi told him.

"What do you mean? Explain this to me, please!" Now Natsuo seemed to be really surprised.

"I'm dead, and you're not. At least, not yet," the woman replied making a face. "You have something in common with your father. And your father's brother knew about it, undoubtedly he also was aware of why Kazue Morosawa had chosen a lonely place to live in. You and he could see the dead, the ghosts of people who passed away long ago, and to you two there had never been any difference between the two shapes. This I saw the day, the only day, you moved away from our home on Hachijō-kojima for our marriage on the bigger Hachijōjima. You saw people who had died long ago. You also briefly talked to them during the party, and to you they looked as if they were alive, still on this Earth. But most of the people you saw that day, and you talked to, were only visible to you. So, I understood then that you could see ghosts the same as you see living beings. This is a strange ability of yours, no other man I know can do this. Your strange power is something unearthly, something other people would be afraid of, and this would make a common life for you just impossible, as a matter of fact."

"What? Are you saying I see ghosts? Why should it be like that? How could I ever do such a strange thing? You know that I never saw the ghosts of my mother nor of my father," Natsuo told her surprised.

"Your father died at sea, and was never buried on Hachijō-kojima. Then your mother died on nearby

Hachijōjima so she too was never buried near your home. Your father's brother was really convinced that you two could only see the dead who were in a place, those who passed away within a certain area or that were buried there. It's just as you today can see the ghosts of those who lived and also died long ago here on Aogashima. So, what did you think when you saw here so many people, dressed in so many varied ways, even wearing clothes from another era?"

"I…well, I don't know…" a dubious Natsuo replied. "Maybe a re-enacting festival? What else could it be? I recognized people dressed in Meiji costumes, and others with clothes from other historical times, actually, maybe from the Muromachi period." The man said this while his thoughts came back to some nights at home, those long hours filled with those strange perceptions of deeply unearthly things that had overwhelmed his mind, at times…

"No, there is no festival today. You imagined that people dressed in old costumes here were part of some historical recurrence, or were doing something connected to the old times. You see the present citizens along with the old citizens who passed away and who now appear in their ancient clothing, the same clothes they wore when they were on Earth. Because it's you that can't differentiate among them, to you they all look like people who are still alive."

"I can't believe this! If it's really so, why did you leave? What's the reason for what you did?" The man looked at the dead wife. "What has all this nonsense to do with why you left? Did you find me mad? Or was it too strange to accept to live with me any longer?"

"First of all, I knew of the complications which might have followed if you went along with me as I moved from one hospital to another within a larger village because of my illness, until I died. Beyond that, I would have never allowed my body to be buried on Hachijō-kojima because, if it had been buried there, you would have always seen me next to you, in that deserted place, thinking that I never really died. And this might have brought you to real madness soon."

"So, you left, without telling me why until today…" Natsuo's tone was high now, and angered. "Is this what you're saying?"

"I died a few weeks ago, while living here, my dear Natsuo. And my grave is in the main cemetery on this island. But to you I'm alive, you see me now as I once was, you can look at my ghost as if I still were alive. If you had been with me in this place until my end, nothing good would have come from your stay. People might have started asking questions about you, they might have even thought of you as a madman, somebody to be forcibly put into a psychiatric hospital for who knows how long…maybe for the rest of your life. I didn't want this for you, I knew what your ability really was, and I thought it was better to leave you there, on that small island, where you might never spot the dead as there was nobody else who, possibly, had been buried there in the past," Kimi told him.

"Now I see what you mean…" the young man said, turning his head to the sky. "You really did it for me. So, what we do now?"

"If you like you can stay with me for a few moments more today, but pay attention: your behavior might appear strange to other people living on the island. Try not to talk to me while somebody else is around, or they could become worried about your mental condition. But for now, you can stand here in this garden and no one else will notice you standing alone and talking to the wind. This is okay," the woman warned her husband.

"As you say," the man told her. "But I would like this moment to never end."

"But it will. And you'll go back to your small island, painting your beautiful scenes of that place again," Kimi smiled. It was a smile that now looked so deeply unearthly to the saddened Natsuo.

"Yes, this is what I'll do. I'll be all right now, being alone there, for as long as I can paint, and live, of course." The man returned her smile and seemed a bit relieved. But, of course, he wasn't. How could he ever be really glad about anything after what he had been told today?

He was the man to whom the Afterlife bordered with the reality of every day. He now felt half dead and half alive!

A Winter's Return
By R.P. Serin

Lee Norton felt as though he'd been driving these narrow roads for hours, though a quick glance at the dashboard clock was enough to rebut that perception: it had not yet been half. Gossamer drizzle – barely seen, save for its shimmering whirl within the glow of headlights - dowsed the windscreen. Wipers swung fretfully from one side to the other.

If the sign hadn't looked so out of place amongst the coarse hedgerows, twisting oaks, and eroded verges, then he would have missed it completely. As it was, the large red lettering, the surrounding border of stylised snow, and the gaudy background of vivid green, demanded the attention of any passer-by.

Christmas Tree
FOR SALE!
Best Quality. Best Price
When It's Gone, It's Gone.

This had to be the place. Clair hadn't mentioned the tacky sign, but she had said the trees were cheap. And no one else around here seemed to be selling.

He'd wanted a real Christmas tree for years. When he was a kid, the heady aroma of fresh pine as he'd bounded down the stairs each morning had been a large part of the yuletide magic. Smells could be so evocative.

This was the first year Clair had agreed to have one. In the past, she'd always managed one excuse or another. *Why should we spend money on a new tree every Christmas when the one in the attic does the same thing?*

This year she'd tried to convince him that they were worse for the environment than the plastic ones. Lee had laughed. *Is that the best you can do?*

'Fine,' she'd said. 'We'll give it a try, just for this year.'

On two conditions: not expensive and not from one of those gargantuan tree farms, the ones that people took their kids to, just to get that 'magical' Instagram pic.

Well, the sign did say they were cheap, and it certainly wasn't a big operation.

Lee came to a large, isolated farmhouse. There was no sign of life, save for a light in the porch. The rest of the house was dark. If he hadn't travelled all this way, in such shitty conditions, he wouldn't have even bothered getting out of the car. But he was here now so, why not?

The front door opened as he approached.

'Good evening, sir,' the man said. His clean-shaven, unblemished face as unreadable as Shakespeare's *Cardinio.* 'You are either frightfully lost, or … you've come to rid us of our Christmas tree.' His shoulders rose and fell as he chuckled, creasing the lapels of his peculiarly formal suit. He held is hand out for Lee to shake.

His grip was soft, his skin softer still. Not like any farmer Lee had met before.

'You got me, I've come to take a look at your trees. Twelve years together, and the wife's only just letting me have a real one.' Lee laughed, but the man didn't return the gesture.

'Tree, sir. We've only got one. You are lucky that it hasn't gone already.'

Not likely, Lee thought. *I can't imagine anyone else being mad enough to drive all the way out here to look at one poxy tree.* 'That'd be great,' he said.

The man led him round the side of the house and into a field. Lee's trainers became increasingly soiled as they trapsed through sodden mud. He could feel the cold liquid filling the spaces between his toes.

He had nearly overcome the politeness that was preventing him from vocalising his displeasure at having not been offered suitable foot ware, when he heard a small 'click'. Ahead of them, no more than twelve feet, two impressive floodlights, suspended within the confines of an open-sided barn, burst into life. The blackness around them was eviscerated.

The barn itself was empty save for a singular tree. Its dense foliage tapering neatly into a satisfying cone. The quintessential Christmas Tree.

'How tall is it?' Lee asked.

'Just over five feet.' The farmer raised his well-manicured forefinger and paused for breath. 'It's a Norway Spruce - you'll notice how fine it looks – a real classic, though a word of warning: those needles can be surprisingly sharp, so be sure to take care.'

Lee laughed at the joke. 'I think we'll be fine. How much do you want?'

'Oh, just a token gesture. £10?'

'I couldn't do that, how about 30?' Clair had been trying to get him to haggle for years, but he'd always resisted. This wouldn't have been what she'd had in mind.

'No, no, I insist. It is the season of goodwill after all. £10 is quite enough. Do you have cash?'

Lee pulled out his wallet and produced a crisp £10 note. 'You're in luck. I stopped by the cashpoint just this afternoon.'

The farmer took it, folded it neatly and placed it into his breast pocket.

***

'Admit it, this looks loads better than the tatty thing in the attic?' Lee held his hands on his hips, grinning like a kid who'd just discovered the joys of picking their nose. The tree stood in the corner of the living room. Two cardboard boxes, filled with an assortment of decorations, had been placed on the sofa. Clumps of fibrous dust swung in the air around them, settling on the leather seats, falling to the carpeted floor. Their two daughters were sat either side. Abigail, eight years old and toying with the notion of being too old for all this festive nonsense, stoically resisted the urge to rummage through the baubles, Santa statues and tinsel. Holly, who had recently turned four, and having no such qualms, was enthusiastically mauling a plush, ornamental snowman.

'Okay, it's pretty good.' Clair sipped her Port as the pseudo-Elvis voice of Les Gray crooned from the speakers, lamenting the fact that Christmas was going to be lonely and cold. 'And at £10, I like it even more. What do you think kids, shall we put the decorations on?'

After just five minutes of hanging decorations upon whichever branches were within their reach, they had both grown bored and disappeared to play upstairs.

'Looks like it's just us then.' Lee carefully lifted a box containing white baubles whose tired foam coating made them look more like an exotic species of fungus than festive snowballs.

'Do we have to put those on?' Clair said, moving across the room to look through the boxes herself. 'They looked awful when we got them. They look even worse now. Maybe we should get some new ones?'

'These were the first decorations we got together!'

The hurt that momentarily shaped Lee's face caught Clair by surprise. 'Why don't we just put a couple on the tree, for old times' sake?'

Lee's shoulders slumped forward. 'I suppose so,' he said, lifting one of the contentious spheres from the box, this time manufacturing the hurt.

'Put it towards the back, where nobody can see it.' Lee ignored the taunt as he reached towards the top, selecting the most prominent branch he could find.

'Flip!' The gaudy bauble dropped to the floor as Lee staggered back, cradling his one hand with the other.

'What happened?' Clair placed her drink down.

He held his finger out. A single green needle extended from the tip, pulling the skin tight where it had plunged into the flesh.

'Ouch,' Clair said, moving in for a closer look. 'Is this part of the *real tree* experience?'

'The guy said the needles could be sharp, but this is a bit much.' Lee tugged at the floral spear and winced when it failed to budge.

'That's stuck in there worse than an Alabama tick.' They both smiled at the reference. 'Let me have a go.'

Before Lee had a chance to respond, Clair had clamped the needle between the fingers of one hand and held his arm steady with the other. She pulled hard, twisting as she did. 'Ow!' He pulled his finger away.

Blood began to flow from the small puncture, coursing down his finger in rivulets, forming small pools in the folds of his palm.

'My God, that was deep!' Clair twirled the needle between her fingers, looking at it with a kind of morbid respect. 'You should go and run that under the tap. The last thing we need is a trip to A&E for an Advent Acquired Infection.' She snorted at her own joke as she left to retrieve the first aid box from the utility.

The rest of the evening passed without incident. Abi and Holly kept helpfully out of the way while their increasingly merry parents finished decorating.

With the last piece of tinsel hung, and with the other three looking on, Lee placed the angel on the top. Then he plunged the room into darkness.

He flicked the fairy lights on, and the December gloom was transformed. A galaxy of stars – red, yellow, blue, and green – gave new life to the trinkets that hung expectantly between them. Wooden reindeer flew within clouds of iridescent brilliance. Icicles made from clear glass reflected the lights as if they were their own; luminous gemstones set within their translucent skin.

There was no carefully manufactured colour coordination here, just a diverse assortment of memories bathed in a harlequin glow. Some people probably thought it was tacky, but it was exactly how they liked it.

***

It was nearly ten o'clock before Lee slid out of bed. Everyone else was already downstairs.

'Afternoon,' Clair said as he stepped into the living room. She was sat next to the kids watching a *Peppa Pig* Christmas special.

'Morning.' Lee's voice cracked as he spoke.

'Wow, you sound awful,' Clair said. 'I didn't think you drank *that* much.'

'Neither did I, but my head's pounding.' He went to the kitchen, filled a glass with water, and returned to sit with his family.

He sniffed, trying to clear dried mucous from his nostrils, and grimaced as he held his nose to his arm pits. 'Is that me?'

'It's not you, it's that bloody tree. I thought that must be the smell of fresh pine you've been aching for. What do you think girls?'

Holly held her nose. 'Pooey!'

'It's disgusting,' Abi added.

If he really tried, Lee could just make out the aroma of pine, but it was struggling to assert itself in the presence of more powerful competition: stale egg; stagnant water; bad breath.

'That is *not* how I remember it.' He'd crossed the room and started running his fingers through the branches, looking for signs of rot.

'Watch it! We don't want another medical catastrophe. Speaking of which, how is the wounded appendage?'

Lee glanced at his finger and pursed his lips. 'A bit swollen actually. Smarts a bit too.'

Holly was pulling at the sleeve of his dressing-gown. 'Le'me see.'

Lee thrust the finger in front of her face. She inhaled sharply, creating the same hiss that she used to do when she fell over and scraped her knees. 'Nasty.'

The annual Santa parade was coming to their street that evening, and the girls spent the rest of the morning whipping themselves into a frenzy of unsuppressed excitement.

Later that afternoon, to help take their minds off it, they took a trip to the local German Market. Lee always enjoyed the idea of it more than the reality. It was too busy, and the stalls were exactly the same as ten years ago. Still, a serving of bratwurst and a glass of glühwein made the trip worthwhile. That, and seeing how much Abi and Holly enjoyed themselves. They wanted to buy every shiny thing they saw, of course, but were surprisingly satisfied with a bag of sugared almonds and a porcelain ballerina that they could hang on the tree when they got back.

The mottled rain that had burdened the air for the past few days had yielded to an icy frost. The skies had cleared too, revealing a more comforting blackness. There was no chance of snow, but at least it felt right for the season.

***

'Is Santa here yet?' Back home, Holly had gone straight to her bedroom and put her *Frozen* Christmas jumper on. 'I can't *wait!*'

'Not long now, angel,' Clair said.

'*What the fuck was that!*' Lee's shouting landed in the room like heavy artillery in a frosty meadow that glistened in the whispers of cautious moonlight.

Clair and Holly listened to the sound of cupboard doors opening and closing, the chaotic rattle of cutlery drawers being searched, furniture being dragged across the kitchen floor.

'What on earth is he up to?' Clair spoke to herself as much as to Holly, who rolled her eyes in response. '*You alright in there?*'

He didn't reply, but the frantic commotion continued as she walked towards the kitchen.

Lee was on his hands and knees, head pressed firmly to the floor, looking beneath the refrigerator.

'I think I can see it.' He shielded his eyes with his hand. 'Pass your phone, I'll shine the torch on it.'

'It's not mice again, is it?' Clair selected the torch icon and passed it over.

'Look, there she is!'

'There *who* is?'

Lee jolted backwards with a jarring sigh, struggling to his feet.

He steadied himself by grasping the sideboard with one hand while the other clasped around his mouth. He pulled it over his chin, stretching his bloodless face as he wrapped it around his own neck, something Clair had only ever seen him do once before: the time Abi had nearly choked on a pear drop. As she had gasped silently for breath, her face turning purple, Lee had become frozen with fear, staring at her with his hands around his throat. Though Clair had been further away, it had been she who administered the blow to the back that had sent the near-death confectionary flying from their daughter's mouth.

'She's coming, Clair. Please. *Do something!*'

Clair stood beside her husband and put her arm around his waist. *What the fuck is going on?* Her confusion was turning to fear. 'Lee, it's okay.'

He had taken his hand from his neck and was pointing to the floor. 'She's under the fridge,' he spat the words out, as if it were they that were making him gasp. 'I saw something scatter across the sink as I came in. A mouse,

I thought.' Clair's mind was racing, what should she do? Call the doctor? Take him to the hospital? She resisted the urge to interrupt. Talking seemed to be calming him down. Giving him a focus. 'I searched all over but couldn't find it. Then I heard the whispers, under the fridge. I looked under and she was there – the ballerina. She was calling to me, saying that we'd all be dead for Christmas. Staring with that fucking porcelain face. Then she started to move.'

Panic began to take hold, spreading down her spine, contaminating her flesh like a rapidly advancing infection. Not knowing how else to respond, Clair lowered herself to the floor. Lee grabbed her shoulder, shaking his head in dismay. She looked into his watery eyes and placed her hand on his. It felt hot. His finger had turned violently red and swollen to nearly twice its size. The rest of his hand was inflamed too, the skin a mottled glaze of purple and white. The infection must be making him delirious; the same thing had happened to her sister when an innocuous looking graze on her knee developed into a life-threatening sepsis. She needed to get him to the hospital.

Hoping to ease his panic before doing anything else, she peered under the fridge.

There was an old diecast mini – upturned like the remains of a long-forgotten wreckage, a half-eaten digestive and a partially decomposed grape, all discarded amidst a landscape of crumbs and dust.

'There's nothing there now,' she said, trying to sound as matter of fact as she could. 'Let's go to the other room – I'll get you a drink.'

Holly had gone back upstairs to play. Lee sat on the sofa sipping his coffee. Clair stood by the window, massaging the back of her neck, avoiding eye-contact.

'I believe that *you* saw what you say you saw,' she said, hoping that she didn't sound as patronising as she feared. 'But I think you should at least consider the possibility that what you saw was not what was there.' The street outside had been transformed into a boulevard of artificial lights and giant inflatables. A bloated Santa Clause and a billowing snow man, each the height of the lamp posts that lined the road, frolicked among an endless cosmos of polychromatic light.

'Why would I make something like that up, Clair?' It was frightening, how rational he sounded, how sure he was of his own experience.

'I'm not saying-' It was no good, they were going round in circles. 'Will you at least let me take you to the hospital to get that finger checked out?'

'I'm not leaving the girls here with that … thing in the house.'

Clair pulled her phone from her pocket. 'Obviously we're not going to leave them. I'll call mum. She won't mind if we drop them off on the way.' She opened her contacts.

'Only if you check the tree.'

'Check it?' Clair selected 'mum' and hovered her finger over the green phone icon.

'To see if that ballerina's still where you hung it. If she is, then I'll go.'

The relief washed over her like a hot shower on a winter's morning, expunging the bitterest of chills. She turned to the tree, holding her phone, ready to make the call.

'Here she is,' Clair said, lifting the decoration so that he could see. 'Just where we left her.'

He shuffled in the chair. 'I suppose you might be right.' His eyes hung mournfully. His top lip was pulled down between his teeth.

After Clair called the girls down, they stood beside the front door, eager to join the festively adorned street that beckoned through its clouded glass. Holly was wearing her knitted elf hat.

Clair wasn't looking forward to what had to come next.

'*That's not FAIR! Why do we have to go? Why?*' Holly had ripped the hat from her head and thrown it to the floor. Her first reaction to such news was usually rage, quickly followed by inconsolable sorrow. Judging by the quiver of her lip and the glassy film coating her eyes, she was already making the transition. Abi had folded her arms. Old enough to realise that arguing would do no good, not too old to sulk.

To make matters worse people were already gathering along the street, smudged figures visible through frosted glass. Their muffled thrum bled through the walls, compounding the nascent disappointment; an airless apparition, seen by none but felt by all.

'I know it's rubbish – I was looking forward to seeing Santa too, but Daddy's finger has made him *really* poorly and he needs to see a doctor.' As Clair spoke Holly began to sob. Abi picked the hat off the floor and handed it to her sister. Clair's chest filled with pride. She had been expecting a fight, though in some ways their solemn acceptance was worse. 'How about we go to *Winter Wonderland* next week instead?'

Holly lifted her head, hope written in pages of her involuntary smile.

Abi managed to cool it out for a second or so before succumbing to her own excitement. 'Do you promise?' she said.

Clair put an arm around her shoulders, pulling her closer. 'I prom-,'.

Lee's anguished wail cut through the affirmation like the strike of a blade upon the butcher's block, dividing the glistening remnants of something that had once been full of life.

Clair told the girls to stay put before dashing into the living room. Lee was lying on the floor, curled into the foetal pose of someone anticipating the impact of a leather boot. Abi and Holly, who had ignored their instruction, filed in behind her.

'Lee?' She knelt beside him. His face was buried beneath his arms, hands reaching over the top of his head, grasping at his hair. 'Come on, let's get you to hospital, the girls are all ready to go.' She turned towards them. They both nodded, clearly stunned by the sight of their dad curled up on the floor, frightened and vulnerable.

Lee didn't react until Clair leaned in to help him up. He pushed his hand into the centre of her chest. She toppled away, as he twisted onto his back. He stared at Clair as though he had never seen her before in his life. She felt like an invader in her own home. His eyes were yellow and bloodshot, his face slick with a viscous residue. The marbled stain of infection had travelled up his arm and into his neck. Clair could almost see his jaw swelling as the poison forged its path.

The girls rushed to their mother's side. Still silent. Still in shock. They had never seen either parent lay a hand on the other before.

Lee stretched the diseased limb out in front of his face. His hand grasped at the air, reaching towards the unseen fabrications of his fevered mind. The palm-side of his wrist, pulled taut by the angle of his hand, seemed to pulsate, as if something beneath the skin was struggling to push through.

With trembling fingers, Clair pulled her phone from her pocket. It was time to call an ambulance.

Abigail was the only one to see the skin of her father's wrist tear apart. She screamed as thick, blood smeared, pus squeezed through the fissure. It fell to the floor in heavy lumps. The smell was instantaneous and obscene.

Lee continued to hold his arm forth as he stared towards some ill-defined part of the room. If he felt anything, it didn't show.

Clair looked up from the phone. As if the sight of her husband's mutilated wrist wasn't enough, she could see movement. A sturdy band of elasticated tendon bulged through the already lacerated tissues. The pressure caused Lee's fingers to contract into a fist before snapping open again as the tapered tip of a milky, almost colourless tendril pierced the overstretched sinew. It extended from the clotted mass with bewildering speed.

Abi pulled Holly towards her chest, a protective instinct that she'd never known she had, shielding her little sister from the horrors that were unfolding.

Her dad's whole body slumped to the floor. His knees were still tucked up, but his arm fell forward, and his face melted lifelessly into the carpet. He looked dead, but his eyes stayed open. Didn't people close their eyes when they died? Abi was sure it was true. Any moment now and her dad was going to stand up and start laughing at his own elaborately planned joke.

The tip of the tendril nearly touched the ceiling. Its opaque stem rose vertically from Lee's motionless arm. The upper third thrashed around wildly.

Clair was up in an instant, pulling her daughters behind her. Holly kept her eyes firmly shut as Abi whispered that everything would be okay.

As the three of them started running for the door the parasite that had violated Lee's body swung around the room, its tip whipping furiously as it reached towards them.

Clair felt it tighten around her ankle. Time moved through a gelatinous soup as she fell to the floor. The detail of every protracted moment was torturous and vivid.

Abi and Holly stopped when they got to the door.

'Keep going girls, get help.' Clair could feel the writhing shackle tighten around her ankle, probing at her skin.

Holly lifted her head from the cocoon that Abi had created, seeing for the first time the appalling scene that was playing out amidst the festive décor.

Her screams, boundless and inhuman, erased all else from Clair's mind. She didn't feel the pointed end of her husband's final gift as it gouged into her ankle and tunnelled up her leg, spiralling beneath the skin. She could only hear the animalistic cries of her daughter, only watch as the child ran instinctively towards her, face twisted with fear.

Lying prone on the floor, limbs splayed at stilted angles, face slanted forward, Clair could do nothing to comfort the little girl who clung to her shoulders, who pleaded between pneumatic sobs.

Please mommy, let's go.

She tried to console her with empty promises, but as the tendrils forced their way out of her wrists, the pain took control.

The parasite worked quickly now, finding each child with impatient efficiency and speed, the thrashing scions formed tight ligatures around their prey. As the periphery of her vision began to fade along with the life from her body, Clair was able to witness the final moments of her children's short existence. In the darkest circumstances hope can take desperate forms, and she found some solace in the fact that each had quickly lost consciousness, collapsing limply to the ground as the tendrils pushed deftly into their soft necks.

Almost as soon as their skin had been breached, new branches of the invading organism emerged from each of their four limbs, waving deliberately in the air like the barbed tentacles of a sea anemone, waiting patiently for its unsuspecting prey.

***

The man with the unblemished face watched from the other side of the crowded street. The acerbic smell of mulled cider and gingerbread was nauseating, but he didn't mind. Overexcited children jostled past, trying to get a better look at the motorised sleigh on which an impressively authentic Santa was sat. A few people gave a sidewards glance as they passed – he probably should have worn a coat – but by and large they were too preoccupied with the celebrations to notice the stranger in their midst.

The curtains of the house were still open, and the lights had remained on throughout, but nobody had noticed what had taken place inside – all attention had been on the big man in red.

Just as he was thinking of walking away – satisfied that his work had been done, ready to let things progress in their own time – something caught his eye. A woman, wearing a formidable looking duffel coat and a yellow and brown bobble-hat, was walking towards the newly fledged arboretum. She produced what looked like a Christmas card from her pocket and slotted it into the letterbox of the front door. She quickly started to struggle, trying to pull her hand away, to gain the attention of those around her. Then she fell limp, swinging into the door – her arm stretched upwards, her hand held firmly by that which was inside. He looked on as fresh tendrils extend from her limbs, reaching hungrily towards the crowd.

It wouldn't be long now, not long at all. He walked away with a smile on his face and a spring in his step. For once, it was beginning to look a lot like Christmas.

A Grave Undertaking
By Stone Wallace

On Halloween Night, teenage infatuation leads to Sidney Underhill's unfortunate participation in . . .

A GRAVE UNDERTAKING

Tires crunched on the loose gravel of the narrow road as the car arrived at its destination and drew to a slow halt, the engine kept running, sounding as a gentle purr.

The boy who sat on the passenger side, Sidney Underhill, a freckle-faced, red-headed youth who just recently celebrated his 17th birthday, was quiet before he slowly pivoted his head and furrowed his brow, looking with puzzlement at the striking raven-haired Cassandra, whose slim hands and long tapered fingers remained curled around the steering wheel in an eleven-to-one-o'clock positioning, a slight caressing to her touch, her green, cat-like eyes not meeting her companion's questioning stare.

Sidney was patient, but then he released a deliberate sigh. He waited for a reaction that did not come from Cassandra, and then he offered an obvious and unnecessary observation:

"This is a cemetery."

Cassandra hesitated before a slow smile crept across her full ruby red lips.

"Of course," was her pleasant if enigmatic reply.

Sidney cleared his throat and fidgeted slightly in his seat.

"And . . . why are we here?" he questioned. A hint of uncertainty filtered through in his words, though at the same time he tried to remain unfazed by this unexpected "detour".

Cassandra finally focused her gaze completely on him.

She spoke her words with a casual, innocent inflection. "What better place to visit on Halloween night?"

"Y'know, this is . . . like, totally weird," Sidney remarked as he experienced a creeping sense of unease.

"Is it?" Cassandra said. She sighed with a subtle satisfaction. "Personally, I like it here." Then, with a gentle shrug: "Especially tonight. It's just . . . perfect." She added with a burst of exuberance: 'Don't you think?"

Sidney nodded absently. "Yeah, well . . ." He discharged a breath. "I mean, do you come here . . . like often?"

Cassandra sighed again, her expression now somewhat downcast. "No. Not as often as I should."

Sidney lifted a quizzical eyebrow. He had no idea what she meant by that. Was there any particular reason for her visit to the cemetery? He wasn't sure if he wanted to find out.

His eyes then stealthily shifted toward the inviting crotch V-line of Cassandra's oh-so-tight black jeans and his misgivings about their rather macabre environment found conflict with his desire to be alone with her – and whatever "Halloween treat" that might offer. More precisely, what *she* might offer.

He took a minute or two to steady the physical manifestation of his urge which could prove embarrassing for him if she noticed, and instead he shifted his attention out the side window. It was mid-autumn; the falling orange and yellow leaves were tapping along the dirt roadway and dancing across the well-manicured cemetery lawn in a slight breeze that interrupted the stillness of their surroundings. Darkness was beginning to shadow the skies accompanied by a smudging of gray clouds. It produced an atmosphere hardly conducive to the possibility of romance.

Trying to redirect his thoughts, Sidney reflected back to where and how this all began. At the same time, he reminded himself that he was where he'd wanted to be – well, yes, but not exactly where he *chose* to be. He was alone with the striking raven-haired beauty with the flawless porcelain skin to whom he'd been attracted since that day at high school when he'd first spotted her, standing alone next to her locker.

It was just three weeks into the new school year and she must have been a late arrival since he hadn't seen her in the hallway before. He was at his own locker a row away collecting his books for morning classes and noticed that she seemed to be struggling with her lock combination. She appeared flustered and he debated whether he should walk over to her and see if he could offer his help. But he hesitated in his decision, and soon it was too late. Another girl came over and gave her a hand opening the stubborn lock. He watched discreetly as the raven-haired girl smiled appreciatively, and with a heaving sigh he shut the door of his locker and started on his way to first period history class.

It was a new experience for Sidney. Whoever this girl was, she'd made a definite impression on him, even though he'd seen her for not even five minutes. As an average maturing boy, he'd naturally felt attractions to other girls, but those were just crushes that generally faded as fast as they came, often once a new face entered the scene and his attention was re-directed to a brand new fetching form. But for a reason even he couldn't completely comprehend the image of this girl had affected him differently and had somehow settled deep into his psyche. For the rest of the school day he had difficulty concentrating on his studies as she had become a steady fixture in his thoughts. At one point he momentarily lost connection to where he was and reactedwith an involuntary but quite audible, "Wow."

This of course drew the quizzical and even smirking attention of his classmates and delivered him a stern, disapproving look from the teacher, who was a humorless warhorse in any regard. Sidney smiled with quiet embarrassment and tried unsuccessfully to hold back the flush from his features.

As time passed, Sidney saw the raven-haired girl frequently and always tried to make it a point to be at his locker when she arrived for morning classes. He noticed that while she too was a "freshie," she seemed to be making friends at a rapid rate – and garnering particular attention from the boy crowd, even those in the upper grades. It didn't surprise him. Each time he looked at her she seemed to get even prettier. She possessed a distinctive look complemented by a contagious glow and perfect smile that couldn't help but gain her an instant and impressive popularity. Sidney observed all of this with a deep inner yearning, though he held onto a personal fantasy that, considering both were first year students, an opportunity might come along where he might speak with her; maybe even get to find out a little about her . . . provided he didn't bungle it by getting over-eager and uttering something awkward or even inappropriate. But it didn't take Sidney long to recognize that his fantasies collided with the reality of the situation. Strike one: They shared no classes together. And whenever their paths crossed in the hallway, she looked to completely ignore him; never giving him so much as a passing glance. With a sinking heart, Sidney slowly accepted that in her world he was regarded as a non-entity, and that was a category with which he was too familiar. High school just presented a new, ego-deflating spin on it.

While he recognized that in a popularity poll he'd rank somewhere in the bottom percent, he could, if weakly, console himself that he wasn't alone in that miserable category. One of the few friendships he'd formed this school year was with a youth who likewise roamed the halls as someone few cared to recognize, and fewer still bothered to acknowledge except to occasionally shoulder-bump him into a locker. His name was Ed Jones, and his looks and personality were just as bland as his name. The difference between the two boys was that Ed knew his position in the school caste system and accepted it, and in a strange way even embraced it. He didn't seem to care if anyone accepted him. Anonymity seemed to be his preference.

Strange guy – yet it seemed to Sidney the kind of person he'd find himself friendly with.

During one lunch hour Sidney opened up about the new girl who had caught his eye and who seemed to have taken up permanent residency in his thoughts.

"But you don't even know her name," Ed stated incredulously, his reedy voice a few octaves higher than most volumes spoken in the school cafeteria.

Sidney almost choked mid-swallow on his sandwich. "Announce it all over the lunchroom, you putz," he grumbled.

Ed responded with a slight lift of his shoulder. He glanced around the cafeteria, noticing just a few sets of eyes on him.

Sidney took another bite of his sandwich and chewed thoughtfully on its contents of whole wheat bread, cheese and a generous portion of lettuce, as his eyes veered in another direction, apparently gazing at nothing.

Then he turned back to Ed and asked, "Do *you* know?"

"Know what?"

"Her name?"

Ed gave a teasing wobble of his head, and then offered a playful grin. "Sure I do."

"Really?"

"Uh-huh. In fact, she's in one of my classes."

Sidney's eyes widened slightly in anticipation.

"Well . . . ?"

Ed stalled and took this opportunity to make his friend squirm a little, settling back in his chair and puffing out his chest, arms lifted and fastened behind his neck. "Some guys have all the luck, huh?"

Sidney looked crestfallen. He turned his attention back to his sandwich, and after brief consideration he slapped its remnants down onto the paper plate before him.

"Look amigo," Ed said, now leaning forward with both elbows resting on the table, "it's okay to dream –

hell, we all do it, but some things just happen to be beyond our reach. And hot chicks, well . . . they pretty well top the 'no-way Jose' list for guys like us."

Sidney eyed his companion critically. He smirked and chimed, "And never was heard an *encouraging* word . . ."

Ed threw himself back into his chair and raised his arms in a surrendering gesture.

"However, never let it be said that Eddie Jones stamped out someone else's fire," he proclaimed.

Sidney frowned. "That the best you can do? And I thought it was 'step on someone's dreams'."

"Whatever, same difference," Ed replied nonchalantly. "But if it'll help you, I can tell you that her name is – get this: Cassandra." He spoke her name with a touch of deliberate mystery.

"Cassandra?" Sidney echoed.

Ed nodded slowly. He grinned. "Bewitchin', ain't it?"

Sidney rocked his head, enticed. "Yeah," he murmured.

"And get this," Ed continued, raising his hand, palm outright, for emphasis. "That is how she insists on being called. She made that clear in the class I have with her, and probably all the others. 'My name is Cassandra, not Cassie,' she said."

"Seems kind of highbrow," Sidney mused.

"Why not? She likely can afford to be."

"Suppose," Sidney said, sounding pensive.

Ed suddenly nudged him under the table and jerked his head to call attention to something behind him. At the same time, he frowned in a gesture for Sidney not to look now. Sidney ignored him and casually glanced over his shoulder. He saw the raven-haired beauty walk over to a table at the far end of the cafeteria that was populated by the school's A-listers. Her pose was perfect, her stride confident. Her lips were parted wide, smiling her 100-watt, ruby-lipped smile, highlighted by blindingly white, perfectly-spaced teeth.

Sidney instantly felt himself surrendering to a sort of adolescent apoplexy. But his momentary "high" dissipated when the school's Grade 11 super-jock and all-round stud, Mickey Treadman, sauntered into the lunch room projecting his customary arrogance and proceeded directly over to the table where Cassandra sat. She clearly welcomed his presence as the two immediately engaged in a friendly, cozy chat.

"Man. Ego just drips off of that guy like sweat," Sidney observed.

Ed noticed the slight tightening of his friend's jaw. Instead of offering support he took advantage of the moment to tease Sidney further. "So tell me Galahad, think you can compete against that?"

Sidney shot him a quick, not amused glance but wouldn't oblige him with a response.

* * *

Grade 10 passed into Grade 11.

Same story. Even though Sidney had hoped that with the first year of high school over, summer vacation might provide enough distractions to keep his thoughts away from Cassandra. He never saw the girl at all during summer break and could only imagine what her own activities might be, and likely in the company of her jock boyfriend. Still, harboring envy and a subtle resentment, he'd never been so eager for the new school year to begin. Though in his more reasonable, rational moments he'd ask: for what purpose? This new year would likely yield the same disappointing and discouraging results.

The school year started in September and much to his disappointment (if not his surprise) Cassandra and Mickey seemed to have further cemented their relationship. Obviously they had been together through at least some of the summer months. Both had matching tans that Sidney surmised were not obtained on individual outings. They were soon looked upon as the school's "dream couple," and were seen together everywhere – and not just within the hallowed halls of Sherwood High. Sidney expected this to be a particularly rough year. It was difficult for him to conceal the jealousy and heartache he felt whenever he spotted Cassandra and Mickey together – which was frequently. It also didn't help that they shared a science class (to which he had hoped to be assigned as her lab partner – not to be), and it almost seemed that she deliberately tried to avoid him whenever he passed a cursory glance her way. In solitary, introspective, and even maddening moments he often asked why he tortured himself – especially when he knew what he had since the beginning, yet stubbornly refused to acknowledge: that Cassandra was beyond his reach. He could create all the fantasies he wanted, but the truth simply could not be ignored. A truth that often slammed into him with the impact of an emotional battering ram.

Despite this disappointment when it came to Cassandra, Sidney wasn't completely without other female options. He'd been aware that there was another girl who he had been told was secretly interested in him. She was a virtual high school "ghost" like himself – not unattractive particularly but nothing to excite Sidney after his long infatuation with Cassandra. A Friday night school dance was coming up and this girl, Brenda, without coming across as too forward dropped hints during their casual conversations that she didn't have a date for the dance . . . and was Sidney planning to come. He was surprised and puzzled when cynical Ed Jones seemed to switch gears and told him it wouldn't look good for him to be seen with "Miss Plain Jane".

"You're singing a different tune," Sidney said. "Or am I guessing *you* want to be my date?"

"Funny guy," Ed smirked. "Sure, I considered it, but on further thought, you just ain't my type."

"So what is your suggestion?" Sidney asked him. "Skip the dance and hang out with you on another dull Friday night?"

"Huh-uh." Unexpectedly, Ed's demeanor turned serious, catching Sidney off-guard. "Look, just wait it out a bit."

"Wait *what* out?"

"Trust me."

"You are making no sense," Sidney told him directly.

Ed simply repeated: "Trust me." He then let out a sigh and responded to Sidney's furrowed brow. "It ain't over till it's over."

Sidney was left scratching his head. Ed was a peculiar sort but whatever he was *not* saying seemed to indicate he'd just jumped a few notches on his personal Weird Meter.

Despite Ed's "advice" Sidney briefly considered asking Brenda to be his date for the dance. But he decided against it. Brenda was nice enough, a sweet girl, but he knew he couldn't be properly attentive to her with the "dream couple" inviting all the attention with their perfect appearance and obvious affection for each other.

While virtually admitting defeat, he continued to discreetly observe the relationship between Cassandra and what appeared to be her steady beau.

And then . . . gradually, it seemed to take an odd turn.

No one could explain why, but from Cassandra and Mickey being the most visible and admired couple at Sherwood High, and seeming to revel in the attention they received, they were becoming distant, even from those who previously had been closest to them. They seemed to be keeping more to themselves, and even outside of school they were avoiding their usual haunts where they'd hang out with the other kids who shared their "prestige". Naturally, this shift in attitude prompted rumors. Hushed conversations among the more gossip-minded in the school. Some were suggesting that Mickey had gone too far with his machismo and gotten Cassandra pregnant; that remained a whispered favorite. A few of Cassandra's closer friends tried to subtly broach the subject with her, but the raven-haired girl would barely speak with them, maintaining an uncharacteristically aloof manner – thus fertilizing the soil for heightened suspicion, while also generating a sort of adolescent excitement among her former crowd.

Sidney remembered overhearing a couple of school jocks and Mickey's "buds"–standing by the gym lockers and presenting their own theories as to the standoffish behavior of their friend.

"They've gotten into some weird shit," one of the boys surmised.

"You talkin' dope? That don't sound like the Mick. Doesn't even smoke straight cigarettes. Drop that idea."

"I'm not talking about *that* kinda shit."

Another boy offered, "I knew something was up. Mickey doesn't show up for gym class anymore, misses wrestling practice. That's not like him. Hell, he barely even comes to school anymore. Can't hardly talk to the guy. Like he's carrying around some big secret. Yeah, been real odd this year. Ever since summer break."

Then a more "perceptive" observation: "They spend a lot of time together at Cassandra's house. You know Greg Aimsley lives across the street from her. He tells me he sees Mick go over there practically every night. Sorta like after dark. Might even be every night, he don't know for sure. Don't think Cassandra has folks; either split or died I figure. Lives with some strange old bird who's probably her grandmother or somethin'. Greg's folks say the old lady rarely comes out of the house. Real secretive shit. That big house and just the two of them. And get this: Aimsley tells me that once he sees Mick go inside, then . . . like clockwork, within maybe five minutes all the lights go out. Tells me the house stays pitch dark except for one light that stays on in the upstairs attic window . . . and he never sees when Mick leaves. That is, *if* he leaves after those visits."

"Creepy," one of the boys uttered.

The group fell silent, each boy now absorbed in his own contemplation.

* * *

It was Monday morning and Sidney was threading his way through the usual mass of student bodies preparing for another week of studies, heading toward his locker.

On this morning he noticed there was a tight congregation surrounding the proximity of Cassandra's locker. Whatever was going on, the conversation seemed intense. Sidney was curious what was up, but understood it was none of his business. And he would be told so in no uncertain terms. He tried not to be obvious – not that any in that group would notice him anyway – but he could not resist casting oblique glances in their direction – along with straining his ears to maybe catch a word or two of what was being said.

In the next instant he felt a tug on his shoulder. His immediate thought was that he'd been spotted eavesdropping and was being called out on it.

Instead, he turned and found himself face-to-face with Ed Jones.

"You heard, huh?" Ed said, his voice tinged with muted excitement.

Sidney shrugged. "Heard what?"

"Not here," Ed said.

Ed gave his head a nudge in a gesture for his friend to follow him. He led Sidney down the hallway toward the stairwell at the far end of the building, where they could talk more privately.

Sidney grew impatient. "What the hell's wrong with you? What's with all this mystery shit?"

Ed glanced around to make sure no one was in earshot.

"Are you ready for this?" he then said.

"Hell, yeah."

Ed still stalled, as if unsure of how to proceed or just aiming for dramatic effect, in either event continuing to frustrate Sidney.

His eyes continued to dart about. And then:

"Guess who bit the bullet on Saturday night?"

"Huh? What do you mean, bit the . . .*what*?"

Ed rolled his eyes. "Got himself killed, you piñata."

Sidney's expression registered his bewilderment at whatever it was that Ed was trying to get across to him.

"Your 'rival' – Mickey, big man on campus."

Sidney's jaw drew slack. "Mickey . . . *Treadman*?" he responded in a whisper.

Ed's grinned. "No – more like Mickey '*deadman*'."

"He was . . . *killed*?"

Ed rocked his head vigorously.

"But . . . how? What happened?"

"Don't know too much. But apparently he was out cruisin' on Saturday and somehow crashed his car. Hey, get this: word goin' around is that it might *not* have been an accident."

"I – don't get you."

"Deliberate," Ed emphasized. "According to people who saw the crash, the way he was driving it was a miracle no one else was killed."

"So – he killed himself . . .?" Sidney uttered. "Was he drunk? High on something?"

"Doubtful. The guy never even touched a beer."

"Then what the . . ."

"From what I hear he was mangled beyond recognition. He musta really totaled that fancy car of his. I mean, what a mess to clean up."

"Shit!" Sidney spat.

"I'm sure there was plenty of that, too," Ed remarked, straight-faced.

Sidney wore a disgusted expression. "Not funny, you ghoul."

Ed smiled deviously. "Maybe not. But there is an interesting angle to it. One that might benefit you, my friend."

Sidney understood where Ed was headed. He frowned in his displeasure at Ed's blatant insensitivity – and at his not so subtle suggestion.

"Man, you really are a ghoul," he said.

"Hey, all I'm saying is that the girl of your dreams is free again."

Sidney spoke incredulously. "Man, you're not only a ghoul but one cold-hearted S.O.B."

"Maybe," Ed said without taking offense. "But I prefer to think of myself as a realist . . . which is why I think you hang around with me. I see things as they are. You do, too – if you'd just open up to it. Man, cut the

Archie Andrews bit and just look at the bigger picture." He paused before resuming. "Look, with the road clear–" He halted and suppressed a smirk. "Uh, bad choice of words, huh?" he said.

Sidney nodded grimly. "No matter how I feel, a guy's dead, and if you think I'm gonna jump in now, at this time . . ."

But even while Sidney considered it not only an inappropriate but morbid proposition, he couldn't deny that he also had briefly given similar thought.

Ed mused: "A little sympathy." Then, with an exaggeration of compassion: "Maybe a little I'm-here-for-you-if-you-need-me concern."

Sidney frowned; he was not about to acknowledge that his strange friend had somehow keyed into his own momentary thinking.

Instead, he addressed him sourly. "You have all the compassion of a wombat."

* * *

The school permitted those students who wanted to attend Mickey Treadman's funeral to have the day off. Naturally a number of students took advantage of this opportunity, though for many it was a convenient reason to enjoy a school break. Sidney debated going to the mortuary chapel, but decided against it – though he likewise took the day off under the pretense of attending the service.

Ed, with his apparent morbid curiosity, went, however, and immediately afterward rushed to tell all to Sidney. Presumably, because of the condition of the body, it was a closed-casket affair. Ed sat with Sidney in his friend's bedroom and pondered what exactly was enclosed in that hardwood coffin. Did the mortician try to reassemble Mickey's damaged corpse but was unable to achieve satisfactory results, thus the reason for no viewing of the body. Maybe the missing limbs were bagged in plastic and placed inside the coffin with what was left of Mickey's torso. It was all morbid speculation. Sidney wasn't eager to discuss postmortem procedure and hastened to change the subject. He wanted to know about Cassandra, how she reacted at the service. Was she in grief? Ed shrugged. He told Sidney that it was hard to tell because the funeral home was filled to capacity and he was seated in a pew near the back. And once the lengthy service (peppered with Bible quotes and personal remembrances from Mickey's friends and teammates) was over, Ed hurried out.

"I'm not much for all that religious stuff," Ed admitted.

"Suppose it doesn't matter," Sidney said neutrally.

The room went quiet for a few moments.

"So the playing field is clear," Ed suddenly said, emphasizing his remark with a sharp clap of his hands.

Sidney looked at him. "You starting this again?"

Once more Ed's voice grew animated. "You gotta wise up. I'm just trying to steer you right. Walk up to her and offer a little friendly compassion. You wait too long and it's a sure bet you'll miss your chance. 'Cause someone else is sure to come along."

"What she's gonna need is some time," Sidney stated.

"Well," Ed breathed, "your decision. But take it from me, she's vulnerable now and that's when a sweetheart appreciates a sympathetic shoulder to lean on."

Sidney's eyes fastened on his companion, and he tightened his brow. It almost sounded as if Ed was intimating he knew something that Sidney didn't.

"Since when did you become such an expert on the needs of the female psyche?" Sidney said, mock critically. "You: Ed Jones."

Ed Jones . . . ?

Now that was a crazy thought.

* * *

Over the next several days Cassandra was absent from school. For the other students at Sherwood High the usual routine was re-established now that the shock of Mickey Treadman's sudden and tragic passing had subsided. The resiliency of adolescence moved the students onward and forward with their lives and activities.

Sidney, though, was restless. He grew continually curious. Certainly it wasn't unusual for someone who had suffered a personal loss to take a few days off from school. But after a week passed without Cassandra attending classes, he began to detour home by walking by her house, hoping maybe to catch a glimpse of her. He only did this for a couple of days since he didn't want to become obvious in his movements. He certainly didn't want Cassandra to finally take notice of him in such a way, as if he were stalking her.

He found it odd that the front window drapes and upstairs curtains were always drawn. It almost gave the impression that the house was vacant. He experienced a queer feeling both times he passed by. Something just didn't seem right to him – and he grew concerned about Cassandra.

Finally, after another week had passed, Sidney was at his locker when out the corner of his eye he caught a familiar figure walking down the hallway. Sidney turned his head, perhaps a little too expectantly, and saw that it was raven-haired Cassandra. Again he feared being obvious so he quickly turned his attention back to his locker, pretending to sort through some of his textbook assignments.

In the next moment came the unexpected –

"I know you've been watching me," a soft and sensuous voice wafted from behind him.

Sidney hesitated before turning.

It was Cassandra, and she was talking – to *him*.

Nervous, uncertain, he cleared his throat and tried to speak without mumbling his words. "You're – talking to me?"

"Of course," she said innocently, her eyes veering from one side of the hallway to the other. "Do you see anyone else around?"

Sidney felt his body temperature heat up. He feared he might start to perspire.

"I know how you've felt for a long time," she smiled approvingly.

"But . . . but . . ."

"Just what I thought about you. You're bashful."

This wasn't a silly teenage girl talking. To Sidney, this was a mature woman expressing herself.

His thoughts were an internal echo of his stumbling words: *But . . . but . . .*

Beyond his bewilderment at her sudden attention toward him, it dawned on Sidney that he'd always only noticed her from a distance; even in the class they shared they sat at opposite sides of the room. Looking at her up close she was even more attractive than he'd imagined. What he particularly noticed was the unique curvature of her eyes. They were oval-shaped, almost feline-like, reflecting a deep clear green. He felt that if he were to gaze into those eyes long enough, he could be drawn into them; they possessed an almost hypnotic effect.

Sidney's breathing started to almost tighten, constrict, and he had to pull himself back in.

"You don't have to be bashful," she told him, mildly, her voice nearly a caress.

"I – I'm not bashful," he said. "Uh, not particularly. It's just that . . . well, you never talked to me before. Don't think you ever even noticed me."

She smiled, almost coyly. "Oh, I noticed you."

Sidney shrugged slightly. "I never thought you did."

"Mmmhmm," she sounded gently.

"But . . . why now?"Sidney ventured. "Why are you talking to me now?"

Cassandra cocked her head. "Isn't that what you want?" she said lowly.

"Huh? I – well, yes, it . . . it's nice."

Sidney turned his head for a moment and noticed his friend Ed standing not far from the two of them, in the middle of the hallway. He was grinning like a Cheshire cat. Sidney was certain he knew something. Sidney even considered that maybe he'd had a hand in setting up this very unexpected turn of events.

A thought he quickly erased.

Ed Jones . . . ?

Cassandra surprised Sidney even more when she asked him outright:

"Would you like to ask me to go out with you?"

"Uh, yeah, sure." Sidney's answer was immediate. Yet he was so overwhelmed he hardly knew what he was saying. And did he respond *too quickly*?

"We could go for a drive," Cassandra suggested.

"A – drive?"

Cassandra nodded.

"Yeah, I'd like that, only . . . I don't own a car," Sidney said. "But maybe I could borrow my –"

Cassandra shushed him. "No need. I have a car."

"Uh, where would you want to go?" Sidney asked.

Cassandra raised her eyes upward and looked to consider.

"You let me decide that," she then said.

This was all so surreal. Within mere moments Sidney's life had experienced a major shift. Everything he'd fantasized about over the past year had suddenly coalesced into a reality. And all the while Ed was standing there, apparently delighting in this development and his friend's obvious perplexity.

He had to have had something to do with this . . .

Sidney nodded. "Okay."

Cassandra smiled. "I *know* you know where I live. I've seen you walk by my house."

"You – have?" Sidney said, embarrassed.

"Do you mind walking over to my house . . . around let's say 5:30?"

"Sure. I . . . guess."

"Around 5:30," Cassandra repeated.

Sidney nodded. "Uh-huh."

Cassandra flashed him a wide, white-toothed smile and then she turned and walked away – but not to where her next class was scheduled. She was heading toward the student exit doors, leaving the school.

Once she had disappeared from sight, Ed sauntered over to his friend.

Sidney just shrugged.

"That the best you can do?" Ed said with a sly smirk.

"She – asked me to go for a drive with her."

"Not necessarily a home run but sounds like second base potential," Ed remarked.

Sidney pointed an accusing finger at him. "You somehow set this up, didn't you?"

Ed spoke in his own defense. "What? Why would I do that? And – do you think that *she* would listen to anything I'd have to say? You're dreamin', buddy."

Sidney remained suspicious.

Ed then said, "Look at this another way, will ya. Seriously, hear me out. Your formerly elusive dream has sorta gotten lower on the totem pole now."

"What's that supposed to mean?" Sidney demanded.

"Simply that she ain't Miss Popularity anymore."

"And . . . ?"

"Well, come on, face it. She had nothing to do with you then. Now that her boyfriend's dead and she ain't exactly chummy-chummy with her fancy high-falutin' group . . ."

Sidney's lips twisted. "Still, why would she suddenly be interested in a schmuck like me?"

Ed rolled his eyes in frustration. "Man, you're a lost cause. Do I gotta spell it out to you in block letters? 'Cause maybe she feels safe with a schmuck like you. She's clearly been observing you showin' some interest in her . . . and let's face it, you ain't exactly someone who she – or really anyone – would see as a threat." He grinned toothily. "Just a nice average Archie Andrews-type guy."

"The second time you referred to me that way," Sidney said." I guess in your own way you mean that as a compliment."

Ed stretched his thin lips in a smile. "How else?"

* * *

"You wanta do *what*?" Sidney exclaimed, astonished at what Cassandra was suggesting.

Cassandra pushed her body closer to his. Still tempted by his desire to actually fulfill what so long had consumed his fantasies, Sidney hesitated only momentarily before biting down on his lower lip and giving his head a slow but deliberate shake.

"No. No, I – I don't think that's gonna happen," he said, suddenly shifting his body aside while pushing out his words in frustration.

"I admit it's a little strange, but . . . so am I. I have peculiar desires."

"I'm okay with that, I guess, that you're as you say a little strange. But this sounds like more than just a 'peculiar desire'."

"Then why did you agree to come out here with me?" Cassandra asked petulantly.

"I – wanted to be with you," Sidney answered timidly.

"And you are."

"Yeah. But I – didn't expect . . .*this*."

Cassandra sighed dreamily. "Well, I find it somehow appealing…even charming."

"So did Dracula," Sidney muttered under his breath.

Cassandra gave him a questioning look. "Hmm?"

"Huh? Oh – nothing. Nothing important. I just think there has to be someplace . . . well, more appropriate to . . . you know."

Cassandra sighed again. "Well, that's too bad you feel that way. Because I know just the perfect spot. . ." She eyed him seductively. ". . . if you're up to it."

Sidney didn't answer. He appeared tentative though the "invitation" was proving hard for his male desires to resist.

"Take a chance," Cassandra gently urged him, penetrating him with her feline eyes. "Prove to me you have an adventurous spirit. You won't be sorry, I promise."

"There are a lot of guys at Sherwood more adventurous than me," Sidney admitted.

"I'm not interested in them," Cassandra said, her voice firm. "Not tonight."

Not tonight . . . ? What was that supposed to mean? Was she looking at him as merely a one night diversion – and why? What did she *really* have in mind?

Cassandra reached across and took his hand. "Just trust me."

Sidney almost recoiled from the touch. Her hand was cold. Her long, tapered fingers felt like icicles against his skin.

Again: "*Trust me . . .*"

Sidney searched for some sort of a stall so that he could regroup his thoughts.

"Do your parents know that we're out tonight?" Sidney suddenly asked her.

Cassandra responded with an expression of surprise. "My parents?"

Sidney nodded and then shrugged. "Yeah, you know, your folks. Just like to know a little about them, that's all. You know, you being their daughter . . . your peculiar tastes, as you put it."

"And that maybe I might not be part of the all-American family?"

"Well, sort of a strange way to put it," Sidney said uncomfortably.

"Is that important to you?" Cassandra asked with a frown.

"No. I – guess not."

"No?"

"Just making conversation, I guess."

Cassandra's attitude darkened. And at that moment, for the quickest instant, Sidney detected a slight change in Cassandra's appearance. Brief, fleeting, but unsettling, like a malevolent shadow passing over her features. He quickly dismissed it as a trick of the shifting light as the shadows lengthened in a prelude to nightfall.

Cassandra's eyes lowered. "I don't like to talk about my parents," she said, the inflection in her voice strange and distant.

Sidney's question was not meant to upset or even offend the girl, yet he now regretted asking it. He felt himself bracing for something unexpected and possibly unpleasant.

The climate in the car chilled. Sidney was now wishing that it was he who was seated behind the wheel. He'd likely throw the car into gear and just drive the hell away from here. Sitting in a lonely cemetery on Halloween night seemed to bring out a weird shift in Cassandra's personality. Something that during his long infatuation with her he'd never have suspected she possessed.

But after several moments the tension inside the vehicle seemed to subside.

Cassandra regained her composure. She turned to Sidney and spoke in a muted tone. "Do you really want to know about them?"

"I – I'm not sure," Sidney said over a reflexive swallow.

"My parents are dead," she told him straightly.

"I'm – sorry," Sidney offered, awkwardly.

Cassandra hesitated, sighed. "It was long ago."

Sidney spoke compassionately. "If it's something you'd rather not talk about . . ."

Cassandra proceeded onward, and her ominous words sent a shiver of dread through Sidney.

"They were accused of being wicked," she began. "And like many others they denied and fought the accusations in an effort to preserve their lives and save their souls from the promise of eternal damnation."

Cassandra paused, and when she resumed, she was as if transfixed in her telling. "But it never made any difference. Punishment would always be delivered, whether they were guilty or not."

Sidney barely managed to control the tremor in his voice. "Guilty . . . of *what*?"

Cassandra slowly turned her face toward him. There was a glow of malevolence highlighted in her eyes. "Practicing the Dark Arts."

"You mean . . . w-witchcraft?" Sidney said with a stammer.

"Yes. That was what they called it."

Sidney found he could barely get his next words out. "Is that . . .how they . . . died?"

"Yes."

Sidney's Adam's apple bobbed, noticeably.

"They were first tortured, made to confess . . . before they were hanged," she said.

"Tortured? Hanged?" Sidney echoed her words in bewilderment. "But – that sort of thing happened centuries ago."

"Yes. Centuries ago."

"I think I'd like to get out and go for a walk," Sidney said before he inhaled and exhaled a forced breath. "It's feeling kinda stuffy in here."

"Of course," Cassandra replied deliberately. "That's why we're here. To go for a walk. A nice walk. Together."

"Cassandra, I gotta tell you – you're really freakin' me out. I mean, this is fun and all; you know, Halloween spook stuff. I get it, but –"

Cassandra seemed not to hear him, consumed as she appeared to be in her own dark utterances. "After they were hanged my grandmother was entrusted with our care. She taught us about who we were. She confessed to us about our parents . . . and their legacy."

Sidney's eyebrows lifted. "*Our . . .?*"

Cassandra gave a very slow nod. "Yes. Me . . . and my brother: Michael."

"You have a brother? I didn't know."

"Yes . . . you do," Cassandra said with a faint, chilling smile. "Only how could you or anyone understand how it really was?"

"I *don't* understand . . ." Sidney said, with emphasis.

Cassandra pumped a breath. "It was my brother who died in that terrible accident."

Michael . . .

"*Mickey Treadman*?" Sidney expelled in a gasp.

Cassandra didn't acknowledge, instead saying: "It wasn't Michael's time. His spirit wasn't ready to depart. But he was afraid. He didn't want to wait for when and however that time would come and so he forced it upon himself to make it happen. And because of that decision, because he chose to leave this life against the natural, his spirit is imprisoned within the confines of the grave. His body must be set free so that he can complete his earthly journey. But that can only be if an exchange is offered." Her emotions lifted in a crescendo. "And what a glorious night it is for him to come home."

Realization once again landed hard on Sidney, manifesting a chill that gripped his body like cold, grasping tentacles.

His fingers slid slowly toward the door handle.

"Michael and I share a special bond. Through these centuries we became closer than you or anyone could imagine."

Sidney couldn't listen to this craziness any longer. He didn't know what she was up to, but he didn't want to be a part of it, Halloween gag or not. She was not the girl he'd expected her to be. The girl who had evolved into his ideal attraction through his active fantasies.

Now he didn't know *what* she was.

He unlatched the handle and pushed open the car door and scrambled out of the vehicle, dropping to his knees with the suddenness of his move but rapidly regaining his footing. But his brain was clouded. He didn't know where to go. Which direction to take. Where to escape from this nightmare. A haunting, prolonged wailing surrounded him, sounding to his ears like the forlorn call of the distant dead, lost souls, emanating from somewhere – perhaps *everywhere* – in the graveyard. He started to run, confused, in a panic. He ran blindly, stumbling as he desperately tried to pick up his pace through the cemetery, dodging around the headstones that projected from the grass and the mud, some recent, some ancient, bent, twisted; finally losing his footing completely and falling face-forward upon a mound of fresh earth. He lifted his head, focused his eyes, and was unable to stifle the scream that ejected from deep in his throat when he read the name and dates written on the temporary grave marker:

Michael "Mickey" Treadman
2005-2022
R.I.P.

"You have nothing to fear."

It was Cassandra's voice, reaching him from behind. Only there was an unnatural cadence to her voice. Sidney didn't know what to expect and could barely summon the courage to turn to face her.

And instantly he wished he hadn't.

A horrifying transformation had taken place. Cassandra's flawless features had twitched and twisted, manifesting into a terrifying countenance, a ghoulish mask of unholy physical desecration. Her feline eyes were hollowed into deep black sockets, her nose had widened and elongated into a cruel hook; her ruby red lips pulled inward to reveal a mouthful of crooked yellow teeth. Her blemish-free porcelain complexion was now embedded with wrinkles and shaded into a deathly gray pallor.

The crone that had once been Cassandra cackled as she stalked toward him, arms outstretched with fingers bent into claws as if reaching for an embrace. She slowly lowered and bent her body toward his and inched her face closer to his, her ghastly mouth open as if to offer a final, obscene kiss.

"It's what you wanted, isn't it, *Sidney*?" she said in a sinister yet seductive intonation. "What you wanted after *. . . all . . . this . . . time.*"

Sidney's mouth also opened – to emit another long, piercing scream, only this time the sound was unheard as it became locked in his throat–

For at that moment gnarled, decaying hands reached out from the grave and clutched at Sidney's shoulders, holding firm.

In the next instant Sidney realized with helpless horror that the hands were not just gripping him, but pulling him *. . . into* the earth. His struggles were futile against the strength of this supernatural opponent, and within moments, as if he were submerging into a mire of quicksand, his body was completely drawn under and the moist ground poured over him like sand draining into an hourglass, and he was gone.

Cassandra's wretched features re-formed into the striking if artificial beauty she possessed. She straightened her posture and stood upright. All was still. She waited for what was to come.

Then: "Hello, Sis."

Cassandra turned. Her brother Michael was standing behind her. His face was mangled, features horribly distorted, yellowed flesh separated and hanging in strands, eyes dull and lifeless; his stance twisted and awkward, body trembling uncertainly as it struggled to regain the flexibility of undead movement.

The two looked at each other briefly before embracing.

Cassandra then stepped back and started to brush away the soil that clumped and dusted her brother's burial suit.

"You always fuss over me," Michael said, his words guttural and issuing out of a lopsided, jaw-twisted mouth.

Cassandra smiled and said simply, "And what else is a sister to do?"

"We should be going home, "Cassandra then said with a hearty sigh. "Grandmother will be waiting for us."

Michael rocked his head.

"Everything has been prepared," Cassandra said.

Cassandra then halted as she sensed a presence. She turned and her stern expression softened into a welcoming smile.

Ed Jones was standing just a few yards away.

Only it wasn't Ed Jones. Not really. What stood in the eerie dusk of the old cemetery was some entity that had masqueraded as the high school youth. A claw-fingered, semi-human creature, a gargoyle that was only faintly recognizable as the boy everyone at Sherwood High knew – or more precisely *didn't* know – as Ed Jones.

"He always said I was a ghoul," he rasped.

"You served us well, Edward. You provided a fine substitute."

"It wasn't hard." Edward then dipped in a respectful bow. "I'm always ready to serve you, Cousin Cassandra."

The blackness overhead would soon be complete, creating a pall that would curtain this lonely stretch of landscape. Cassandra and Michael walked through the cemetery arm-in-arm, once again happily reunited, their forms gradually consumed by the deepening shades of a Halloween nightfall. Edward remained behind, watching them leave, content that his efforts had pleased them. He then focused his attention on the burial plot, the surface ground neat and undisturbed. He spoke to what lay within its depths.

"How were you to know, Sidney, that not only does nature abhor a vacuum . . . So does the grave."

The helpless and hopeless screams were not heard. Nor would they ever be. They could not penetrate the coffin imprisoned forever within the dark, dank earth.

The End

OTHER HELLBOUND BOOKS

The Toilet Zone: Number Two
"Restroom reading at its most terrifying!"

Imagine, if you will, you're traveling through the unknown, hellbound, with no roadmap or stars to guide you. The light fades as you descend into a shadow realm where supernatural terrors make their lair and evil lurks at every turn. Here, dead things don't always stay dead, for this is a world where things that shouldn't be... *are*, and things that should be are not.

In this world, it takes between 2,500 and 4,000 reading words to pay a visit to the smallest, but terrifyingly necessary, room, and stories are written precisely to chill the bones as you wait for nature to make its call.

You open up the book, and one of the 32 tales skulking within its hellish pages chooses you…

It's too late to turn back now. You are about to set foot into another dimension, so best watch out for that signpost up ahead...You've just crossed over into... The Toilet Zone

The Horror Zine's Book of Ghost Stories

"This collection of ghost stories is fresh, varied, and entertaining. Perfect company for a long winter's night." – Owen King, co-author with Stephen King of the New York Times #1 Bestseller Sleeping Beauties

Twenty-six brand-new tales of ghosts, spirits, and the afterlife to chill even the most hardened reader to their very marrow. Grand masters and newcomers alike serve well to petrify with stories to keep you laying awake in the dead of night - long after the last of the light has died - listening for that telltale scratching at the door, a soft whisper of disembodied voices, and the icy caress of long-dead fingers upon your ankle…

The Horror Zine's Book of Ghost Stories is delighted to present to you original, never before seen, spine-tingling tales from Bentley Little, Joe R. Lansdale, Elizabeth Massie, Graham Masterton with Dawn G. Harris, Tim Waggoner, and the very best up and coming writers in the genre. Includes a foreword by Lisa Morton.

"An incredibly creepy collection of stories of the recently and not so recently dead, written by some of the finest writers in horror. I suggest that when reading, do so in the daylight, because reading these at night will only make you more aware of your own, unempty house

Blood and Blasphemy

If you enjoy your horror dipped in buckets of blood and sprinkled with generous amounts of blasphemy, then you've come to the right place!

Blood and Blasphemy is a collection of over thirty of the most sacrilegious horror stories ever written.

Within these irreverent pages, you will encounter a priest that keeps his deformed spawn chained in a root cellar, a convent where a poisonous species of salamander is worshiped, a demonic altar boy, possessed religious relics that kill, blood-drinking clergymen, a Son of God who feeds on sin, an unsuspecting couple who run afoul of religious lunatics in a small town, the divine (and deadly) turd of Christ, and other terrifying tales guaranteed to make church ladies faint and nuns clutch their rosaries.

Schlock! Horror!

An anthology of short stories based upon/inspired by and in loving homage to all of those great gorefest movies and books of the 1980's (not necessarily base in that era, although some do ride that wave of nostalgia!), the golden age when horror well and truly came kicking, screaming and spraying blood, gore & body parts out from the shadows...

This exemplary 80's themed/inspired tales of terror has been adjudicated and compiled by one Mr Bret McCormick, himself a writer, producer and director of many a schlock classic, including *Bio-Tech Warrior, Time Tracers, The Abomination, Ozone: The Attack of the Redneck Mutants* and the inimitable *Repligator*.

Featuring stories from: Todd Sullivan, Timothy C Hobbs, Mark Thomas, Andrew Post, James B. Pepe, Thomas Vaughn, Edward Karpp, Jaap Boekestein, Lisa Alfano, L. C. Holt, John Adam Gosham, Brandon Cracraft, M. Earl Smith, Sarah Cannavo, James Gardner, Bret McCormick, and James H. Longmore.

Graveyard Girls

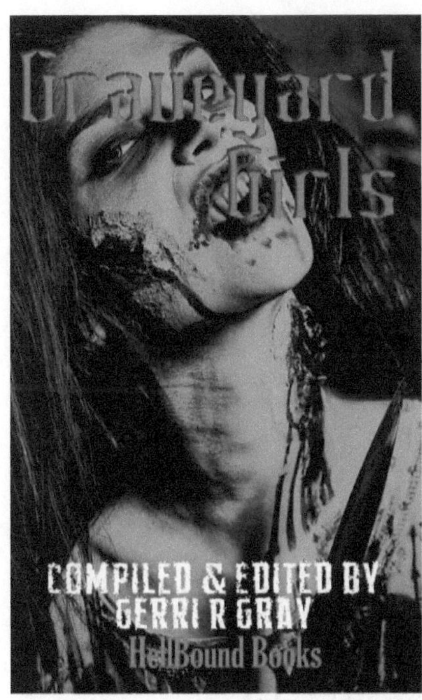

Female authors + Horror = something spectacularly terrifying!

A delicious collection of horrific tales and darkest poetry from the cream of the crop, all lovingly compiled by the incomparable Gerri R Gray! Nestling between the covers of this formidable tome are twenty-five of the very best lady authors writing on the horror scene today!

These tales of terror are guaranteed to chill your very soul and awaken you in the dead of the night with fear-sweat clinging to your every pore and your heart pounding hard and heavy in your labored breast…

Featuring superlative horror from: Xtina Marie, M. W. Brown, Rebecca Kolodziej, Anya Lee, Barbara Jacobson, Gerri R. Gray, Christina Bergling, Julia Benally, Olga Werby, Kelly Glover, Lee Franklin, Linda M. Crate, Vanessa Hawkins, P. Alanna Roethle, J Snow, Evelyn Eve, Serena Daniels, S. E. Davis, Sam Hill, J. C. Raye, Donna J. W. Munro, R. J. Murray, C. Bailey-Bacchus, Varonica Chaney, Marian Finch (Lady Marian).

**A HellBound Books LLC
Publication**

http://www.hellboundbookspublishing.com

Printed in the United States of America

www.ingramcontent.com/pod-product-compliance
Lightning Source LLC
Chambersburg PA
CBHW060723190726
48285CB00001B/45